USHER'S HARBOUR

Barry & Darls Epstein

USHER'S HARBOUR

Barry & Darls Epstein

iUniverse, Inc.
Bloomington

USHER'S HARBOUR

iUniverse books may be ordered through booksellers or by contacting:

iUniverse
1663 Liberty Drive
Bloomington, IN 47403
www.iuniverse.com
1-800-Authors (1-800-288-4677)

ISBN: 978-1-4697-9091-6 (hc)
ISBN: 978-1-4697-9090-9 (sc)
ISBN: 978-1-4697-9092-3 (e)

Printed in the United States of America

iUniverse rev. date: 4/18/2012

Dedication

To my wife, my companion, my collaborator and co-author, the love of my life.

"Thou …..".

(James Clavell, Shogun)

CHAPTER 1

THE PLAGUE

Winter, 2089

Where once stars had twinkled in the night sky, the Earth was now enveloped in an unremitting blanket of clouds. Pollutants defiled the atmosphere, thanks to humanity's greed, arrogance, and neglect. One could forgive the citizens of Richmond, Virginia for failing to recall those halcyon starlit nights of bygone times, especially now that a thousand fires blazed all around them, sending up pillars of black smoke that blotted out the merest suggestion of a sky above. A storm approached. Its cloaking clouds glowed red and angry, reflecting the light from the conflagration …

… and in that savage light, Mark Wells stood on his balcony high above the blazing city, clutching the railing in a death grip. Far below him, the clamour of sirens and klaxons, each conveying its own particular message of panic and distress, all but drowned out by the angry cries of the rioters, the shattering glass, the screams of the victims of rape and pillage. He could see the flames rising from the burning buildings, the firestorms that engulfed the industrial areas, and the funeral pyres on the city's periphery, but the stench of searing flesh and the reek of decaying bodies in the shattered buildings and ruined avenues below had not yet reached that high.

The ravening mobs moved from street to street, looting, burning, and clashing violently whenever they chanced to meet. Drunk, enraged, caught up in the mob hysteria; it didn't matter. The end result was the same. There was neither rhyme nor reason to their actions, save for the terror all felt as civil society collapsed. The plague, lethal and inescapable, fell upon them, as governments stood powerless against it. Born of the overcrowded camps, where interned eco-refugees thronged together in their misery as they fled the rising oceans and the desertification of their lands, it spread rapidly, a story repeated the world over.

Riot police fell back in the face of the relentless power of the marauding gangs, many of them deserting the ranks to guard their own families, some even joining in the mayhem. Military forces were confined to their bases, held in reserve to mop up and restore order after the rioting abated. Inevitably, they too would be drawn into the madness, the death throes of the damned.

Tears rolled down Wells' cheeks. It wasn't just the smoke from countless fires befouling the air that caused him to weep. His wife and son lay dead in the penthouse behind him, victims of the deadly disease. Incurable, it took them in a matter of days. He whispered low, "What have we done?" Then louder, "What have we done?" Then in a gut-wrenching scream, "What have we done?" He collapsed to the floor, his cheek against the railing, his body racked with sobs.

"We failed," he moaned in anguish. "How could we have been so arrogant? To imagine that we could change the world." He sighed deeply, forlornly. "But we tried." Now in a whisper, "At least we tried." Old age had taken his friend Jace near a decade before, and D.J., the third member of the Founders, had drowned attempting to save a friend in peril. Now only he remained, a ruined shadow of his youthful self, as the nucleus of an ever expanding group dedicated to saving mankind from itself. Failure weighed heavily upon him.

From his lofty perch he was unable to hear the mob breaching the building's defenses, overwhelming security, breaking through the iron gates and locked doors. He didn't hear the final panicked announcement as the concierge tried to warn the residents even as the mob surged over him. He didn't hear the building's alarms as danger drew ever closer. At last he became aware of the looters' presence when they battered down his door, flooding into his home, his last refuge. They tore the place apart, destroying what they couldn't carry away. The bodies of Wells' family were tumbled indifferently to the floor, evicted from their beds and kicked aside as their mattresses were appropriated by the looters. Wells tried in vain to stem the tide.

"No," he screamed. "No. You don't understand." His entreaties were ignored as two of their number pushed him back, picked him up and hurled him from the balcony, laughing in derision at his terror. As he fell, he had only moments to lament the sad fate of his kind before he crashed to the pavement below, to join the detritus of a failed world, a failed vision.

Later that evening, torrential rains pounded the city, sweeping clean the blighted air, extinguishing all but the most entrenched of the fires as it sluiced down hills and gutters and rooftops, temporarily cleansing the streets and forcing rioters and defenders alike to seek shelter, save for the maddest and most frenetic of them. Sadly, the rains did not make an end of it. Tomorrow would be another day, and the violent appetite of the survivors was far from being assuaged.

Summer, 2089

There was little cause to celebrate the nation's birthday, yet they did. The plague had taken most of the world's populace in a mere ten weeks. In the United States, a scant twenty-two million survived, scattered over the land in cities, in towns, and on farms. Of Richmond's inhabitants, only a few thousand remained. Those pitiful few, the plague's survivors, had dragged themselves from the ashes and tried in vain to rebuild. The extent of the damage and the hundreds of thousands of rotting corpses finally persuaded them to abandon the effort. Most of the city was gone, the charred and twisted wreckage attesting to weeks of rioting and looting.

They'd salvaged what they could from the rubble and built shanty towns of tents and huts and lean-tos in parks and fields. On the Fourth of July they'd found flags and bunting and decorated their hovels, to celebrate their elation at being amongst those who yet endured, still joyous to have their freedom and the bounty that the government pro tem was even now showering upon them. Few would admit that they were the damned, condemned to live out their lives in privation and misery unless they found a way to resurrect the comfortable civilization they'd helped to destroy.

The members of the federal government and others of wealth, rank, and privilege had taken refuge in bunkers and had managed to ride out the crisis in relative comfort. After the calamity they had emerged to govern a blighted land. They'd promised much, for of necessity there was much to be done, the feeding and re-housing of millions being a priority. For now, there was an abundant supply of food, in houses and supermarkets and warehouses that had survived the worst of the fires and the looting and destruction. Even now, survivors scrabbled for sustenance in the cellars of gutted homes and the wreckage of commercial buildings. Farms and ranches, whose owners had succumbed to the plague or to looters, were repopulated by grateful refugees from the ruined cities, and the government sent out teams to train them in the agricultural sciences. The massive recovery effort had begun.

Like North America, South America, Australia, Europe and Asia had begun their own recovery programs, but normal would never again be a state to which any of them could return. Africa was already lost, with no hope of aid or surcease, as the plague decimated populations and ancient intertribal rivalries took care of the rest. Only isolated populations in areas verdant and fertile would survive there. So much more had to be done, and the solution lay in the past and in the near future.

Decades before, a chance meeting on the Galapagos Islands would have repercussions for centuries to come. Wells had not died in vain. His legacy and that of so many others would bestow upon mankind a gift given to few species on the brink of extinction; a second chance.

CHAPTER 2

THE FOUNDERS

Spring, 2057

Mark's feet scrabbled for purchase on the smooth rope lava as he plunged recklessly down the slope towards the distant shoreline, fleeing for his life. The fact that he was running towards what he most feared was irrelevant, for that way held the best chance of escape. He gasped for breath in the fetid air and cursed himself for not keeping his thirty year old body in better shape. His final expedition to the Galapagos might well be his last anywhere.

He'd cut it too close, his leave taking. The three day permit issued by the Ecuadorian government's administrative center on San Cristóbal had expired a good ten hours before. It wasn't the deadline that propelled Mark to flee, but the fact that the once inactive volcano on Isla Bartolme had recently decided to come back to life. Bartolme was on the opposite side of a broad bay from Isla Santiago, where Mark had been completing his work. In spite of many warnings by geologists, he'd taken his life in his hands to carry out a final study of the few species that remained on the island, before an eruption might well wipe them out. Even to the untrained eye of a humble ornithologist, it was evident that the penultimate moment had arrived.

Once he reached the shoreline, he realized that in his haste he'd taken a wrong fork in the trail halfway down the slope, and was now on the edge of an unfamiliar cove. His Zodiac was in the next inlet over, just around the promontory to the north. He had three untenable choices; try to make it over or around the point, attempt the dash overland to the distant cove to the west where his ship was anchored, or take to the waters and swim for his life. None of these options appealed to him, yet a choice had to be made smartly.

Debris from the mounting eruption was beginning to rain down; ash accompanied by rocks of various sizes, as it began in earnest. Lava was not a consideration… yet. His biggest concerns were the toxic sulphur gases that were even now fouling the air and the possibility of pyroclastic flow, from which there was little chance of escape. There was no safe haven on the relatively barren shoreline. Mark knew that he had only minutes to make a decision. A marked increase in the rumbles and booms across the channel impelled him to immediate action.

Three days earlier:

The equatorial sun blazed hot in a hazy blue sky, onto the clear greenish-blue waters of the cove on the south end of Isla Santiago. The bay provided safe harbour and was far enough from the burgeoning volcano to ease a mariner's fears. Sea turtles and Galapagos penguins swam gracefully beneath the hull of Mark's boat, as mockingbirds took respite on the radar mast, and gulls alternately begged and scolded from a safe distance, circling before landing on gentle swells to await due tribute. A few of the surviving feral goats grazed high on nearby volcanic slopes.

"Ahoy, The Beagle," a cheerful voice hailed.

Mark was in the process of ensuring that his anchors were set and loose lines coiled and stowed when he became aware of the graceful sailing vessel that had managed to glide unnoticed into the cove. Fifteen meters long and gleaming with lacquered simwood and polished brass, the yacht executed a graceful arc aft of the Beagle III, as its skipper pressed a button that rapidly collapsed and stored the sails.

Mark straightened, and shaded his eyes to get a better look at the intruder, as the skipper hailed him once more, "Ahoy, The Beagle."

"Ahoy," Mark returned, giving a friendly wave. The gesture was reciprocated by the deeply tanned, white-haired senior at the helm, wearing only shorts, deck shoes, and a skipper's cap.

"Permission to come aboard?" the newcomer shouted, his request almost drowned out as his diesels kicked in. Mark nodded, and the yacht crossed the intervening space on the calm waters of the sheltered cove. It hove to on his starboard side, gentling itself against Mark's vessel by means of underwater jets, as large inflatable bumpers deployed automatically.

Mark threw him a line, then another, and the two ships were quickly twinned as the stranger tied off. The older man vaulted nimbly over the railing, landing with a gentle thump on the deck. He strode towards Mark, his right hand extended, eyes twinkling above a broad grin that emanated from a face as craggy as the nearby volcanic slopes.

"Jason Moorehead the Fifth," he said in a cultured British accent, his voice deep and strong. His agility and energy belied his evident physical age. As young and vigorous as Mark was, he understood that he might meet his match in any physical contest with Jason.

Mark shook his hand, noting the strength in his grip. "Mark Wells the First and only," he said. The older man's smile widened, and he chuckled.

"I get a lot of that. Sounds somewhat pompous, doesn't it? The Fifth part, I mean. Call me Jace."

"Perhaps just a little," Mark responded. "Jason Moorehead? Your name sounds familiar, Jace. Aren't you the British construction mogul, the one who sold his international enterprises and retired a few years back?"

"That would be me. How could one forget a name like Jason Moorehead the Fifth? Now I'm free to wander the world on permanent vacation. And you are Mark Wells, yes? A biologist, yes? I took a few moments to look you up on my comlink as I was sailing into the bay. I queried Beagle III. Aren't you worried about the volcano?"

"Who wouldn't be? The geologists have promised at least a week free and clear. In any case, I only have a three day permit. I'll be out of here well before it goes."

"If the experts are right. Shame that all of this might vanish within decades, notwithstanding the volcano. The oceans are rising. The waters here are already showing signs of pollution, and the air as well."

"Yes. The greenhouse effect, climate change, is raising temperatures above the tolerance level of many of the indigenous species. Food webs are collapsing. That's why we have to monitor the progress of the flora and fauna here. There's too few of us and too little time." Mark was aware of a scattering of scientists on many of the other islands in the Galapagos group, toiling to study and preserve the endangered ecosystems.

"Why don't we chat about this later? I'll be hanging around for a few days. Perhaps we can get together this evening for dinner and drinks. My treat. I'm a half decent chef. Pan fried turtle O.K. with you?" Mark blanched. "Just kidding. I've turned vegan in my old age. Healthier, you know. I'll let you get to your work while I set my anchors over there. See you later."

"Later it is then," Mark replied. "I'll be there will bell peppers on." He laughed as Jace grimaced at the pun.

Jace turned and, grasping the handrail of his yacht, made an impressive leap that landed him on his own deck. He cast off the lines and went aft. Behind the wheel once more, he restarted the diesels and retracted the bumpers, moving slowly some 50 meters away before punching the button that ejected his anchors and set them automatically.

Mark loaded his equipment into the Zodiac in the Beagle's aft bay before deploying it. He took it out and around the southeast end of the island, making for the shore of Sullivan Bay hard by Isla Bartolme, which made an exclamation point into the bay. His primary objective was to have a closer look at some of the fourteen species of finches that were unique to the Galapagos, those having evolved from a single species in the distant past.

Most of the protected species on these islands would likely survive the imminent cataclysm, with the exception of those that had chosen to concentrate their nesting areas and habitats on these particular slopes and on those of Bartolme itself. Many of the local species of giant tortoise had gone extinct decades before, despite the best effort of the biologists to preserve their environment or to raise them in captivity. Air and water pollution was devastating the delicate ecosystem, and the Humboldt Current that had once tempered the equatorial heat had slowed to the point where temperatures increases now had a marked effect on all of the species in the area.

The Zodiac glided gently towards the shallow beach, as Mark cut the motor and let the momentum bring him up the shore. White coral sand slid between his toes as he stepped out of the boat, lugging his pack and camera along. He pulled the boat a little further up the beach, put on heavy socks and hiking boots, then set out along a trail well-worn by eco-tourists, up the slope of a fissure volcano. It was disconcertingly close to the newly reviving cone on the opposite shore that rumbled and belched steam with alarming regularity. Lava lizards hurried to get out of his way on the barren slope as he strode briskly along, then peered at him suspiciously from the cover of lava cacti. He inhaled the fresh, relatively untainted air, took a long look at the scenery then began to set up his kit. Dark-rumped petrels and frigate birds circled overhead, while startled ground finches and tree finches chided him from nearby. It promised to be a productive day.

On his return to the Beagle III, he plunged naked into the warm waters of the bay to wash off the dust and sweat of an honest day's labour. Jace hailed him as he clambered back aboard. "Worked up an appetite yet?" he shouted.

"I'm ravenous," Mark replied. "Be there in ten." Water sprayed everywhere as he shook his blonde hair and toweled himself off. With his rugged good looks he could easily have been the poster boy for a fitness club.

Once he came alongside in the Zodiac, Mark threw the painter to Jace who tied it off and hoisted Mark aboard by way of a small platform that rose smoothly from sea to deck level. Jace stood smartly by at the rail, still wearing his shorts, shoes, and cap, but now with a small white towel draped across his left arm. "If sir will kindly follow me, I'll show you to your table," he intoned solemnly.

Mark played along. "Nice joint you've got here," he said.

"We prefer to call it a spliff, sir." Jace grinned. And indeed there was one beside each of their plates, Mark observed, as Jace seated him at a cloth-covered table with real china and crystal and cloth napkins. "Straight from the Islands, mon. The very best ganja. Good for the appetite. And it's organic." Jace sat down opposite. "Would you care to indulge before supper?"

"I don't normally partake, but since this is a special occasion …"

Jace snapped a barbeque lighter in Mark's direction, then lit himself up. A few tokes later his grin was wider and dreamier. "Best get the food while I still can," he said as he rose and vanished inside.

The table was on the shaded afterdeck, where they could watch the tropical sun lower itself behind the slopes of Volcan Darwin on nearby Isla Isabela. Mark wondered when the other Galapagos volcanoes might reassert themselves.

Jace reappeared bearing a huge tray loaded with a selection of steamed and pan seared vegetable dishes, rice, yams, and fruits. He placed the tray on a sideboard and invited Mark to help himself, in the meantime taking a bottle of white wine from an ice bucket and expertly uncapping it. He poured as Mark returned to the table with a heaping plate. Jace loaded his own plate, then both dug in, enjoying the fine food, the wine, the tropical ambience, good company, and the warm glow of the ganja buzz.

"You travel alone?" Mark asked.

"Who would put up with me? My wife passed on over two decades ago, and she was a saint to have endured my nonsense for nearly 30 years. Our kids are scattered over the globe, with lives of their own. I was immersed in my work until three years ago, when I decided to hang it up. What about you?"

"Not married yet. Maybe someday, when my life becomes more settled. Right now I travel a lot and I'm away from home for months at a time. What woman needs to deal with that? As for kids, why would anyone bring children into this mess we've made for ourselves? What kind of legacy are we giving them? Besides, what with the chemical and radioactive pollution from the Second Civil War in the U.S. and the lingering aftereffects from the worldwide Water Wars, I'm not even sure I can still reproduce. The latest stats show that the fertility rate is only about 40 percent now and populations everywhere are declining. Sorry. I do go on."

"I understand," Jace said. "It's not right, you know. A sad state of affairs, the massive, self-inflicted decline of our planet. We've batted the issues about for over half a century, and still we do too little to save ourselves. What do you think, Mark?"

"As you say, too little done by too few. Politicians do what's politically expedient, and businessmen do what makes them the maximum profit. Like it or not, those are the people who run our world, and what can us ordinary folk do about it?"

"Surely you've heard of the French Revolution? Mahatma Gandhi? The fall of the Berlin Wall and the Soviet Union? Nelson Mandela and the ANC? The Velvet Revolution? The Madrid Coalition? Ordinary folk have done plenty throughout history. They just have to organize and make demands and be willing to make sacrifices. Much of the time it succeeds."

"So how many people were needed to make those changes successful? A thousand? A million? You need big numbers to affect change."

"Not so big as you might imagine. If you have a plan and a big voice, you'd be surprised at what you can do. Start with the seed of an idea, and if it's appealing enough it can propagate endlessly."

"But these days you need tons of money. Lots of contributions from a lot of people. You need massive amounts of cash to organize and publicize a real movement."

"Or some rather large contributions from only a few people. In case it escaped your notice, I have a ton of money and nobody but myself to spend it on. Oh, I make the usual philanthropic bequests and donations, but I can do better than that. I'm not bragging, just setting the scene."

"So what do you have in mind?" Mark asked.

"Have you heard of the Illuminati?" Mark shook his head. "For decades, even centuries, people have been postulating that the recent evolution of society has been carefully planned by a few men behind the scenes. The modern group supposedly consists of politicians and businessmen who run the world for their own benefit or for our benefit, depending on who you believe. It's been variously postulated the Illuminati is run by Jews, the Catholic Church, the House of Windsor, the Bilderberg Group, and on and on. No real evidence has ever emerged concerning such a group, other than the accounts of the original group founded in Bavaria in the 1770s."

"How does this relate to anything we've been discussing?"

"I'm proposing to establish an Illuminati-type group that would resolve many of the world's problems and determine the future course of mankind. It would be open and aboveboard, an international think-tank that accepts and considers any and all proposals and welcomes the participation of anyone who cares to contribute. Even politicians and businesspersons would be welcome, without special standing. I'd like to recruit mainly scientists, economists, educators, engineers, philosophers, and political scientists. We'd also need a wide-ranging group from other diverse disciplines. What do you think?"

"It's rather ambitious, isn't it, and I know such a group would provoke resistance from the establishment. I like the idea, but I wonder how practical it would be. Where would you garner the support? What incentive would people have to back you?"

"For the same reasons that they contribute to charities; altruism, or possibly self-interest. Two sides of the same coin. People would join the group so they could safeguard their own future or that of their loved ones or of mankind in general. Human beings have diverse reasons for contributing their ideas, their labours, their monies, or even their lives if necessary. It all works out the same in the end."

"So you think that maybe we could be the core of this new group of .... what? ..... Illuminati?"

"Perhaps we shouldn't actually call it that. Might scare folks off, or attract the wrong kind. We can work out the name later, but yes, we two could build great things."

The ganja had done its work well. Drifting on a cloud of unfettered ideas, Jace and Mark and others soon to come would form the nucleus of a group that would ultimately be the salvation of mankind. Of course, they couldn't know it then, but they did have high hopes.

Over the next two days they engaged in a serious discussion of the proposed objectives of the group and the actual mechanisms that might generate sufficient interest to pull people in. And so great movements are born of small ideas, by men and women plotting amongst themselves in clandestine gatherings in darkened back rooms, or perhaps on the aft deck of a luxury yacht under the tropical sun.

* * *

The clear waters of the inlet closed above Mark's head as he dove in to join the turtles and penguins frolicking innocently below. He broke the surface just in time to see a personal hovercraft sweep around the point and head rapidly in his direction.

"I figured I'd find you somewhere around here. Jace sent me. Need a hand?" the newcomer shouted as he approached.

"Sure could use one," Mark sputtered, treading water. The stranger cut power and the hovercraft slowed, descending to the surface only meters from the swimmer. He helped Mark aboard and made sure that he was secured in the second seat before applying power and retreating from the bay, skimming the tops of the waves and swerving south and west, away from Bartolme and its deadly threat.

The machine's roar barred any possibility of normal conversation while it covered the intervening distance to the cove where the Beagle III lay anchored. A third vessel had arrived in the cove in Mark's absence. It was, like the Beagle III, a converted trawler, those boats having become dirt cheap upon the complete collapse of many fish species over the past few decades. Jace was waiting anxiously on the bow of his yacht, and his body language conveyed considerable relief when the hovercraft bearing two riders rounded the point.

The craft powered down near the center of the triangle formed by the three ships and settled onto the water's surface, drifting in Jace's direction. "Glad to see you're safe and well, Mark," Jace shouted. "Have you met Derrick? That's Derrick James Carver. Just call him D.J. We were chatting when Bartolme began to blow its top. When you didn't show up here in a reasonable time, I was going to come to your rescue, but D.J. offered his hovercraft as the speedier alternative. Want to come aboard?"

Mark turned to his rescuer and shook his hand. "A genuine pleasure to meet you, and thanks for coming after me."

"It's nothing," D.J. responded. "Glad I could help." D.J. was slight, dark skinned, and far from what one might call handsome, his oft broken nose lending him a sinister air.

"Thanks, Jace," Mark called out, "But I think we'd all better get a move on out of here before something really nasty happens." He looked over his shoulder just as an immense black cloud appeared beyond the eastern part of Santiago, accompanied by a particularly loud boom and a mounting shower of debris."

"Capital idea, my friend. What say we meet in Puerto Baquerizo Moreno? Darwin's Refuge, on the docks. I'm buying."

D.J. dropped Mark off on the Beagle III then hastened to his own boat for the short voyage to the administrative capitol of the Galapagos. The yacht steamed out of the cove on diesel power, leading the other two boats. They stood a safe distance out to sea for a while to watch the sound and light show, and Mark had ample time to reflect on his narrow escape. Once clear of the ever-widening danger area, Jace hauled sail and the three proceeded, each at his own pace, towards their rendezvous.

* * *

It would take the better part of a day running at less than 15 knots before the three were reunited at Darwin's. Jace and D.J. were already into their second round when Mark finally showed up.

"Wonky diesel," Mark said by way of explanation. "Good swift kick got it going again." The others looked skeptical. Thanks to an attentive server, a cold mug of beer appeared before him as if by magic as he seated himself. "What's up?"

"We were just continuing the discussion you and I started back at Santiago," Jace said.

"Sorry we didn't have time to get to know each other back there," D.J. said to Mark. "Jace tells me you're an ornithologist. I'm a civil engineer by training." He dropped his voice, leaned in conspiratorially, and continued in a stage whisper, "And now, a member of the Illuminati."

The others chuckled at the remark. "Let's bear in mind that we don't want to be secretive," Jace said. "We want as many people as possible to know about us, and to that end we have to get out there and beat the cyber-bushes for eager acolytes with specialized skills and cognitive abilities. We need thinkers and visionaries and risk-takers who are willing to imperil their own futures for humanity's sake."

"We can expect thousands of applicants. How can we vet so many? Weed out the screwballs, the egotists and the just plain iniquitous?" D.J. asked.

"By directing our message to the type of people we need," Jace replied. "That would reduce applicants to a manageable number. It can be done, it must be done. D.J., your C.V. shows that you have experience in media relations. You must know a few people who can help us there. We also need to round up a couple of experts in cyberspace communications."

"First we'll need a mission statement," Mark put in. "If we're to attract the kind of people we want, we have to let them know exactly what we're up to."

"Let's keep it simple, just what we've been discussing," said Jace. "How about something like 'For those who see the world not as it is but as it could be, we offer this singular opportunity to join us in shaping it for the benefit of all mankind.' We would go on to state more specific objectives, such as restructuring the social order, reforming governance, ending pollution, increasing food production, ameliorating housing conditions, enhancing reproductive technologies and so on."

"Excellent," D.J. said enthusiastically. "Rather than casting a wide net, we set a lobster pot to draw in the best of the best. Speaking of which, this establishment serves a mighty fine thermidor. Anyone game?"

"I'm in," Mark said.

Jace drew back in mock horror. "I'll opt for the tofu loaf and steamed veggies, while you two carnivores gnaw away on our friends from the deep which, by the way, are becoming scarce," he scolded.

"Then we'll just have to add that to the list of things that need fixing," D.J. rejoined.

The three settled in to enjoy the comestibles of their choice while continuing to discuss those weighty matters that would ultimately impact upon the future of mankind. It took them several days to work it all out, but that which was brought forth through necessity would bear fruit in years to come, and the three would long be remembered and honoured for the work they did at that time, in that place.

CHAPTER 3

CENTENNIAL

July 6, 2204

The cold, dispassionate eyes of the GOES-XV series weather satellite peered down on the Earth and dutifully recorded and reported conditions below. It neither knew nor cared about the environmental changes that had and were affecting the past, the present and the future of mankind. Through the persistent veil of cirrostratus clouds, the haze of pollution and ground level dust storms, it observed the blighted lands below, the coastlines of North America transformed by the rising oceans, the remains of ruined and abandoned cities, and the Domes that dotted the landscape, the last refuge of the survivors.

Tourists circled the lower observation deck in the central tower of RichmondDome. They marveled at the wondrous construct spread out below them. The parklands and the habitats of the first completed city of the 22nd century were historical treasures, the city an engineering marvel of its time. Advances made in building techniques and creature comforts by this, the beginning of the 23rd century, did not in any way diminish the spectacle below, the precursor of modernity. An eddy of color and motion among the trees and across the lawns and the plazas in one of the parks drew the attention of the observers, and they dialed up the magnification on their com-helmets in order to get a better look.

Bells jingled and finger cymbals clashed as a sinuous line of chanting Hare Krishna meandered its way fluidly across the south plaza of SeabrookRound, under the feeble glow of the late afternoon sun filtering through the Dome. Diners watched, as they sipped their soy shakes and munched on synthburgers at the nearby eatery, while passers-by, loungers, and children at play stared at the dancers, amused by their flowing saffron robes, their infectious smiles and their shaven heads. Most couldn't help but spare a grin for the youngsters. No proselytizing, pamphleteering, or importuning spare change for these youthful and harmonious imposters. Their mission was merely to celebrate life and to share their joy in it. They had studied the Hare Krishna movement of the 1960s, and had taken from it that which they most admired and enjoyed. They might mimic the religiosity of yore, but they were not of it.

This sort of spectacle was not all that unusual, even at the dawn of the twenty-third century. The tweenies, having studied twentieth century history in school, had become fascinated by Flower Power and the decade of permissiveness that had been the 1960s and, not for the first time in the annals of the Domes, had made it their own. Many dressed the part, with bell-bottoms and tie-dyes, sandals and kaftans. Hair grown long, flowing locks head-banded, gypsy-scarved, ponytailed or left to blow free in the artificial breezes. The music of the Beatles, Bob Marley, Janis Joplin and Elvis resonated from youth gatherings, and contemporary folk music vied with the tunes of Woody Guthrie and The Kingston Trio on numerous makeshift stages. Many parents, as they had in ages past, looked askance at the fashions and the music, but took a softer line as they recalled their own flirtation with the Vow of Poverty fad and the mournful Gregorian chants associated with it, culled from the archives of the 2020s.

Still, a goodly number of the younglings and most adults eschewed the latest fads in favor of more modern clothing; flamboyant multi-colored tunics and tights, or the technophiles' robes that changed shape and hue on keyed verbal commands. The very height of fashion for both males and females was the brightly toned close-fitting helmet-like headgear that incorporated communications devices and information systems in a package only millimeters thick. These helmets were sometimes left unadorned, or were more often embellished with painted designs, faux-fur or colorful plumes.

The only colors forbidden by custom and decree were solid red and royal blue. These were reserved for the robes of the Futures and the Compilers, those select few who were as royalty in the New Social Order. The Compilers had laid the foundations for the New Society that had been humanity's salvation, and the Futures continued to provide competent and responsible governance under their guidance. Even now, several Futures passed through the plaza and strolled the pathways of the surrounding Seabrook Park. The pseudo-Hare Krishna gave due deference and made way. Common citizens halted in order to let them pass. Children gawked in awe. Young lovers, lounging on the grass in the dappled sunlight beneath the trees took a moment from gazing into each others' eyes to note with respect the Futures' proximity.

As if the relative brightness of the day were not enough to tempt the citizens of the Dome to gather in the parks, plazas and eateries, the Guardians, governors of the Dome, had declared a year long celebration of the hundredth anniversary of its completion. SeabrookRound Plaza, like plazas throughout the Dome, was alive with jugglers and acrobats, singers and musicians, magicians and mimes and all manner of traditional festive amusements. Vendors promoted their wares; clothing and souvenirs, ersatz food from bygone days, toys and balloons, gewgaws and gimcracks and every conceivable sort of time-honoured carnival merchandise that might have been served up or hawked since street fairs had begun centuries before.

Exotic aromas drifted among the stalls, competing for the attention of the shoppers, tempting them; retro foods, incense, fragrant soaps and candles, flowers from roof gardens. Spicy soy-sausages were consumed with gusto, washed down with beer or lemonade, and cotton candy and candy apples were a particular hit with the youngsters. Aromatic and scintillant T-shirts, ponchos and shawls were bartered for food or merchandise or exchanged for time credits.

In due course, the swirl of humanity in the plaza and in the adjacent park abated. Dusk approached as the dancers moved on, singing to the strains of 'Penny Lane' that emanated from their wrist pods, and the good citizens of the Dome went about their evening's business.

* * *

High above the dispersing celebrants, Quinten Braxton paused for a few moments to collect his thoughts before facing his first class of the new semester. The main campus of the university girdled a privileged space just over half way up the Dome's central tower, affording a spectacular view of the metropolis. Looking out over the city, he stood with his back to the entrance of the lecture hall. Rocking back on his heels, he mused on the wonders of science and technology that had allowed the creation of this engineering masterpiece and on the marvels of social engineering and genetic manipulation that had rendered modern society so vigorous, tranquil, and secure. How fortunate they were to be living here, protected from the capricious ravages of climate change and ozone depletion, celebrating the benefits of the New Social Order.

Serried ranks of housing marched downwards towards the Dome's perimeter. High rises gave way to low rises which in turn yielded to multiplexes, with dual level townhomes on the periphery. Here and there, roof gardens satisfied the primal needs of some to cultivate the soil. Broad, tree-lined avenues separated the six wedge-shaped districts that made up the city, each district identical to every other, with duplicate facilities for the convenience of the residents. Parks, plazas and green spaces provided ample room for the citizens to stroll and to gather together in the controlled climate under the Dome. Quinn surveyed his surroundings for a few moments more as he considered how far society had come in the past century. Satisfied, he took a deep breath and turned away. Behind that door, some 200 students awaited their professor's arrival with eager anticipation.

* * *

He entered the Great Hall of Scholars and strode briskly to the podium. Instant recognition; black suit, turquoise lapels, turquoise piping, emblematic of his rank and his profession. Immediately the hubbub of conversation ceased as the assembled students craned to catch a glimpse of their instructor on this, the first day of Biology 103. As stated in the university's prospectus, he was the son of two Futures of distinction, and had significant qualifications in his own right; a PhD in reproductive biology and a masters degree in criminal psychology, as well as awards and honours in both academia and community service.

Professor Quinten Braxton was taller than average, just over 2 meters, with grey eyes, ash blond hair and a firm and muscular physique that attested to his dedication to fitness and a healthy diet. He evinced a shy smile and a gentle demeanor coupled with a sly wit, all of which served to endear him to his students and colleagues, not to mention his many female acquaintances. Having gained tenure the year before, he had only two classes; Biology 103, considered to be a soft class, and a seminar class in forensics and criminology. Consequently, he had extra time to pursue his studies into the history of deviant criminal behavior and to write learned papers on that subject. In addition, he was on an informal contract with the Sentinels to act as a consultant on difficult criminal cases, of which there were, fortunately, very few. He had been called upon only twice; once to trace a missing person, and a second time to hunt down an aberrant citizen, one Ujo Vreem, whose antisocial tendencies were irritating the authorities.

By the advent of the twenty-third century, deviant criminal behavior was virtually unknown, and even crimes considered to be antisocial were relatively rare. The Compilers' New Society was tightly controlled, but in a discreet manner. The inhabitants of the Domes were satisfied that their world was being administered for their benefit, and the Councils of Guardians did their best to provide them with a benign regime. The Sentinels were charged with keeping peace and order, which they did with all the dedication and vigour that the law allowed. Thus dissent was virtually unknown, and antisocial behavior was more likely to be treated rather than punished.

Professor Braxton synched his wrist pod with the projection system built into the podium, then briefly introduced himself. Many young ladies in the class, and even a few of the young men, struck by his evident charisma and attractiveness, drifted off into fantasy and almost missed his opening remarks.

"Good evening. I'm Professor Braxton, and I'll be directing your progress through Biology 103, an introduction to the science and technology of artificial and enhanced human reproduction. The course includes details of the human genome, genetic engineering, epigenetics, gene splicing, and cloning technology, with a historical overview. There will be one formal class and a minimum of two labs a week, and if time and circumstances permit, tours of commercial labs, reproduction facilities and Safe Harbours. The bulk of your work will, of course, take place in your habs as self-directed learning, research, and through somno-teaching. The main purpose of our weekly gatherings here will be for instruction, elucidation, and discussion. This is the only evening class to which I'll subject you. Future classes will be held every Monday morning at 0900 sharp.

"Early in the twentieth century, some years after the triumph of the Wright brothers, when biplanes were beginning to fill the skies, a scientist, or so he called himself, asserted that airplanes could never fly faster than three hundred miles per hour, because no material known to man could stand up to the stresses that they would undergo beyond that speed." The podium projected a flow of tri-d illustrations in the air above his head; the Wright brothers early efforts, Fokker D.VIIs, Spad XIIIs, and Sopwith Camels, dashing and soaring through the skies at speeds up to two hundred miles per hour.

"If you are ever to be scientists, you must overcome your natural prejudices and become forward thinkers, allowing for every possibility, examining and giving due consideration to every new idea. Our skeptical scientist apparently did not even consider materials such as plywood or aluminum, which existed in his day and were to become integral parts of the structures of future planes." More images appeared; the Hawker Hurricane, the Messerschmitt Bf 109, the Douglas DC-1, the

Boeing 727, and the X-1, all speeding along at well over three hundred miles per hour.

"Late in the twentieth century, scientists succeeded in cloning a mammal, thus producing Dolly the Sheep. Mind you, this came after many unsuccessful attempts, in which sheep were stillborn or were brought forth as monstrosities that could not possibly live and which had to be destroyed. Sadly, Dolly had the shortened telomeres of her adult parent and also developed arthritis at a young age, but she was dying from lung cancer when the scientists finally put her down. Her autopsy revealed she was normal in every other way.

"Soon afterwards, many scientists asserted that humans could never be cloned, because people would never stand for the risk of creating clones with grotesque deformities, and the consequent predicament of having to decide how to deal with them. Subsequently, they managed to clone mice, cats, and dogs. Research continued, and difficulties like DNA methylation, among others, were ultimately solved. Now, two centuries later, we have perfected the techniques of epigenetic manipulation, gene snipping, and cloning, which can be used to produce perfect human babies and to repair potential defects. Once again, the early scientists were wrong, because they were not forward thinkers, because they did not have the farsightedness to envision extraordinary solutions." Images of the cloning process were followed by Dolly the sheep, Snuppy the dog, Deena the Kitty, L.C. the cow and Kevin Eleven, the first successfully cloned human.

"We now have the means to do what those pioneering biologists so many years ago could not. Thanks to their efforts, the Human Genome Project, the development of genetic engineering, and embryonic efforts - no pun intended - at cloning, we have been able to advance the methods and means of human reproduction and, in so doing we have contributed to the advancement of society itself. Safe Harbours store memories and DNA and use them to reproduce near-perfect human beings such as the Futures, those select few who are capable of guiding us forward. Those of you who, after taking this course, feel inspired to move on and to continue this noble effort will one day be looked upon as pioneers in your own right, and heroes of science and modern civilization."

The professor continued with his introductory speech, endeavoring to motivate his students to put forth their best efforts both in their studies and in their future careers. He assigned readings from their textchips, and a term project to be researched.

"Just one more thing," Professor Braxton said. "Before I dismiss you, there're a couple of things you need to know about me and about yourselves, if you don't already know. The purpose of teaching and learning is for all of you to achieve. A teacher's greatest reward is the success of his students. A student's greatest reward is to achieve that success by way of the knowledge imparted by those teachers that touch his life. You will realize your dreams through hard work and by connecting the various fragments of knowledge you've absorbed over the years, and then by extrapolating those links to solve new problems. You can do it, in that I have complete faith. Excellence is within your grasp. Seize it. Dismissed."

The students left the lecture hall that evening, their heads awhirl with enthusiasm over what they had heard, with trepidation at the workload ahead, yet inspired to put forth the effort required to fulfill Professor Braxton's expectations of them. Success would be theirs.

By the time Quinn ended his introductory lecture, the sun was setting in shades of bright red and mauve, a multiplicity of colors produced as the waning light was scattered by the suspended particulates in the air. As the students dispersed to their habs, they were blissfully unaware of the terrible tragedy that was unfolding nearby, an event that was to consume the attention of the citizens of the Dome for some time to come.

* * *

A handful of stars twinkled in the sky, more or less directly overhead. The insistent cloud cover and the haze of pollution shrouded the vastness of the firmament, obscuring the view of stars at lower inclinations and reducing the moon's brilliance to a pitiful ruddiness. The Dome sheltered the city from the worst effects of pollution, from the extremes of weather brought about by climate change, and from the intense u.v. radiation resulting from the depletion of the ozone layer.

Still, the Dome couldn't protect the innocents inside it from the worst that humanity had to offer.

She was young, only twelve years old, but she strode briskly and with self-assurance through Seabrook Park, confident in the ability of the Council of Guardians and the Legion of Sentinels to protect her. In this Age of the Domes, however, there was little from which she needed to be protected, and she knew it. Storm O'Reilly was all too aware that she had overstayed her time at her friend Jade's hab. Absorbed in a game of 3-D Mah Jongg on Jade's holoplayer, she'd lost track of the time and would have been there yet had her mother not commed her. Now she hurried to her own hab just across the park. She followed the rambling pathways that twisted and turned between patches of hardy shrubbery and sheltering trees that absorbed carbon dioxide, produced oxygen, and allowed the citizens to remain emotionally attached to their past.

A gentle breeze stirred the leaves as enormous pumps circulated purified air around the Dome. The lights were already dimmed, in part to bolster normal human circadian rhythms, but primarily to conserve precious energy resources. The city's inhabitants were encouraged to be abed early, for the same purpose. As a rule, few people wandered the park's pathways after dimming time, except for lovers seeking privacy and romance under the few stars that remained visible. When daylight faded, the city basked in a half-moon glow from the phosphorescent coating on the Dome's supporting members. The shadowed lawns and woods, so familiar and welcoming in daytime, took on an air of menace in the muted light, though citizens out for a late stroll felt not in the least imperiled. Nevertheless, Storm moved forward, unafraid.

Just beyond the faint radiance of dimmed gloworbs floating above the pathways, a night thing prowled the underbrush, hoping for a chance encounter, an opportunity. It called softly to the girl as she passed nearby, youthful and trusting. The natural curiosity and naiveté of youth would ensure the success of its hunt. Death lay in wait. It was July 6, 2204, the day after the child's birthday, and her last day on Earth.

CHAPTER 4

THE DARKNESS DESCENDS

July 6, 2204

He had waited so long, so very long. Self-discipline, absolute strength of will had ruled his life for over a decade, and even prior to that he'd restrained himself of necessity. He deserved to be rewarded for his patience. Now was his time. The fruits of his meticulous preparation and planning were about to be realized. His needs would be denied no longer.

She came along the path in his direction. Peering through the foliage, he waited until she was almost abreast of his hiding place in the bushes, then called to her softly, in an old man's voice, "Help me. Can you help me please, youngling? I've managed to get myself caught on a branch and I can't get free. It will take only a moment."

She stopped, cocked her head then moved cautiously toward him. "Where are y….", she began, as he stood up and seized her quickly and firmly, his arms encircling her. She managed only a small cry as he pulled her into him, muffling her voice in his thick clothing. From his right hand, the subcutaneous microjet spray penetrated her neck, taking effect almost immediately. He held her tight against him until he was sure that she was unconscious. As he pressed her soft and burgeoning body against his groin, he felt the familiar stirrings. "Aaaah," he gasped, his breathing becoming ragged.

He carried her to a clearing further back in the woods. Laying her gently on the ground, he quickly removed her clothes and tossed them aside.

His head pounded, the beginnings of a headache ravaging his brain. The hammering increased as he removed his own clothing and positioned himself above her. He was dimly aware of what happened next, but was conscious of little else until after he had emptied himself in a series of body-wrenching spasms.

The headache had not abated by the time he had finished with her. If anything, it was worse. Awareness returned and with it the realization that his hands were clamped tightly around her throat. "Look what you made me do," he growled. "You drove me to this. It wasn't my choice. It's your fault. Bitch! Whore!" By now he was shouting, his fingers squeezing ever tighter. "You betrayed me. You deserve whatever you get!" The red rage penetrated his consciousness, overpowering what little was left of rationality. Releasing her, he stood up and ground his knuckles against his temples, moaning in anguish.

The child was just beginning to come around and whimpered in pain. He bent over and hit her across the face with an open hand, again and again, back and forth until she slumped once more into oblivion. Kneeling astride her, he hit her with closed fists, pounding her head and torso repeatedly. Rather than sating his rage, the violence inflamed it. He picked her up by the waist and swung her around until her head contacted the trunk of a tree with a sickening crunch. He didn't stop, but kept swinging her until she collided with another tree. Only then did he release her, and she went flying, fetching up against the base of yet another tree some meters away.

Gasping for breath, he went down on one knee, and remained there, sobbing, until his head began to clear. He stood up and went to the girl. Kneeling beside her, he gently stroked her hair, weeping, yet the tears he shed were not for her. When a semblance of composure returned, he regained his feet and went in search of his clothes, then returned to the body. In his hand was a length of red ribbon. He lifted the girl's head and gently encircled it with the ribbon, tying it in a bow over her eyes after he'd lowered her head, allowing it to rest on a root. Once again he stood and, after dressing himself, simply walked away. He did not look back.

July 7, 2204

Quinn was stirred from a sound sleep shortly after 0400 hours by the insistent trilling of his com; an emergency call. He tapped the device at the head of his sleep shelf.

"Speak," he said sleepily.

"You're needed. Seabrook Park, south entrance. Now!" The com went silent.

Quinn had recognized the urgent voice of Director Camus Benwright, regional head of the Sentinels. If he was involved in this situation and at this early hour, it must be serious indeed.

Hurriedly, he threw on his working unisuit, grabbed a sampling kit, and rushed to the nearest transport station. He summoned a floater and spoke his destination as he boarded the transparent globe-shaped craft. It drifted smoothly towards the distant vault of the Dome, crossed a segment of the city, then downwards, depositing him within minutes on the circle walkway at the southern edge of the park. Several Sentinel floaters were tethered at the entrance. A cerulean-clad Sentinel scanned the identity chip implanted in Quinn's left earlobe and passed him through the portable metaplas barriers that had been set up to keep out the curious. Quinn scanned the area, looking for Director Benwright, who soon emerged from the nearby shrubbery. Unmistakable in appearance; he was short, slightly pudgy, and with a shaven head surmounting an unexpectedly cherubic face.

"Thanks for your prompt attendance," Benwright said, greeting him formally just a few meters down the pathway. "She's over there." He pointed in the direction of a half-circle of Sentinels nearby, facing outwards as if protecting a dignitary. A distraught man in a tight sportskin was being interviewed by one of them on a nearby bench. "The fitman over there found her," Benwright continued. "He was doing a late night rush around the park, stopped for a drink and spotted her foot protruding from the bushes. The p-meds have already examined him and administered a tranq. He was quite hysterical when he commed us, no less so by the time the quick response team arrived."

"She? What have we got here?" Quinn inquired.

"Young girl, eleven, twelve years old. Beaten, probably raped, murdered. I've secured the scene, protected the forensic evidence. Can't believe this has happened. First homicide ever under the Dome, and so young, too. What kind of recessive degenerate could have done a thing like this?" It was evident that Benwright was shaken to his roots, yet he managed to maintain his professional composure.

The Sentinels opened a path for them. Quinn stopped just inside the cordon and took in the scene. Still on the path, he was able to see a gelshoe-clad foot protruding from the bushes just a couple of meters from where he stood. Portable gloworbs floated over the scene, illuminating it to daylight brilliance.

Quinn put on the 'spider shoes', his own invention for use at crime scenes. They had eight thin and springy downward curving brackets attached to each sole, which provided support but caused minimal disturbance to surfaces due to the tiny pads at their ends. Above his right ear, a personal holocorder tracked everything he observed as he kept up a running commentary.

What he saw turned him sick, his gorge rising. He was forced to pause to regain his composure before he could continue. Never in all of his experience had he witnessed anything approaching the raw brutality of the scene before him. He had come across similar horrors, complete with pictures, in his historical research, but none of those images had prepared him for this.

The girl was semi-prone and unclothed, except for her shoes. Her body had fetched up on its left side against the base of a tree, head bent forward, left arm beneath her trunk, right stretched straight out from her body, legs askew. It appeared that the fragile corpse had been hurled there from a distance. As Quinn moved around the body, he was startled to observe a wide red ribbon tied around her head, a bow covering her eyes. Her body was a mass of bruises and welts, her hair matted with blood. There was blood between her thighs. Partial footprints were only just visible in the dust-covered packed earth near the corpse.

Rage was an emotion only slightly tempered by the genetic manipulations that led up to the creation of the New Society, yet Quinn could not hold back the surge of anger that passed over him at the outrage that had occurred here. He could, he would track down and bring to justice the monster who had committed this appalling crime. That was the promise he made to the young victim as he bent to the task of looking for clues that would lead him to the perpetrator.

Quinn performed a scan to ascertain the body temperature and residual neural activity in order to determine the time of death, then lifted her gently and looked at the ground beneath her. He found nothing. Examining her left side, he detected scrape marks where she had impacted the ground and slid into the tree. He lowered the tiny body back to its original resting place. A scan of the identichip in her left earlobe would reveal her identity, stored in the Dome's central database.

Probing outward in the direction the right arm pointed, Quinn found more footprints and signs of a struggle several meters deeper into the underbrush. He placed markers around the evident imprint of a small body on the earth, and then searched the ground in concentric semicircles away from what appeared to be the primary crime scene. Articles of her clothing were scattered about, and he dutifully flagged them.

Hurrying back to the area of the struggle, he bent to examine it more carefully. The red ribbon would merit closer scrutiny. The ends appeared to have been cut from a longer roll. Suddenly he straightened up and cursed. A gentle rain had begun to fall, dripping off the leaves and settling onto the earth at his feet. Simultaneously, a light misting of water rose up from jets embedded in the ground.

"Benwright," he shouted. "Get the sprinklers turned off, now!" He grabbed a thinsulate blanket from his kit and threw it over the girl's body.

Knowing that it would take too long to contact the park attendant at this hour, Benwright tapped the temple switch on his com-helmet. A menu appeared before his eyes. Quickly, he barked out a series of commands, "Access code AM5691Q. Seabrook Park; sprinklers; off!" He saw the menu scroll rapidly to the required screen, then confirm compliance with the command. The sprinklers, some buried and others located on supporting ribs of the Dome high above the park, shut off. The entire process took less than thirty seconds.

"Sorry about that, Quinn," he apologized. "I forgot about the automatic sprinkler program. Somebody should have been on top of that."

"We all should have been," Quinn said grimly, regaining the pathway. Water was still dripping from the foliage, imprinting tiny craters in the dust below. The smell of damp earth that arose was an unwelcome reminder that valuable evidence had been obliterated. "Well, that's it for the crime scene. Any footprints or drag marks are gone. The scuffle marks might have told us something, but I've got them recorded anyway. Have the body taken to the morgue and I'll look at it there, and bag and transport her clothing. When the marked area dries, have your people go over the ground looking for anything I might have missed. Did you get anything useful from the fitman?"

"Only that he noticed her around 0330 hours, and he didn't see anyone else in the park. Other than that, he didn't have much to contribute."

"From the scan data, I put the time of death between 2205 and 2210. You might want to review the surveillance vids in the area. If you get anything, let me know. For now, I'm through here. I'll be in touch."

Benwright saw how shaken Quinn was. They all were. "I'm sorry I had to drag you into this. If we'd had a professional criminologist on staff, I wouldn't have needed your expertise, but you're all we've got."

"I know. Forget it. We all do what we must. It's just part of being a responsible citizen. I have to get some sleep, and then I'll look at this thing with a fresh eye in the morning. Send me the reports. S'long."

"S'long," Benwright responded to Quinn's retreating back. He knew that there would be no sleep for either of them this night. For them, and perhaps for the citizens of the Dome, the Era of Tranquility had ended.

On the way back to his hab, Quinn mulled over what he'd observed. A senseless, brutal murder had occurred; something that might have been common more than a century earlier, but practically unheard of today. A lot of rage there, as evidenced by the bruising and the way the tiny body had been hurled a distance from the primary crime scene. The perpetrator had used her, venting his fury on the tiny victim, and had angrily discarded her like a used and broken toy. And the red ribbon... that signified something, but what?

Sociopathic behavior at this level had been virtually unknown since the establishment of the Domes. The Compilers had created a well-ordered society, using a combination of genetic and social engineering to quell humanity's baser instincts and to elevate its higher attributes. While emotions like love and anger, necessary for the survival of the species, had been left more or less untouched, those who lived in the Domes had been cleansed of the genetic predilections that created the kind of mayhem that had been common prior to the 22nd century, and were conditioned from an early age to conform to the current social standards and mores that bring about a peaceful and cooperative society. Virtually all of the anti-social behaviors in recent decades had come from those who chose to dwell outside of the Domes, and who had committed their acts either outside the Domes' protection, or had infiltrated these sanctuaries to defile their social order.

There had been a few unfortunate incidents with the hard-working, hard-drinking, hard-playing construction workers in the early days of Dome construction, but those days were long gone, as the Dome had been completed a century before. Now, only small crews of trained and well disciplined workers laboured to expand the ancillary service and light manufacturing domes on the peripheries of the city.

Quinn returned to his hab and attempted to get a couple of extra hours of well-earned sleep before he had to go to his campus office to organize the day's work. He tried to close his mind off from the gruesome incident he had just investigated. It soon became evident that sleep would be impossible.

Finally giving in, he got up and went to his comcenter. "On," he instructed. He synched and downloaded the contents of his holovid and examined the crime scene more closely. It didn't add much to what he already knew. There were few evident marks of a struggle; the child had been subdued easily, and the few visible footprints were indistinct and unidentifiable.

Next, he used his high level authorization to access the park's security camera records and quick-scanned from 2100 hours onwards, stopping only when a citizen appeared onscreen. At 2151, a young girl came into view, hurrying along the pathway. She paused close to the spot where he had later entered the woods. Cocking her head, she moved slowly towards the shrubbery beside the path then vanished from the sec-cam's view. Quinn called up several different angles of the scene, but the sec-cams lost her a couple of meters into the woods. He brought up the sound level, and was able to hear what he thought was a muffled cry. Lacking the expertise to do a more in-depth analysis, he decided he'd better let the lab boys work on that later.

He tapped into the coroner's digicam system. A holo of the examination room sprang into view before his eyes. With minute hand gestures, he was able to rotate the image and zoom in. As he'd anticipated, the girl's autopsy was underway. The red ribbon and each item of her clothing were individually bagged on a side table, The monotonal drone of the coroner's voice came from the image, "….of a twelve year old female, Caucasian, shoulder length auburn hair, height one hundred thirty-five centimeters, mass thirty eight point five kilos, no obvious scars. Visible evidence of massive trauma with bruising over the entire body. Bruises on the throat, a fractured hyoid bone and petechial hemorrhaging suggest strangulation as a possible cause of death. Sexual trauma, as evidenced by bruising on the inner thighs, vaginal intrusion and the torn hymen is …". Quinn muted the sound and dejectedly watched the visual as the body was automatically scanned and electronically probed, samples removed and stored for later biopsy. He'd read the report later.

As the autopsy continued, Quinn's mind wandered. In a recent paper he'd read on the history of deviant sexual behavior, the subject of pedophilia had been given some prominence. It had not been unusual for children to be kidnapped and molested, then murdered either for thrills or to keep the child from bearing witness against the offender. This particular crime did not seem to fit exactly into either mold. It appeared to be a crime of directed and passionate violence. The rage implicit in the way the girl had been beaten then hurled aside suggested a crime inspired more by anger than by sexual desire. The most puzzling aspect of the murder was the red ribbon.

Quinn searched his memory for similar cases. There were many throughout history, instances where corpses had been laid out in various poses or had had words or symbols written on or carved into their skin, eyes or other body parts removed, objects inserted or laid on or around the body. He was trying to slot the murder into a category when he drifted into a troubled sleep on the couch.

A strangled cry awoke him a short time later. Instantly alert, he shot up and turned to see his sister Sera frozen in mid-step just inside the entry portal, her horror-struck gaze locked on the comcenter projection where the autopsy was still in progress. The look on her face told him all he needed to know.

"Off", he commanded, and the ghastly images vanished. "Sorry, I wasn't expecting you," he said as he rose and walked to her.

She stood, still frozen in place, gasping, her mouth attempting to form words. He enfolded her in his arms and held her close. "It's all right," he murmured.

"It's not all right," she said, finally regaining her voice and pushing him away. "What the frik was that?"

"Sorry you had to see it," he apologized again. "A young girl was murdered tonight. Benwright called me in on the investigation. I was just viewing the autopsy. I thought you were staying with your friends for a few days."

Quinn and Sera shared the hab they'd been brought up in, the same one that their parents had occupied during their short but happy existence in the Dome. It was now divided into two smaller habs for privacy, but they shared a common entrance.

"Murder? Under the Dome? Impossible!" Sera said. She was shaking now, and Quinn wanted to hold her and comfort her, but she moved away and threw herself into a sling chair across the room. "I can't believe it," she continued, bent over, covering her face with her hands. "A murder. Who? How?"

"We don't know much yet. It was a cruel and violent crime. The victim was a young girl. It'll take a while to gather the evidence and analyze it."

"Well, better you than me. I don't think I could handle it. It's just too brutal. How do you manage deal with something like this?"

"If I hadn't spent years studying deviant criminal psychology, I wouldn't be able to. I was exposed to some of the worst atrocities man had perpetrated against man. I saw the photos and watched the vids. It's not an academic exercise I'd recommend to the faint of heart."

"I can't stand it. I just can't. I've been working on my research project all night and I'm exhausted. I'm going to bed. I need to get away from this. Com me if you need me."

Obviously shaken, Sera went through the portal to her private space, leaving Quinn to try to sort out his feelings and the mystery of the senseless crime that would embroil him for a long time to come.

* * *

The autopsy report had arrived at his desktop comcenter by the time he got to his office, somewhat later than usual. He called it up and gave it a quick read-through. The girl's name was Storm O'Reilly, twelve years old, survived by her father, a lab tech, her mother, a licensed mentor, and her 18 year-old sister, a nurse-intern at Delphi district hospital. Other than that, it told him little that he hadn't observed at the crime scene, except to confirm that the little girl had indeed been raped, though there was no semen present, nor any evidence of a lubricant such as might be found on a condom. Puzzling. She'd been alive through the beating, though probably unconscious. There were evident finger marks on her throat, but no fingerprints. The cause of death was trauma to the head, confirmed by the deep lacerations in which fragments of tree bark were embedded. Her skull had been bashed in against a tree before she had been flung to her final resting place.

A memo from Benwright was appended, informing Quinn that the Sentinels were continuing to examine the crime scene and that a tri-d reconstruction of the probable progression of the murder would soon be available. The forensics team was also examining the girl's clothing and effects, with special attention being given to the red ribbon. The body had been checked for trace, but nothing was found except a few synthetic fibers in her mouth and nose. The report on those was also to follow. It was only with a great effort that Quinn was able to tear his mind away from the crime in order to focus on his day job. His efforts to temporarily distance himself from the crime lasted only until the full forensics reports arrived an hour later.

"I can't deal with this alone," he thought, as he studied the reports arrayed on the screen in front of him. He punched his com button and spoke, "Sera," into it. Within moments, his sister responded.

"How're you feeling?" Quinn inquired.

"I'm all right," she said. "I'm just coming to terms with my feelings about this. I think maybe I can deal with it now. How are you doing?"

"I'll be fine. I could use some help."

"I wondered how long it would be before you called. I assumed you'd be busy, so I didn't want to disturb you."

Sera Braxton, Quinn's sister, a year his junior, was as brilliant as he. She had degrees in microbiology, biophysics and biochemistry and, like Quinn, taught two classes at the same university. Her research dealt with cell structure and the ways in which cells interact in order to carry out their many functions within the body. Her interdisciplinary degrees allowed her to study biomolecules for the purpose of manipulating their functions to produce technological breakthroughs in the field of bio-robotics. She had already devised ways to direct benign bacteria to perform useful functions beyond what they normally did. Now she was working on constructing biological nanobots that could be custom grown within the human body to perform multiple specialized tasks.

"So you know what I'm up against," Quinn said. "I may need some of your expertise on this one, but for now I need your insights. If I copy the files to you, will you have time to go over what we know so far and share your thoughts?"

"Sure," Sera replied. "I'm on my way to a seminar right now, but if you've got time, we can go over the case over lunch."

"Good. I'll meet you at the Retro-Fit Café around 1230. Out."

Two hours later, Quinn strode onto the patio of the Retro-Fit, at the base of the central tower. The caf was decorated in the gaudy primary colors popular after America's second civil war, complete with the pennants and flags of the blue and the red states. Soothing music, intended to stimulate the appetite and relax the patrons, emanated from the acoustic walls. The menu included a lot of dishes using soy, alfalfa sprouts, and hydroponic vegetables. Quinn craned around and finally located Sera at a table far from the door to the caf.

"You'll be waiting a while for service, sitting way over here at peak hour," he commented as he seated himself opposite her.

"I don't have to quiz the roboserver today," Sera replied. "I don't really care too much for food right now. Just a couple of nutri-wafers and a fruit juice to keep me going. I'll use my com to order." This told Quinn a lot about Sera's state of mind. She loved her food, and almost never substituted the wafers for a good meal.

"Sorry I had to drag you into this," Quinn told her. "It's just that …"

"Never mind. I know. If it's for the common good, every citizen must do his duty, however abhorrent." Quinn thought he saw a hint of a tear in her eye.

He added an alfalfa-bean sprout-nut salad to Sera's order, along with a carrot nutri-shake, and within minutes their lunch arose from the table's pedestal centre. The table read their identichips and deducted the appropriate charge from their time credit accounts. Aromatic edible flowers garnished his salad, and Quinn inhaled deeply, appreciating the entire experience of dining on natural food. It was likely to be the only experience he'd enjoy this day.

Sera munched her nutriwafer despondently. "I looked over the files," she said, popping a holoscreen up from the table's surface and synching it to her wrist pod. Like her brother, she was one of the minority who chose to use the wrist device instead of the com-helmet, preferring to feel the artificial breezes tousle her shoulder-length raven hair. "This is just horrible," she continued, scrolling through the documents and vids. "Excuse me. I'm still having trouble dealing with this atrocity." Tears welled up, in spite of Sera's determination to remain strong.

"Look, we can do this another time if you like. I'll put together a report for the meeting, and we'll talk later on, O.K.?"

"No. No. I'll be all right," she said, regaining her composure with some effort. "Let's do it now. Any ideas?"

"To say I'm clueless would be an understatement. The perp left us almost nothing. The fibers and particles are quite ordinary, so they're virtually useless unless we can match them to a person, and we can't do that if we don't catch him."

"Let's go over what we have," Sera suggested. "There are the footprints that you caught on your holocorder, so we can get an approximate shoe size. There's the particulate evidence you mentioned, although of limited usefulness for now, but we can conjecture a psych profile by making a few assumptions."

"I've got a meeting at the Sentinels' H.Q. in less that an hour. Even with all that, it leaves us almost nowhere."

"True, but we must make the best use of what we've got. I have to get back to work, but I'll help you summarize these reports for the meeting first." Sera gritted her teeth and plunged in.

* * *

Later that day, a meeting was convened in a conference room at Sentinel headquarters in the Dome's administrative centre in the Central Tower, to go over the evidence gathered thus far. In attendance along with Quinn were the coroner, a forensic technician, Director Benwright, Commissioner Chaz Earl, who was Benwright's superior in the Command and Control sector of the Dome security branch, and two representatives of the Dome's governing body, the Guardians; Guardian Isomoto and

Guardian F-Kilmara. All had accessed a summary report on their info screens or helmet projections, detailing what was known about the victim, the probable progression of the crime, and evidence that might point to a suspect. Benwright chaired the meeting, but it was Quinn they were all waiting to hear from.

"News of the crime was all over the tri-d's and the Net before breakfast," Benwright began. "People are frightened and horrified. We have to give them something quickly, a suspect, a lead, anything. Everyone knows that this kind of thing just doesn't happen, hasn't happened in over a century. What can we tell them?"

Quinn stood up. "We can tell them pretty much nothing. I've studied the evidence that has been gathered and analyzed so far, and there's little to indicate where we can go from here. There are scant leads.

"The victim's name is Storm O'Reilly, age twelve. Her parents, Sean and Greta, live in a two bedroom hab in the third ring in Seabrook District. He's a lab tech in the physics department at the university. She's a licensed mentor with the Seabrook Elementary School system. Both are Sociocultural class 1A. Storm had an 18 year-old sister.

"Fibers found in the girl's mouth and nose are common synthetics found in most clothing, and the color is unremarkable. The fibers themselves hold no trace of DNA or anything that might lead to the wearer. The red ribbon was cut from a longer roll, but what it means, if anything, is unclear. There's only one manufacturer of that particular ribbon, and anybody can requisition it. It's widely available, and is used mostly for home decoration or to make a fashion statement. Blood screening, coupled with the circular bruise on her neck, indicated that she was tranq'd as the perp took her." By way of illustration, Quinn called up the security vid from the park. "Right there," he indicated, as the girl disappeared from the camera's view into the woods, and her last words, amplified, were cut off suddenly. "That's when he tranq'd her to keep her quiet and to control her."

"In the absence of semen, how can you be sure she was raped and not merely violated with an object?" Guardian Isomoto asked uncomfortably.

The coroner spoke up. "Bruising on the inner thighs and lower abdomen indicate a ferocious pounding, as if an adult male had repeatedly thrust himself against her. Vaginal tearing is consistent with a violent rape. It would have had to have been a fairly rough object to have caused that kind of damage, and odds are that it would have left some fragments inside her. We found a tiny amount of particulate matter present, which forensics hasn't as yet been able to identify. These particles were recovered from both the vagina and the bruised areas adjacent. Could be some kind of condom, but that doesn't explain why we haven't found any hairs or epithelia on the body."

"As to those particles," the forensics tech said, rising at his place, "We think it may be some kind of synthetic plastic, but it will take another day or two to type it with any certainty. We've identified the tranq he used as a quick acting hypnotic commonly used in hospitals and by p-techs."

By this time, many of the participants at the meeting were looking somewhat ill, the unaccustomed details of a grisly murder impacting on psyches that had been insulated from such horrors all of their lives. Had it not been for their strong sense of civic duty, they would have wished themselves elsewhere.

"The only thing we can be fairly certain of is that this was a crime of opportunity," Quinn observed. "The girl was not targeted personally, since nobody except her parents and her friend's parents knew where she'd be at that time, and all of them were in their habs during the assault. It appears, then, that the perpetrator was either in the right place at the right time, or that he stalks young girls. Since this has never happened before, either conclusion is feasible.

"I've examined the killer's footprints as best I could from my holocording of the crime scene, and they, too, are unexceptional. They could have come from any number of shoe types worn by most citizens. Without more detailed measurements of tread dimensions, I'm afraid they can't be narrowed down."

"Professor Braxton. Would you care to speculate on what we should be looking for?" Guardian F-Kilmara asked.

"What can I tell you? A moderately strong male with a messed up psyche. Could be a citizen, or even an Outlander in the Dome for the Centennial celebrations, perhaps a vendor or a performer in the parks. We'll be checking every possibility and hope we catch a break. Until we know more we can't narrow it down further."

Benwright arose, "Thanks, Quinn. It's less than twenty-four hours since the crime was committed, too early to conclude that we're at a dead end. Examination of the evidence will continue, and we can only hope that something comes of it. I've asked Quinn to take the lead on the investigation, because of his expertise in the field of deviant criminal behavior, so he's to be cc'd on all reports. Let's meet again tomorrow to see where we stand. With the approval of Commissioner Earl, I'm asking all of you to assist me in coordinating a task force to catch this homicidal maniac. We'll meet regularly to assess the information we've obtained and to decide on a course of action. Thank you all for coming. Quinn! A moment?"

"We have much to do," Benwright said as he pulled Quinn aside. "We're going to be interviewing everyone we feel might be directly or peripherally involved in this. Can you sit in on the interviews?"

"I'll do what I can. I expect you want me to prompt your interviewers when appropriate, and to help evaluate the results."

"I'd very much appreciate it. It would be a great help to us and it might also help you to gain some insight and get a better overall picture of the investigation," Benwright replied.

"When can we begin?"

"A soon as my people put together a list of interviewees. I expect it'll be a short one; the parents, the fitman, anyone we can identify as having been in the vicinity around the time of the attack."

* * *

Less than 24 hours after young Storm O'Reilly had met her fate, Quinn, accompanied by ACS Egon Travio of the Sentinels' special squad, arrived at the portal of the modest family-4 hab where her parents Sean and Greta lived. The portal confirmed their identities and admitted them after Sean granted permission. The hab was decorated in subdued colors with soft materials on the walls and furnishings. Subtle nature smells and muted birdsong filled the air as the hab's A.I. detected the mood of its occupants and attempted to compensate.

Sean and Greta O'Reilly sat on the sofa clinging to each other, suspended in time, cosseted together in their anguish. Their red rimmed eyes attested to their grief. Storm's sister Gale, heavily tranq'd, had taken to her sleep shelf.

"So sorry to bother you at a time like this. Our condolences on the passing of your daughter," ACS Travio said. The couple nodded slightly in acknowledgement.

Travio continued, "We're in the process of gathering any possible information that might lead to the perpetrator of this appalling crime. To that end we would ask that you cooperate by answering a few questions."

"Anything we can do to help," Sean said, his voice breaking.

Greta sobbed softly. "How could you have let this happen? We expect to be watched over by the Guardians and protected by the Sentinels under the Dome. Things like this just cannot occur!" she moaned.

Quinn stepped in. "If ever we had imagined something like this could happen, we would have taken measures to prevent it. I commiserate with you in your pain, but we must find the perpetrator and prevent anything like this from every happening again."

Greta continued to sob, and Sean comforted her as best he could. "Please ask your questions quickly then, so that we may be alone."

ACS Travio took the lead in the questioning, with Quinn prompting him from time to time. The parents' answers revealed nothing useful, except to solidify the timeline they had already established. Examination of Storm's space likewise uncovered no further clues. Quinn and ACS Travio reiterated their sympathy and left.

Their next stop was Jade Choy's hab across the park, the inquiry there similarly yielding no useful information. It turned out to be a long evening. None of the subsequent interviewees was able to cast any further light on the case, so they wrapped up that phase of the investigation for the time being. ACS Travio returned to his office to summarize the results, such as they were, and to fill Benwright in, and Quinn went home to get some much needed sleep.

July 14, 2204

A week and several meetings later, it was apparent that they were indeed at a dead end. Neither Quinn nor anyone else associated with the investigation had moved so much as a millimeter closer to finding the killer. No new forensic evidence had been uncovered. Everyone who had been identified as having been in the park that evening had been interviewed, as had Storm's friends, their parents, and anyone who worked at the park or at the adjacent plaza. Examination of floater trip records revealed nothing. Nobody was able to add anything meaningful to the file.

Yet, there was a single, mysterious and tantalizing bit of evidence that haunted Quinn's thoughts day and night. The tiny particles recovered from the girl's vagina and torso had been identified as being a spray-on synthskin, often used in burn treatment. That, at least, was a lead worth following.

CHAPTER 5

AT HOME WITH THE USHERS

July 16, 2204

"Hey, I was watching that," Desert protested as the holovid image winked out.

Bedtime, youngling," her older sister River declared. "You've got to be up bright and early tomorrow."

"Rosieee," Desert appealed to her mother. "Just another half hour, just until 'Tween Image' is over. Pleeese!"

"Mind your sister, DD. She's just looking out for you."

"Oh, all right. But why do I have to go to bed so early and Daniel doesn't?" she complained.

"Because you're thirteen and have science camp in the morning, and he's 16 and his next college class isn't until Tuesday," Rosie explained. "Now, off with you, and make sure you straighten up your sleep shelf in the morning before you go out to breakfast. You won't have time later."

Daniel, occupied with completing a calculus assignment, took time out to smirk at his little sister before going back to his computations. She returned a scowl before reluctantly slouching off to her sleep alcove in the next room, where she changed into her jams and slipped under her huggie. After tuning her wrist comp to x-pod mode, she drifted off to the gentle soughing of whisper tunes, the latest fad among tweenies.

Evening at the Ushers' was family time, when everyone congregated in the gathering room to pursue individual or group activities. Familial closeness kept the lines of communication open and strengthened bonds of affection that the Ushers shared. Eventually, Daniel put his assignment aside and took some time out for recreation. While he and River engaged in a challenging round of the ancient game Go, Rosie and Gus discussed business. They owned a very successful Harbour located in RichmondDome.

"By the way, Rosie, where's Jon tonight?" Gus inquired. "I thought he wanted to be in on this discussion."

"Had a date," she answered. Their oldest son, Jonathan, was a partner in the family firm, and as such had a right and a responsibility to be in on business-related decisions. "Marvey's being transported to the Antarctica science Dome tomorrow, and it's the last chance he'll have to see her for a while. We can fill him in when he gets home, if he gets home tonight!"

"That boy? Not likely!" Gus snorted. "Anyhow, if we want to apply for expansion space for next year, we have to do it before the end of the month."

"Unless you're really close to developing the 'tens', I can't see why we'll need it for a while. It seems to me that we can get along just fine with the space we have now. It's not as if the Guardians are approving a whole lot more Futures' licenses lately." Gus was working on a process to accelerate the growth of Futures clones by up to ten years and, anticipating increased business as a result, would need much more space if he were to succeed. Besides, their major competitors, the Stildenbachs, were constantly expanding their own Harbours empire.

"They could if they'd lighten up on the qualifications for Futures candidacy. After all, nobody's perfect, or almost nobody. Anyhow, I'm very close to solving the 'tens' problem. I just need a little push to get over the last hump, that's why I've asked Quinn to come over tomorrow. He has a good deal of expertise in theoretical reproductive biology, areas where I'm a little weak. My strength is in the application of theory. He can look at my work and perhaps suggest ways in which I might tweak the genome to produce the result I'm looking for."

"Better keep an eye on that one. Have you noticed the coy glances that River throws his way whenever he's around? He has, and I daresay he's returned more than a few when he thinks we're not watching."

Gus and Rosie had met Quinn years before through a mutual friend, Pierre Adler, an eminent Arbiter, at one of Pierre's frequent open house gatherings. Even though the Ushers were senior to Quinn by more than a decade, they'd hit it off immediately through their common interest in reproductive technologies. Quinn often visited Usher's Harbour, getting firsthand pointers on the practical aspects of the applied sciences involved, and sometimes bringing his classes in for tours. Gus and Rosie returned the visits, frequently winding up in late night gab sessions with Quinn and his sister Sera in the hab the siblings shared.

As the years went by and Gus and Rosie's daughter River matured, Quinn couldn't help but notice how the gawky teen had blossomed into a gifted, vibrant and lovely young woman. Her intelligence, her innate curiosity, and the intellectual stimuli provided by her parents, combined with the academic nature of RichmondDome, had inspired her to pursue a career in anthropology.

For her part, River's teenage crush on 'Uncle Quinn' had grown into so much more. She couldn't deny her heart, and her scientific training told her that Quinn compared more than favorably to the best phenotypes of centuries past. Their parents had instilled in them some old fashioned values, and for a long time they denied their mutual attraction for the sake of propriety. That state of affairs could not be sustained forever.

"Our daughter could do worse," Gus replied. "He may be a few years older than she is, but I can really see them as a good match. He's intelligent, successful, well-respected, and a really decent and likeable guy, not to mention his genome is first rate. After all, both of his parents were Futures. Getting back to the problem at hand, if I do get it solved,

I'll need the space in less than two years. It'll take me the better part of a year to get set up."

"All right, I take your point. We should apply as soon as possible. I'll download the forms tomorrow and get them filled out. I should be able to upload them to the Space Allocations Division before noon."

July 21, 2204

As it turned out, it would be several days before Quinn was able to free himself up from his other duties to visit Gus. The murder investigation had stalled and he was anxiously awaiting follow- up reports from Sentinels' interviews and forensic analyses.

Rosie welcomed Quinn as the entry portal admitted him just after midday. "Come in, Quinn. Lovely to see you again. How are you? How's Sera doing? How's the investigation going?" she asked.

Quinn was always amused at the way Rosie greeted people with rapid fire questions as to their state of well-being and that of their loved ones. "I'm fine, Sera's fine, and the investigation is going nowhere. Thanks for asking."

"Oooh, I'm sorry to hear that, Quinn. I mean, about the investigation, not about you and Sera." She grasped his arm and tugged him into the gathering room. "Guuus," she called. "Quinn's here."

River looked up from the virtual spiral galaxy she had been constructing inside an energy globe. She hit the save button and turned it off. The stars winked out.

"Lo, Quinn. Good to see you again," she greeted him.

"Lo, River. That looked interesting."

"Just helping DD with a science project. Something to fill in the time. Nothing to do, nowhere to go." She sighed. Quinn failed to get the hint.

"You could've just commed me," Gus observed as he entered the room moments later. "You just enjoy using full voice, Rosie m'love. Lo, Quinn, it's been a while. We hear you're up to your knees in it these days."

"Gus. You're looking good. I assume you mean my involvement with the murder investigation, and, yes, I'm in it well beyond my knees by now, heading rapidly towards my neck."

"Such a terrible thing this is," Gus remarked. "Should never have happened under the Dome, under the protection of the Council of Guardians, under the vigilance of the Sentinels."

"Yet it has, and we must deal with it. This creature cannot be allowed to disrupt the order of the Dome, but I doubt he can stand against the forces being brought to bear for long. Don't worry. He'll soon be caught and dealt with." Quinn could not know how wrong he was.

"How will you catch him?" asked Rosie.

"Detective work," Quinn replied. "Twenty-first century investigative techniques. We put together a list of suspects, and narrow the list down by analyzing the forensic and physical evidence we're gathering."

"As simple as that?" Gus asked.

"By no means simple," Quinn answered. "It'll take work, a lot of drudge work and a lot of legwork. Right now we have half a million suspects, and we haven't managed to narrow down that list by more than a few dozen."

"Are we on that list?" Rosie inquired.

"Of course not. In reality, we're eliminating all females and all males under or over certain ages. Then we'll look at the databanks to determine levels of physical ability in order to eliminate anyone who could not possibly have overpowered or savaged the girl so brutally. There's more we can do, but narrowing the list to a manageable length will take some time."

"And in the meantime?" Gus said.

"We work, we wait, and we hope it doesn't happen again."

"Do you think it might?" said Rosie.

"No. I think it's unlikely. I think it was probably an Outlander, and he's almost certainly long gone. We may never actually solve the crime, but we won't stop trying."

"At least that should go a long way to alleviating the panic people are in over this," said Gus.

"Well," Quinn said, "We're not yet ready to state that publicly. We have a long way to go before we can reassure the citizens that the perpetrator is caught or that it won't happen again."

"I can't bear to think about that poor girl any more, or the monster who killed her," Rosie interrupted. "Did she suffer much, Quinn? No. Don't tell me. I don't want to hear the details."

"If it's any consolation, Rosie, we don't believe she suffered. The killer tranqued her before he assaulted her, She may never have know what was happening to her."

"Let's be thankful for that, then. I've heard enough. Her parents must be in a terrible state. As a mother I can only imagine what they're going through. Can we please discuss something more pleasant and productive? I'll order up some refreshments from the dispenser before you get down to work."

"Right," Gus said. "So, Quinn, if you can just look at my research logs and see what I've been doing on the 'tens' problem, maybe you can make some suggestions or point out where I might be going wrong. If I can speed up the growth of the recipient bodies by just a decade, I can make the process more efficient and less costly. After that, perhaps ordinary people might have access to it."

Gus brought up the logs on his comcenter. Together, they did a quickscan and settled on some of Gus' more recent efforts. Rosie slid a tray of drinks and nutri-snacks between them, and then retired to the lab to clean up.

"Here," said Gus. "This is what I mean. Of course, I've been using pig ova and DNA and nurturing the resulting pig embryos. Growth can be slowed down or speeded up using hormones. I've had some limited success, but I have to balance out the benefits with the risk of damaging the growing bodies. If I can't speed the process up by at least ten years then the advantage of accelerated growth will be limited."

"According to your notes, you administer the growth hormone in measured doses. Have you tried giving it continuously?"

"No. Even with sophisticated techniques I feared lack of absolute control over the dosage, which must be monitored and changed continuously in response to increasing body mass and biological maturity."

"Well, here's another little problem you might not have considered. As you know, with human subjects, their memories are played back in real time and imprinted on the brains as their new bodies mature in the sensory deprivation tanks. If you speed up their growth you'll have to precisely match the speed of the memory download. It's important that their life experiences correspond to their physical maturation, or else psych problems may develop."

"Ach, another headache," Gus exploded. "As if I needed more problems."

"We'll work on it together, Gus, as soon as I can get clear of this murder case. Don't get too concerned. I'd enjoy the diversion of working on something new and challenging with you."

"Thanks, Quinn. If I could get those problems under control, I could get Ted Williams out of storage and revive him."

"Really? You could do that?"

"Quinn. You're too easy. Ted Williams was revived over a century ago."

"He wa ......? O.K. You got me again, Gus," Quinn laughed. Gus was quite a joker, and enjoyed making Quinn the butt of his gags. Fortunately, Quinn had a fine sense of humor, and gave as good as he got. "I've some thoughts on the subject that might help you. If you give me a copy of your records, I'll toss some ideas around and get back to you as soon as I can."

Gus copied the records of his experiments onto a memory crystal and handed it to Quinn, who put it in his waist pouch for safekeeping.

"Thanks Gus. Thanks Rosie. See you soon," he called down the passageway connecting the living quarters to the labs. "I'll be in touch. Bye, River."

"Bye, Quinn," River replied, casting him a steamy look. "Give me a call if you need help with your science project."

Quinn laughed as he reached the portal. "I'll do that. Be seeing you." Then he was gone.

River humphed grumpily, then went back to Desert's science project. "Things will be different next time, buster," she resolved.

CHAPTER 6

THE RISE OF THE COMPILERS

Autumn, 2072

One fire flared and, shortly thereafter, another. From the Right Bank, black smoke swirled and billowed across the Seine. FNN reported that demonstrators had set fire to the Parisian City Hall in the Place de l'Hotel de Ville, just across the river from the Quartier Latin where Emile sat at his comcenter. Through the window of the compact flat overlooking Boulevard Saint-Michel, he could see, beyond the Île de la Cité, the glow of the fires across the Seine, accompanied by the braying of klaxons as fire engines and ambulances converged on the scene. Police were already on hand, trying in vain to contain the rioters as they split up and dashed north towards the Pompidou Center and northwest to the Forum Les Halles, smashing and looting and setting fires as they went. It was not altogether clear what the demonstrators wanted, other than free electronic gear and appliances. Caught up in mob hysteria, logic occluded by anger, the protesters surged through the heart of the city in chaotic patterns that converged and parted at random, leaving destruction in their wake.

The 'whik, whik' of police stunners echoed in the streets, but as quickly as immobilized demonstrators were scooped up, others replaced them. The comcenter's split screen displayed the FNN broadcast, as well as the two friends that Emile was currently communicating with; Ranjit Singh, a fiftyish medical doctor in Chennai, India, and Brad Colchester, in his late twenties, a psionic engineer in Silicon Valley, California. The three were part of the larger group of forward thinkers coordinated by the Founders, who regularly networked, exchanging information and ideas.

"Are you seeing what I'm seeing?" Emile asked. "Sacre Coeur! They call themselves L'Espoir Nouveau, the New Hope. It's madness. What do they want? What has the world come to?"

"Seems more like Le Désespéré Ancien, the same old hopelessness," Ranjit replied. "They want what we all want, a better life. They just don't know what to do about it. Half of them lack the education or the opportunities to better themselves, and the other half are just along for the ride. It was ever thus."

"We've been getting some of that over here, too," Brad replied. "Fires all over South Central, and so soon after they had finished with a major reformation of the entire area. So sad, and for what?"

"Governments and society had the means to nip problems like this in the bud over half a century ago, but they lacked the will to be proactive." Emile said despondently. "We must work faster. Events have been spiraling out of control for decades and nobody knows what to do about it. We have to consolidate our ideas into a form that appeals to everyone before we can even begin to have an impact."

"And that's what we're trying to do now," Brad interrupted. "We can make a difference, if we can get them to listen."

"Ah, the idealism of youth," ventured Emile, all too aware that he was rapidly approaching his fiftieth year. "If only we could make them listen. That's what the mob destroying my city is saying, and that's what disenfranchised peoples have been saying for ages. If only we could make them listen. Once we have a plan in place, we'll have to find a way to make them listen, and that will have to be part of the plan. If we leave it up to the powers that be, they'll never listen, because then they'll cease to be the powers that be, with all of their attendant wealth and privilege."

A massive light flared across the river opposite Emile's window, then a concussive wave, an explosive thunderclap that shook the building . Yellow and orange flames lit up the night sky.

"Matharchod!" Ranjit exclaimed. "Did you see that on FNN? What was that?"

"I can see it from here," Emile answered. "Looks like a gas pipeline went up near Les Halles. They're still at it."

"Where's Maria tonight? She said she'd be online with us," Brad said.

Ranjit replied, "I got a message that she's tied up in traffic. Seems that the same sort of thing is going on in Santiago. The police have cordoned off the area where she lives. She said she may not be able to get home tonight, so she's going over to a friend's place and she'll try to contact us from there."

* * *

Back in 2057, Jason Moorehead, Mark Wells, and Derrick Carver had founded a group to provide leadership and guidance for the peoples of a troubled world. They had worked tirelessly, recruiting dozens to their cause, rejecting others who would have disrupted their efforts either through malice or self-interest. Now, in 2072, the next generation of crusaders was taking over.

This particular group had been formed in the late 2060s when half a dozen students met for a seminar class in sociology at the prestigious École Normale Supérieure in the historic Latin Quarter, under the tutelage of Professor Emile Vaillencourt. Prompted by the invitation issued by the Founders, they began to discuss the human condition, both in and out of class, their professor often joining their off-campus discussions. Most evenings they met informally at a café in the Latin Quarter, near the university.

"I sometimes feel," began Maria Sanchez, an exchange student from Santiago, Chile, "that we take and take and take and give back so little.

Society is collapsing of its own weight, because people aren't contributing enough, not even their fair share. So many people expect others to carry the burden of making society work, and still others plunder the wealth of the world and ignore the plight of those who must bear the cost."

"What's your point?" asked Lee Hang, a refugee from the Sino-Taiwan War. "Civil society has been on the decline for decades in many parts of the world. Are you implying that we few can do something about it?"

"Yes," Maria continued. "You see, the rift between the haves and the have nots has been widening for the better part of a century. It started to narrow after the beginning of the industrial revolution, but then it began to widen again by the end of the twentieth century, through exploitation of the masses. Corporate executives began to loot their own companies by way of outrageous salaries and bonuses, if not outright theft. Corporations began to shift their manufacturing and service bases to underdeveloped countries, and to exploit cheap labour by economic and political refugees in their home countries."

"But that supported and improved the economies of the underdeveloped countries and allowed the people to raise their standard of living," Brad Colchester protested.

"It allowed developing countries to join the global economy in a significant fashion, and hastened the growth of democracy in many countries under autocratic or one-party rule," Ranjit Singh added. He was on a one year sabbatical from his clinic in India, and chose to spend some of it auditing university classes in Paris. "In my country, there was an upsurge of industry in a way that had never before been seen. Other countries in Asia saw similar benefits."

"And few ordinary workers saw the direct benefits. As always, the major benefits went to rich industrialists and foreign corporations," said Marie. "Those who had the opportunity to become well-educated thrived, while others fell by the wayside and benefited only peripherally from those economic improvements."

"You seem well versed in economics, young lady," Emile interjected. "What's your background?"

"My mother is a government economist. My father is a political scientist who was one of the founders of the Chilean Workers Equity Movement. I've been steeped in history and economics since I was a child."

"What's the guiding principle of the movement?" Emile asked.

"A more equitable distribution of resources and equal educational opportunities for all, combined with universal healthcare and an absolute guarantee of proper nutrition and adequate shelter for everyone. If our programs were implemented it could wipe out poverty and disease and inequity in our country."

"Think bigger. Think worldwide," added Jasmine Burke, a transplanted Iranian with an English father. "If those principles could be applied across the board, the human condition could be improved all over the planet."

"You're all so young and idealistic," Emile commented. "I don't want to put a damper on your enthusiasm, but you're not the first to get this far, then, faced with the exigencies of your own lives, look only to your own backyard once you get home."

"But it doesn't have to be that way," Maria protested. "We have the technology. The Founders showed the way. We can network. We can organize. We can clamor for attention. If nobody does anything, then nothing will ever change, or things will get worse. We have to do something."

Her passion was infectious, and the group nodded in agreement. They continued to debate and to discuss well into the early hours of the morning, as students are wont to do. When they finally parted, they had resolved to replace talk with action. True to their word, they continued to meet throughout the remainder of their university courses, and, upon returning to their homes, they communicated on the Net. They blogged and they posted their ideas on accessible websites. They harassed and harangued governments and corporations in person and through the mass media. Over the next few years, word of their aims spread, and they were joined by others determined to make a difference.

Individual meetings in chat rooms, and on other social media and dedicated websites had resulted in the coalescing of a group of dozens of like-minded individuals from all over the globe, along with a group of lurkers and hangers-on numbering in the thousands. Daily, they used their comcenters and handhelds to communicate with each other, to discuss weighty matters that involved the future of mankind. They thought of themselves as futurists, examining their present world of the early 2070s, hoping to design an idealized world of tomorrow by combining forward thinking with the best ideas from the past.

The group was attempting to take every factor into consideration; nationalism, climate change, pollution, population increase, technological progress, resource management, ozone layer depletion, macroeconomics, microorganisms, and everything, in general, that might affect the planet for good or ill. They were endeavoring to plot scenarios for manipulating those factors that might ameliorate the human condition, but realized that their greatest challenge lay in trying to predict the vagaries of human nature, and to direct them for the benefit of mankind. Current events were conspiring to thwart their efforts.

* * *

"Are you safe there, Emile?" asked Brad.

"As long as they stay on La Rive Droite. If they start to cross the bridges, all bets are off."

"Getting back to my earlier issue," Ranjit put in. "We must consider scenarios that include random and unpredictable factors. Those are the very things that could completely sabotage our most carefully laid plans."

"Examples?" Emile asked.

"Wars, natural disasters, terrorism, pandemics, the discovery of intelligent life elsewhere in the universe, a rogue comet or asteroid," Ranjit replied. "Any of those, or something else totally unexpected. There're so many things that could derail us."

"Or even the discovery of intelligent life on Earth," Brad said, laughing. "Seriously, though, we can only do what we can do. There are so many things beyond anyone's control that we just can't make allowances for. We can project contingencies for certain disasters, but location, magnitude, available resources .... well, it's just not possible to foresee every eventuality."

"O.K. Let's just work with what we can estimate with reasonable certainty and make our plans accordingly. By the way, I have an inquiry here from an architect in England who would very much like to join our group. He'd be a good counterpart for Ivana, the civil engineer from Minsk in Belarus. They could work together on future housing, and I think there's an urban planner in Kansas who's expressed interest. That could work well for us."

That night was neither the first nor the last of the urban revolutionary movements, and demonstrations would continue throughout the world for years to come. Whether the insurgents called themselves L'Espoir Nouveau, The Earth Liberation Front, Para Hacer Cosas Mejor, or any of the dozens of other armies, brigades, avengers, swords of, and countless splinter organizations that perpetrated acts of urban mayhem, they all characterized themselves as freedom fighters, seeking to liberate their fellow citizens from that to which most were never quite able to put a name. Their aims were unclear, and eventually the revolutions simply ran out of steam. A few fanatics took to the forests and the hills and the mountains, to live out their lives in communal privation. At least they weren't making miserable the lives of others.

Year by year the group expanded. Piece by piece their plans for the future fell into place. By 2077, the active members of the assemblage had grown to well over three hundred individuals from every walk of life. Jason Moorehead died that year, passing the torch to the heroes who would follow. Mark and Derrick continued the crusade, supported by an ever growing cadre of volunteers. There were doctors and scientists, engineers and builders, philosophers and theologists, mathematicians and theoreticians, agronomists and agriculturists, artists, law professors, historians, industrialists, economists, psychologists, and political and social scientists.

Some of the original members proposed a conference so that they could get to know each other face to face, as real live flesh and blood individuals, the better to formulate realistic strategies for shaping a future world. They settled on Geneva as a convenient and central location, mindful of its symbolism in human affairs, and scheduled the convention for late

September. The members would have to bear the expense of their travel and accommodations, but not one expressed any reservations about doing so.

* * *

When the delegates finally arrived at a modest lecture hall at the University of Geneva, they were greeted by demonstrators who mistook them for international bankers and economists, which therefore must be protested no matter what the objectives. The police were very helpful in getting the members through the picket lines which, in a very Swiss manner, were peaceful and respectful. When they had finally seated themselves and the gavel sounded to open the conference, they could not suppress a cheer and a round of applause that seemed to go on forever. They were about to reshape the world.

On that historic day, September 26, 2077, Emile Vaillencourt was introduced at the podium by Ranjit Singh. Emile began, "First, I want to thank Founder Mark Wells, who's with us today, Founder Derrick Carver, who is too ill to attend and, in memoriam, our late Founder Jason Moorehead, for establishing this group for the benefit of all mankind." Mark Wells rose from his seat to thunderous applause, waved to the assemblage, bowed to the podium, and sat back down so as not to detract from the importance of Emile's address.

Emile smiled, inclined his head in acknowledgement and continued, "This assemblage, we dedicated few, have gathered here to bring our collective minds and expertise to bear on the problems afflicting our planet. We must, in the short time given to us, begin to prepare a document for the ages, a declaration of true human rights and freedoms for all. But further to that, we must prepare a plan to implement such a declaration in an ever changing and chaotic world, where wealth and power have for too long frustrated efforts to promote mankind to the level of nobility of which it is capable. Before we return to our home countries, we hope to have in place a framework on which we may rebuild our world according to the vision of history's most forward thinkers. Now, here's our proposed agenda …."

The meetings, initially scheduled to last three days, went on for six. The first order of business was to elect an executive. Emile was acclaimed as chair and Ranjit as co-chair. Other members from the original core group filled the remaining positions. Subcommittees and study groups were formed. Similar disciplines were at first grouped together, then mixed with variants to provide a diversity of ideas. Each group ultimately tendered their proposals to the oversight committee, who submitted a consolidated report on the last day of the conference. It was given to Ranjit to present the final document.

"I have in my hand the final draft of our inaugural report to the world. You may review it on the comscreens in front of you, or on your handhelds on the way home. Copies will be distributed to the media, and they will hopefully disseminate our vision to the world. We had not hoped to achieve perfection on our first try, and no doubt you will all continue your good works once you get home. I'm counting on everyone to recruit more members, so that when we meet again, we might fill this hall to overflowing. With that, I present our report."

The presentation took almost three hours, during which time the delegates listened in rapt silence. The document began with a statement of human rights, culled from many similar declarations from governments and revolutionaries of the past, and from more than a few idealistic works of fiction. Following this there came a model for a new society that would support the declaration. Housing, agriculture, education, science, and the arts had been scrutinized, and recommendations made. Medical care, transportation, government, and economics had been dissected and reassembled in a more rational and equitable manner. Resource management and ecological responsibility were given a high profile, with mandated guidelines and accountability established.

The delegates had done their work well. The intention now was to put the document forth to governments and ordinary people, for commentary, criticism, and suggestions for improvement. In the year following, the core group of thinkers more than doubled. Naturally, there were special interests and fanatics who opposed many of the proposals, but the suggestions were generally well received. The press had, characteristically, given the group a name, The Compilers, due to their inclination to cull the best of what history had to offer and to compile it into a document for the ages.

"We've done it, mes amis," Emile exclaimed when the group was again assembled at their comcenters some months later. "They're beginning to listen. Even those so-called powers that be realize that the present state of affairs can't hold sway much longer."

"Yes," Maria added. "Governments are appointing committees to look into our proposals, and some are even starting to present bills to implement our best ideas."

"Don't break out the bubbly yet," Brad interjected. "We've got a long way to go, but more are joining our cause every day. In the end, we will have made a difference."

By the time the second conference convened in Geneva in 2078, they had already outgrown the lecture hall, and the university magnanimously allowed them use of the historic Great Hall. The ranks of the Compilers had been swelled by urban planners and civil engineers, teachers, philanthropists, anthropologists, linguists, environmentalists, climatologists, and so many more, who were clamoring to be a part of their noble endeavor. With a structured group and a framework to build on, progress was much more rapid, and they were able to reduce the length of the meeting to a mere four days, after which they issued an amended manifesto.

Suggestions from the general public and from new members with unique expertise had contributed to the shaping of the ground-breaking document. In particular, advances in science and technology were brought to bear on innovative ways to implement the original suggestions for molding a new society. Developments in materials technology, social and genetic engineering, alternative energy sources, clean air and water initiatives, agriculture, aquaculture and hydroponics and a host of other technologies were now being included in the Compilers deliberations.

At the end of it, they had moved a giant step forward in the achievement of their goal of an idealized society and a peaceful and prosperous planet. They could not know of the impending disaster that would very nearly undo their hard work, but would, paradoxically, wind up assuring that their efforts would at last come to fruition.

CHAPTER 7

GUS AND ROSIE

Winter, 2179

August William Usher was in a foul mood as he approached the offices of Brandon & Ripley, Certified Mediators. He mulled over the reasons why his life thus far had turned out to be less than ideal. Having married in haste a year before, at age 19, he had been a victim of lust and infatuation. The object of his affection was one Sissy Nisbitt, a longtime schoolmate and friend. The relationship had turned passionate when she seduced him on a weekend outDome spelunking trip with a group of college chums, and he succumbed to his inner beast, as youthful hormones overcame good sense. They were wed within weeks, over the objections of both of their families. Reality set in as they were forced to face the exigencies of everyday married life. They lived in Gus' bachelor hab for most of the eight months of their marriage, until they grated on each other to such an extent that Gus volunteered to move out. A legal separation quickly followed, and divorce proceedings were instituted.

Now Gus was about to face the consequences of those proceedings. The mediators' offices were decorated in earth colors, with dimmed lighting and soft music, the better to encourage amicability and a tranquil mood.

Brandon and Ripley sat on opposite sides of the large, round table, with Sissy and Gus facing each other between them.

"We understand," began Ripley, "that your differences are irreconcilable and that you are both agreed that permanent legal separation from each other is the only course you wish to pursue."

"Yes," said Gus and Sissy simultaneously.

"Then it only remains for us to advise you that we must deal with your shared issues," Ripley observed. Community property was no longer a concern in the 22nd century, as physical property was shared or freely available to anyone who cared to requisition what they might need. Specialty items obtained by individuals either through barter or extra work-time credits became their exclusive property until they expressed a desire to divest themselves of them.

That first night of passion, camping under minidomes in the caves, had yielded progeny in the form of a boy child, one Jonathan Calum Usher. The couple had informally agreed on joint custody, pending a legal settlement.

"I don't want the brat," Sissy shocked the mediators by declaring of the now six month old Jonathan. "All it does is eat and cry and make disgusting messes. Besides, I have a career to pursue, and I can't deal with motherhood at the same time." Gus adored the child, and was perfectly willing to be a single father. The custody agreement was quickly signed to the satisfaction of both parties, with no visitation rights accruing to Sissy.

So it was that Gus and his son were cast adrift on a sea of uncertainty. Gus' parents helped out where and as they could, by babysitting their much-adored grandson, and Gus was free to date again. In his spare time he volunteered at a district spiritualism and meditation center, helping to minister to the emotional needs of his community. It was there, two years after his divorce, that he met one Rosalind Marie Kelly Wilson, nee Stildenbach, who had recently lost her husband to one of the few hereditary diseases that science had not yet conquered.

The first things he noticed about her were her large, luminous green eyes and her exquisite smile. The second was her petite but voluptuous body. The third, upon formal introduction, was that she was sister to the Stildenbach twins, each an owner of his own Harbour, and bitter adversaries of and competitors with his parents. Rosie, like Gus, was a Harbour tech, working for Mellow Stildenbach until such time as she could decide what career path would be her destiny.

Rosie was attracted by Gus' easy and sincere manner, his athletic physique, his vid-star looks, and his full head of wavy black hair. She wasn't the least put off by his relationship to the Usher family and their Harbour.

For the next two years, as friendship gave way to courtship, this was to be a secret relationship. They were certain that neither family would have approved. When at last Gus' parents met Rosie, they were so taken with her that they barely commented on her lineage. The Stildenbach brothers were not nearly so reticent or forgiving. They denounced the relationship at the outset, and so remained estranged from their sister thenceforth.

Gus knew from the start that Rosie had a child from her previous marriage; a daughter named River Elizabeth who was one year younger than Jonathan. Inevitably, Gus proposed to Rosie, and the two families were happily merged. By now, Jonathan was four and River was three. They had taken to each other the first time they met, when Gus and Rosie had begun their secretive trysts, and were inseparable from then on.

The technology for artificial human reproduction had been perfected in the latter half of the 21st century, and government run Safe Harbours had sprung up in every major population center. By the time the Age of Chaos had ended and the Domes were being established, governments had decided that they no longer wished to be in the business of recording memories and reproducing individuals from stored DNA, so they sold all of the Harbours to private enterprise. Few major corporations had survived the challenges of the Great Plague, with its attendant economic collapse and labour shortages, and the remains of those few were in decline, their functions being taken over by governments. Accordingly, it fell to individuals and families to take the plunge and purchase the Harbours.

Gus' great grandparents had purchased the only one in Richmond, Virginia, and had moved it to the new RichmondDome as soon as it had been completed. The elder Usher had owned a chain of funeral homes, and reasoned that a Safe Harbour was a naturally related business. "We get 'em coming and going," he was often heard to say. He was able to hire former government trained employees to run his Harbour and to show him the ropes, then he sent his son, Gus' grandfather, to university to learn the science behind the technology so that the family could run the Harbour by itself. Gus' father had followed in his father's footsteps, as had Gus, and they made a decent living restoring past lives, earning double time credits for providing an essential service.

In the normal course of time, Gus' parents passed on, and he inherited their Harbour. He and Rosie worked side by side to ensure its success, and as the years passed they prospered. A few years later, Rosie gave Gus a son, Daniel and three years after that a daughter, Desert.

The approach of middle age had done nothing to diminish Gus and Rosie's love and passion for each other. In spite of excellent diet and a rigorous exercise regime, Gus was showing a slight tendency toward an apparently unavoidable middle-age spread. Rosie found him as attractive and desirable as ever she had, taking full advantage of the extra leverage Gus' love handles afforded during moments of intense passion. For her part, Rosie managed to remain relatively svelte, priding herself on being able to wear any of the latest fashions sported by much younger women.

When they secreted themselves in their private haven, she still wore her most seductive lingerie, the better to inspire Gus. As for Gus, he needed no extra encouragement. When he massaged the love of his life with warm and fragrant oils, in the love grotto that Rosie had designed and built years before, he was as amorous and energetic as he had been on that night when they had at first so eagerly explored each others bodies.

They lavished love equally upon their four children, and enfolded them in an atmosphere of mutual caring, respect, and intellectual and spiritual stimulation. Sheltered under the Dome, the family would prosper and endure, secure in the knowledge that their world was shatterproof. It was to be an example of the injustice of existence that the tranquil lives of such a decent family should be rent asunder by circumstances beyond their control; with the added irony that Gus would become an unwitting instrument of that tragedy.

CHAPTER 8

MORE TROUBLE IN PARADISE

August 6, 2204

If the opportunity had not presented itself, he would have had to have created it. It was, after all, the sixth day of the month, and there was a schedule to keep. He was on the prowl well before dimming, with the full expectation that his chosen hunting ground would yield the desired prey. There were more than enough innocents in the area to make it easy for him to cut one from the herd. He watched, he waited.

* * *

While their parents lingered over the remains of the evening meal at the Farside Cafe, relaxing as they sipped glowberry wine or an exotic liqueur on the plaza bordering the park, the children took advantage of the remains of the waning light to play jet darts on the park's adjoining lawns. Twelve year old Kym Wolenz was among them. Her parents had already gone home after their dinner, and Kym had obtained permission to stay on for an hour so she could play with her friends.

"You must be home before dimming," her father had told her sternly. Her vigorous nod was her promise to comply. That she might be in the slightest danger did not occur to any of the adults. Even as the shocking event of the previous month had begun to fade from memory, everyone now assumed that it had been an isolated incident. Surely nothing like that could ever occur again, the absence of an arrest or even of a suspect notwithstanding. It was widely assumed that an Outlander had infiltrated the Dome and had fled back into the wilds, beyond the pale of civilization, after committing his heinous crime.

Soon enough, Kym's team was down by eight points. Two more and they would be obliged to resign. Her next throw was high and wide, the dart soaring past the defenders and into the woods.

"Hey, you did that on purpose, just because you're losing," Samara Keeno cried. "You go get it."

"O.K., O.K.," Kym said, shrugging resignedly. "I'll find it." She slouched off into the underbrush and was quickly lost from sight. The remaining youngsters sat on the grass and proceeded to dissect the most recent plays and to argue over strategy.

The adults were ready to leave, and they summoned their offspring to the plaza on the opposite side of the lawn.

"We can't go yet," Sammy called back. "Kym's looking for my dart."

"You can get it from her tomorrow. Come on, let's go," his father replied impatiently.

"Kym. We're going now. Bring my dart back tomorrow," Sammy called into the woods. Sammy, his brother, and the Casmirik triplets shambled unhurriedly over to the plaza, occasionally glancing over their shoulders in the hope of sighting their stray friend. They could not know that they had seen her for the last time.

The watcher had taken her from behind, before she even knew he was there. He had quickly rendered her unconscious, dragged her deeper into the undergrowth, and had tied her hands to a stout overhanging limb. He cut her clothes away, and then sat down to watch her until the park had emptied and dimming time was upon them. Oblivious, bound and gagged, she swung there, awaiting his pleasure, as he ran his finger repeatedly along the knife's edge in anticipation of what was to come.

*   *   *

"She promised," said Marco Wolenz, aggravated. "I'm giving her another 15 minutes, then she's constrained for a week." Kym, independent and headstrong, had a history of testing her boundaries, so Marco and Selena Wolenz were not overly concerned when she was a few minutes late. Twenty minutes later, annoyance had given way to concern, and shortly thereafter, to alarm. They attempted to com their daughter, and having failed to get a response, they contacted the Keenos and found out where and when Kym had last been seen.

It was only half a kilometer from their hab to the park, but they covered it in record time. Selena searched the pathways, calling to her child, but it would be Marco, combing the woods, who would find her beaten and lifeless body slumped against the bole of a tree, a red ribbon tied over her eyes. His wails of grief and despair could be heard across the plaza.

*   *   *

"We've got another one," Benwright's voice issued from the comcentre, overriding the audio on the holodocumentary Quinn was viewing. "Gundy Park, Venicia District. Plaza entrance. How soon can you get here?"

"Since you asked so politely, maybe fifteen minutes. Out!" Quinn replied. He was getting a little irritated with Benwright's assumption that he was available every moment of the day or night, as well as with his abrupt style. Nevertheless, he resolved to behave in a professional manner, and was aboard a floater, kit in hand, within minutes. While en route, he mulled over his complete failure to track down the source of the synthskin, or even a reason for its presence on the body. With the cooperation of Benwright and his security network, every conceivable avenue of inquiry had been exhausted, yet not a scrap of useful information had emerged. It was baffling and frustrating in the extreme.

Venicia District was adjacent to Seabrook and the transit to Gundy Park took slightly under ten minutes. Quinn was passed quickly through the Sentinels' cordon, arriving at the crime scene barely twenty minutes after Benwright's call. It was just after 2230 hours.

"Same thing?" Quinn inquired, as he exchanged fist-tap with the Sentinels' chief by way of greeting.

Benwright nodded. "Over there," he said, pointing to an area of the woods beyond a line of grimfaced Sentinels. "Same M.O. as before. Seems to be a little more violence involved this time, but I'll let you be the judge of that. Her father found her around 2140. Poor guy. The parameds had to tranq both him and his wife and transport them to a medcenter."

Quinn rapidly donned his working clothes. "Sprinklers off?" he asked.

"One of the first things I did after I got here," Benwright affirmed.

"Right, then. Here we go." He took a deep breath and plunged through the Sentinels' line, walking with his head bent forward, examining and recording as he went. The path the child had taken into the woods was clearly defined, and he paralleled it all the way to the crime scene. This time, the progress of the attack was evident in the marks made on the dusty, lightly packed earth. Another set of tracks, larger, curved inwards from her right, merging with hers from behind. Her track vanished as if she'd been lifted from the ground, then carried forward, deeper into the woods. Here, she'd been set down, and had collapsed, an outline of her tiny body unmistakably delineated. The larger footprints circled the outline, and a number of scuffed prints a short distance away indicated activity of some kind.

The unclothed body was a few meters further on, lying on its back where the distraught father had reluctantly left it. Quinn was not surprised to see the red ribbon encircling her head and tied in a neat bow over her eyes. The father's footprints came in from a different angle, straight to the base of a nearby tree. The disturbance there in the dust told the story of his discovery and embracing of his daughter's corpse. Blood and shattered bark on the tree's trunk revealed how the girl's life had probably been ended. The finger marks on her throat indicated she'd been choked, just like the first victim. The killer's footprints left the clearing in the direction opposite to the father's, and the marks were far apart, possibly indicating that he had fled quickly even as the father had approached.

As before, Quinn scanned the body to determine the time of death. The instrument indicated that it was between 2125 and 2130. Now he looked more closely at the corpse, and observed small cuts on her torso, and ligature marks on the wrists. He stood up and looked back towards the clearing where she had first been dropped. A stout limb protruded above it, and Quinn saw the place where the bark had been slightly abraded, as if a rope had recently been tied there. The full picture was beginning to emerge. The killer had captured her, probably rendered her unconscious, and had strung her up on the limb. He had then leaned against a tree close by, studying his handiwork, as evidenced by his footprints. How long he had lingered there was unclear, but what was apparent was that he had taken his time with her, cutting her and probably raping her before finishing her off in the same manner as his first victim. There was absolutely no doubt in his mind that this was the same perpetrator.

Quinn shook his head sadly as he opened his forensics kit. First, he did a thorough study of the body in situ. Next, he took blood and bark samples from the tree against which she had last rested, and as he did so, he spotted a tiny strip of yellow gelplas, no more than a centimeter across, wedged into the bark at the base of the tree. It appeared to be a fragment from a gel-shoe. He made sure that its location was recorded from several angles then marked its position before retrieving it and placing it in an evidence bag.

"Are you almost done in there?" Benwright called from the edge of the woods.

"About ten more minutes," Quinn replied, as he poured quickset epoxy into the clearest of the killer's footprints. He did a rapid sweep of the area, attempting to locate the girl's clothes, but found nothing close by. Gathering up his kit, he took one more look around to make sure that he had sampled everything that he needed to, then exited the trees the way he had come.

"Get your team to search for her clothes, will you," he said to Benwright. "I can't locate them in the immediate area. And have a look at the sec-vids.

Get me a report as soon as possible. I know that two murders don't make for a serial killer, but I don't like the beginnings of the pattern I'm seeing here. The same M.O., the same victims' profiles, the same date. I have a feeling it's going to get a lot worse unless we catch this guy now!" Even as he said this, he knew in his heart that they wouldn't be catching this depraved creature any time soon.

'O.K., Quinn. We should have a report to you in a few hours. Can you give us any preliminary findings?"

"Not much that I haven't told you already. The cuts on the body seem to have been tentative, somewhat reluctant. She wasn't cut deeply. It almost seems as if he's experimenting with a new level of violence. He has to be stopped quickly, before he escalates."

"Agreed," Benwright said. "When this gets out, the whole Dome will be in a panic. First thing we're going to do is to close public access to the parks after the onset of eve. I have a hunch it won't stop this guy, but there's not much else we can do by way of ensuring public safety. I'm calling another meeting for tomorrow afternoon, after we've had a chance to sort through the evidence. I'll see you there."

The more Quinn found, or more to the point didn't find, the greater his fear. It was a level of anxiety he had never before experienced. He understood then that he might never again know true peace.

August 7, 2204

Quinn arrived back at his hab in plenty of time to get a good night's sleep, but it was not to be. His first thought was to wake Sera up and share the latest news with her, but upon reflection, decided that bad news could wait until morning. She was normally an early riser, so a voice message on her com asking her to meet him at his office would suffice. He slid into his sleep shelf and spent several restless hours reviewing the facts, but making little progress towards a resolution. He drifted into a troubled sleep just before dawn.

A few hours later, only slightly refreshed, he arrived at his office, where Sera was already waiting. "You look like you've been dayburned and smog-choked," she commented, upon seeing his red-rimmed eyes and grim expression. "I brought you a soylatte and a plankton rollup. Thought you might need some nutrification before we get to work."

"I tell you, sis, this is really wearing on me, and I think we're a long way from the end of it. I'm glad I have you to lean on."

"Just like when we were younglings. We sustained each other through the hard times and the good times. We were always there for each other, especially after dad and mom died."

Quinn smiled at his sister, drawing strength from their lifelong bond. The tragedy of their parents' death had affirmed their closeness and their mutual support.

CHAPTER 9

THE MAKING OF FUTURES

Spring, 2073

A late spring day, and Londoners strolled the Thames Embankment, enjoying the sunshine and the fresh breezes. Their senses were tickled by the fragrance of early blooming primrose and dew dampened earth, spring birds feeding, building nests and singing their joy at the turn of the seasons. They would not have too many more years to enjoy this sort of pastime, as climate change and environmental rapaciousness and indifference took their toll on the biosphere. Yet today, looming catastrophe was ignored as they took pleasure in the here and now.

Ada Meeks ambled slowly along the promenade, lost in thought, preoccupied with images of formulae and diagrams associated with her research work at the Ministry of Health. She had only recently been seconded to the communicable diseases section, and had a lot of catching up to do as she struggled to acclimate herself to her new situation. So distracted was she, looking down at the river and up at the trees, that she failed to notice the young man walking towards her, equally preoccupied with images of a historic documentary that pulsed from his handheld.

Their destinies collided, literally, near the plasteel replica of Cleopatra's Needle, where a gentle bump resulted in a mutual exchange of apologies.

"Excuse me."

"I do beg your pardon."

"My fault entirely."

"Close one," he commented wryly, as they disengaged. "Nearly a nasty accident. Wasn't watching where I was going"

"I'm so sorry," she said, stepping back, her cheeks aflame. "I was a world away. Sorry," she repeated.

"Relax. Perhaps you should have a seat," he said, indicating a nearby bench. "You look all shook up."

"You're American," she observed as she took him up on his invitation. He made himself comfortable beside her.

"Abram Braxton, late of Boston, Mass," he said by way of introduction, and offered his hand.

"Ada Meeks, presently of London, England," she responded as she shook it. "A pleasure to meet you. I'm such a klutz. So sorry."

He chuckled disarmingly. "Stop apologizing. No harm done. In truth, I'm not used to women accosting me on the promenade. It's a refreshing change."

He was tanned and handsome, lean and muscular, and so charming that Ada had trouble imagining that women were not in the habit of falling at his feet. His blond hair was slicked back in the fashion of the day, and he affected a modest mustache, which gave him an air of Teutonic nobility.

For his part, he couldn't believe his good fortune in this chance encounter. She was dark and demure, lithe and lovely, as fresh and warm as the Spring day itself, and he was immediately taken with her.

"Are you visiting here?" she asked.

"No, not really, well, sort of. I'm here as a visiting professor at London University, lecturing in the dreaded poly-sci. I love it here. I may just stay on after my term is up and apply for a permanent position somewhere."

"Aren't you a bit young to be a professor?" Ada inquired.

"A child prodigy or an idiot savant, depending on whom you ask. I was a much advanced student, and entered my chosen field early. I taught in the public school system for several years then, when I got a chance to profess, as it were, I jumped at it. Now here I am and here I hope to stay."

"You couldn't hope to find a more cosmopolitan city. I'm sure Boston's a fine place, but here you'll find culture, entertainment, intellectual stimulation. It's been so much better since the government cracked down and got rid of the less desirable elements that were ruining our lifestyle and security."

He was aware of the gangs that had once roamed throughout the metropolitan area, bullying, molesting, and robbing anyone who had the misfortune to cross their paths. It was a not uncommon condition in many cities, but London had taken a hard line and, in spite of the protests from self-styled civil libertarians, had rounded up the miscreants as quickly as they revealed themselves, and had exiled them to redemption camps in the countryside.

"Tell you what. If you have time why don't we go to a … ah … tea room for a coffee or tea or whatever," he offered. "How about it?"

They had not taken their eyes off each other since the moment of their rather unconventional meeting. Even though she was due back at work after her lunch hour, she was quick to accept his invitation. In a quaint, glass-enclosed Victorian tea house in the nearby park, they shared tea and pastries and life stories. They spent most of the afternoon together, talking and laughing, getting to know one another, and at the end of it they exchanged contact information. Her more observant colleagues would subsequently remark on her exuberant mood as she returned to her job near the end of the workday, especially when the cause of her euphoria was later revealed.

Abram and Ada went out on their first formal date the following evening, and it was just short of sunrise when they at last parted. The following night they could not bring themselves to take their leave of each other and, as passion overcame restraint, they spent the hours before dawn making love tenderly in his bed. That night he found out to his delight that she was not nearly as reserved as he had at first thought. After that they were seldom apart, except for the hours they spent of necessity pursuing their respective careers. It was not long before they made the decision to move in together, and shortly thereafter they affirmed their love legally, in the joyful bonds of marriage.

Their love remained undiminished over the years, even as their careers evolved. Those who knew them would often remark on their closeness and their consideration and respect for each other. That was how they conducted their life together and it was how they related to others; coworkers, friends, acquaintances, and students. Their warmth and sincerity, their caring and compassion for others were qualities that made them loved and respected by all who knew them.

Ada went from success to success in her field, then came to the notice of the Minister of Health herself. At this point her career took a sharp turn as the Minister, impressed by her credentials in the medical and biological sciences, asked that she join the scientific investigations section. She was placed in charge of the Center for Disease Control, a position of considerable prestige and responsibility. She felt gratified that all of her education and experience had converged in a place where she could be most useful.

As for Abram, his decision to remain in England turned out to be as fortuitous as his chance encounter with Ada. He became a British citizen and thus became eligible to run as a candidate for the House of Commons. His prominence as a lecturer and academician and the respect accorded him by the residents in his riding assured his election on his first attempt to secure a seat. He was reelected four years later, and was appointed Deputy Minister of Homeland Security.

Their success had enabled them to purchase a home in the country, minutes from a maglev station which could deliver them to any part of the capital in under an hour. They were thus able to spend a great deal of quality time together, and to pursue their leisure activities. Bike rides between rustic hedgerows and ancient stone walls, and quiet walks by sylvan streams kept their love alive and strengthened their bonds. In the quiet of the evenings, they played backgammon and chess and Scrabble by the fire, over a glass of wine or a cup of hot chocolate, as the mood struck them.

Abram catalogued his stamp collection, and Ada pursued her hobby of pottery making. She spent hours tempering the clay and throwing pots on her wheel in the concrete floored room attached to the rear of the house. French doors opened to a rear yard on one side, giving ready access to her kiln, and another set at the far end connected to Abram's study, so that they could enjoy their diverse interests while remaining in close proximity to one another.

By the early 2080s the musings of the Compilers were being widely disseminated and seriously considered. Their proposal to record memories and to store DNA for a select few, then to reunite the two in a cloned body, was endorsed by the International Science Council, then adopted by most national governments. The objective was to cultivate a cadre of moral, ethical and competent leaders with a proven record of public service, and to store them away to be resurrected later to serve mankind. Only the very best would be selected. The honour would be conferred solely on those deemed most worthy by their coworkers, their friends, and their communities, for it was those that knew them best who would be most qualified to determine their destiny. The Futures, as they were called, were to be the leaders of the Compilers' New Society.

The Compilers recommended the establishment of foundations that would combine the collection and storage of both memory crystals and of the DNA of successful applicants, against the day when they would be cloned, brought to term, and Awakened. These establishments, dubbed Safe Harbours, would also be authorized to engage in research in order to improve the process leading to Awakening, so that it could be rendered faster and less expensive. A New World was dawning, and the infrastructure, the societal structure, and the leadership would all be available to ensure its success.

In the warmth of their bed one winter's night, the glow of passionate lovemaking still upon them, Ada's mind wandered to the matter of her biological clock.

"Abram," she whispered, "Don't you think it's about time we had a child. I think we owe the world a greater legacy than just our insignificant efforts."

"Have you looked around at our world lately?" Abram replied. "Do you really want to bring a child into this world, such as it is? Wars, pollution, climate change, ozone layer depletion, water shortages, crime, famine, disease. As much as I'd love to father a child with you, I don't think that this is a world I'd want to pass on to my offspring. Maybe someday things will be better, and then we can be the best parents the world has ever seen."

Ada couldn't argue with Abram's logic, but her heart ached as she relegated the idea to the hope chest of her reveries.

* * *

When it became apparent that a worldwide pandemic had begun, early in 2089, Ada and Abram discussed the possibility of having their memories and their DNA stored, against the time when they might be called upon to further serve their world. Accordingly, they both applied for the newly created status of 'Futures' and, after a rigorous vetting process, both were approved. They went together to the nearest government-run Safe Harbour and were quickly processed, their memories locked electronically into artificial diamond matrices and their DNA stored in stasis. They had stipulated that they must be Awakened together, a request to which the authorities were glad to accede.

A new and most virulent strain of influenza was spreading rapidly through the overcrowded cities and refugee camps of Europe, and farther, as people fled on foot and by any means available in a vain attempt to escape the plague. Air travel ensured that many of the infected would unknowingly pass the virus on to others in far off countries within hours of their embarkation. The authorities tried to stem the tide, to quell the stampede, but to no avail. They banned air travel, but it was already too late. The disease was airborne, and took its victims in a matter of days. It spread unimaginably quickly and was seemingly unstoppable. The mortality rate exceeded ninety per cent.

Abram was charged with the responsibility of attempting to keep refugees fleeing mainland Europe from entering Great Britain. It was a futile task. Desperate families found their way onto the island nation by whatever means was at hand, and in so doing, sealed its fate. They fled into the countryside, spreading the disease wherever they went. Those who couldn't be stopped on the coast were rounded up, as Brits everywhere turned them in. As head of her nation's Center for Disease Control, it fell to Ada to try to halt the spread of the plague. Refugees were placed in quarantine, where they died by the thousands. It was too late; Britain was doomed. There was little immunity and no cure. Great Britain shared the fate of Europe and the rest of the world.

It was fortunate that Ada and Abram had been preserved as Futures, because the virulent plague took them quickly. Eschewing the option afforded to government ministers and the wealthy, of hiding in bio-proofed bunkers, they chose to serve their countrymen and to share their destiny. They were just as defenseless as any ordinary citizen, and once infected, they had no more than a few hours to say their goodbyes before they too succumbed, together in death as they had been in life. They were buried with full honours in their beloved London, but the mourning was brief as there was so much death all about.

Before the Great Plague was over, most of Earth's inhabitants lay dead. Chaos reigned in all but the most stable societies, and governments collapsed as senseless and uncontrolled rioting, looting and lawlessness swept through large cities. Populations, seeking safety from the pandemic and its aftermath, sought refuge in neighboring countries where conditions were no better than in their own. Cities lay in ruins. Many survivors starved or died of exposure. At the end of it, a scant billion people were left to pick up the pieces that remained of a ruined and decimated planet.

Autumn, 2173

An unfamiliar voice spoke softly, "Welcome back. Joyous Awakening to you." Abram opened his eyes to see an orange clad female tech bending over him. "Can you understand me?" she asked.

"Of course I can," he responded grumpily. He attempted to sit up, but fell back, too weak to move. "Where's Ada?" he demanded.

"All's aright. If you turn your head to the left, you'll see her," the tech responded.

He did, and was gratified so see his beloved wife smiling at him from the next couch. "Well don't this just beat all!" he offered.

"Grammar, young man!" Ada admonished lovingly. They both laughed with the heady joy of reunion.

"Move me closer to her," Abram demanded, and the tech complied, sliding his 'wakening pod' closer to hers. They reached out to touch one another.

"Together again at last," she murmured.

"You're as lovely as ever you were," he replied. "I can't wait to get my hands on you."

"And do what? We only just arrived at whenever we are, and already you're cultivating the image of a dirty old man."

They looked exactly as they had been when their DNA had been stored, at their prime, each near forty years old. It would be a while before their brains and their newly animated bodies completed the neural connections that would allow them to operate synchronously once more, and for them to regain normal strength and muscle tone.

The tech intervened. "Your new identichips are in place and functioning correctly. There are things you must do and things you must know before you can resume a normal life. We can begin now."

It was obligatory to inform them of their ultimate fate following the recording of their memories at the Safe Harbour; of events subsequent to that they knew nothing. It was also necessary to reeducate them; to bring them up to date on the history and technological achievements of the eight decades since their passing. Society had moved on. It had survived and evolved. Their lives had been suspended through most of the Era of Tranquility and Reconstruction. After the Great Plague, humanity had no choice but to pull together in order to survive.

The year was 2173, and, as promised, they were together once more, the remainder of their life's story yet to be told. In the days to come, their rejuvenation was accomplished with nourishment and exercise, and their love life found renewal as soon as fitness permitted, no pharmacological enhancements required.

Upon their Awakening, the supervising Harbour was required to destroy any DNA that might remain of the revived Future. In addition, the memories held in their crystals were eradicated by carving them into signet rings, which were then given to the Futures as a mark of their eminence, always to be worn and never removed until their deaths. Before they were released from the recovery facility, Abram and Ada were presented with their rings, which they wore proudly from that day forth.

They were sad to hear how their world had been laid waste, but gratified at how resilient the peoples of Earth were. Now it was their turn to begin to repay the favor of continued life that had been granted them. A new form of government had evolved while their essences had lain dormant, and they were eager to become a part of it.

Citizens placed absolute trust in the integrity and competence of Futures, and with their customary foresight the Compilers had suggested that local governing bodies consist of equal numbers of appointed representatives and Futures. The invaluable guidance of the Futures provided direction and balance to eager but inexperienced councilors. Each Council of Guardians that governed a Dome was comprised of twenty Futures who served six year terms in rotation, as positions became available. The other twenty seats on the Council were filled by ordinary citizens, each serving a two year term, and chosen by computer lottery according to their credentials, such qualifications being determined by their record of competence and benefit to their Dome. Service on the Council was mandatory, deferments being granted to those in essential occupations, those terms to be served after the citizen retired. Everyone contributed, everyone benefited.

Abram and Ada began their government service in LondonDome, but the climate, often cold and gloomy in their past life, had turned positively morose and melancholic. The northern hemisphere now suffered from the full effects of polluted air and climate change, and the complete cessation of the flow of the warm waters of the Atlantic conveyor. The Dome was covered with snow all winter, and rain clouds in summer frequently obscured the sun. It was utterly depressing. Accordingly, in 2175, they decided that they would prefer a more southerly location, and requested a transfer to RichmondDome in the North America Federation. Futures' requests were almost never denied. After wrapping up their affairs, they boarded a westbound shuttle the following month.

A more temperate climate was not the only reason they wished to move southwest. In their early 40s, they were about to become parents, and they were determined to provide all the best for their offspring. Their new home was in a university Dome, and the cultural and educational opportunities available there were among the best in the world. Somno-orientation was quick and convenient, and it wasn't long before they were able to take their places on the Dome's Grand Council of Guardians, as soon as Futures died or moved on to other vocations as their terms expired. Abram found new and challenging hobbies to occupy his free time, while Ada joined a pottery group at a district leisure center, where she was able to access a communal electrokiln and pursue her favored hobby.

Abram and Ada were warmly welcomed into the council. Every member had been, as custom dictated, apprised of their record of public service and of the high esteem in which they had been held. That veneration would now be passed on to a new generation. The couple embraced the opportunity to fulfill their destiny.

* * *

Quinten Lemay Braxton was born to the overjoyed parents early in 2176. Just over a year later, Sera Ellen Braxton came into a society that was close to idyllic, where the vision of the Compilers had at last been realized. They would want for nothing, and nothing would harm them.

Everyone in the New Society willingly contributed where and as they could, to the best of their abilities. In return, society provided for all of their needs. They had only to ask. Efficient, government-run facilities produced all of the goods and services required. Shopping for citizens under the Domes consisted of browsing on their com-center or com-helmet projections, then requisitioning the necessary items. Malls in each district provided communal space for socializing and storefronts where selected merchandise could be viewed and ordered for later delivery. In addition, a limited number of luxury items were available to all, and private enterprise was permitted solely for arts and crafts merchandise, exchanged through barter or for time credits. Intellectual properties were public domain, in order that everyone should benefit.

The Compilers oversaw the secure and comfortable world of the Domes, governed by Councils of Guardians and safeguarded by the Legion of Sentinels. For the descendents of the survivors of the Great Plague, their way of life was superior to any civilization in the history of the planet; no poverty, no strife, no hunger. But for the fact that, by necessity, they must live under a Dome in order to enjoy the benefits of the New Society, the people of the 23rd century were very well off.

Quinn and Sera had the additional benefit of being brought up in a loving home. Not that it was unusual, for the New Society nurtured in its citizens an inborn desire to conform to the ideals and mores that the Compilers had deemed to be most desirable for peace, security and harmony. Ada and Abram gave them unconditional love and capable guidance from the moment they were born. The quality of education in the university Dome was the best the New Society had to offer, and the siblings grew up in an ethos of intellectual motivation and cultural stimulation.

Artifacts of their parents' hobbies surrounded the children, encouraging them to select their own. Ada's pottery occupied shelves and ledges, along with framed displays from Abram's early stamp collection, and his later electronic tonal compositions periodically emanated from the acoustic walls. Quinn took pleasure at an early age in caressing some of his mother's creations and connecting their shapes and textures to that of his father's musical works. There was a definite correlation, as if two like minds had conceived different incarnations of the same concept. When he pointed this out to Sera, she joined him in exploring the idea. Ada and Abram arrived home to find the siblings sitting together on the couch, listening to music and fondling a variety of pottery. Upon hearing the explanation, Abram said, "It's good that you're willing to explore a diversity of ideas. Question everything, accept nothing at face value. You'll have a richer, fuller life."

As the years passed, both Quinn and Sera excelled in all of their endeavours. They were as devoted to each other as any siblings could possibly be, always at each others' side, sharing every joy, every triumph, every sorrow. They completed one another, even as each was challenged to surpass the other. Their mutual interest in the sciences, their competitive natures, and their parents' wise counsel inspired them to excel in their education, and to set the stage for success in their future lives.

* * *

Abram and Ada garnered ever more respect and honours in the service of their Dome. Thus it was that they were chosen to attend the 2189 Grand Congress of the Councils of Guardians, convening that year in far off MumbaiDome. They arrived at SebringPortal in a government floater, bag, baggage and children in tow. A close family friend, Aunt Aggie as she was known to the siblings, was there to attend to the children while their parents were away. The group passed through the exit portal to the nearby transport terminal, where a flyer awaited to take Abram and Ada halfway around the globe. Even though they would only be gone for a few days, Ada and Abram said tearful goodbyes, for they had never in thirteen years been separated from their offspring. They boarded the craft along with seventeen other passengers who were also Mumbai-bound.

It was over India that disaster struck. At the request of his V.I.P. passengers, the pilot slowed the aircraft and descended so that they could view the Taj Mahal at Agra, Shah Jahan's fifth century monument to his cherished wife. It had been preserved, hopefully for eternity, under its own weatherproof dome. The romantic in both of them dictated that they not miss out on this singular opportunity.

"Isn't it lovely," Ada observed as the transport flew low around the shrine. "I wonder how they keep it so white."

"I'd build you one, had I the means," Abram replied tenderly.

"You have already, in my heart," Ada responded.

It was a pleasurable interlude that did not last long, as the pilot excitedly interrupted their idyll.

"We must leave immediately," he announced. "An anomalous weather system has sprung up nearby. Strap in, everyone. This could be a very rough ride."

Too late he attempted to gain altitude. Turbulence in the heated and unstable atmosphere had spawned a series of tornados, several of which converged on the area. The graceful craft soared towards the stratosphere where it might gain safety, but well before it could achieve altitude, the F5 winds tore it asunder, rendering its high tech safeguards ineffective and hurling it aside like a broken toy. Airfoils shattered and useless, the jumpjet plunged earthward, Ada and Abram clinging to each other in terror. They had only moments to once again say their goodbyes and to vow their eternal love.

"Beloved," he whispered, caressing her cheek.

"Beloved, forever" she returned, her face streaked with tears, just before the craft crashed to the ground and exploded in a ball of flame. There were no survivors.

Their funeral was conducted with appropriate state honours. Deaf to the praise heaped upon their parents as friends and dignitaries eulogized them, and blinded by tears, the children were bereft and inconsolable. Aunt Aggie tried to comfort them, but even as the flyer has been torn asunder, so had the lives of the two youngsters. Respecting tradition, their parents' Futures rings were presented to the grieving children as a remembrance and a token of respect.

"Why can't they just bring them back, like they did before?" Quinn sobbed.

Sera hugged and comforted him. "You know. You have the answer in your hand, the essence of what they were," she said, pointing to the ring that Quinn held. "They had only one chance at a second life. Now others will have their opportunity."

Emotionally, Sera's answer didn't mollify him, but he knew rationally that their parents were gone forever and that he would just have to accept it.

Quinn, now a mature thirteen year old, petitioned the Guardians for permission to remain in the family hab and to raise his sister. After friends and neighbors vouched for their competence to take care of themselves, and with a special recommendation from Pierre Adler, an Arbiter and friend of Abram and Ada, their request was granted. Aunt Aggie would keep a close watch on their progress, but their inner strength, their maturity, and their love for each other would ultimately carry them through.

Time passed and pain faded, but never the love and regard they had for their parents, whose ashes resided, commingled in a common urn, on a shelf in their gathering room. The two grew even closer, filling the gap now left in their lives. He was her protector, she was his rock. Together they felt invincible.

As they passed from high school to university, their common paths diverged somewhat. Quinn majored in reproductive biology with a minor in psychology, while Sera pursued studies in physics and microbiology, leading her to a career in nanotechnology. The skills they acquired would serve them well in the terrible times to come.

* * *

They were the same, yet so different. Quinn was an intellectual, taking delight in his career and his various interests, secure in his masculinity, confident that the world about him was stable and secure and that he understood it.

He knew he was attractive to the opposite sex, but he didn't quite know why. As far as looks went, he perceived himself to be average. He didn't think he was anything special. Rather, he thought it might be because he actually liked women, less for the erotic encounters than for the way their minds worked. They were different. Somehow their logic was completely illogical; but even so it brought the world into a kind of cohesive focus. He knew that the woman he admired most in the world, his mother, would have understood. Yet he chose his paramours with care, giving more attention to their minds than to their physical attributes. He was truly a gentleman of the old school.

Women viewed him in a whole different light. Female colleagues, friend and acquaintances, and most of his female students saw a ruggedly handsome man with a quiet, self-deprecating and gentle manner, gallant and courteous at all times. Those who were so inclined envisioned the ecstasy of being bedded by him; his tender caresses as he explored every nook and cranny of their bodies with his hands, his fingers, his lips, his tongue, his … By this time, they were almost always flushed, damp, and breathless as their fantasies played out. Those few who had indeed experienced his sexual attentions could attest to the reality of the fantasy. Even so, when women got to know him, they realized that he actually paid attention to what they said and valued their opinions, taking pleasure in their company.

His early sexual fumblings more often than not resulted in embarrassment on both sides, but he had the good fortune to be taken in hand by an older woman. He was sixteen, she nineteen and with considerable experience to her credit. What she taught him about pleasure and gratification would earn him praise and gratitude from his future conquests.

Like her sibling, Sera was highly intelligent and curious about everything. Her inquiring mind often led her to studies that bordered on the esoteric. While her career combined physics and biology, her wide ranging interests focused on sociology, but also included parapsychology, mythology, and many other arcane subjects. She and her friends indulged themselves in these fads, and even went so far as to take classes together in their current area of interest. These generated many nights of endless debate and discussion in cafs and gathering rooms and student lounges, with the lead most often being taken by Sera.

She had always been a talkative girl, often to the annoyance of her teachers. She took delight in answering questions in class, and teased her professors by commenting on the subject then asking questions designed to draw them off-topic. Many professors purposely avoided asking Sera to respond to their questions in order to avoid problems, but her classmates, knowing the game, often deliberately refrained from volunteering answers so that the professor was forced to go to the girl who was grinning and swinging her arm wildly in the air.

Frequently, Sera became so absorbed in her own little world that she would sit and stare off into space, deep in a trance-like state. On one occasion, she and her friends were in the student lounge, discussing the decline and fall of the world's religions in the 21st century, as their lack of relevance and rationale became apparent to the vast majority of the populace. A random thought captured Sera's attention, and she mentally pursued it through the torturous passageways of her mind. She went into her trance-like state, a state from which her fellow students were unable to rouse her.

"I swear you could set off a bomb in here and she wouldn't notice," her best friend Adrian commented.

"I'll bet we could dance naked around her and she wouldn't come out of it," Miriam countered.

A sudden silence fell on the room. They looked at each other, grinning mischievously. It wasn't long before clothes were flying in all directions. A few minutes later, when the new dean entered the lounge to introduce himself and his wife to the students, they were both taken aback by the sight of a half dozen students cavorting naked around a very pretty girl sitting cross legged and oblivious on the carpet. The dean and his wife beat a crimson faced and hasty retreat after he assayed a concise but pointed lecture to the students on the subjects of propriety, decorum, and restraint.

Sera returned to an awareness of her surroundings at some point in the dean's brief tirade and noted with interest and delight the variety of interesting genitalia at her eye level. She was not without sexual experience, and even as she explored her intellectual interests, she was similarly liberal about the exploration of her sensual being.

Her first sexual awakening, at age fourteen, had been with a female neighbor, as they played in her hab while Quinn was away. Imitating a romantic holovid, a gentle kiss turned passionate, and this aroused such intense feelings in both of them that they were soon satisfying their curiosity about each others' bodies. Her investigations in that area continued until she discovered the wonderful world of boys a couple of years later, leading her first real beaux on a forced march of mutual exploration. He was surprised and delighted at her enthusiasm and vigor, she no less so at his stamina and willingness to experiment. She was thrilled that her choice of potential sexual partners had now doubled.

* * *

"What's that you're watching?" Sera asked as she walked into the gathering room. It was now almost a decade since the loss of their parents. Quinn had completed his education and, following in his father's footsteps, had secured a position teaching at the university. Sera, on the verge of graduation, was considering her career options.

Quinn paused the comcenter display. "It's an old crime drama from the early twenty-first century called CSI, Crime Scene Investigation. It was probably the finest series of its kind, interesting and instructive, if somewhat unrealistic. There were a number of offshoot series and imitators, but the original was the best. It's amazing how violent people were back in those days, and astounding how much criminological expertise we've forgotten because we didn't need it."

"Was it really necessary for them to show objects and projectiles going through flesh like that? It's a bit grisly."

"Probably not, but it's useful to know what kind of damage various weapons make. From that, it's often possible to identify the type of weapon and often, the specific weapon. I can also access databank files on the subject, as well as on gross anatomy and criminology. All of that kind of information would be helpful if it were ever needed, but it doesn't replace hands-on experience in the field."

"If you ask me, that's some bizarre hobby you have. I don't understand your obsession with violence."

"To tell the truth, neither do I. I've only just begun to look into deviant criminal psychology. I guess it's a kind of passion for understanding how the human mind works, in all of its manifestations. We know so much yet so little about it. It's an interesting avocation, if not particularly useful. At least it keeps me out of trouble."

In the not too distant future, Quinn would have cause to recall those words, and not in a good way. Over the following years, he would often be called upon for his unique expertise in criminal psychology. Many investigative skills had been lost to the authorities in the quiescent years following the virtual eradication of violent crimes, and Quinn's unique knowledge of the past would serve society well.

* * *

A few years on, Quinn was now content and secure in his position, teaching biology to aspiring doctors and scientists. Sera had opted to do research in her chosen fields, where opportunities abounded. He pursued an extracurricular interest in deviant criminal psychology, drawing on the historical archives available in the Dome's vast databanks. She developed an interest in contemporary sociology, and used her friends as research subjects, engaging them hour after hour in dialogue and provocative debate.

"You wouldn't believe some of the notions they cling to," she told Quinn in one of their daily conversations.

"For example?" he asked.

"They think all Outlanders are societal rejects. They refuse to even consider the available literature and vids that show most are people like us, just trying to get by from day to day and wanting the best for their families. Just because most of them chose to live outside of the Domes, refusing to accept the edicts of the Compilers and their rigid controls, my friends think they're lesser beings than we are. It's the Outlanders who do the rejecting."

"You're right about the Outlanders being little different from us, but they're not doing themselves any favors by declining the benefits and opportunities of the New Society and spurning the wisdom of the Compilers," Quinn responded.

"Don't you think the Compilers might be just a little too .. ah … forceful in imposing their edicts on us?" Sera asked.

"I wouldn't call it forceful. Perhaps merely vigorous. If standards are not set and enforced, you have anarchy. That's just the way civilization works."

"So you like being controlled?" Sera asked.

"Not so much controlled as informed and persuaded," Quinn replied testily, not appreciating having his values challenged. "The Compilers realized that people living together in close quarters, as we half million do under the Dome, must engage in voluntary compromise. For the common good, the masses under the Dome are influenced to be respectful, respectable, and productive citizens."

"Controlled," Sera insisted. "And I'm not the only one who thinks so."

Quinn opened his mouth to dispute her once again but, realizing he was getting nowhere, settled for a drawn out sigh as he shook his head in exasperation.

Sera wanted to continue the debate, enjoying the intellectual stimulation of the exchange, but recognized that Quinn was in no way receptive to the undeniable logic of her arguments. She let out a mocking sigh and shook her head in imitation of her brother. They both collapsed laughing, knowing that even philosophical differences could never come between them.

The siblings held their long departed parents dear to their hearts, and the memory of their love and their insightful wisdom would stay with them and serve them well for the rest of their lives. Ada and Abram's influence had shaped their psyches and made them the strong and honourable people they had become. Now, they were determined to give back to society, just as their parents had before them. That opportunity would not be long in coming even as, unbeknownst to them, a dark shadow was falling upon the Dome.

CHAPTER 10

A WARRANTED ASSUMPTION

August 7, 2204

"Let's get moving on this," Quinn said, pulling up the files on his comcenter. He briefed Sera on the available specifics of the case and showed her the vids from the crime scene and the sec-cams. "Any thoughts?" he asked.

"Not much in the way of forensic evidence. We're developing a new kind of scan that types a person's particular mix of skin bacteria. If the perpetrator left his precise mix of bacteria on the girl, we can type it. The downside is that we can only identify him after he's caught."

"It always seems to come back to that. We're going to have to do the kind of old-time detective work they used to do more than a century back. Legwork, paperwork, and profiling; skills that have practically been lost."

"Speaking of profiling, do you have any insights?"

"Just this. He's confident and clever. If we're dealing with an old fashioned sociopath, there's a whole catalog of behaviors we can expect. At least we have an idea of what we're looking for. Once we can develop a short list of suspects, either from evidence or from a criminal profile, my studies will help us narrow down the probable perpetrator. Right now, we have to sift the evidence for clues. There's not much in the way of physical evidence, except for the ribbon segments, synthskin particles, and the gel-shoe fragment. We have to review the sec-cam vids and taskforce interviews. I'm very much afraid that this guy is too clever to reveal himself carelessly, and we can't count on him to do so. Unless we're very lucky and stumble on a clue, there's little hope that we can stop him from killing again."

They studied the autopsy report, which indicated that the girl had been murdered in much the same way as the first victim. Again, the violent rape. Again, the child's head bashed against a tree. The cuts were a new twist; perhaps an addition to the culprit's growing catalog of sadism, or perhaps merely a means of whiling away the time, waiting for the park to clear out. And once again the maddening, tantalizing fragments of synthskin. That lead had fizzled out as it became apparent that the product was commonly available, but the question of its presence on the bodies still remained. Perhaps the perp was a recovering burn victim. Easy enough to query the med centers on that score, although burn victims were a rare breed in such a safety conscious society, and even among the Outlanders. An unlikely scenario.

"How about this," said Sera after several hours of sifting through the available information. "I know it won't be easy, but perhaps we should go through the files of every male under the Dome. We can probably eliminate everyone under 15 and over 85, based on the strength and knowledge needed to commit the two crimes. We can also eliminate all of the Futures."

"And that should leave only, oh, about 200 000 males," Quinn sighed. "Not to disparage your idea, but I think we have to narrow down the possible suspects further before we begin to examine files. Time is our enemy here, and there just isn't enough of it or of human resources to carry out that plan."

"What about the red ribbon?" Sera asked.

"Ah, now, there's something interesting, that strip of red ribbon. The ends of the pieces recovered from the first and second bodies matched. This is compelling evidence that the two crimes are linked. Now all we have to do is to find the owner of that particular roll."

"What do you make of its presence on the body? What does it mean?"

"It appears to be ritualistic. Some serial killers in earlier times liked to leave a distinctive signature, usually something related either to their past or to a message they think they're sending. Most often, the significance can't be determined until the killer is questioned or until he contacts the authorities to make his intent clear."

The forensics team's report contained what could be an important lead. The small fragment of yellow gelplas and the tread marks were from a particular make and model of shoe commonly worn by citizens in the Dome. However, this particular shoe was part of a faulty batch that had received a special experimental coating to increase wear resistance. That batch consisted of some 10 000 pairs of shoes, all of which had been distributed only locally, and had been recently recalled when it had been determined that the coating was too rigid to bond permanently to the flexible shoe, causing the edges of the soles to peel back and chip. Public service messages were being circulated on all broadcast media, urging the public to heed the recall and to return the remaining shoes. At least the special taskforce investigative team now had something to go on.

They reviewed the security cam records from both crime scenes once more. Nothing resonated with either of them. "Quinn," Sera said finally. "All of these sec-cam images. Do you think the Guardians might be watching us too closely? Are we being too ..... controlled?" She had broached the subject with Quinn in the past, but faced with the massive evidence of domestic surveillance, she had decided to approach the issue more directly.

"Please don't start that again, sis. They do what must be done. It's for the common good. We all benefit. Those who have done nothing wrong have nothing to fear. You worry too much; analyze everything to death. Accept what is. Take joy and comfort in it. The Compilers, in their wisdom, bestowed on us a perfect society."

"Or so we are to believe, but just think about it. There's surveillance everywhere, even more than the public is aware of. You told me so yourself. Don't you ever get concerned?"

"You know, dear sister," Quinn replied in a slightly exasperated tone, "We've got a pretty good life here. Imagine what it was like to live in the cities of the twentieth and twenty-first centuries. Filth and decay and neighborhoods into which it was unsafe to venture. Being afraid to go out at night. Lawlessness the authorities were unable to control. I'd rather have someone watching my back than to be constantly looking over my shoulder. However, if you're really that concerned, you could always go and join an Outlander colony. Live underground. Wear a rebreather and a radsuit every time you venture out onto the surface."

Sera shuddered as she considered the prospect. Only the most committed fanatics chose to live outside of the protection of the Domes, for either religious or philosophical reasons. A few were exiles from the Domes, expelled for a variety of severe antisocial behaviors, a measure that was as uncommon as it was extreme.

She persisted nonetheless. "It's like a religion to you, isn't it? Blind faith in the Creators, sorry, the Compilers. Aren't there questions in your mind, too? You're a scientist like me. We're trained to question everything."

"You really think I'm a true believer? I'd have thought you knew me better than that. Of course I have doubts, but I balance them against the greater good. Are you going to waste your life challenging every norm of civil society?"

Satisfied that he had put the subject to rest, Quinn continued to examine the evidence. Sera was not nearly so sanguine. She had a jaundiced view of the world order and a suspicion and mistrust of authority. She, too, had an abiding interest in the past, and what she'd found out about governments and the abuse of authority, wealth, and power shaped her views of the present. When she got together with her friends for informal gatherings, she expressed her views freely and entered into discussions that prompted discord as often as they produced concord. They all understood that a degree of conformity and consensus was necessary for a society to be able to function, but at what cost? Nevertheless, she abandoned the contentious dialogue for the sake of the investigation. Several hours spent going over the evidence resulted in a report that might impress the oversight committee, but moved them no closer to finding the identity of the perpetrator.

* * *

On his way to the task force meeting, Quinn hopped a floater to Gundy Park. He wanted to view the crime scene by the light of day. Barriers were still in place around the scene, superfluous now, as ordinary citizens had forsaken the park's once welcoming greenery. They stayed away in fear and horror of the event that had transpired here. The only people in evidence were Sentinels and forensic techs.

Quinn identified himself and walked down the pathway and into the woods, being careful not to interfere with the techs' ongoing investigative work. He stood there, where he had stood the night before, between the place where the child's corpse had lain and the tree bough where she'd been strung up. Closing his eyes, he attempted to envision what had transpired there; the killer carrying the girl into the dimness of the woods, tying her hands and suspending her from the limb. Quinn moved to where the perp had stood. The images following did not come easily. The girl stripped of her clothing, dangling helplessly. A knife, small bladed by the size of the cuts, wielded hesitantly, cutting here and there. Quiet in the park, the light fading. The knife slashing across the rope, leaving a score mark on the bough, the unconscious girl falling to the ground, the monster looming over her, preparing ....

He could bear no more. The images were too real. He didn't want to envision the outcome. The techs would prepare a sim-vid from the evidence gathered which would, thankfully, feature only generic mannequins. Even that he would have a difficulty watching. Time to go. He had a meeting to attend.

* * *

"It would be premature to conclude that the two killings are the work of a serial killer," Quinn began, as he addressed the meeting of the homicide task force later that day. "Having said that, I feel that we must consider it a strong possibility. If it's true, then we have to stop him before the sixth of next month."

There were nods of agreement around the room.

"If he is a serial killer, Quinn, what should we be looking for?" Benwright asked. "Nobody alive today has had any experience with this type of crime. Even your expertise comes only from studies of historical cases."

"If you'll look at your data screens, you'll see that I've included a page of typical behavioral characteristics of sociopaths in the file. Keep in mind, these are only guidelines. Each individual may exhibit different behaviors. It's almost certain that the motivations for his actions are based on things that happened to him in his youth. If we can't find him through his psych profile, we may be able to track him down from his background. So, here it is. He obviously has a complete disregard for societal norms and rules, and a callous indifference for the feelings of others. He appears to have a low threshold for discharge of aggression. The very violence of the crimes attests to that. He probably has no capacity to maintain enduring relationships, so he's likely to be single. Most especially, he'll have problems relating to adult females in any normal kind of romantic or sexual way. It's also likely that he has an inability to experience guilt."

"O.K.," Benwright interjected. "We might be able to observe most of those things after we catch him. Other than his being single, what might we look for?"

"He's likely to be glib and have a superficial charm," Quinn continued. "He will almost certainly have a grandiose sense of self-worth."

"So, a charming overachiever?" Guardian Isomoto asked.

"Could well be," Quinn replied. "He'll be a pathological liar, cunning and manipulative. If we have a suspect, we'll be able to profile him by his childhood experiences and behaviors, which will probably include behavioral problems, impulsivity, irresponsibility, and a history of juvenile delinquency. He may have been abused by his parents or siblings, and as a result will have a poor sense of self-worth, although child abuse of any kind in this day and age is practically unknown, as is juvenile delinquency."

"Doesn't that contradict his grandiose sense of self-worth?" asked Security Commissioner Earl.

"Bear in mind," Quinn said. "He may exhibit only some or even many of these characteristics. His sense of self-worth may be poor or grandiose, or that may not even enter into it. These aren't hard and fast rules. The one thing that we can be certain of is that, since this type of crime has been unknown for over a century, the perpetrator is either some kind of mutated deviate or possibly a gene-altered throwback. Nothing in our experience could have predicted the genetic error that spawned this creature. He probably has a reckless disregard for consequences. He'll act as he wishes to act, and will assume he won't get caught unless he wants to get caught. What we're dealing with here may be well beyond our level of comprehension."

"Any guesses on age or physical description?" Guardian Isomoto asked.

"Hard to pin down either right now. Mass probably about 75 kilos, estimated from the size and depth of some of the footprints. Age indeterminate, but most likely between 18 and 50, considering the state of physical fitness required to handle the girls, and his access to tranqs coupled with the knowledge of exactly how to use them. I know it's not much, but it's all we've got."

"What about the shoes," Guardian F-Kilmara asked. "How do we know that the yellow fragment wasn't there before."

The forensics tech spoke up. "I can answer that one, Guardian F-Kilmara," he said, using the honourific F-, in recognition of the Guardian's status as a Future. "First, we know that the killer's tracks are consistent with that type of shoe. Second, there was blood spatter on the tree, some of it beneath the fragment, so we know that this particular piece of the shoe got wedged there after the girl was murdered. There was little time between the murder, around 2127, and the time that her father found her, at 2133, for anyone else to have wandered around the murder site and deposited it."

"Good," Quinn said. "The task force is working on that clue. They should be able to track down everyone who requisitioned that particular model. At least we'll have a list of suspects, however long it may be."

"Assuming the shoes were worn by the original requisitioner," Guardian F-Kilmara interjected.

"We can only hope," Quinn replied. "We may have to seize, identify, or track down every pair. It'll be arduous work, but it has to be done, and quickly. We have less than thirty days to catch this creature."

"And synthskin was also present this time," Commissioner Earl stated.

"Yes. It remains to be seen where that might lead us. Obviously, these are pieces of a puzzle that we're only just beginning to put together. The girl's clothes were found in a refuse bin near the north end of the park. It appears that he had them in his hand when he apparently heard the father approaching, and forgot to drop them in his rush to escape."

"Just to fill this task force in," Benwright said. "After the first murder, we sent troops of Sentinels to the Outlands to check out the two nearest Outlander colonies, and one band of nomads less than 15 kilometers from the Dome. They were discretely armed with stunners, in case of trouble. Interviews in the two colonies yielded no information, and the nomads scattered as the Sentinels approached. We're still pursuing stragglers, but we're having no better results there. That line of investigation is ongoing."

When the meeting finally wrapped up, Benwright took Quinn aside. "What next?" he asked. "Are there any resources you need, off the record? I know someone who can get you anything you need. We might have to take some shortcuts to get to the bottom of this."

"Thanks," Quinn replied, "But given the status of the investigation, I think we're going to need more information before we can decide just what resources we need and where to allocate them."

Benwright nodded. "You're right, but if you need more help, your friend Pierre Adler is not without influence. Have a talk with him."

Pierre Adler was a member of the Council of Arbiters, well respected in the community, and with access to a considerable range of resources, both on and off the books. Pierre had been a good friend of Quinn's parents, and was the siblings' godfather. He had been active in the children's upbringing after the death of their parents, and had maintained a continuing interest in their careers. Both Quinn and Sera had sustained the relationship with Pierre to the present day, enjoying his company and valuing his wise counsel. They frequently attended gatherings at the judge's home where community leaders mingled with anyone who cared to show up.

"I will," Quinn said. "Com me if you get any new leads." He'd be ready to call for Pierre's help as soon as he could determine exactly what he might require. Until then, he was determined to gather facts and to settle on a course of action that would bring the person responsible for the recent heinous acts to justice.

CHAPTER 11

RIVER MAKES HER MOVE

August 12, 2204

"Back so soon, Quinn?" said Rosie as the portal slid aside. "Doesn't time just fly away! It seems like you were here only last week."

"Last month," Quinn corrected her. "There's been another murder since I was here last."

"Yes, so sad. Those poor children … and their parents. What must they be going through?"

"I've talked to all of the parents. It's not something any parent should ever have to experience, and it's not something I would ever again wish to go through with them. Is Gus here?"

"Sure," Rosie replied. "Guuus! Quinn's here to see you!"

"One day you're going to strain your vocal cords doing that. We do have coms, you know," Gus reproached her playfully as he entered the gathering room.

"And I do have a good set of lungs, which I know how to use."

"You do indeed," Gus replied, grinning as he playfully poked her breast.

"Gus! Not in front our guest! Shame on you!"

"Can't help myself, m'love. It's the horny adolescent in me."

"Ahem!" Quinn interjected. "If you two are quite through, I have some information that might be of benefit to your research, Gus. Or would you prefer some private time?"

"Yes," they both said simultaneously, then burst into laughter.

"But that will have to wait. It wouldn't be polite to our visitor," Gus said to Rosie. "What do you have for me, Quinn?"

"I've been tossing ideas around with Sera, and she's been working on a promising line of research that might be of help to you. One of your problems was the delivery of growth hormone in a timely manner, and I think we've come up with a solution. Sera's been working on developing nanobiobots for various specialized purposes. She thinks that she can tweak them to manufacture and deliver the hormone on demand, from inside the body. The 'bots would also detect the degree of growth and regulate the speed of delivery of memories from the crystal. She'd be happy to work with you on such an experiment."

"That's wonderful news, Quinn. It would be the ideal solution if it works. How soon can we get started?"

"Almost immediately. I'll ask Sera to com you."

"Excuse me, Gus, Rosie. I finished prepping F-Werner for Awakening and laid out the old hardcopy files for archiving. Is there anything else you need before I go home?" A slight man, apparently in his early twenties, had entered the room. He affected a retro unshaven look that had been inexplicably popular early in the 21st century. It was an incongruous contrast to his technophile robes and high tech com helmet.

"No, that's fine, Gabby. Just make sure you're here early tomorrow for the Awakening," said Rosie. "Where are my manners? Quinn, this is Gabriel Iano, the new tech-trainee we just took on board as part of the university's intern program. Gabby, this is Quinn Braxton, a family friend and a professor at the university."

"A pleasure to meet you, Gabby. You're lucky to have found a position in the best Harbour under the Dome, and with the best family anywhere."

"I'm well aware of how fortunate I am to be working here, professor. I'm really enjoying it," Gabby replied politely. "I've signed up for your seminar class for next semester. I'm really looking forward to it. And I want you to know that I share your interest in deviant criminal psychology. I've followed your works in that area closely. Maybe we can discuss it after classes. Nice to meet you in advance. Well, folks, I'm off. I'll see you bright and early."

Gabby activated the portal and left. "Nice boy," Gus commented. "He's eager to learn and a hard worker. Doesn't mind doing scut work during his internship. He should do well. A little backward socially, though. Now, where were we?"

Just then, River walked into the room, and Gus immediately lost Quinn's attention.

"Lo, stranger. What a nice surprise. It's been a while," she said breezily as she strolled by Quinn, offering him a hint of her perfume, and plunked herself down in a balloon chair. She was dressed casually in filmy black pantaloons that were cinched tightly at the ankles and ballooned slightly before they once again tightened above her slim and sensuous hips, forming a V that plunged below her naval. Her flaming red hair flowed free, spilling over a short black turtleneck, sleeves ballooning slightly on her upper arms, like the trousers, and ending at the elbow, with the front cut short, exposing the pale half moons of the lower part of her pert breasts. Her bare midriff was accentuated with a black pearl in her naval. Flared black ankleboots and fingerless wrist gloves completed her ensemble.

She wasn't fooling anybody. Quinn's presence was no surprise to her, since she'd heard his initial greeting to Rosie, and she'd chosen her outfit quickly but carefully, for eye appeal.

Quinn noticed. "River," he greeted her. For all his sophistication, her name nearly caught in his throat. She was stunning to behold, and the effect on Quinn was exactly what she'd intended. Her decision to abandon sweet and coy and to embrace the direct approach seemed to be paying off.

"I'm in the mood for a soylatte. How about it, Quinn? Feel like going to The SkyLounge? I'm buying." The title 'Uncle' Quinn was long gone.

"Now just a minute, young lady," Gus began, frowning. "Quinn and I were talking shop." He was anxious to continue the conversation they'd begun.

"You two go and have fun," Rosie interjected. "You fellas can catch up on shop talk later." Gus was still grumbling in the background. He'd give Rosie what for later.

"Do I get a say in this?" Quinn asked, pretending reluctance.

"No. Grab your stuff and come on," River informed him. Quinn took the updated memory crystal that Gus grumpily proffered, then hurried through the portal in River's wake. He would review the research later, but in the here and now, his mind was elsewhere.

* * *

"Bold move," Quinn commented finally as they walked to the floater station. "You're a little firebrand when you want to be."

"If I'd waited for you to make a move I might die an old maid."

"So now you're proposing to me?" Quinn said, laughing.

"Get over yourself, buster. You still have some work to do to impress me that much. Just for now, I'll allow you to take me out occasionally and prove yourself worthy of me."

"Well who needs to get over herself now? Really, you're forthright and self-assured beyond your years. I had it in mind to approach you sooner or later, but having been a family friend for so long, I've been reluctant to cross that line. It's my conventional upbringing."

"You're forgiven. Let's make up for lost time, starting right now."

They summoned a floater, and rose to the very top of the Dome. During the short journey, the two made small talk to pass the time. The craft soon docked at the observation ring encircling the top of the Dome's central tower. The lower level of the ring provided a view within the Dome; the upper level, above the Dome's covering, offered a spectacular panorama of the surrounding countryside when climatic conditions were favorable; the mountains to the west and the ocean to the east. The

SkyLounge was located within the upper ring, which slowly rotated, providing an ever-changing view.

River led Quinn to a vacant banquette that seemed to float above the Dome's summit. They ordered drinks from the roboserver and sat back to enjoy the vista. It quickly became obvious that the view might not be theirs to enjoy for much longer. A storm was rumbling in from the west, and by all indications it was going to be a bad one. The city, alerted by weather satellites, was beginning to make its preparations. Harvesters and dredgers offshore rushed for the sanctuary of coves or dove deep to the safety of the aquaculture farms. The wind farm to the south retracted its vanes and grounded its towers. Protective walls rose from the ground on the windward side of the Dome, almost to its full height. The flexible walls consisted of a series of huge, horizontal, angled baffles designed to deflect high winds up and over the dome, and to gather energy from those winds using small impellers dotting their surface. The inhabitants were little concerned, since the Dome had been designed to withstand weather much more severe than it would ever experience. The storm promised a spectacular light show, and River and Quinn watched until at last the torrential rains obscured their view.

They spent the rest of the day in rapt conversation, getting to know one another in depth. They explored each other's likes and dislikes, opinions, hopes and dreams, and, after the storm had passed, watched the sunset through the tainted grey gloom of the early August sky. When they parted at last, outside the Harbour late that evening, they embraced, and he kissed her gently and tenderly before reluctantly releasing her, but only, he promised her, for a little while.

August 13, 2204

He was scouting. Only a week after his last assault he was already picking a location for the next one. The park in Hanover would seem to be ideal. The general layout of the commons was the same from district to district, but they varied in their sweep and flow around lakes and ponds and streams and woods. The flora was richer and thicker here, the gloworbs making little headway against the shadows, and HanoverRound plaza was more remote from the most heavily wooded area than were plazas in other parks. On the day, he would have to seize his prey early, before the curfew.

Nonchalantly, he strolled the pathways at eve, searching out just the right place to replicate his triumphs of the past.

"After all," he reasoned, "why argue with success?"

Examining each prospective location, he paused to visualize the progression of his next crime. At one point, he was peering at a clearing barely visible between the trees when, abruptly, he realized that he was becoming excited, and the evidence of his arousal had been noticed by a young couple walking towards him, their fingers entwined. The girl giggled and her swain glared as the pair moved quickly by.

Too late he realized what a mistake this had been, this foray in public, in broad daylight. He hadn't even bothered to change out of his professional attire and into his civilian clothes. What if he were recognized? Glancing over his shoulder at the retreating lovers, who were in turn looking back at him, he straightened his back and moved rapidly off in the opposite direction.

"Why worry?" he told himself. "Who would they bother to report me to, and why?" Still, he would have to exercise much more caution in future, if he expected to live to a ripe old age. He knew from past experience that luck comes to those who make their own. He hurried out of the park and boarded a floater at the nearest station, ordering it to drop him in Lowertown. "Best be away from this place as quickly as possible," he thought.

August 14, 2204

"Who's winning?" Quinn asked as he arrived home after a long day at the university. Splitting his time between teaching and trying to solve a seemingly unsolvable series of murders was wearing him down.

"Avotech," Sera replied sourly. The comscreen holo showed two aceball teams jockeying for position, as two blues rushed around opposite ends of the green clad defenders arrayed in front of them. The defense split and, their attention thus diverted, one of the blues darted up the middle without being netted and sprang nimbly up to the next level, scoring 5 points.

"Tied," Quinn observed.

"Not for long," Sera countered.

"Now, for half a point and the right to attempt a conversion," the head referee called to the successful blue, "Name the 12th president of the United European Federation."

The blue furrowed his brow in concentration. "Malachi Umberto," he shouted from the platform high above the field of play. "Correct!" the referee confirmed. "One half point!"

"Ha!" Sera exclaimed triumphantly.

Darting across the platform, the blue vaulted into the air, did a forward somersault, and landed on a higher platform.

"Half-point," the referee declared as the time clock ran out. "Servotech is affirmed the winner by one point."

Cheers arose from the stadium as the home team achieved victory. They were on their way to the championships.

Quinn grimaced, and groused, "Lucky shot. Malachi Umberto! Who ever remembers him?"

"My team, apparently," Sera crowed, and doubled over with laughter.

"Wasn't that funny," Quinn said, scowling.

"Oooh, such a sourpuss. Get out on the wrong side of the sleep shelf this morning?"

"O.K., O.K.," Quinn laughed. "I guess I'm a bit stressed with all of this workload, and the fact that the investigation is moving glacially slowly.

We can't seem to get any traction in finding clues. I'll be back to my jolly old self as soon as things start to break for us."

"And when do you think that might be?" Sera asked.

"Soon, very soon," he replied confidently.

While Sera occupied herself with the post-game wrap-up, Quinn commed River.

"Hi," she said brightly as soon as they were connected. "I was just thinking about you.'

"I must have picked up on that, then. Want to get together for supper? I could use some pleasant company."

"Hey, what am I? Chopped tofu?" Sera protested in the background.

"Don't pay any attention to her," said Quinn. "My little sister just likes being a pest.

Sera made a playful face-scrunch at Quinn and went back to her game review, where the media-bot was interviewing the water boy and the towel boy. They had some incisive opinions on the players' relative degrees of thirst and levels of cleanliness. Sera shook her head and switched off. "Idiots," she muttered.

"I'll meet you at BelleWeather in an hour," River said, and rang off. "Our first official date," she thought. "The world is unfolding as it should."

" 'Bout time," Sera admonished him. "That girl's been mooning after you for years. How could you have ignored her for so long?"

"So was I the last to know? And I wasn't ignoring her. I was being circumspect, properly respectful."

"If you say so," she grinned at him mischievously.

"Umph," he grunted. "I've got a date to keep."

A quick sono-shower and facial depilation was followed by a lengthy deliberation on which outfit would be most appropriate for the occasion. "I've nothing to wear," he thought, rotating the rack of sports, work, and formal clothing in his storage cylinder. He finally selected a snappy black jacket with white piping over a tight orange turtleneck, with stylish white jodhpurs and black knee boots, then allowed the cylinder to retract into the wall.

"Have fun," Sera called after him as the portal swished open. He waved backhandedly as he stepped into the corridor and made his way to the dropshaft. Seven minutes to spare. If a floater was on station, he'd arrive about a minute late, so as not to look too eager.

He was deflated when he got to the BelleWeather and River was nowhere in sight. She arrived a minute after him, thus winning the 'not-too-eager' sweepstakes. She wore a diaphanous white dress, sleeveless and open-fronted in the Greco-Roman style, which threatened at every moment to slip from her bare shoulders. Gold sandals and a thin, corded gold belt completed her ensemble. Quinn was electrified.

"Hi, you," she said coquettishly, though that ship had long since sailed.

"Hi, yourself," he responded, putting an arm around her and giving her a respectful peck on the cheek. She turned, pulled him to her, and gave him a full-on kiss on the lips that lasted for nearly half-minute, causing him to re-evaluate the efficacy of wasting time being circumspect and respectful.

Once River had disentangled herself from him, Quinn was finally able to take a breath. "Wow," he gasped. "When you go for it, you really go for it, don't you?"

"At least I know how to attract a crowd," she replied, smiling acknowledgement at nearby diners, who grinned and nodded their approval at the handsome couple.

"Perhaps we should find a table," said Quinn, guiding her by the elbow towards the rear of the room. The caf was lit by walls glowing in muted colors that gently swirled and flowed. Soothing sounds, both natural and musical, emanated from tri-d audial projections in the air itself.

Quinn chose a hush booth at the rear of the caf, where ambient sound was muffled by cleverly designed baffles, so that they could talk in peace and quiet. They sat close together on the banquette, no more than a hand's breadth between them.

"I can help, you know," she said, after they'd keyed their orders into the menu screen.

"Help with what?"

"Your investigation. You know I'm an anthropologist by training, with a minor in psychology. Cultural and social interactions are my specialty.

The man you're looking for is trying desperately to fit into our society, even though he's in no way mentally equipped to do so. He's faking it, making the people around him believe he's one of us when he's clearly not. Nobody who's done what he's done could ever be one of us."

"Good analysis. I agree, but how does that move us closer to catching him?"

"In the short run, it may not, but he's bound to give himself away. Perhaps you should also be looking for people who've noted odd or anomalous behavior in one of their male colleagues or acquaintances. Unless he's well versed in wearing the mask, he will stand out."

"You're quite the romantic when you want to be. If this is you're idea of pillow talk, I must say it's not really stimulating me."

River flushed and laughed. "O.K. I hadn't meant to swerve off into that area. It's just that the thought had occurred to me, and I wanted to let you know I was available to help you out. Care to show me the files one of these days?"

"I'll do that, but right now, let's just enjoy this meal and talk about us." A roboserver in formal attire had trundled up and was discreetly and accurately distributing their order. The server gave a little bow and withdrew.

"In the old days servers expected a gratuity for bringing your meal. Of course, they were all humans then," Quinn told her.

"Really? And what of the people who actually prepared the meal?"

"In most cafs, they had some sort of equitable sharing arrangement. That depended on the honesty of the server who collected the tip to accurately report the amount. Servers were among the lowest paid wage earners in society, but of course you'd know that."

"Yes. The least valuable in society, like entertainers and athletes, were among the highest paid, and the most valuable, like doctors, teachers, and firefighters, received only average remuneration. I'm glad we don't have to deal with money anymore. It's so much more efficient to have your work time fully and automatically credited to your account, and special purchases or exchanges debited. By the way, is this your idea of pillow talk?"

"Sorry. Just a random observation. I'm prone to do that." With a couple of quick hand gestures he dimmed the wall behind them and raised a privacy screen, then moved closer to her. "Trade you a couple of baby carrots for an asparagus spear," he whispered.

"Now you're talking," she murmured, slowly and sensuously swirling her tongue around the rim of his ear before nipping his lobe and pulling away. "There," she said, "The appetizer. You'll have to wait for dessert."

"I'll be sure to save some room for that." They carried on with light banter for the rest of the meal, accompanied by intimate touches and caresses. By the time they were finished, they had sated their appetite, but not their hunger. That would come later.

CHAPTER 12

QUINN MAKES HIS MOVE

August 16, 2204

"Hey babe, what're you up to?" River's image appeared on the comscreen as soon as Quinn acknowledged the incoming call.

"The usual. You know. If I'm not grading papers, I'm slogging out the murder investigation. Want to come over and take my mind off things for a while?"

"As fast as I can get a floater to move," River replied. "I'll be right there."

Quinn barely had time to finish his marking when River pinged his portal, requesting admittance. He waved his work files closed even as he commanded the portal to open.

"Remind me to enter your access code so you won't even have to ask to be admitted in the future," Quinn said as the entry slid closed behind her.

"Ooooh. Giving me a key already? Wow, do you move fast!"

Quinn reddened. "Just a convenience," he managed to stammer. "So that you know you're always welcome here." He felt like an adolescent caught stealing glances at an elegant and lovely woman, and for good reason. No other female had ever had such an effect on him. He'd squired around some of the best that RichmondDome and nearby Domes had to offer. Intellectually gifted, fair of face and form, personable; artisans, scientists, educators, builders, but none the equal of the young lady who now graced his hab.

She wore a sheer pale green peasant blouse that exposed her shoulders and flared around her arms, ending just below the elbow. It was cinched at the waist by a silver wire linked belt, its end trailing downwards to the hemline. Hunter green pleated pantaloons ended just below the knee, revealing taught calves adorned with a silver chain anklet above high-heeled green sandals. The colors nicely set off the red hair that framed her face and cascaded over her bare shoulders. The top was just filmy enough to suggest that she wasn't wearing anything beneath, but modest enough to signify that her assets would only be available to a most worthy suitor. The scent of cinnamon and vanilla drifted lazily around her, spicy and sweet. The metaphor was not lost on its principal target.

Quinn was utterly enchanted and almost forgot to breathe as he drank in her spectacular beauty. She was well aware of the effect she was having on him, and for the first time experienced the thrill of having captivated a man to the point of intoxication. Nor was she immune to his charms, having been infatuated with him since the time she was old enough to notice men. The boys she was used to going out with just didn't measure up.

"Let me get you a drink," Quinn offered. "I've some ice wine that just came in from an agri-Dome up country."

"Love some," she responded. "Can we have a fire?"

"Sure," said Quinn, and called up a virtual campfire, a holo-projection in the middle of the room. With the lights lowered, the leaping flames and the crack and sizzle of the virtual wood enhanced the romantic atmosphere. "Privacy," he commanded, and a blue energy screen glowed softly into being, closing off the gathering room from view should Sera use their habs' common entrance. A simple gesture caused soft classical music to emanate from the acoustic walls, compositions culled from the best that centuries past had to offer; Mozart, Brahms. Gershwin, Vatu, Krishnamuri.

River curled up on the couch and patted the space beside her after Quinn had uncorked the wine and poured. She accepted the glass, touching his hand sensuously as she did, and swirled the wine, inhaling its aroma appreciatively as Quinn slid in close. They sipped the wine, its warmth spreading through their bodies, relaxing them, removing the last of the inhibitions that might have given them pause.

"Missed you," she whispered, closing the gap and turning to him.

"If I hadn't been so busy, you wouldn't have been able to pry me off you." Quinn put his glass down and turned towards her, taking the glass from her hand and setting it aside. He took her face in his hands and gently caressed her lips with his. She pressed back harder, more urgently.

Abandoning their wine, they flowed into each other, a reciprocal embrace, their bodies pressed together with increasing ardor. What heat the virtual fire lacked they more than made up for in the intensity of their passion. Their hands caressed here and there, exploring, disrobing each other. Fastening strips dissolved at a touch, and clothing flew in every direction. He tasted her skin as he moved down her neck and lower, tongue and fingertips tracing the contours of her body, probing her vibrant mysteries. She moved her body fluidly in response, pressing against him. Soon he reached her core, the heart of her sexual being, and probed deeper, savoring her essence, her taste, her scent. She moaned in bliss.

"Too soon," he whispered, and moved higher, once more meeting her lips. She sighed and stroked his cheek. Before long their naked bodies were intertwined in an unrelenting, passionate kiss. River allowed Quinn to take the lead, his solid and muscular body moving tenderly but firmly against her softness. He lay back on the couch and pulled her onto him. His legs trapped hers and she moved against him, letting him feel her wetness, smell her musk. She pulled back and rose up on her knees, allowing him to penetrate her as she lowered herself onto him, feeling his hardness inside of her. He gasped, she moaned, and they moved together as he caressed her breasts and thrust upwards. Her hands were on his chest, then moved lower as their movements became more insistent. She clutched his waist and pulled him upwards, hard into her, her moans becoming more urgent, his gasps turning to groans, then to gutturals. She climaxed seconds before he, her fingernails penetrating his flesh, the pain giving him a few moments pause, followed by euphoria as he erupted inside her. She collapsed onto his chest, the sweat of their exertions intermingling as they shared a final, passionate kiss.

"Wow. Oh, wow!" she exclaimed as she lay by his side, one leg over his.

"Wow doesn't begin to describe it," he countered breathlessly. "I hadn't realized I had a tiger by the tail."

"You're the one with the tail," she said teasingly as she flipped his limp member with her finger.

"Hey, treat my friend with more respect if you want good service in the future."

"You've spoiled me. I've now come to expect great service, and just how long do I have to wait for a repeat performance?"

He didn't reply, but covered her mouth with his and soon enough her question was answered with ardor reawakened, and yet again before dawn the consummation of their passion would provide the distraction Quinn needed to ease his mind and soothe his soul. By first light, murder was the farthest thing from his thoughts.

August 23, 2204

In late August, the task force report arrived at Quinn's comcenter. Most of the information contained in it was a rehash of Quinn's own findings and the coroner's report. The interesting part was the results of the investigation into the gelshoe fragment. The team had been able to track down every citizen who had requisitioned that particular model. They had interviewed practically everyone on their list, with the exception of seven Futures who were, of course above reproach. All interviewees had either returned the faulty shoes for exchange or had thrown them away, and all had been cleared on the basis of gender, age, alibi or lack of opportunity. They were back to square one, and with only a fortnight to go until the anniversary date of the first two killings, Quinn was getting worried and frustrated.

"Talk to the Futures," he told ACS Travio, the leader of the group assigned to track down the shoes. "Find out if they still have their gelshoes, if they threw them away or perhaps gave them to somebody else. We need to know where all of those shoes are."

Travio raised his eyebrows but refrained from comment. He'd do his job, no matter what oddity might present itself.

CHAPTER 13

A LOCKED-ROOM MYSTERY

September 6, 2204

The parks were closed to ordinary citizens after dimming, by order of the Sentinels. "No matter," he thought. "The entire Dome is my hunting ground."

He was adaptable. He knew things that nobody else knew. His will and his resources were practically limitless. He hadn't survived this long to be stymied by such a minor impediment to his purpose. It was the sixth of September, precisely one month after the second murder. The authorities were no closer to finding the stalker, and he was once again on the hunt.

The monthly fitness run was coming to an end as the sun plunged towards the western horizon. On the last day of the first week of each month, citizens were invited to challenge themselves and each other by running the perimeter road inside the Dome. They called it 'Running the Dome'. Only those with exceptional ability could run the entire 30 km, but others were able to choose whatever segment they felt they could handle. It was normal for several hundred residents of all ages to turn out for the event.

Thulia Traynor, age thirteen, was trailing far behind the pack on her first attempt to Run the Dome. Even her best friend Marissa had easily outpaced her. The rest of the runners were out of sight around the curve of the road, and Thulia had slowed her pace practically to a walk. She ambled along, past an area where low-rise housing was being reconstructed and reconfigured to accommodate the changing needs of the populace. At this late hour, few people were about, and Thulia sidled over to a metaplas barrier fencing off the renovation site. She rested against it and drank deeply from her sportskin's built-in power juice reservoir.

The stalker had mapped out his territory in advance, and when she came into view, he was ready. Like a predator in nature, looking to cut a weak straggler from the herd, he had planned for this very contingency and moved to cut off his prey's escape. If a victim had not wandered onto his range, he would have amended his strategy to ensure that one would. In any case, the youngling had accommodated his plan in a most convenient way.

He crept along the other side of the barrier until he was at the nearest opening to the place where Thulia was resting. Looking around, he determined that there was nobody within sight, then quickly and quietly slipped around the edge of the barrier and confronted the startled young girl. She stood up, alarmed at the sudden appearance of the menacing adult, and prepared to take flight. She was always mindful of the two murders that had taken place, and the warning issued by the Sentinels to beware of strangers. Too late she turned to run. He had her. As before, he quickly placed the microjet against the girl's neck, and she fell unconscious against him within seconds. He carried her behind the barrier and between the habs under reconstruction. Her body would not be found until the next morning.

September 7, 2204

The call came while Quinn was conducting an open forum with his biology class. "The Golden Age of Life Sciences came at the expense of manned space exploration. After the disastrous Mars mission, in which the lander failed to return to orbit and the entire crew was lost, followed closely by the loss of the International Space Station and all 200 crew on board, when an out of control robot cargo carrier crashed into it at speed, the world lost interest in sending manned missions into space. Funding was diverted to life sciences such as biology and psychology. By the middle of the 21st century, the development of stored memories, advanced cloning techniques, and genetic and social engineering were …."

The trilling of his com interrupted the discourse. "I'll be finished here in a few minutes. I'll get over there as soon as I can," he told Benwright. It took only moments for him to punch the weekly assignment into the comnet and to dismiss the class with apologies for having to cut it short. Grabbing a unisuit and a forensic kit from his office, he rushed to the nearest floater station and was soon on his way to the address Benwright had given him in Kula District. It turned out to be a small government stockhouse where furniture and fixtures were stored for quick distribution to area homes and businesses.

Benwright greeted him at the door and escorted him to a tiny back room. "Her name is Thulia Traynor," he said. "Her parents reported her missing late last evening. She was Running the Dome yesterday. Never crossed the finish line. Vanished in the final few kilometers. We've had teams out all night looking for her. A workman made the discovery this morning when he came in to retrieve his tools."

The girl's body lay supine on a sleep-pad, arms crossed over her chest, legs together, and the now-familiar red ribbon over her eyes. She was nude, her clothes piled neatly beside the pad. It took only a glance for Quinn to determine that she had fared no better than the other two. There was blood between her thighs, finger marks on her throat, and evidence of head trauma, but none of the cutting evident in the second murder.

"Fourteen hours," he informed Benwright when he had completed his examination. "That's how long she's been dead. Abused just like the other victims. He took his time with this one, no doubt because he wasn't concerned about being interrupted. Bag the clothes and the ribbon, and transport them along with the pad. I can't find anything on the floor, but I want your boys to vac the area and send everything to forensics."

"Kind of a locked-room mystery we have here," Benwright informed him. "The building was sealed by the workman before the girl went missing. No signs of tampering with the access panel, and there are no windows nor any other doors, and nothing on the street surveillance cams. Access records in the panel verify that nobody came in and nobody left after the portal was locked."

"That in itself is a clue," Quinn responded. "He must have got in and out somehow. Check every centimeter of this place until you find out how. To enter unseen carrying a presumably unconscious girl was quite an accomplishment. If we can determine how he did it we'll have some insight into how he operates and even who he might be."

Half a dozen Sentinels swarmed over the building, carefully examining it inside and out. They found no conceivable source of access, and reported their failure to Benwright, who passed the report on to Quinn, already in transit back to his hab.

"Not good enough," Quinn told Benwright as he read the report on his wristcomp. "Either there's a problem with the security 'corders or your men failed to find what must be there. He couldn't have teleported himself in and out. We're all missing something. Until we get to the bottom of this, I want the building sealed and under guard." Quinn's level of frustration was increasing.

Benwright shrugged. "I can't disagree with you. Our people have little experience investigating major crimes. If this were a century ago, we would have the resources and the skills to properly investigate a crime like this. The Sentinels basically keep peace and order under the Domes, but we lack much of the knowledge and training to combat such a criminal. We're all sort of learning on the fly."

The forensic report yielded little useful information. The child had, like the other two, been raped and brutally beaten, but this time she had been strangled to death. The head trauma seemed to have been incidental and wasn't the cause of death. The ribbon was determined to be the next section on the killer's roll. The only difference between this killing and the other two was that the girl appeared to have awakened from the tranq before the perp was through with her. She had tried to fight back, but was apparently beaten unconscious as the killer accomplished his goal. Evidence of this was the particles of synthskin beneath her fingernails, deposited there as she had attempted to stave off her attacker.

"Try this," Quinn said to Benwright. "Check the vids of the last part of the run. We know where she wound up, but we don't know where she was taken. We just assumed it was in the area of the storage building as she may have taken a shortcut on the way home. It could have been anywhere in the last few kilometers of the run."

"Brilliant," Benwright responded. "Why didn't I think of that? I'll have a result for you within the hour." Benwright always marveled at Quinn's analytical skills and clarity of mind.

He commed Quinn back not long after. "Have a look at this," he said, calling up a vid and sharing it with Quinn. "This came from a location 300 meters back along the road, before the stockhouse. You can see the girl trotting along the course, there, then she moves over to the barrier, just on the edge of the sec-cam's field of view, then you can see a figure looming over her, then they're both gone. Finally, we get to see the perp."

"How much can you enhance the image?"

"Here it is. You can see a bundled figure here, who appears to be a slim male, just under 2 meters tall. He's hooded, so we never get to see his face. There's a brief flash of his right hand as he injects the tranq into her neck. That's about all we can see."

"Is this the only angle you have?"

"No. There's one other, but it's not much help. You can see the top of his hoodie here, just on the other side of the construction barrier. He moves along, just to the edge of the field of vision then moves inward, deeper into the construction site. If the barriers hadn't been there, he'd have been right out in the open."

"Or somewhere else. He selected this site carefully. He knew what he was doing. I hate to ask this, but do you have any way of tracking the locations of people through their identichips? I heard you were working on it."

"Not yet. Only the newest models respond to signals at long range. We can send out a signal to the latest model of transponder and it sends one back to the central computer through the nearest sensor. Older models only respond at short range, so we only use them for security at the outer and inner portals of the Dome. We're hoping we can extend the range of those by installing powerful transmitter-receivers at all surveillance locations, but that'll take months."

"And then you'll be able to track the location of every citizen in the Dome?" Quinn asked uneasily, mindful of his earlier conversation with Sera.

"We could if it ever became necessary," Benwright responded guardedly, and Quinn sensed that his response was both evasive and cautionary. What might someday be was perhaps what already was. This was information that he was definitely not going to share with Sera.

* * *

"What do you make of this?" Quinn asked Sera when he commed her a few hours later and shared the security vids.

"Not much there to see. He's probably wearing a disguise, just in case somebody spots him. Other than that, at least we can rule out people who are too tall or too short or too rotund."

"Agreed. We're moving in the right direction, but too slowly. We need a big break, and soon." He briefed her on the locked room aspect of the case.

"You had them check the common service conduits?" Sera asked.

"Of course. The dust wasn't even disturbed. There're huge gaps in our investigation. If we could fill in just one of them we'd be very much closer to catching him. It's so exasperating."

Sera tried to be encouraging. "You can only do what you can do. He's only human. We will get him."

"We will. Let's hope it's sooner rather than later. One thing I've noticed, though. He seems to be going through the districts in a clockwise manner; first Seabrook, then Venicia, then Kula. If he keeps following that pattern, then he should be in Hanover District on October 6. We can be ready for him."

"Let's hope it doesn't take that long," Sera said.

September 7, 2204

It was a dispirited and dejected group that gathered that afternoon at command headquarters. Another killing, and the Task force was no closer to catching the perpetrator. Once news of the latest murder spread, the Dome would be in a panic.

"Thank you all for coming on such short notice," Benwright began. "I'd like to welcome a new member to our group. Guardian F-Kilmara was called away on personal business, so Guardian F-Kerrick has volunteered to take his place. Guardian F-Kerrick."

F-Kerrick rose from his place at the table and made a half-bow to the group before resuming his seat, as they acknowledged his presence with welcoming nods. Quinn took an instant dislike to the man. Most Futures were fit and trim. F-Kerrick had let himself go. He had a paunch and his face was plump and ruddy, his thinning hair unkempt, and his appearance made all the more absurd by the retro sideburns that he affected. The small effort of rising from his chair had caused him to breathe heavily, and a sheen of perspiration appeared on his upper lip. The Guardian reclined in his chair, his hands folded over his protruding belly, his red robes draped carelessly about him. He lacked the presence and the bearing of a Future.

"Thank you for allowing me to serve on this committee," Guardian F-Kerrick remarked, leaning forward. "As a newcomer to the task force, it would be improper for me to criticize the progress made thus far. Having said that, I have to wonder why this massive effort by so many people has yielded so few results. I've read all of the reports, and it seems to me that many of your resources are being misdirected. If I may …"

"Guardian F-Kerrick," Benwright interjected. "If you would bear with us, at least until we've summarized the information on the latest murder, then perhaps we can discuss your no doubt helpful suggestions."

F-Kerrick merely humphed, scowled, and gathered his robes more closely about him. It was not appropriate to interrupt a Future, even in such dire circumstances as the present emergency. Quinn now liked the man even less.

Quickly, Benwright outlined the details of the latest death, including the locked room mystery aspect of the crime and the singular lack of forensic evidence, apart from the matching ribbon end and the synth-skin under the victim's nails. He showed the assembly the pictures from the security cams, and outlined the description of the perpetrator that they were able to infer from the images. F-Kerrick leaned forward, peering intently at the images.

"Slim, male, under 2 meters tall, young and fit, judging from the way he moves. That's about all we can get from these pictures."

Quinn took over, and reported on the condition of the body and the similarities to the other two murders. Footprints in the dust were identical to those at the first two murder scenes. He outlined the necessary progression of the investigation for the near term, and some suggestions for a longer term search for the culprit, should that become necessary. It had come down to this; the meetings were becoming routine and formulaic. Not a good sign.

"On a hopeful note, I can inform you that we might have a chance to get him before he has a can strike again," Quinn said. "It appears that he's set himself a pattern as to the timing and location of his crimes, and if he holds to it, he should strike in the Hanover District on October sixth. The next time we can be prepared."

In spite of the hint of optimism, F-Kerrick continued with his intrusive questioning throughout, endearing himself to no one. His constant challenges and his superior attitude, Futures status notwithstanding, were quickly getting on everyone's nerves.

"What of the pursuit of a suspect in the Outlands?" he asked.

"Nothing has come of that," Benwright informed the task force, "With the exception that we've aroused the ire of the Outlander colonies. They're never happy with what they regard as government intrusion into their lives, even at the best of times."

F-Kerrick humphed. "That we might have to wait for an entire month to trap this criminal, thus risking the life of yet another young citizen, is far from encouraging," the obnoxious Future observed. "If we need more resources, let's get them and move on with this. He's only one man, and we should have him in a matter of days, not weeks."

Though they couldn't disagree with him, by now everyone was uncomfortable and more than ready to end the session. As the meeting was breaking up, ACS Travio slipped through the portal of the conference room and placed a report in front of Quinn.

"I thought you'd want to see this immediately, so I hard copied it and brought it personally. It's the result of my interviews with the Futures."

"Thanks," Quinn replied as he scanned the report. His brow furrowed, then he looked up at Travio before allowing his gaze to drift elsewhere in the room. He had a lot of thinking to do.

September 10, 2204

Rosie, dressed in pink work coveralls, was relaxing in a sling chair opposite Quinn, who had chosen a faux-antique ladder-back. The chair perfectly suited his tense mood. Rosie was trying to relax him with a cup of ginseng green tea and some soothing words.

"Come now, it's not all that bad. You've barely begun to investigate these murders, and you have precious little to go on. You can't expect to solve this thing overnight."

Quinn was hardly mollified. Scant evidence was just what was disturbing him. He was impatient, and wanted to get on with finding out who was committing these heinous acts under the Dome, then make an end of it. Infuriatingly, no end would be in sight without better information.

"I take your point," he told Rosie. "Tell you what. I'm going to take today off and get my mind away from the problem. Perhaps I can go at it again tomorrow with fresh insight and a more positive attitude."

"That's the spirit," Rosie said. "River's at work. Why don't you com her and arrange to meet afterwards? Gus is in back with Gabby and Jon, finishing up an Awakening, so he'll be free soon. Choose a more comfortable chair, put your feet up and relax."

Quinn complied, and after arranging to meet River later on, he felt much better. "I'm just going to check up on the Awakening," Rosie announced. She activated a scent orb, and the relaxing aroma of sandalwood filled the room. "You just sit and unwind. Nap if you feel the need. I'll be back in a while."

The portal shooshed open as Desert arrived, fresh from school, her learning module strapped to her back. "Uncle Quinn," she said, beaming with delight. In typical tweenie fashion, her volatile mood was on an upswing this day, and a visit by Quinn always brightened her disposition. "Just wait 'til I change and get rid of this. There's something I want to ask you." She was wearing the standard school tunic, the unflattering grey-green knee length uniform for both boys and girls in the education system; loathed, reviled, and mandatory. Desert hurried away to rid herself of the despised garment.

When she returned to the room dressed, ironically, in desert camo shorts and blouse, she sat opposite Quinn on the same ladder-back he'd recently vacated. She leaned forward, brow furrowed and lips pursed in adolescent seriousness. "I have a secret," she said hesitantly.

"You have a swain," Quinn guessed, teasingly separating each word.

Desert blushed beet red. "Wonder what gene causes that," Quinn thought reflexively.

Quinn lowered his face closer to hers and looked her straight in the eye.

"Well, yes … I just …How did you know?"

"Is he handsome?"

"Handsome? I don't really know. He's just so nice. He listens to me and he gets me."

"Ah," Quinn said. "You're seeing him with your inner eye, as he really is. Good for you."

"Don't tell Rosie or Gus yet. I need more time."

"Don't worry. Your secret's safe with me. Will you tell River?"

"Of course," Desert said, shocked at the idea that she would withhold anything from her sister.

"So what was it you wanted to ask me?"

"His mother is a Future. Since I'm an Ordinary, could our kids have perfect genes?"

Quinn suppressed a laugh. Desert was highly intelligent, and the questions she asked, pointed and direct, fulfilled her pursuit of knowledge.

"Being a Future isn't just about having perfect genes. There are many more factors that are considered, and all Futures living today came from Ordinaries, at least those that proved to have nearly perfect genes. There's no evidence that your parents or you have any genetic defects. I'm sure that the Dome's databank would have notified Gus and Rosie if there were any significant deviations from the norm. Don't worry. I'm confident that whoever is lucky enough to have you as a mate will sire perfect children with you. O.K.?"

"O.K. Uncle Quinn. I feel better about that now. Do you think that Ordinaries will ever be able to live again, like Futures?"

"Perhaps some day, thanks to procedures like the ones that Gus is working on. If the process is faster and less expensive, then many Ordinaries may be granted a second life. Still, it won't ever be approved for everyone. One of the main things that landed us in our present situation was overpopulation and the stripping of Earth's resources. Our forebears pumped pollutants and greenhouses gases into the air to satisfy the imagined needs of ever growing populations. They raised animals that they knew could breed viruses that could and did kill so many of them. That can't ever be allowed to happen again. We won't survive it a second time."

Desert gave him a funny look and he realized he'd slipped into his lecture mode. Of course, she already knew what had caused the disastrous decline of mankind, from which it had barely managed to resurrect itself. "I understand, Uncle Quinn. Thanks. Gotta go. I'm meeting Kyle at Campbell's Super for lunch. See you later."

She skipped happily out of the hab with typical youthful exuberance, replete with the knowledge that her world would unfold as it should. At that moment, Rosie returned from the Awakening.

"Was that Desert? She flits in and out so quickly I barely have a chance to talk with her these days. Tweenies! They're in their own little world. I can barely remember what it was like for us back then. Sorry, Quinn. I didn't mean to bring back bad memories."

"Not at all, Rosie. My folks were still alive when I was a tweenie. Those were good times. Those were the times I remember and treasure. Anyway, the aceball finals are being held in a couple of weeks and I've managed to get hold of a block of tickets. We could go as a group, you and Gus and River and the kids. Sera's favorite team is playing. How about it?"

"We could sure use a diversion from everything that's going on these days. Will Sera bring Maggie?"

"Probably not. I'm pretty sure she's not with Maggie any more. I think she said she's back into her 'male craving' mode.

"Don't you envy the bi's? Life seems to be so much more complete for them".

"And complicated," Quinn replied. "Dealing with one gender is quite enough of a problem for me, thank you." Rosie laughed. "I think she's seeing some aceball player now," Quinn continued. "He's on one of the teams that'll be playing in the finals. Rafi Jojimba. Heard of him?"

"I think so. That would be a fun outing for all of us. I'll talk to Gus and we'll make a day of it."

"Great. I'll make the arrangements and we can all meet in StadiaDome2, perhaps at GoodSports Lounge for lunch?"

"It's a date. When is this game going to be?"

"Sunday, September 23. The autumnal equinox. A good portent for the home team, under the sign of Libra. Not that I believe in such things."

"Of course not. Just another one of your hobbies?"

Quinn laughed. "Just keeping my options open. I'll be in touch. S'long."

"S'long, Quinn," Rosie waved him out. "Don't be a stranger," she added with a chuckle. Rosie knew that as long as River was residing in their hab, Quinn wouldn't be absent for long.

September 23, 2204

A sumptuous lunch at GoodSports made for a promising start to their afternoon outing. Quinn and Sera and the Ushers joined the growing crowd streaming into the stadium, the excitement building in anticipation of the competition to come. Supporters on both sides clutched banners and light batons and screamers denoting their particular allegiance. Many had dialed their clothing or had changed the colors of their com helmets to correspond to those of their teams.

Despite the growing apprehension caused by three killings in as many months, people were embracing the opportunity to break the cycle of gloom, to forget their cares and enjoy themselves for a time, however brief. Some 50 000 citizens, a tenth of the Dome's population, were expected to fill the sports stadium to capacity. Every seat was spoken for.

The Braxtons and the Ushers took their turn at one of the entrances as a box floated up, accepted their admission passes, and granted them boarding privileges. When the box had reconfigured itself to comfortably accommodate the eight of them in form-fitting flex-foam loungers, they seated themselves and the box drifted off to join thousands of others jockeying for position around the bubble covering the playing field itself. Some preferred low, others high, and a brave few above, tilted to view the playing surface below them. Everyone was thus afforded an equal view of the game. Friends, acquaintances, co-workers and longtime fans greeted each other as the floater boxes passed by, kept at a safe remove by the proximity sensors that guided their course.

"Professor Braxton! Gus! Rosie!" The salutation emerged from the babble of excited voices surrounding them. A shortbox drifted closer, configured for three passengers; two giggling teens accompanying Gabby Iano. The latter waved enthusiastically and Quinn and the Ushers returned the greeting in kind, with amiable salutations as their box passed near.

"Really! This is too much of a coincidence," Quinn thought. "He can't be following me, can he?" As Gabby's box moved out of sight, Quinn was distracted by River and Sera, talking animatedly about the game, and he lost his train of thought concerning the young Harbours tech. Soon enough the players took to the field and everyone's domely cares dissolved under a barrage of animated cheers, chants, hoots and taunts that left the participants weak with laughter and the renewed joy of carefree being. Baseless optimism aside, their joy would not be unconfined for long.

Servotech took an early lead and their supporters went wild. The Einsteinium fans scoffed at them, promised quick reprisal, then whirled their screamers in derision. Sera nudged River, who returned her grin with a mock glare. Einsteinium scored and Servotech lost the lead, prompting a new round of chants and yet another exchange of good-natured taunts and insults. So it went until halftime, when the teams were in a virtual tie. The fans needed a respite almost as much as the athletes, having worked themselves into a fine lather for over an hour.

Boxes docked themselves along the promenade and supporters debarked and headed for the personal sanitation booths and refreshment kiosks. As Quinn escorted River and Desert along the walkways, Gabby once again appeared nearby.

"Professor, are you enjoying the game?" he asked, an affable grin on his face.

Quinn was now getting quite concerned about Gabby's persistent proximity, which he felt must be more than happenstance, given the large numbers of fans eddying about the concourse. "Very much so, Gabby, and you?" he responded politely, having no valid reason to be rude or stand-offish.

"Splendid, and how are River and Desert today?" he said, addressing the two Ushers. "How about you, little one. Having fun?" he continued, giving Desert a big wink as he chucked her under the chin, a gesture that offended her sense of burgeoning womanhood and her personal space. The two murmured courteous responses as Gabby continued on his way.

"Bizarro," Desert declared as soon as Gabby was out of earshot.

"But a good worker," River added. "Even though he works for the family and Gus and Rosie seem to like and trust him, I get an odd vibe when he's around. I can't quite warm up to him."

"No matter," Quinn said. "He's gone. Let's just enjoy the day."

They returned to their box hefting food carriers of stadium exotics sufficient for all; soy burgers and tube hounds and corn nachos covered with spicy peppers and ersatz cheese in the time honoured tradition, with nutrishakes, ale, and smoothies to wash it all down. No sooner had they been auto-slotted back into the position they'd saved at the end of the first half than the game resumed in earnest, as did the enthusiastic cheering and jeering. On this day, at least one conflict would be resolved, while another would carry on for some time to come.

CHAPTER 14

THE COMPILERS: A VISION FULFILLED

A.D. 2080

By 2080, the Compilers not only had a worldwide following, but were rapidly becoming celebrities and the current media darlings. Futurist aficionados carried around the little green book entitled 'The World According to the Compilers', and wore T-shirts bearing the likeness of Mark, D.J. and Jace, along with Emile and Ranjit and others of the original group, displaying the slogan 'Ad Futurus'. Some bore slightly more irreverent slogans like 'The Compilers: Masters of the Universe!', 'Compile This!' and the ever-popular 'My Folks Went to a Compilers Symposium and All I Got Was This Lousy T-Shirt', but all well-meant, with adoration and respect for their heroes.

For their part, the Compilers were uncomfortable with the acclaim and recognition. All they desired was to have their ideas, not themselves, acknowledged. For the Originals, it was hardly possible to go out in public without being asked for an autograph or being swarmed by the media.

Governments were rushing to implement those of the Compilers proposals that made sense, or that benefited their political agenda, or that were not vigorously opposed by big business. They cherry-picked the manifesto, but overall, wound up giving the people what they demanded.

Even so, the Compilers still had much to do. There were many areas of social and economic development that needed amending in response to rapidly changing conditions. Many others, such as human reproduction and environmental change, they had barely begun to address. It was a tremendous undertaking, shaping a new society, integrating many disciplines so that each worked smoothly without disrupting or derailing others.

* * *

Research labs all over the world had been sharing the results of their various projects, and their combined knowledge inspired new ideas, which ultimately resulted in innovative techniques for reproducing humans, both naturally and artificially. It was thus fortuitous that, by the late 21st century, a confluence of ideas was available to the Compilers, and enabled them to frame an ideal structure for their New Society.

Fertility enhancement, artificial insemination, in vitro fertilization, and surrogate motherhood had been available as reproductive techniques for many decades. Now, advances in genetic engineering could be used to virtually eliminate hereditary diseases and birth defects through selective gene snipping and manipulation. Hormones were being enhanced, suppressed, and better controlled to aid the physical and mental functioning of the human body. The human race quickly became healthier and more robust. Meanwhile, research in the esoteric field of cloning was continuing apace, and the results were encouraging.

Speculative fiction had long posited that someday it would be possible to record and store all of a person's life experiences. By the mid-21st century, such technology did indeed become available. People who wished to take advantage of it were able to go to secure storage areas and download their accumulated memories into cubes made of artificial diamond containing appropriate impurities to render them electrically active. These virtually indestructible crystals were then stored in secure, environmentally controlled and electronically shielded underground vaults. The memory cubes could be updated at any time, and people were eventually permitted to download their life stories even on their deathbeds. Regrettably, no mechanism yet existed for reading the contents of the cubes, except to upload them into a living being. When one brave but foolhardy scientist tried it, the sensory overload rendered him incurably insane. Nobody was reckless or courageous enough to try it again. Even so, many felt that the memory crystals gave them a sort of immortality. Research on memory transfer continued for many years, until success was finally achieved.

A quarter of a century later, a convergence of technologies provided a practical use for the memory matrix. Advances in psionic engineering had rendered memory storage retrievable, but only if downloaded into a blank and receptive vehicle. In addition, the achievement of human cloning that was successful and perfect every time gave the Compilers the last piece of the sociological puzzle that they were seeking.

Now the Compilers would have available to them the means to create a committed and morally superior group of humans who could show others The Way to the Future. The method was far too expensive and time consuming to be used for ordinary reproduction, nor would it automatically be available to those with extraordinary influence or means. The Compilers decided that only the DNA of people of exceptional character, accomplishment and dedication to public service should be accepted for cloning. To this end, they codified a set of regulations and qualifications to ensure that only the very best of the aspirants would be accepted to safeguard the future of mankind.

Their idea was that, many years later, the stored DNA would be inserted into a carefully selected and prepared ovum, and the process of restoration would be underway. Once the fetus was brought to term in a nutrient bath, it would be placed into a sensory deprivation tank, where growth hormones would accelerate its development. Its memory crystal would be attached to the tank, and sequenced memories would be downloaded into the developing being so that, upon Awakening, the individual would have the full memories of a life well lived. The process was technically complex and could take up to thirty years. After Awakening, the revived individual would be indistinguishable, physically and mentally, from the original. He or she would then be briefed and prepared to take his place among the elite of future society.

QUALIFICATIONS TO BECOME A FUTURE

1. The candidate must have led an exemplary life, and must not have committed any crime or significant misdemeanor that might have brought him or her to the attention of law enforcement, the judiciary, or the governing body of the day.

2. The candidate's genome must compare favorably to the ideal Human Genome, except for the most minor, harmless and inconsequential variations, in order to ensure that genetic defects are not passed on.

3. The candidate must be of high intelligence and of good character, as exemplified by his contributions to the community, and as attested to by his contemporaries.

4. The candidate's qualifications must be submitted to the government of the day for approval. If such approval is granted, the government will then pass the application on to a special judicial council. The candidate must then, if able, appear before the Special Council for final approval of his or her application. His genome and his memories will then be submitted to an approved Safe Harbour for storage until required for his Time of Awakening.

Winter, 2089

"Emile, are you available?" Brad messaged. "I need to discuss the situation with you."

"I'm here. Ca va?"

"Ca va bien, mon ami, mais je suis triste. Et vous?

"Me aussi. It's a sad situation."

"It's a disaster. The plague is spreading at an alarming rate, and nobody knows how to deal with it. Quarantine is only marginally effective, on a small scale. People are traveling, running to get away from it. Many of the refugees are infected, and only hasten the spread of the plague. It seems unstoppable."

"I agree. Pharmaceutical companies and independent and government labs are all working on a solution. There's been little success so far. Civil society is collapsing in the areas most affected. Millions will die, and it might turn out to be much worse than that. The only encouraging note is that a small segment of the population seems to have a natural immunity. They're being studied for a possible cure. I fear it will be too late."

"In the meantime," Brad said, "what can we do? We have no resources, no structures or agencies that can lend a hand. We're merely a think-tank. I feel so helpless."

It was 2089, and the original Compilers were older and wiser. Brad was in his late 40s, Ranjit over 70, with Emile not far behind. All of the originals had been approved as Futures by their various governments, their memories and DNA safely stored in Harbours. Other members of the Compilers had already joined them, and still others were in the vetting process. Of the three Founders, only Mark had survived to see the beginning of the end of mankind, but he had gone missing before he could get to a Harbour.

"All of our work is being undone," Brad continued. "Nations are in chaos, our reforms in ruins."

"It's not the end just yet," Emile said. "If the worst occurs, at least the world will have the methods and the means to rebuild and restructure their societies along the lines we suggested. We just have to go one step further.

We have to figure out how to ensure the survival of those who remain. Social structures can be restored and we have the proposals for replacing the infrastructures."

"The Domes?" Brad asked.

"Indeed, the Domes. All of the plans are complete; designs, architecture, materials. It only remains to convince the surviving authorities that it's the only way to secure the continued existence of mankind."

"It's a huge project. There's likely to be resistance."

"Yes, and it will take decades, but it's a matter of life and death, and what alternatives are there? They must move forward on this. And don't forget, we have our ace in the hole."

"Doc," Brad replied.

"Yes, Doc," Emile responded. "Following our victory in the last election, we now have a formidable opposition in the House. With Doc's cooperation we can move ahead. If the United States signs on to most of our reforms, the world must follow. I'm very optimistic about our chances, assuming our organization and humanity survive the crisis. It may take some years, but it will happen."

Even though much of the world was being won over to the Compilers' vision of the future, progress on implementing the suggestions in their manifesto had been painfully slow. Had it not been for the events of 2089, their vision might have been fragmented and ultimately forgotten. The Great Plague only served to make implementing their ideas more logical and urgent. The continued existence of mankind was in the balance. Without the complete cooperation and compliance of every government and independent group, the effort would be doomed to failure.

Sadly, the majority of the Compilers would not survive the plague to see their dream fulfilled. Like any ordinary citizen, they were as susceptible to the virus as anyone else, and only a handful would live to fight on and to help to organize the reconstruction effort. Even so, they would one day be Awakened to serve mankind once more, and that day would not be long in coming, for they were to be Earth's salvation.

THE FUTURES' MANIFESTO

1. A Future must, at all times, comport himself in a conscientious and principled manner in order to set an example for the masses. His conduct must be seen to be above reproach.

2. A Future must, when in public, wear the Red Robes of Honour, in order to be easily recognized by the populace, and to command the respect due him or her.

3. A Future may not, at any time or for any reason, remove the signet ring presented to him at Awakening. It is a mark of his status and his office.

4. A Future must always put the well-being of Society ahead of his own.

5. A Future must come to the aid of the community at large, or of any individual who requests such aid, as long as the request does not conflict with his duty to Society as a whole or cause harm to any innocent individual or group.

CHAPTER 15

A GATHERING

October 1, 2204

It was Founders' Day, an annual celebration in recognition of the formal creation of the group that would soon thereafter become known as the Compilers. On this day in 2077, they had announced their first manifesto to the world, thus laying the groundwork for their later accomplishments; the salvation of mankind through the establishment of the Domes, the structure of a new and more perfect society, and the creation of the Futures. Given the mood of anxiety that blanketed the city, the festivities were more somber than usual.

At Pierre's invitation, friends and colleagues came together in his hab to pay homage to the Compilers and to the Founders that gave rise to them. Quinn had invited River to come along, but she'd been obligated to attend a community service meeting that night, and begged off. Upright and conscientious citizens took their responsibilities to society seriously.

"Welcome, welcome," Pierre greeted each new guest passing through his portal. Sera and Quinn arrived together. "It's so good to see you both again. I've missed your company. Here, have some aerie-wine and tell me about yourselves." The aerie-wine, so named because it came from grape vines nurtured in the hydroponic gardens near the apex of the Dome's central tower, was sweet and fruity. The hydroponic gardens were also a source of many of the home grown comestibles Pierre served at his gatherings. His guests had come to expect a well-stocked table when they attended Pierre's soirees, laid on as it was with an additional selection of imported exotics seldom seen in RichmondDome.

A variety of guests was in attendance, from neighbors to civil servants, from students to teachers, from fellow Arbiters to Guardians. An eddy of red robes in one corner of the gathering room caught Quinn's eye and, much to his disgust, he spotted Guardian F-Kerrick, holding forth amid a group of young and impressionable wabs, all eager for pointers on how to emulate their heroes. He resolved to make an effort to avoid that particular guest for the balance of the evening.

Gabby Iano detached himself from the other wabs and came over to Quinn. "Professor Braxton. How good to see you again. Can I assume that you're hot on the heels of the villain that killed those three girls?"

"Not quite yet, Gabby, but we're getting closer with each passing day. Thanks for your interest."

"Our shared interest, professor. Perhaps when you have time we can sit down and have a talk about the kind of person you think might be committing these antisocial acts, and how he can be so clever in evading capture. I have some ideas that may be of value to you."

"Of course, Gabby. I'd appreciate your insights," Quinn said. There was something about the young man that made him uneasy. Perhaps it was the way in which he was somewhat overeager to please, or perhaps a certain air of conceit and superiority he exuded. No matter. He was obviously highly intelligent and would be a good student.

Gabby wandered off to rejoin the wabs mobbing F-Kerrick. Quinn turned back to Pierre and Sera as the three made their way to the centre of the gathering room.

Guests congregated in pairs and groups to share gossip or to exchange ideas. Nearby, several students were arguing the relative merits of quantum computers versus the newer models with biogenic processors and memory. Others discussed a range of topics including a possible resurgence of religion, resuming manned space exploration, and encouraging government reforms. Many talked in hushed tones about the horrible events of the past few months and the seeming inability of the authorities to do anything to protect the children.

The music that emanated unobtrusively from the acoustic walls belied the somber mood, attempting to infuse false gaiety into the proceedings with holoshow tunes and the thrushsong warblings of Valine Maionne, current darling of fans of the vocal arts. Soothing colors swirled leisurely across the walls as nature's scents, injected into the air ducts, sought to bring the natural world into the artificial atmosphere of the Dome. The scents of new-mown hay, cherry blossoms, and rain-dampened earth were meant to transport the guests to a world few of them had ever known.

"I guess I don't have to tell you how the investigation is going," Quinn said to Pierre. "With each murder, we're moving only incrementally closer to identifying the perpetrator. We have little chance of stopping him in the next few days. He's displayed cunning and resourcefulness well beyond our expectations or control."

"Yes," Sera added. "He's quite clever, and knows full well that we have little experience in dealing with this kind of crime. He's running rings around us. Any suggestions?"

"I only wish I could help. You're the experts. There haven't been any murders since the end of the Age of Chaos; never one under the Domes. Violent tendencies have been genetically engineered and bred out of the human race. If this felon came before me on the bench, I'd be hard pressed to decide how to deal with him. The only case law we have for this kind of crime is outdated, pre-Compiler. Come now, let's lighten the tone and put aside our Domely woes. How are you two doing? What's new in your lives?" Pierre genuinely enjoyed his family time with the siblings.

Sera was about to mischievously spill the beans on Quinn and his new love interest when she saw out of the corner of her eye a red-gauntleted hand being laid on her brother's shoulder. "What peculiar manner of Future is this?" she thought.

"My, my, Professor Braxton, you do get around. Please introduce me to this lovely lady."

Quinn stiffened as he turned and found himself face to face with Guardian F-Kerrick.

"Guardian Kerrick," Quinn said, purposely omitting the honourific. "What an unexpected delight to see you here. This is my sister, Sera. Sera, this is Guardian Future Kerrick." This time Quinn went overboard, as if to make amends for his previous slight, but in the process intentionally compounding the insult.

F-Kerrick's face began to pucker into a frown, but he stopped himself and beamed at Sera. "Young lady," he said, as he executed a half-bow and, taking her hand, pressed it to his lips. "What a genuine pleasure to meet Professor Braxton's sister. I have no doubt that you are quite as brilliant as he, and so lovely, too. We should talk, to get to know each other better."

He moved his hand to her elbow and gently but firmly escorted her away from her bemused brother. Sera turned slightly and gave Quinn a half-shrug as the Future led her out onto the balcony overlooking the greenbelt and gallantly seated her on a divan before taking his place beside her. The greenbelt encircled the Dome between the first and second ring of habitations, connecting the major parks in each sector with a stream, pathways, and greenery. Now the pathways were patrolled night and day by Sentinels armed with stunners. Sera was baffled as to how she had allowed herself to be maneuvered into this situation.

"You might want to start defending your sister's honour," Pierre suggested.

"She can take care of herself. Don't forget, we've been self-reliant since our parents died. I'm not worried. Besides, Futures are above reproach. What's your opinion of Kerrick?"

"I sense that you don't much like him."

"He's too imbued with a sense of his own importance. He's not like any Future I've ever met. I get the feeling that he's the type who has a craving for power. It's fortunate that our checks and balances would never permit that."

"My impression exactly. I had occasion to check his background, purely out of curiosity of course. He was a decent, honest and upright citizen in his past life, a hero to many, as were all Futures, naturally. Perhaps he's merely unable to help his appearance and his superior attitude."

"Well, let's not let him spoil the evening, old friend. I see you've laid on the usual enticements. I swear you'd tempt a fitman to gluttony," Quinn laughed.

"I'm not going to force you to the groaning board," Pierre teased. "Nor will I hold you back. Let's test the famous Braxton mettle, shall we?" He slapped Quinn on the shoulder in a display of camaraderie and familial affection.

Quinn chose a middle path, sampling a few of the gustatory delights without going to excess. Even had he not possessed a strong will, he was mindful of the rotundity of the likes of F-Kerrick, an image that should dissuade any responsible citizen from overindulging.

"How's Sera's work going? I hear she's on the brink of great things, some advances in nanotech that might be of significant benefit to medical science." It was evident that Pierre was bursting with pride at his goddaughter's accomplishments.

"So she tells me. I understand that she's managed to develop directed nanobiobots, but I should let her explain it to you. It's really quite fascinating."

Quinn let his gaze wander to the balcony. Sera was still sitting on the divan talking to Kerrick, who was now leaning casually on the balustrade, turned sideways so he could still converse with Sera, but apparently peering with interest at something below.

Quinn's curiosity was piqued. "Please excuse me. I think that perhaps I should check on Sera," he told Pierre, who grinned and nodded. Quinn made his way to the balcony and moved up on F-Kerrick's blindside. He glanced down but saw nothing of interest, save for the service alleyway running between the greenspace and the back of the low rise row housing that constituted the outer circle.

Sera had stopped talking as Quinn approached, and F-Kerrick turned, following her gaze.

"Ho, Citizen Braxton," he said. "You gave me quite a start, coming up on me like that. Perhaps you should be wearing the red, the better to be spotted."

"Maybe in another life, F-Kerrick. What's so interesting below?"

"Oh, ah, nothing in particular. I was just observing the flow of the greenbelt as it connects the parks around the Dome. I don't often have the opportunity to view it from this perspective. What a wondrous construct we live in, don't you agree?"

"Most remarkable," Sara contributed. "The people who conceived and built the Domes left a truly momentous legacy. We have the Founders and the Original Compilers to thank for all of this, and for the safe and secure society in which we live. It's fitting that we pay them deserved tribute on this day."

F-Kerrick completely missed the sardonic tone in her voice. "Well said, my dear. I was a contemporary of the original Compilers, you know, and of the Founders, and I made the acquaintanceship of more than a few of them. Not to blow my own horn, but I did manage to make my own modest contribution to their final manifesto and to the advancement of their cause."

Quinn did the mental equivalent of an eye roll, and ratcheted the Future down another notch in his estimation. "What a pretentious blowhard," he thought.

"I remember now," Sera said. "You were the minority house leader of the Compilers' Party when they finally managed to gain access to the United States Congress and became the official opposition."

"Kind of you to recall that, my dear."

"In fact, you became somewhat of a heroic figure. You vanished on a humanitarian mission in Europe, didn't you?"

"So they tell me. My memories include only those that were in this crystal, of course" he said, tapping the bulge in his glove where his diamond Futures' ring resided.

F-Kerrick, despite his appearance, rose in Sera's estimation, but dropped even further in Quinn's. For him, past accomplishments mattered less than present actions.

"Your sister and I were just discussing the terrible events of the last few months," F-Kerrick said, turning to Quinn. "How sad for the families of those poor girls. They must be devastated. As a senior representative of the Dome's governing body, I feel personally responsible for our failure to protect those good citizens who've put their trust in us. I can only pledge that we Guardians will place all of our resources behind ending this reign of terror, though not to in any way diminish the considerable contribution you, yourself are making to the effort, professor. Sera tells me that the two of you are working together to aid the Sentinels, but that your progress is somewhat hampered by lack of evidence."

"Sad but true, F-Kerrick. As you observed at our recent meeting, we're struggling not only with a lack of clues, but also with our own somewhat deficient investigatory skills in this area. Our adversary is undoubtedly quite well aware of that and takes advantage of our inadequacies. If history teaches us anything, though, it's that creatures like this inevitably make mistakes, and then we'll have him. It's only a matter of time of which, unfortunately, we have precious little. If he continues his pattern, more innocents will die before he's brought to justice."

"But brought to justice he shall be," Pierre cut in, having followed Quinn to the balcony and listened in on the conversation. "He can't be nearly as clever as he imagines himself. We'll get better as he gets worse, you'll see. Sera, my dear, come and tell me of your scientific accomplishments. I've heard good things and I'd like to understand your work better."

Having rescued Sera from F-Kerrick, Pierre took her to a corner of the gathering room where they engaged in earnest conversation for much of the evening. For his part, Quinn was desperately searching for a way to extricate himself from any further colloquy with the dislikable Future. It wasn't that easy, as F-Kerrick seemed to have taken a liking to the professor turned criminologist. He questioned Quinn incessantly about detection techniques and forensic procedures.

"You understand that I have little knowledge of these things, and I feel that I need to know more in order to fulfill my responsibilities as a Guardian and as a member of the special task force. We shall all get to the bottom of this thing together." He prattled on while plowing through a plate piled high with provender from Pierre's table, broadcasting crumbs far and wide.

Quinn had little choice but to answer his questions and to put up with his occasional disparaging remarks about the ability of the Sentinels to protect the citizenry. It was turning out to be a very long evening.

When at last the gathering broke up and most of the guests had departed, Quinn and Sera were able to say their private goodbyes to Pierre. Sera was momentarily pulled off to one side by an earnest young man that she worked with, so Quinn took the opportunity to speak with Pierre in confidence.

"Sorry you got stuck with Kerrick," Pierre said.

"Could've been worse. On the plus side, I was able to learn a few things about our red-clad friend that don't appear in his record. The man's just rife with braggadocio. And on that very subject, perhaps you could use your influence to do me a favor." Quinn quickly spelled out what he needed from the Arbiter.

"You're sure about this?" Pierre asked.

"Quite certain. You mustn't let anyone know about it. And no, I can't tell you why. Just trust me. I'll explain when I can."

"I always have, my dear young man. I'll let you know when it's done."

As Sera rejoined them, Quinn said, "When we have more time, we should have a talk. I'll com you soon. Thanks for having us over. As always, it's been a pleasure."

"Drop by the lab sometime, Uncle Pierre," Sera added. "I'll give you the ten credit tour."

"I'd enjoy that. You know you're both welcome to drop by anytime. I'll see the two of you soon. S'long." Pierre made a mental note to take time out from his busy schedule to visit the Braxton homestead and Sera's lab.

CHAPTER 16

THE CRISIS DEEPENS

October 6, 2204

RichmondDome had gone into lockdown mode after the third killing. Younglings were forbidden to be out of their habs unescorted after 1800 hours. Fear gripped the citizens, as it became apparent that neither the Guardians nor the Sentinels had the power to protect their children.

On this sixth day of October, the Sentinels employed a new stratagem. Anticipating the date and place of the next attack, they became proactive. In Hanover District, several female decoys were sent out; petite but strong volunteers, dressed in the mod fashion of young girls, who would walk the streets and parkways under close surveillance, from early eve to past dimming, in the hope of luring the killer. Realistically, they had little faith that their scheme would succeed, as everyone in the Dome knew that children were forbidden to be out that late. Still, they had to do something, anything, to try to trap the fiend.

Citizens were particularly watchful and fearful on this day. They had been forewarned, and took extra precautions to safeguard their loved ones. Everyone was hopeful that the anniversary of the killings would pass uneventfully, so it was an even greater shock when yet another incident was reported.

* * *

Benwright commed Quinn just before midnight, while he and Sera were trying to keep their minds occupied by watching a late night unreality program. It was a call that Quinn had both dreaded and half expected. Their conversation was brief.

The floater set him down at a station near the central administration tower, within sight of a group of Sentinels gathered at the edge of Central Park, the greenspace that surrounded the tower. They were setting up barriers and marking the area with tape. Portable gloworbs illuminated the woods.

"What do we have?" Quinn asked, as Benwright separated himself from the Sentinels and stepped forward to greet him.

"More of the same. Another youngling, over there in the shrubbery. Best guess, she was taken earlier in the day, when everyone had their guard down, and dumped here, on our very doorstep later on, as a show of defiance to the authorities. Now he's taunting us."

"Didn't her parents report her missing?"

"Not until early evening. She was supposed to be staying with relatives overnight. She wasn't missed until her father tried to com her. Each family thought she was with the other."

"O.K. Let's have a look," Quinn said glumly, donning his forensic gear. The Sentinels parted to let him through, and he followed a trail of yellow tape right to the scene, recording as he went. Gelshoe imprints led directly to the broken body, unclothed and sprawled on her back, the inevitable red ribbon covering her eyes.

"About six hours dead," he soon called out to Benwright, who was waiting nearby. "You were right. She wasn't seized or killed here. The only evident marks are the impressions her body made, and the trail of footprints in and out. The killer couldn't have done such a complete cleanup without risking being observed. We have to wonder how he could have carried a body in here, in such a public area, without being seen. Better check the …"

"Secvids," Benwright provided. "I'm on it. There're enough cams around here that one or more should have caught a useful image."

Quinn continued with his recording and evidence gathering, although there was precious little to be gleaned here. Nothing around the body, nothing evident on the body, other than the ribbon and the evidence of the terrible beating to which she'd been subjected. Her torso was a mass of bruises and there was blood between her legs. The lab would check for trace when they got her back there, and the techs would do a more thorough sweep of the area. Still, Quinn was not optimistic.

She was in much the same condition as the others. Obvious signs of rape and strangulation, but no head trauma this time. A small contusion on the side of the neck where the tranq had been administered by microjet. Quinn suspected that asphyxiation would be determined as the cause of death. He took an impression of a footprint, then wrapped up his examination and rejoined Benwright.

"Identichip says she's Viola Secouri. I assume she's the girl reported missing?"

"That's her. Born in 2191. Father an airplant maintenance mechanic, mother a hydroponics plant tech. No siblings. Lived in DelphiDistrict, third ring. Last seen around 1630 hours when she left her hab to go to visit with her uncle and aunt in AlbanDistrict. Parents told her to be there by 1700. She was supposed to travel by floater, but there's no record of her boarding one. She may have gone elsewhere, but it's certain that she was taken within an hour of her leaving home. We'll try to track her movements with sec-cam and portal records. I've got people examining them now."

"Who found her?"

"Sentinel patrol. We've got them out in all the parks. Found her around 2330."

"So we have to find out where she was for about 7 hours. I assume the Sentinels didn't see anything useful?"

"Of course not. Nobody lurking around where they shouldn't be. No clues."

"O.K. You can let the lab boys loose on the crime scene now. Keep me posted. I assume you'll be convening the task force this afternoon."

"We will. You'd better get some sleep. It's going to be a long day."

October 7, 2204

"Well?" said Sera, who had waited up for him, knowing that he'd need some emotional support.

"Another one, just like the others," Quinn replied. He looked careworn and disheartened. "No new clues. We're just hoping that something shows up on the secvids." He dropped onto the couch.

Just then his comlink chimed. "Lo," he said.

"It's me." He recognized Benwright's voice. "Got something for you, but you're not going to like it. We managed to track Viola from her hab to the entrance to AlbanMall. The portal transponder recorded her identichip. She went in at 1644, but she vanished somewhere between the portal and the mall itself. Secvids show her making a sharp right into the public 'fresher, but she never came out. Naturally, we don't have surveillance in there. "

"So, no clues as to who took her or how?"

"It gets worse. We had a look at the secvids around Central Park for the period between 1700 and 2330, when she was discovered. There's no sign of anyone carrying anything large into the park. No suspicious persons loitering nearby. We can't figure out how she got from the mall to the park. We have people examining the 'fresher in AlbanMall now, trying to find out how she vanished from there."

"Terrific!" Quinn exclaimed sardonically. "Get back to me if you find out anything useful."

"Bad news?" Sera asked.

"Nothing but," Quinn replied. "A girl just vanishes, then her body reappears as if by magic in the middle of the Dome. First the locked room mystery, now this. This guy is running circles around us. Look, you might as well get some sleep. I've got a lot of work to do, starting with reviewing my holocam recordings. We'll talk in the morning."

"O.K. If you're certain." She gave him a reassuring hug and a kiss on the cheek. "I have confidence in you. You'll come up with something sooner or later. G'night."

"G'night" he acknowledged gloomily. He unpacked his holocam and synched it with the comcenter, then viewed his own progress across the grass, and along the trail of footprints up to the area of the body. The cam scanned around the area, just as he had done, then centered on the girl. He watched his hands go through the forensics routines, then pack up his gear. The cam tracked his course as he returned the way he had come.

Something struck him as strange. He went back to the beginning and watched it again, then once more, concentrating on the beginning and the end of the recording. There it was. The perp's footprints went to and from the grassy verge surrounding the bare earth of the wooded area, but no more and no less. Except for his own footprints and those of the Sentinels and Benwright, the grass remained undisturbed. It was crushed down by their heavy feet, and would take hours to recover, but the footprints of the killer nowhere impinged on the lawn.

"I've been reading the evidence backwards," he thought. "He didn't go in and out, he went out, to the very edge of the shrubbery, and back in, but he didn't tread on the grass. That's why he didn't show up on any sec-cam." Now he went back to his scans of the area surrounding the corpse. The dusty ground had been disturbed beyond what the investigators had caused. It had been swept along a certain path, probably with a branch, the sweep marks barely visible as dust had settled on them. The killer had wiped out the footprints he had made from a different direction.

Quinn quickly commed Benwright, who sleepily answered, "Lo."

"Quick. Stop the techs working the crime scene and ask them to withdraw immediately. Meet me there and I'll explain."

He hopped a floater and arrived back at Central Park only moments before Benwright.

"Follow me," he said as he walked past the bemused group of techs standing idly by on the lawn. The body had been removed, but Quinn moved carefully past her outline in the dust and further into the bushes.

"Just as I thought," he said to Benwright over his shoulder. "Have a look at this." He pointed to a hatch set into a low slope behind some bushes some twenty meters from the crime scene, a hatch used by maintenance workers to access utilities serving the park and the nearby administration tower. There were sweep marks on the hatch itself, and evidence of an attempt to eradicate the remaining footprints by the hatch, probably from the inside.

"Can we get this open?"

"I'll have to get the codes from the central computer. You think this is how he did it? He'd either have to be a tech or have high level access to get those codes."

"Suppose he didn't need codes. Suppose he accessed the hatch from inside."

"He'd have to get into the belowground system somehow," Benwright answered. He punched in the entry codes when his com received them, then summoned two Sentinels from the cordon by the street and instructed them to go into the tunnel and look around. The lead Sentinel wore a bright light and a cam that transmitted what they were seeing to the wristcomps and helmets of the watchers outside.

The tunnel was grey and gloomy, laced with pipes that carried water, sewage, and ground up recyclables, along with various power and communications conduits. The floor was plain carbocrete, and the light revealed that the dust there had been disturbed. The Sentinels followed the trail to the first four-way intersection, where the trail faded to nothingness. There, carbocrete dust hung in the air, settling slowly onto the footfall traces.

"Clever," Quinn commented. "He somehow stirred up the dust in the tunnels to cover his tracks. He may have used some kind of blower, or perhaps he accessed the ventilation fans and briefly set them to a higher speed. Tell them to follow the tunnel where the dust appears to be thickest."

After a false start down a tunnel where the dust had already settled, the view moved into a tunnel headed southeast where the dust cloud was slightly denser. At the next intersection, a cross breeze stirred the dust only slightly, clearing the air, and the trail was lost. No amount of forward and backtracking could pick it up. The Sentinels were recalled.

"If this guy knows the tunnels, he's probably engaging in misdirection anyhow," said Benwright. "There're hundreds of kilometers of tunnels below, on several levels, according to the city's schematics. He could have gone anywhere."

"So let's start at the tunnels feeding the AlbanMall, then move outwards from there," Quinn suggested.

Benwright put in a call to the Sentinels unit closest to the mall and ordered them to begin a sweep of the tunnels in that area. The result was the same. The killer had covered his tracks in a most cunning manner. They were able to ascertain no more than that entrance to the tunnels had been gained from a utility room adjacent to the 'fresher. A maintenance portal between the two rooms had been forced open, but no trace evidence had been found, since the cleaning bots had done their job efficiently and thoroughly. Yet another dead end.

* * *

Late that afternoon, the special task force gathered in the meeting room in the central tower. The windows of the room overlooked Central Park, where metaplas barriers and yellow tape were still in place. Members of the group gathered there needed no such reminder of the gravity of the situation. A fourth child had been murdered, and they were no closer to catching the killer. He had managed to thwart their best efforts, and even now the evidence of their failure mocked them from below this very room.

"As much as it pains me to admit this," Benwright began as the meeting came to order, "We're amidst the greatest crisis the Dome has ever suffered, and we appear to be helpless to do anything to end it. Our proactive efforts to stop this killer seem to have been pointless. He somehow managed to circumvent us. I have no doubt that a resolution will be achieved eventually, but for now we're in a dire situation. Quinn, would you please summarize where we stand." As he finished, his com pinged, and he busied himself with the urgent call.

At that moment, F-Kerrick huffed into the room. "Apologies for being late," he gasped, struggling to catch his breath. "Have I missed much?"

"I was just about to report on the latest crime," Quinn said, irritated not only by Kerrick's tardiness but by his very presence. "Viola Secouri, thirteen years old. Murdered around 1930 hours last night. C.O.D. asphyxiation due to strangulation. Beaten and raped prior to death. She was evidently taken in the public relief facility at AbanMall, but was assaulted and killed elsewhere, then dumped in Central Park, perhaps as a message to us. It appears that the perpetrator accessed the service tunnels beneath the Dome and used them as a throughway to and from the park. We don't know how he was able to do that, but we're adding it to our investigation. At this moment, we have no clues, other than the presence of the ribbon, and a few footprints that are consistent with the size of those we've observed at previous crime scenes. We hope that the lab and the coroner will have more information for us when they complete their procedures."

F-Kerrick spoke up. "The reason I was late is that I had to push my way through crowds of demonstrators moving through the streets towards this administrative center. The floaters have been overwhelmed by the volume of traffic moving towards the city center. See for yourselves."

Members of the group craned their necks to make out the circle avenue below, and observed a spontaneous outpouring of citizenry converging on the Central Tower. A steady stream of floaters filled the air and disgorged more citizens at nearby stations. Such a demonstration was unheard of. No sound could be heard at this elevation, but media reports on their coms and deskscreens informed them that the protesters were demanding action to protect their children. Anger and frustration were palpable in the mob, as recorded and reported by mediaorbs floating above and interviewing individuals. A line of Sentinels kept the crowd away from the building.

"The Sentinels have the situation in hand," Benwright reported. "We're going to have to make a statement soon. The media are demanding more information. What can we tell them?"

"Allow me to compose an announcement," F-Kerrick offered. "I have some considerable experience with the media and with relating to the masses. I know how to tell them what they want to hear. Leave it to me."

"Thank you, F-Kerrick," Commissioner Earl said. "I'll assist you and we can decide together how much we can reveal." The two retired to an alcove to draft a statement that would mollify the masses, while the others continued the meeting.

"We can only surmise that this beast has some kind of special access to the tunnels," said Quinn, continuing his report, "Either through his job or by some method of gaining entry into the main computer to get the portal codes. This information may help us to narrow down the suspects. We're in the process of interviewing the relatives of the latest victim, as well as her friends and anyone we could identify as coming in contact with her yesterday. No leads there as yet, unfortunately, but it fills out the flow chart I'm building to correlate the connections among the victims. You can access that information in the main file."

The meeting continued until there was nothing left to discuss. The task force members broke up into smaller groups, many drifting over to the windows to watch the mob below and to discuss developments. F-Kerrick was in the hallway, reading a statement that was being broadcast throughout the Dome, pleading for calm and requesting the indulgence of the populace, promising that action was imminent, and then suggesting that the mob disband and return to their habs. The throng seemed to be placated by his words, and shortly thereafter the Sentinels set about breaking up the demonstration. The mediaorbs caught much muttering and grumbling as the crowds dispersed, a reflection of the uncharacteristic discontent among the citizenry.

"Such a display is most unusual," F-Kerrick commented to Quinn as he returned from the hallway after his speech.

"They're terrified," he answered. "They don't know what to do or where to turn. They want answers and they want their children protected.

Historically, such fear and unrest have often led to the breakdown of civil society, as you no doubt experienced in your time."

"Yes," F-Kerrick replied. "Many of the riots of 2072 and beyond had similar root causes. Uncertainty in a time of crisis brings out the worst in people. They become irrational and self-destructive, then follow anyone who promises them solutions, no matter how far-fetched or extreme. Sometimes such actions even result in a change of regime, although the Compilers would never allow such a thing here."

"Well, they've been promised action now and we'd better deliver, although I'm at a loss as to how."

"It will come to you, my boy," F-Kerrick comforted him. "We have utmost confidence in you, and with our combined efforts, we'll get through this." He patted Quinn on the arm paternally. Quinn briefly wondered if he could have misjudged the insufferable Future. Perhaps Pierre was right. Maybe he just couldn't help the way he was. He resolved to reserve final judgment until after the crisis reached its conclusion.

* * *

October 8, 2204

F-Benito, president of the Council of Guardians, tapped the gavel pad firmly with his middle three fingers, generating a whiplash crack that was as much felt as it was heard in the hubbub of excited conversation among the council members. The sound brought all discourse to an abrupt halt.

"This emergency meeting of the Council of Guardians is hereby called to order. We are gathered here to discuss the weighty matter of the crisis afflicting the Dome. Not only do we have a series of unsolved murders that have gone on far too long, but it appears that we may be on the brink of some kind of insurrection. I've been informed by the special task force that they are not much closer to apprehending a suspect than they were after the first murder occurred. I have also been told by reliable experts that, if no resolution is forthcoming, the populace may panic and act inappropriately.

Yesterday's spontaneous demonstration, although peaceful, is evidence of that. I will now open the floor to discussion."

Guardian Secord's light flashed atop the display board, indicating that he had been the first to press his signal button to request recognition by the President. F-Benito highlighted his name, and a chime sounded in acknowledgment, granting him permission to speak. "Ahem," he began, clearing his throat and taking a sip of water before addressing the council. "I've received representations from various ad hoc citizens' committees demanding urgent action and full public disclosure of the status of the investigation into this series of crimes. As one, they demand to know if suspects are under surveillance and if an arrest is imminent. Can we confirm F-Kerrick's public statement? What are we to tell them?" He resumed his seat.

"I've requested the presence of the chief investigator, Director Benwright, to answer any such questions," F-Benito answered. "I now give the floor to Director Benwright."

Benwright arose from his place near the Chair's podium and made a small bow to the twenty red-clad Futures and the twenty Ordinaries in front of him. "Honourable Councilors," he began. "I must be honest, for to be any less would dishonour this assembly. The task force has gathered much evidence, and each clue brings us closer to ending the recent violence that has beset our beloved Dome. Using profiling coupled with the physical evidence and the security cam images, this is what we know. The perpetrator is a male, between sixteen and sixty years of age, most likely between twenty and forty, massing approximately seventy-five kilos, under two meters tall, and fairly fit. He is most likely unmarried, and likely does not relate well to adult females. We conjecture that this killing spree had its genesis in something that happened to him in his childhood, and was triggered by some recent event in his life. As of this moment, we have no viable suspects. That concludes my report. If there are any questions, I'll try to answer them."

A hubbub ensued among the councilors, and many lights flashed in rapid order on the display board, councilors clamoring for recognition. The President tapped the gavel plate to restore order, and the uproar died down.

Guardian F-Iofida jumped up the moment the President granted him the floor. "That's not very much to go on, and far from encouraging. That description, according to the information that I've just accessed from central database, covers about fifteen per cent of the males under the Dome. That's some 38 000 individuals. Are you telling us that's the best you've been able to do thus far?"

"I fear it's true," Benwright answered. "We're attempting to track the whereabouts of as many of those males at the times of the murders as we can, but given our limited resources, we need more clues before we can narrow our suspect list down further. We do have physical evidence from the second crime scene, a gelshoe fragment, and a list of those individuals who requisitioned that particular shoe. That clue has narrowed our list of suspects to fewer than 1200, and we're following up on that."

The rest of the meeting was not pleasant for Benwright, as councilors challenged and beset him from every quarter. He fielded their questions as best he could, but in the end the task force did not come off looking good. In the absence of viable alternatives, the Council reluctantly gave the task force a vote of confidence for its efforts, and more time to proceed with the investigation.

"Thank you for your attendance and your cooperation, Director Benwright. You may leave." Benwright retrieved his file folders and gratefully exited the hall. Guardian F-Benito waited until he had gone, then said, "If there are no objections, I would like to make representations to the Council of Compilers, soliciting their help and advice. I know they're reluctant to interfere in local matters, but they must be aware of the situation, and no doubt view the situation as grave. I'll keep the Council informed as to the progress in this matter."

The formal meeting was adjourned, but committees quickly formed to monitor developments. A considerable and ever growing force was being brought to bear against a single perpetrator, yet it was he who still prevailed.

October 23, 2204

More than two weeks after the latest murder, after the demonstrations had subsided, he lazed in his hab, savoring his triumph. The Sentinels were no closer to catching him, as he ran circles around them, and he enjoyed the game almost as much as the pleasure he took in the recollection of his deeds. He replayed the killings over and over again in his head, stimulating himself as he recalled the rapes and the beatings, quickening as the inevitable conclusion of each assault approached, climaxing as the life went out in the eyes of his young victims.

He would continue to stalk his prey, culling the herd as they grazed stupidly all about him, until his pain was assuaged and past wrongs were put aright. This was his due and his destiny, and no lesser being could stop him.

"Sister, oh sister, what have you done to me? If only you had begged forgiveness when you had the chance. Too late now. The saga must play itself out," he thought. "Too dramatic? Perhaps, but life is either drama or farce, and this is no comedy. It can only end badly for all concerned. At least I'll be remembered; oh how I'll be remembered."

He drifted off to sleep, his head filled with dreams of triumph and glory, his heart still filled with hate.

CHAPTER 17

A SIGNIFICANT BREAK

November 7, 2204

"No, not again," Quinn moaned as the com pinged annoyingly shortly after 0300 hours. He had been lying sleepless for hours, tossing and turning in anticipation of this very event, and hoping that it would not occur. He activated the device, "Lo, Benwr...."

That was as far as he got before Benwright's excited voice interrupted him, "You'd better get over here. You're not going to believe this one."

"Where?"

"Behind Pierre Adler's hab .... and the girl's alive!"

Quinn nearly choked. "I'll be right there. Out."

He shot out of bed, threw on a unisuit, and grabbed his forensic gear in record time. Pierre's hab was only a few hundred meters away, in the next ring out, so rather than summon a floater, Quinn sprinted the distance. He was there within minutes of the call, and was greeted at a public walkway between buildings by a surprised looking Benwright, who took in his disheveled appearance and breathless aspect and figured out what he'd done.

"Through here," he said, escorting Quinn past a grim looking knot of Sentinels. Benwright took him to the serviceway in back and pointed to the large recycling container that served several of the habs in the row. A paramed floater was tethered next to it, and the medtechs were hunched over a stretcher, ministering to a small figure under a thermal blanket. They had her ventilated and wired up, and were carrying on the work of attempting to revive her.

"Reported about an hour ago. A service tech, Max Ford, was checking out a power surge in this sector when he heard a groan from the recycling container. He looked in and found her there, barely alive, laid out just like the others. He immediately commed emergency services and got her out. He's pretty shaken up."

"She'll be all right?" Quinn asked.

"The medtechs think she has a decent chance of survival. We've tried to preserve the scene as best we could so you can work on it, but saving the child came first."

Finally, some good news. Quinn felt a great sense of relief. "Do you know who she is?"

"Identchip says she's Vale Chang, age eleven. Now get this. Her parents are Jamieson Chang and Shaniqua F-Chang."

"A Future? You're telling me he went after the child of a Future? Either he made a huge mistake or he's trying to send another message."

"The message could be that he thinks he can do anything he wants to and we can't touch him. And perhaps we're still underestimating this guy's resourcefulness. When Viola Secouri was taken, we had anticipated that he might strike in Hanover next, and we were prepared for that. It wasn't information that we provided to the public. He circumvented our preparations and went back to Alban. Now he's back in Seabrook."

The medtechs were still hunched over the motionless form of the latest victim. They were making encouraging remarks that gave Quinn and Benwright to understand that the child had a good chance of surviving her ordeal. At last they stood up and began to load the stretcher into their floater.

Benwright hurried over. "How is she? What are her odds?"

"Fair to good," answered one of the techs. "She has extensive trauma and probable psych damage, but we've managed to stabilize her so she can be transported."

"When can I interview her?"

"Most likely not for a while, perhaps several days. She's out of shock, but comatose. It'll take some time for her to be in good enough shape to tell you anything."

Benwright cursed mildly. What the child might have seen could put an end to the reign of terror. He would have to pressure the doctors to bring her back to consciousness quickly. There was too much at stake to delay.

Quinn set about the work of gathering the forensic evidence. He secured the inevitable red ribbon that the medtechs had left on the ground where they had been working, then carefully examined the narrow strip of pavement alongside the container, and the ground on the margins of the greenbelt. Nothing unusual presented itself. Next, he began to process the container, first recording it from every possible angle, inside and out, before removing its contents piece by piece. Another long night stretched ahead. The nature of the grounds, the container, and the recyclables virtually precluded the gathering of any useful information, and the contents of the bin turned out to be unremarkable. As a precaution, Quinn asked the Sentinel techs on the scene to bag everything and to transport all of it to their own lab for examination, including the bin itself, without much hope that anything worthwhile would come of it.

It seemed evident that the crime had been committed elsewhere and the body dumped in the container. But why bother moving the body? That was out of character, even given what the perp had done with his previous victim. And why dump the body in this particular location? Either it had some particular significance or the killer was taunting the authorities by placing it behind an Arbiter's hab. Quinn was struck by the irony that the girl was alive and in a recycling container.

"I'm accessing all available secvids for this area," Benwright informed Quinn when he announced that he had finished processing the scene. "There must be something on one of them that'll help us."

"I'd be willing to bet you'll see something. He's getting more arrogant, more defiant…"

"More careless?"

"No, not careless. That would imply that he wants to get caught or doesn't care if he's caught. I'd characterize it more as imprudent, more like a display of 'I'm all-powerful and you can't stop me no matter what you do!' If he keeps this up it will surely lead to his downfall, although he doesn't think so. Remember, 'grandiose sense of self-worth and reckless disregard for consequences'. I'm thinking he imagines he's on some kind of a mission and doesn't want to get caught until he feels he's accomplished his goals, if then."

Benwright synched his wristpod display with Quinn's and brought up the archived view from a sec-cam near to the path in the greenbelt. It showed a figure moving stealthily along the night-lit pathway behind the habs, towards the recycle bin. He was wearing loose fitting trousers and a hooded jacket. He moved in a lithe manner, in spite of the 40 or so kilos of deadweight that he was carrying slung backwards over his left shoulder. When he reached the bin he punched a button with a gloved hand and a side access panel slid upwards. He was lost from view for some minutes as he entered the container and concluded his business there. When he reappeared, he looked around cautiously, closed the panel, then retraced his steps until he was out of the range of the sec-cam. The date-time indicator read 07-10-04 / 02:13:17.

Benwright let out a whooshing breath. "Well, you were right. What do you make of that? He must have known he'd be in the range of a sec-cam somewhere along his path. Why would he risk it?"

"I don't know. There's something here we're missing. We surely won't be able to identify him from these images, so perhaps he feels he has nothing to lose by letting us see him. He appears to be strong and athletic by the way he moves, even encumbered as he was. We can approximate his height against that of the container as he came out and straightened up to look around. It appears that he's right-handed. That description might narrow our suspect down to a few tens of thousands of men in the Dome. We still need more."

"We have the list of people who req'd the faulty gelshoes. That's already narrowed our suspects down to mere hundreds. We could do a database match on males with a body type in the range of the suspect versus those on that list."

"We could, and that would narrow the suspects immensely. The only problem I see is if those few gelshoes we weren't able to track fell into the hands of unknown individuals. Let's try it anyway and see what we come up with." Something was still nagging at the back of Quinn's mind, and the piece of information he was temporarily concealing from Benwright didn't help either. It was time for another discussion with Sera. Perhaps she could provide some focus.

* * *

"Why aren't you sharing that information with Benwright?" Sera demanded. She was sitting opposite Quinn, the two bent over their work table where hard copies and photos of the evidence were spread out. The sec-vid was running in a continuous loop on the nearby comcenter.

"Because it's only speculation. I have only one source for it, and I don't want to move the investigation off track by getting Benwright stirred up. If he had this report, he might divert resources away from the solid data we have now. I'll look into this myself. It may come to nothing. Let's discuss yesterday's events."

"I still think you're making a mistake, but it's your decision," she replied, unwilling to press the issue. "Do you think he's getting bolder, exposing himself to the sec-cams like that? Do you think he wants to get caught?"

"Yes to your first question, no to the second. He's not looking to get captured. He's having too much fun, but he does seem to think he's invincible, untouchable. Sooner or later he'll trip over his own arrogance. It's only a matter of time."

"Time we don't have. Is there anything useful we can glean from this latest incident?"

"Maybe more questions than answers," Quinn replied. "Three significant things stand out. First, he broke his pattern. We were assuming he would strike in Alban or Hanover, which was where we'd placed the bulk of our resources, but he skipped back to Seabrook. Why? Only the

Sentinels and the Guardians knew we were expecting an attack elsewhere, and prepared accordingly. Does he have an inside source, or was there another reason he switched to Seabrook?

"Next, the girl survived. Why? She sustained significant trauma, just like the other three, yet she's alive. Beaten, raped, and choked, but no head trauma. He obviously wasn't rushed, because he moved her from the primary crime scene, which we haven't yet located, to the recycling bin, after he had finished with her. Surely he knew she was still alive when he put her in there. Perhaps he had already written her off as too far gone to survive.

"Finally, one of the girl's parents is a Future. Was that a personal choice on his part or did he make a mistake? His previous selections of victims were seemingly random, so did he depart from his pattern this time? Was it deliberate? In any event, all hell is breaking loose over this one. The Guardians are in an uproar now that one of their own has been targeted. It's a double outrage, against society and against a Future. Oh, and I almost forgot what may be the most important clue of all. Why did he dump her behind Pierre's hab? Was that a coincidence? Unlikely. It's almost certainly of major significance, if we can only figure it out. We have more questions than answers, but if we can resolve even a few of them, we'll be a lot closer to ending this mess.

"We know only a little bit about the timeline of the latest crime. What we know is that Vale Chang was in the back part of the family hab, located in the second ring backing onto the greenbelt, almost a kilometer from where she was dumped. She was studying, and her parents had just told her to go to her sleep shelf. She kissed them goodnight, then they heard her in the 'fresher, then she was quiet. That was about 2130. They assumed she had gone to sleep. Somehow she either got outside or somebody went in and took her, some time between 2130 and midnight as near as we can reckon. I have ACS Travio and a psychologist standing by to interview her as soon as she regains consciousness.

"I've been forced to call in a favor from a C.I. of my acquaintance, a rather shifty character that I'm usually reluctant to have any contact with."

"You have a confidential informant?" Sera asked. "What for?"

"Information, naturally. In the course of previous investigations, I've had need of sources that circulate more or less unnoticed in the general population. This one was a subject that I investigated some time ago. He's been known to come up with some interesting tidbits of information that I wouldn't normally have had access to. I recruited him during a study I did on the role of C.I.s in 20th and 21st century criminal investigations. Very interesting stuff. Petty criminals were actually paid off in cash or kind, and their minor offences excused in exchange for their informing on bigger criminals. This guy has often provided the Sentinels with useful leads in exchange for preferential treatment in some minor matters related to his mildly antisocial tendencies. I don't expect that he has any solid evidence that would help us, but he always has his ear to the ground and might come up with something sooner or later."

"Sooner, I hope," Sera said. "I don't think I can add much to what you've already inferred based on what we already have. Let's sum up. We have some kind of a psychopath, a sociopath, a serial killer who targets young girls, around twelve or thirteen years old, seemingly at random, with one possible exception. He drugs them, strips them, rapes them, then brutally murders them. He ties a red ribbon over their eyes and makes his escape."

"This one's only eleven."

"She looks older. It seems that he's estimating their age from their height and overall development, so I don't think he knows them or targets them in advance. I'd guess that he has a particular interest in girls of a certain age because of something that happened to him before, probably in his childhood, something that may have triggered his rather specific predilection for the type of victim and crime."

"That's a rather good analysis, Sera. I think we can use it as a working hypothesis. Now if we can only track the genesis of the triggering event. The problem is, if it relates to some kind of dysfunctional family or some mistreatment he received in his childhood, those types of social abberations are so rare in our society that they should have been noticed, reported, and corrected. We should access the Dome's databanks and see if they contain a record of interventions by social agencies in the range of, say, 15 to 30 years ago. If they exist, there won't be many, but at least it's a starting point.

"I've started a flow chart, just like they used to put up in the detectives' squad rooms, so that all of the clues can be tracked, and the interconnections more easily visualized." He brought it up on the comcenter to show Sera.

"His first crime seems to have been the most violent. Subsequent attacks seem to have diminished in violence, as if he got out a lot of pent up rage in the first one, then suppressed or rechanneled it in other attacks. The small knife cuts in the second attack have not reappeared, so that was likely just experimental. I've highlighted all of the commonalities in the attacks, and you can see times and locations of each incident, and all relatives and anyone else connected to them. This should be useful at the next task force meeting, for brainstorming purposes. Speaking of which, it's scheduled for early in the morning, and I still have materials to put together."

"Anything I can help you with?" Sera asked.

"No. I have to load and correlate a few details for my report to the task force then I've just got to get some sleep. Go and get some rest yourself, and thanks for your help. G'night, sis."

Sera couldn't help but notice how drawn and tired Quinn appeared. She was beginning to be quite concerned about his state of health, both physical and mental.

"You should really get some rest yourself. And consider asking for a leave of absence from the university, at least until this thing is over. You're stretching yourself too thin. See you tomorrow."

After Sera left, Quinn called up images of the victim taken by hospital staff after she had been admitted and made comfortable. She lay in an intensive care pod, wired to a lifeforce monitor and connected to breathing and intravenous tubes. Scrolling back, Quinn examined full body images of her, front and back. They showed extensive bruising and swelling over most of her torso, and on her arms and legs. A small bruise on the side of her neck revealed where the tranq had been injected. There were close-ups of the finger marks on her throat. The tri-d images showed only smooth marks, no fingerprints, as if the perp wore gloves. He stored the images for closer examination later on.

November 7, 2204

Grim. That would best sum up the mood of the participants as they gathered yet again to dissect the information that was accumulating in the file now labeled 'Suspect X'. Notwithstanding the fact that the latest victim had survived the most recent attack, less than 24 hours ago, the task force was cognizant of the fact that their combined efforts had gone for naught. They were also well aware that Suspect X must be apprehended before anyone else fell prey to his psychosis. The madness could not be allowed to continue. The only problem was that nobody knew what to do about it.

Benwright once again chaired the meeting. "Thank you all for attending. I have a message from the Compilers. They're sending a representative to attend tomorrow's meeting. They'll be monitoring our progress carefully. Let's hope that little Vale Chang will undergo a full recovery and that she will be able to provide the information we need to capture the predator. Quinn, would you please summarize the most recent events."

Quinn stood up. "I'm sure we all wish Vale a rapid and complete recovery, and we send our heartfelt sympathies to her parents. That one of them is a Future makes this crime all the more shocking. Piecing together all of the accumulated information and extrapolating from that, we can infer that Suspect X now believes that he is in charge, and cannot be dislodged from that position. He appears to have become delusional, if he wasn't before. For the time being, we are withholding news of the latest crime from the public, but only until we have a better understanding of what we're dealing with, and what our next step should be.

"We now conjecture that we're dealing with a psychopath suffering from grandiose delusion, a disorder in which the suspect believes himself to have special powers, such as invincibility. We intend to use this against him."

"Your pardon, Professor Braxton," F-Kerrick interjected. "Have you considered that Suspect X is playing with you, that he knows all about grandiose delusion and is acting in such a way as to mislead you into believing what he wants you to believe? In that way, he might well render your actions against him relatively ineffective."

"We've been in consultation with the best psychologists in the Faculty of Medicine at the university," Quinn answered. "Dr. Jared Acton is with us today. Doctor, would you care to explain?"

"Thank you, Professor Braxton. Yes, well, now, to answer the question, it is our opinion that it doesn't matter if your Suspect X is indeed suffering from grandiose delusion or is just pretending to. The result is the same. Based on his actions over the past few months, he truly believes he's indomitable, that his intellect is vastly superior to our combined intelligence, and no matter what action we take, his deeds will continue to reflect that attitude. It will inevitably lead to his downfall."

F-Kerrick waved a red gloved hand in the doctor's direction. "It seems to me that this task force has been of the opinion for some time that the suspect's arrogance would eventually lead to his capture. It has yet to happen. How can we be sure that your analysis is correct, and that it will lead to the desired outcome?"

"Nothing in this world is certain, but it is the considered and firm opinion of the best minds in the field of psychology that this creature's ego will lead him to ever more audacious and defiant undertakings. You'll have him soon."

"Before anyone else dies?" F-Kerrick sneered.

The good doctor was somewhat nonplussed by the question, the way in which it was asked, and the source. Carefully evading the main query he replied, "Bait him and he's yours." He resumed his seat.

"Thank you, doctor," Quinn said as he stood up. "The progression of the latest crime appears to be this; Vale Chang was known to be in her hab at 2130, when it's assumed she went to bed. Her father looked into her alcove at midnight, and found her missing. He reported it to the Sentinels immediately, and an alert was issued.

"She was placed in the recycling bin at around 0210 hours. She had been sexually assaulted and viciously beaten. As you can see," he continued as he brought up the sec-vids, "the perpetrator made no effort to hide from surveillance. We reviewed records from other sec-cams in the area, but he seemed to have just vanished. He's about 1.9 to 2 meters tall, massing about 75 to 80 kilos, and is fairly athletic and fit. Indications are that he's right-handed. His clothing is common and unremarkable."

"Was she abducted from her bed or did she wander outside," asked Guardian Isomoto.

"I wish we knew. Unless she walks in her sleep or decided to take a late evening stroll, it's more likely that she was indeed taken from inside the hab. If so, then it appears that entry to the hab was probably gained through the rear portal. As you know, private portals are keyed to open in response to the identichip implant of one of the residents, to a command from within the hab, or to an entry code stored in the Dome's main databanks. That brings up all sorts of questions and possibilities we haven't even contemplated yet. As for forensics ...." He nodded to the tech representing the newly constituted crime lab.

"As for forensics, regrettably there's little to report," the tech began. "No DNA trace, no hairs, no fibers, nothing we can expect to connect to the criminal or the actual crime scene. No sign of lubricant in the vagina, nor semen nor saliva anywhere on her body. The remains of the usual hypnotic in her blood. Traces of synthskin on her thighs. Finger marks on her throat again, as well as extensive bruising on the arms and the torso. Some odd imprints on the torso, but we can't match them with any tool or weapon. The ribbon is the next segment from the same roll ...."

"Excuse me," Benwright interrupted. "ACS Travio just alerted me that Vale Chang is awake and ready to be interviewed. The psychologist is with her now, to make sure she's in a stable mental state. If so, Travio will be able to talk to her in a matter of minutes. We'll stream the interview directly to your data screens and com-helmets as soon as it begins. In the meantime, let's review. Professor Braxton has prepared a chart for our convenience, if you'll kindly access file QB1373."

Quinn sat back as Benwright went over everything that was known about the five crimes and the suspect. On his private screen, he accessed the intake photos of Vale Chang, with special attention to the bruises on her torso. There was something about them that bothered him. He messaged the hospital, requesting an update on the pics as soon as possible. He wanted to get a better look at the pattern of the bruising as soon as the swelling went down.

A live feed of the start of ACS Travio's interview with Vale Chang overrode the file he was viewing. The child was still in the care pod, wired and tubed. Her parents sat miserably on adjacent chairs in one corner, holding each other close. The psychologist sat at one side of the bed, holding her hand. ACS Travio sat at the other, leaning close to the girl.

"Do you remember anything of last night?" he asked gently.

"Not … much," she replied in a soft and hesitant voice, valiantly attempting to overcome the shock of what had happened to her and to fight past her drugged state. "I got into my … sleep shelf, then went … to sleep. I woke up …. I remember …. pain … somebody …. doing things to me …. on top of me ….. hurting me …. so much .. pain …….. hurting me …. between my … legs .. then …. everywhere." She began to sob, and the psychologist bent close to comfort her.

When she had calmed, Travio asked, "Did you see anything? Can you describe him?"

"It was … almost dark. Soft and … slippery … underneath me. Felt like indoors. Light … behind him. Tried to … push him … away. Made him … angry. More … pain." Once more she wept. When she had composed herself, she continued. "Hit me … again …. again. Woke up .. in dark .. .can't see …. man came in … carried me out … then … here."

"The same man?" Travio asked. Max Ford, the service tech who had discovered her, had not yet been eliminated as a suspect.

"No ….. different smell."

"Smell? What do you mean by that?"

"Last man smelled … green. Bad man … smelled ….. red." She began to cry again, this time her small body was racked with sobs.

The psychologist bent close. "I think you'd better leave her alone for a while," she said. "I'll stay with her and let you know when she's in better shape to talk to you again."

In the meeting room, the screens went back to their default menus. Everyone was talking at once. Benwright rapped the gavel for attention. "Two steps forward, one step back," he commented. "I'm not sure how helpful that was. Any observations, analysis, anyone?"

Doctor Anton spoke up, "I would have expected the girl to be in a dissociative fugue due to the trauma she suffered, but she appears to be quite lucid. In spite of her distress, she was apparently quite articulate and coherent, with the possible exception of that last part. We have to examine more closely what she meant by smell. It may be a delusion on her part or … perhaps … well, there are recorded cases of people whose brains are wired so that they can apparently see music or feel or smell colors. This youngling may be such a person. The condition is called synesthesia. We could easily test her for it."

"Would that put us any further ahead, if we find out that she can actually smell red?" Quinn asked.

"I don't know. It would depend on the relative significance of the perpetrator smelling like red."

"Could she just have smelled the red ribbon?" Benwright posed.

"I don't think so. She appeared to be linking the smell to the man at the time of the assault, not to the red ribbon, which was placed on her after she was put in the bin unconscious."

"Oddity piled upon oddity," F-Kerrick added, shaking his head. "What next?"

"From her interview, it appears that the perpetrator may not have invaded the hab," Quinn said. "We must ask the Changs if their daughter has ever been known to walk in her sleep or goes outside without telling them. I doubt it. His motivations are so alien to us that we have trouble imagining why he does the things he does."

"Since he's broken the pattern, we can no longer count on being in the right place at the right time," said Benwright. "But given the increasing body of evidence we now have, we can eliminate a host of suspects and begin to narrow down the list. We have his general size and body type, and we can infer from his behavior something about his past history. Quinn is looking into that more closely. We are developing plans to entrap him, and I'll report on those at the meeting tomorrow. In the meantime, those of you actively engaged in the investigation have your assignments on your coms. Interviews are ongoing, as is forensic examination of the Chang home and the physical evidence. Again, we'll have a more complete report by tomorrow."

The attendees scattered or broke up into smaller groups to discuss the events of the past night. Quinn and Benwright were going over the schematics of the Chang home, trying to decide if the girl had been taken from inside or outdoors. Her sleep shelf was located near the rear portal, in a room that doubled as an info center and entertainment room. It would not have been difficult for someone with the proper access code to slip inside unnoticed and abduct the child without her parents hearing anything. They could easily have missed seeing the green light on the hab status board that indicated the rear portal had been opened. Even now, the Sentinels were going over the hab and accessing its portal's stored data. They would soon know.

November 6, 2204

It had been just that easy. Using priority access to penetrate the central administration's databanks, the stalker had obtained the code for the Chang's rear portal, along with a schematic of the hab, then he had erased all traces of his search.

At precisely 2300 hours he had used the information thus gleaned to enter the hab and, moving silently and stealthily on padded soles, had within minutes tranqued the girl and spirited her away into the semi-darkness of the greenbelt. That was where his unique knowledge of the Dome's substructure came in handy. One of the reasons he'd chosen and stalked the Chang girl, apart from her obvious appeal to his perverse desires, was the ready access to a service tunnel entrance, just meters from her hab. Again he used a pilfered code to gain entry and, following a preplanned route, took her to a place that afforded the privacy he desired to satisfy his hunger.

"Fools," he thought. "Did they really believe they could entrap me with patrols and decoys? How gravely they've underestimated my talents for deception and evasion. Knowledge is power, and that's the huge advantage I have over them."

In the dim light of the hidden room, once again he felt the rush of adrenaline, the pounding of blood in his head, the burgeoning headache, the surge of desire beyond his control. Stripping her, he had thrown her onto a plastic covered mat and begun his ritual. As he quickened, she awoke, and he was forced to subdue her violently, savagely beating her back into unconsciousness. It only added to his pleasure, his desire, his wrath. As before, as in the recent past, as in days long gone, he choked her into oblivion, only achieving his release as the last breath passed her lips.

He collapsed on top of her, his chest crushing her as he quaked and sobbed in his personal agony. He rose and straddled her, pounding her torso with his fists in frustration and anguish, inadvertently and unknowingly resuscitating her, allowing her a reprieve from death. Her first long, gasping intake of breath was lost in his wails, and her shallow breathing went unnoticed.

When at last he had finished with her and had regained control of his disobliging brain and body, he set about the final task of disposing of her in a way calculated to discomfit his enemies. In the full knowledge that she was the offspring of a Future, he would place her so as to give them a lesson in power and privilege, a primer on how even the ruling class could be ruled by someone with the will and the determination to put them in their place. While he was primarily motivated by his depraved animal desires, an impetus to which even he would admit, defiance of the established order played into the gratification he felt each time one of his victims was discovered, and the panic that it spawned.

He retraced his path along the service tunnel, the apparently lifeless body of Vale Chang slung over his shoulder. The Sentinels' patrols were on a rigid schedule, as he had observed over the past few days. They worried him not in the least, as they could easily be avoided. Emerging among the shrubbery, he quickly made his way to the bordering pathway. He was aware that he was under observation, or soon would be. He didn't care. Let them try to identify him from the sec-vids. They would not.

He had briefly considered laying the child's body out on the grass at the edge of the pathway, in full view of early passers-by, but deemed that an all too crude indignity both to his victim and to his incontrovertible brilliance. Having scouted the recycle bin earlier, he reasoned that she would be discovered in good time, while he savored his victory and his retribution. To gratify his unnatural desires, exact his vengeance, and taunt the powers that be was so sweet a diversion. They, too, knew that they were being mocked. The game was on.

* * *

"It's confirmed, then," Quinn told Sera later that day. "The Changs' portal records verify that someone accessed the rear portal at precisely 2300 hours, then again at 2302 hours. That was when Vale was kidnapped."

"O.K. We know the when and the how, but what about the who?"

"Wait till you see this," Quinn replied. He called up the comcenter projection of the latest images the hospital had sent over. Vale Chang's young body was laid out on a white sheet for better contrast, as per Quinn's request. Sera briefly averted her eyes in shock and disgust, but soon returned to the holo-image floating before her. The swelling on Vale's torso had reduced markedly, and the black and blue marks stood out. Quinn zoomed in on the odd but familiar markings he had been unable to identify from the previous images, due to the distortion caused by the swelling.

"I wracked my brain to try to match these markings to something recognizable, then I used enhancement and mirrored the image. This is what I came up with."

The picture on the screen changed; enlarged, reversed, enhanced, and was clearly recognizable.

Sera gasped. "It's the imprint of a Futures' signet ring, the one they make from the memory matrix and present to each Future upon Awakening; the one that each Future is expected to wear for the rest of his life and never remove under any circumstances. Mom and Dad both had the identical ring. You remembered!"

"I recalled how Mom worked the clay for her pottery. No matter how she turned her ring, it would always leave an impression somewhere in the clay. Finally, she gave up trying to conceal it and used it as a signature of her work. I shouldn't take all of the credit for recognizing it. Sooner or later some software program somewhere would have identified it."

"We didn't see these marks on any of the other victims."

"We didn't notice them on any of the other victims. We'll have to go back and have another look at the records."

"This guy has been very clever, very cagey in masking his identity and misdirecting us. Maybe this is one more of his schemes to divert us from his true identity. Who's going to believe that a Future is capable of these kinds of atrocities? They're above suspicion. They've all been through a battery of tests prior to their approval for Futures status, their backgrounds examined in minute detail, friends and colleagues interviewed, and their psyches probed after Awakening. No, I don't think it's possible. It's not logical. I flatly don't believe it. Are you sure you're not being influenced by your dislike for Kerrick?"

Quinn was somewhat taken aback at his sister's refusal to even consider the possibility that a Future could be involved. "Ridiculous. What happened to the open-minded Sera who challenges preconceived notions and societal beliefs? Have you suddenly turned conformist?"

"No, no! If you weigh the physical evidence against the rigors of the Futures selection process and the high profile aspect of Futures, your conclusion doesn't hold up. He's just throwing us a red herring, and, come to think of it, I'll bet the red ribbon is one, too. He wants you and the Sentinels running off in all directions, and it appears he's succeeding.

"O.K. Taking that into consideration, what do you make of this?" Quinn held up the report that Travio had given him weeks before, the one he had withheld from Benwright, the one containing the results of his interviews with the Futures who had req'd the suspect gelshoes. "According to this, there were two pairs of shoes owned by Futures that are unaccounted for. Each claimed that they sent them for recycling when they failed. The two Futures in question are F-Garrett and F-Kerrick. I've personally checked their whereabouts at the times of the attacks, and only F-Garrett has a solid alibi. F-Kerrick was determined to have been alone in his hab at those times, but we have no way of verifying that."

"You asked them?"

"No. I was more circumspect than that. It would be improper at this time to get Futures stirred up, not to mention tipping Kerrick off that he might be suspect. I used indirect interviews to track them, as well as databank records from public portals and floater stations."

"And does F-Kerrick resemble, in any way, shape or form, the suspect we've seen on the sec-vids? I still think you're wrong. Unless he has an accomplice, it's not possible that he's involved. I think we're being subjected to a lot of misdirection and artifice. Consider the possibility that someone who has access to a Futures ring committed the crimes. It could be a relative of a deceased Future. We have our own parents' rings right there on the shelf. Forget about the Futures angle and concentrate on what we really know. And here's a thought; why don't you try accessing F-Kerrick's portal data to see if he went in and out on the nights in question? That should set your mind at ease."

"Good idea, Sera. Thanks. But that data can only be retrieved from the portal monitor inside the hab. It has no link to the central databank. I'll have to get in somehow."

"You're not serious! You're really going to do that? You are personally going to invade the privacy of a Future? You must love trouble. Wouldn't it be better to present your findings to the task .... ? Never mind. I forgot. F-Kerrick is on that panel. How about discussing it with Benwright and get his ideas on the suspect?"

"Are you kidding? He's even more closed-minded than you are. He'll dismiss the idea out of hand. No, this is a lead I'll have to follow up on my own. If anything comes of it, then I'll bring in Benwright. It should take only a few days."

"In the meantime, the rep from the Compilers is arriving today. How are you going to handle that?"

"The Compilers have requested observer status at the meetings. If I'm successful in corroborating my suspicions, I'll request a private meeting with the Compiler and Benwright, and we'll see where we go from there. If the killer is a Future, we have a serious problem on our hands, one that will merit the involvement of the Compilers themselves. They're the ones who set the rigid standards for Futures' candidacy, so they must be apprised of any possible shortcomings or loopholes in the rules and standards."

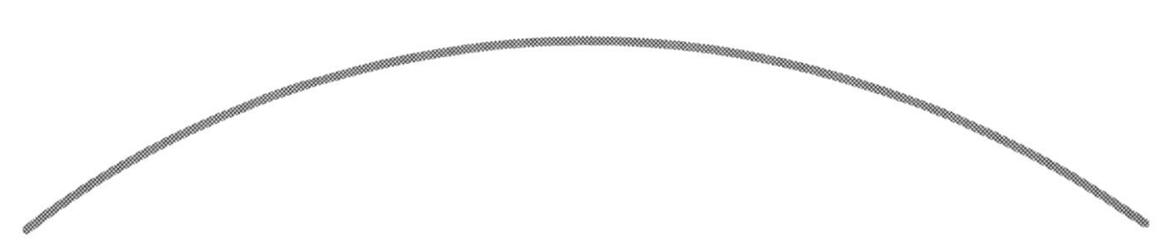

CHAPTER 18

A VISITOR

November 8, 2204

An official visit by a Compiler was most rare, though informal visits by them to the Domes were not uncommon. They enjoyed seeing the results of their efforts, well over two centuries in the making. Those original Compilers, those few who managed to survive the Great Plague, had been unanimously granted permanent Futures status by the Grand Council of Guardians, and each was Awakened repeatedly. The Council of Compilers had been expanded to include a rotating membership of 20, all of them selected from the ranks of the Futures. Now, one of the Originals had been dispatched from the Compilers' seat of government in GenevaDome to investigate the situation in RichmondDome and report back.

The flyer was trundled from the tarmac into a nearby hangar dome to avoid the necessity for the Compiler to have to don a rad suit and rebreather. From the moment the aircraft's pod door opened, the gravity of this visit was apparent to all. The figure that stepped onto the hanger's polished floor, the figure clothed in the deep blue robes of an Original, was Maria Sanchez herself.

C-Sanchez now had the aspect of an Elder, creased and graying, but with the sharp eyes and regal bearing of wisdom and authority. Each resurrection had taken its toll, as years added upon years between new Awakening and new death. Eventually, even the original Compilers would succumb. Recent advances in the technology suggested the possibility of being able to download the contents of an updated memory crystal into a more youthful and vigorous body, but they were not quite there yet. For Compilers, the DNA codes from previous incarnations were still preserved, and the possibility of immortality existed for them alone, a potential reward for their service to mankind.

A deputation from the Council of Guardians was on hand to greet the arrival of the hover plane from the Compilers' headquarters in GenevaDome. The small delegation stepped forward to receive her; F-Benito, President of the Council, and Commissioner Chaz Earl of the Security Branch, with F-Kerrick, hovering in the background. Several other members of the Council of Guardians were also present, and an honour guard of Sentinels preceded and followed the party.

"Welcome, C-Sanchez," F-Benito greeted her, exchanging wrist-grasp. "Your visit honours our Dome. I only wish it could have been under more auspicious circumstances."

"Thank you, President F-Benito. It's good to see you again," she responded. "I, too, would have hoped for a less dismal state of affairs. Rest assured that I'm here merely as an observer, and I'll report my observations impartially to the Council of Compilers. I'm also here to offer any assistance you might request from the Compilers, such assistance as might be in our power to give."

The Compiler's eyes shifted to something behind the Dome's delegation. They turned and saw a media-orb hovering there, levitation and transmission energy waves coruscating beneath its opalescent surface, its red eye fixed upon them.

"Compiler Sanchez," it said. "How do you feel about the latest criminal attack in the Dome?"

F-Kerrick groaned inwardly. "Not the 'how do you feel?' question again! Can't the media come up with something more incisive than that?" He felt embarrassed for them, just before he suddenly realized that news of the assault had leaked out to the media, in spite of their best efforts to temporarily suppress it. Disaster!

"The Compiler has no comment at this time," he intervened. "We'll be holding a formal media-con later today. Please stand by for further information."

The delegation quickly escorted C-Sanchez to ground transport, which whisked her through a main portal and into the Dome, then down one of the broad, tree lined avenues that divided the districts, ending at the foot of the central administration tower. The group made its way from an underground entrance to the meeting room, where the task force was already assembled. President F-Benito ushered C-Sanchez into the room, then took his leave to attend to administrative duties. After Commissioner Earl completed the formal introductions, C-Sanchez was seated at the conference table, and the meeting started.

"There's been a serious development," Benwright began. "The media have somehow got wind of the latest incident, and are even now disseminating the news. I fear what the panic will do to the citizens, especially with no solution in sight, and in view of the unfortunate demonstrations that resulted from the last such occurrence. Since the fifth attack there have been demands for immediate action, and a few requests for transfers to other Domes. Many citizens have taken their children and gone on extended vacations to visit friends and relatives elsewhere. This news could precipitate a stampede."

F-Kerrick heaved himself up from his chair. "With your indulgence, Director Benwright, perhaps I might make a suggestion. If the issue is public panic, maybe we could announce the detention of a suspect, or at least put forth that we have a break in the case, and that an arrest is imminent. That would buy us some time. Surely the resolution of these crimes, the capture of the criminal, cannot be far off."

"And if the public finds out we've deceived them, then what?" Benwright asked. "Our credibility would be undermined, and would reflect unfavorably on the Sentinels and on the entire governing Council. It's too dangerous a game to be playing. The panic would be multiplied, as the perception that we're all helpless and desperate increases. We need a better way."

"F-Kerrick may have a point," Quinn observed. "Without lying outright, we could use the media to instill in the public a sense of confidence that we may be close to an arrest. This kind of manipulation was common two hundred years ago, using mass marketing techniques to sell everything from political candidates to government policies. Rather than actual prevarication, we sell the idea that we're on the job, protecting the populace. It might even put Suspect X off his guard, if he thinks we're looking at somebody else as the prime suspect."

"I'm still quite uncomfortable with the idea," Benwright said. "Perhaps we should put it to a vote. Does anyone else have any thoughts on the proposal?"

Many in the task force shifted uncomfortably in their seats. C-Sanchez looked as if she wished to speak, but held her counsel, adhering to her role as an impartial observer. Her com-helmet live-linked the proceedings with the Compilers in Geneva, but the physical presence of a Compiler in the meeting was meant to validate the actions of the task force, in addition to adding a cautionary note to their deliberations. Even as C-Sanchez restrained herself from counseling discretion in the matter, her cohorts back home were likewise curbing their desire for direct involvement. Things would unfold as they must.

"No one?" Benwright confirmed. "Then an e-vote, please. Yea or nay.... Thank you. And the result is that a small majority favors the proposal by F-Kerrick. We'll call a media-con after we finish here and announce that we have a suspect and that an arrest is at hand. That will buy us a few days. At worst, we can say later that the suspect has fled the Dome and is being actively pursued. If he strikes once more, though, the consequences will be grave."

"And what progress in the investigation?" Guardian Isomoto asked.

"We're continuing to interview Vale Chang," Quinn answered. "Though she has contributed little other than her insistence that the kidnapper 'smelled red'. We're testing her abilities in that area, and if true, we'll have to figure out if there's any significance to it or if it even gets us any closer to Suspect X. We've located a service tunnel entrance near the Chang hab that was accessed about the time of the abduction, and

Sentinels are combing those tunnels for further evidence. We are making progress, but we can't be assured of an early resolution to the crisis."

As the meeting adjourned, once again without a satisfactory outcome, Commissioner Earl, Benwright, and Quinn conferred privately with C-Sanchez.

"We'd value your input, Compiler Sanchez," Commissioner Earl said.

"I'm somewhat distressed by the length of time this investigation is taking," she began. "I understand that you feel overwhelmed by events and are at a loss as to how to handle them. With your permission, I'd like to call in a panel of experts from other Domes. My colleagues in Geneva tell me that they have a database of citizens who have a deep understanding of forensics and investigative techniques, from historical studies similar to Professor Braxton's. With apologies and all due respect to you, Professor, and your expertise in this area, I feel that two or more heads are better than one. If you'll allow me, it would take only a matter of days to assemble such a group. Now, I know I said I'm just here as an observer, but I deem it my duty to offer solutions where possible."

"Might I suggest a middle course," Quinn said. "It's a fact that any help we could get would be most welcome, but rather than have them come here, we could submit all of our data to them for examination. I fear that if we permit such a gathering here, it might scare off our prime suspect. We don't want to drive him to ground before we have the evidence we need to apprehend him. We'd appreciate the input of your experts so that we can better understand our Suspect X. Let's just keep it among the three of us."

"You have a prime suspect, then?" C-Sanchez asked.

"Actually, several. We're just in the process of narrowing the list. I'm afraid there may be a leak in the task force or in the Sentinels, and I don't want the perpetrator frightened off by your experts."

C-Sanchez nodded. "Understood. I'll send the contact list to your 'pods and let you set it up. Please keep me informed. In the meantime, I'm here for the duration, so com me if you need me. I'll see you all at tomorrow's meeting." With that she took her leave.

"Suspect list?" Benwright asked. "When did we get a suspect list? Did you just lie to a Compiler?"

"No, no," Quinn answered. "We've narrowed the suspects down to a relatively small demographic, and with Vale Chang's help, we hope to narrow it down even further. Confidentially, I have my own short list, but I need to investigate further. I'll let you know."

Quinn headed rapidly for the exit before the two bemused Sentinels could react. He had no wish to reveal his suspicions prematurely. That would come soon enough.

As he walked down the hall, Quinn observed C-Sanchez and F-Kerrick conferring quietly in an alcove. What mischief was Kerrick up to now? Yet another matter for him to worry about.

* * *

"You actually advocated lying to the people?" Sera said, outraged. "What's happened to you? Are you still the person I grew up with?"

"Relax, dear sister. Let me explain. It was our friend F-Kerrick who suggested the idea. Perhaps he does have the interests of the citizenry at heart, but I think it's more likely that he'd like things to calm down a bit, if he really is Suspect X, and in that event, the general public would be more likely to let down their guard and increase his opportunities. By my supporting him, it's even less likely that he'll think I'm looking to connect him with these crimes. I won't confront him until I have better evidence that he's the one."

"We've already discussed this. He looks nothing like the suspect in the sec-vids, and there's no evidence against him. Unless he's enlisted a confederate who's bringing him young girls to torture and kill, he's not the one. It's not likely he'd seek the help of somebody else who might slip up or sell him out, and with his high profile, it just wouldn't be worth the risk. I still think you're on the wrong track."

"Tonight," Quinn responded. "He'll be at a council meeting. I obtained his portal code from the main databanks using my high level access, and I'm going in to check his portal records. We'll know soon. If I am able to break his alibi, I'll enlist Benwright's help, or failing that, Pierre's."

* * *

The arrival of the Compiler and the survival of the Chang girl caused Doc to reflect on recent events. His survival instincts kicked in, and his natural arrogance surfaced.

"Do I fear the Compilers? Of course not," he thought. "They hold no more sway over me than do the Guardians or the Sentinels. Perhaps a demonstration is in order, while the Compiler is still under the Dome. An object lesson, perhaps? No. I think not. It might stir things up overly much. The Compilers might engage with a vengeance. Best to let sleeping Gods lie.

"I was careless, letting the Chang girl live. Not at all like me. Well, no matter. She can't tell them anything useful. No need to panic. Just be more thorough next time."

* * *

Quinn arrived at F-Kerrick's portal at 2010 hours, minutes after the Council of Guardians weekly assembly went into session. He wore his com helmet in order to keep track of the meeting in real time, thus ensuring that he wouldn't be caught unawares by the premature return of the subject of his investigation. It took only moments to punch in the access code and step through the portal as its panel swished smoothly aside. Though the Future may have been careless about his personal appearance, the way he maintained his hab belied that tendency. Undoubtedly, the cleaning 'bots kept the place spotless, but the degree of orderliness seemed fastidious almost to the point of compulsiveness. "A place for everything ….," thought Quinn.

Without delay, he accessed the portal's records, downloading them to his com for later scrutiny. His live link showed F-Kerrick still at the meeting, so Quinn decided to take the opportunity to look around. He was most careful not to displace anything for fear of tipping his hand. A quick scan showed no spy devices or electronic detectors, so he felt free to examine the contents of cubbies and sliders. He found fairly ordinary casual clothing alongside extra sets of red robes, some rather commonplace entertainment chips; games, e-books, and 'zines. He even found a few chips labeled as family albums, which he would have dearly loved to access, but was constrained by the fact that the chips would have retained an inerasable record of his intrusion.

There was a personal exercise gym built into the wall. Quinn turned the panel on and read the usage record. It appeared that F-Kerrick exercised regularly, for 30 to 45 minutes at a time. Curious that such attention to fitness yielded such poor results. Another bit of information for the 'Suspect X' file, though Quinn now thought of it more as the 'F-Kerrick' file.

He took another quick look around the hab before leaving, and stopped, frowning. Something was wrong. The size, the angles of the hab were slightly off. Quinn had rarely been in a standard bachelor hab before, but he had the sense that minor alterations had been made. Each resident was free to modify his living space within its confines, but Quinn sensed that something more had gone on here. A cursory examination of the walls revealed nothing. He used the sensors in his com helmet to take measurements of the space for later comparison with the standard specs for such a hab. "Just what kind of bolt hole do we have here, anyway?" he wondered.

Quinn removed any trace of his incursion from the portal's records and left. As he exited the hab, he sensed momentarily that he was under observation. He turned, and looked directly at the portal on the opposite side of the corridor, grinning at the knowledge of a shared secret, then shrugged and made his way down to the street. In this particular area, Lowertown was not a welcoming place. It had an air of cheerlessness and squalor, in spite of regular maintenance and repair by the Dome's engineering department and the best efforts of the city planners to enrich all of the living spaces. "Odd that somebody who shows so much pride in his hab and who could have chosen to live in the Futures bachelors' quarters would choose to live in this neighborhood. I wonder why."

* * *

"Well?" Sera asked.

"Patience," Quinn said as he scrolled through records, calling up dates and times and transferring the information thus gleaned to a separate database file. "It appears that our friend utilized his portal on the nights in question, on the sixth of every month for the last five months. The times are compatible with times bracketing all four attacks. We have him now."

"Did you check nights other than those of the attacks?" Sera asked.

"Well… no. Give me a minute."

Sera sat patiently as Quinn re-examined the records. "The results are unsystematic," he said finally. "He came and went at random times on other nights. The frequency of his outings might cast doubt on his culpability in the crimes. It could be argued that his excursions on the sixth of those months could have been coincidental, but I know that they're not."

"So you know, do you? Even though you don't have any solid proof, you still think you can go after him?"

"I'm going to go to Pierre for help. I have to bypass Benwright, because if word of what I'm doing leaks out in the task force, Kerrick might get wind of it."

"I hope you know what you're doing. If you're wrong, it could ruin you, and the real culprit could escape."

"And if I'm right, which I am, lives will be saved. I have no choice but to take the risk. Potential damage to my reputation would be the least of my worries, and in the unlikely event that I am wrong, the real killer might get overconfident and reveal himself inadvertently. The probable gains far outweigh the possible risks."

"Anything else?" Sera asked.

"Some anomalies in the dimensions of his hab. I overlaid my measurements onto those of a standard bachelor hab, and his appears to be slightly smaller. There may be secrets behind those walls. I have to go back in."

"Is it wise to venture in once more?"

"I'll have to wait for a time when I know that he'll be otherwise occupied for a sufficient length of time. Could be a few days. Just a matter of getting hold of his schedule or shadowing him."

November 9, 2204

Pierre Adler rolled over and looked at his chrono when the main portal queried for permission to admit a regular visitor. "Who comes calling after midnight?" he groaned.

After throwing on a robe he gestured his consent and was taken aback when Quinn crossed the threshold.

"I apologize for coming at such a late hour, Pierre, but I need your help urgently," he said.

Pierre yawned and stretched. "Concerning Suspect X, I'm guessing?"

"Yes," Quinn answered. "I'm certain of his identity, though Sera disagrees. I don't have enough to present to the task force or to ask Benwright to arrest him, so I need your help to get more evidence."

Quinn continued, laying out his case against F-Kerrick. He offered the evidence gathered thus far; Kerrick's unsubstantiated alibi, the portal records, the Futures' ring imprints, the missing gelshoes.

"Pretty thin, isn't it?" the Arbiter commented. "Not too much to go on, certainly not enough to make an accusation."

"True, but I'm convinced that I'm right. Will you help me? I need the services of a few Shadowmen, just 'till he either tips his hand or attempts to strike again. If he's under observation at all times, he can't do any more harm. I can't go to the task force, or even to Benwright, because Kerrick might find out. I need those Shadowmen, off the books. Even the commissioner has to be kept in the dark."

"Risky," Pierre responded. "If this goes wrong, all of our careers will be down the dropshaft. On the other hand, if it goes right, lives will be saved and tranquility will return to the Dome. In truth, I never liked that Kerrick character. I'm with you. Have you investigated his background, his past, before he became a Future?"

"Only the public records. There must be more. If he is what I believe him to be, then how did he ever pass the scrutiny required of a Futures candidate?"

Pierre shook his head. "Who knows? I'll do what I can. My influence only goes so far. I'll call in some favors and let you know in a couple of days. Now go home and get some rest. You look terrible."

Quinn did go home, but once more sleep eluded him. He tried white noise, nature sounds, and somno-tones, all to no avail. He spent too much time contemplating his options. "What if Sera's right? What if Kerrick had nothing to do with the murders? I could be wrong, yet I'm certain I'm not. I don't know how he's doing it, but I know he's doing it." A thought that had been niggling at his mind came to the fore. He recalled one of the last lines on his lengthy list of probable sociopathic behaviors: "It is not uncommon for a sociopath to attempt to insert himself into the investigation."

"Ah, there it is," he thought. He resolved to start afresh the next day, to go back and begin at the beginning.

Exhaustion took him in the small hours of the morning, and he almost missed his first class of the day.

November 9, 2204

Of necessity, bachelors' quarters were small, but still contained all of the amenities deemed appropriate for the comfortable lifestyle accorded to each and every resident of the Dome. Doc valued his privacy, so, paradoxically, had chosen to live in the more crowded inner ring, close by the central tower. Here, he hoped to achieve anonymity by blending in with the crowd, just one more tree in the forest, inasmuch as a bright red tree could ever go unnoticed. He had no true friends and few acquaintances, other than those whom he deemed to be useful to him.

Ujo Vreem would have been recognized in another age as being from the other side of the tracks. One of the less desirable traits that the

Compilers had failed to breed out of humanity was laziness. His ferret-like face and stooped posture contributed to the air of seediness that he exuded, and he was not above trading favors in order to shirk his duties to society. He was of a type who would expend an extraordinary amount of effort in order to avoid honest labour in favor of illicit gain, even to the point of toiling harder than he would have at respectable work that might have yielded greater rewards. He couldn't help himself; it was just his nature.

Ujo's new hab was across the corridor from Doc's. He was thus able to keep track of his neighbor's comings and goings through his portal monitor. In the circle of friends and acquaintances in which Ujo traveled, it was always useful to know what was going on around you. Information spelled self-preservation and profit.

"Good eve to you, Citizen," Doc politely greeted Ujo, arriving at his portal just as Ujo exited his.

"And to you," Ujo returned. "I'm off to supper. Would you care to join me?" he offered. Ujo never passed up an opportunity to curry favor or to accrue opportunities for future gain. The two men had a nodding acquaintance over the past few days since Ujo had moved in, but had not heretofore socialized.

"Why not," Doc replied. "It's been a while since I've had company at a meal. You're new here, aren't you? I hadn't noticed you until recently." It wasn't that Doc had any great regard for Ujo, but he had immediately recognized in the man a kindred spirit, conniving and soulless. He had also heard, with a characteristic ear to the ground, the rumors that Ujo was a snoop, and he was interested in any information that the man might have gathered on his neighbors, and especially on Doc himself.

"Just a bit of luck for yours truly. I was living in communal digs in Lowertown," Ujo said, referring to the less desirable bachelors' quarters at the base of the taller buildings of the inner circle. "But a friend with some small influence managed to find me a recently vacated hab here." Ujo did not know nor would he have cared that the previous resident of the hab had been relocated closer to his work at the data reclamation center, as per his long standing application, which had suddenly and mysteriously jumped to the top of the heap.

"Well then, welcome, neighbor," Doc said. "I'm ….."

"No need, sir. You're well known in these parts, gracing our humble borough with your presence as you do. I'm Ujo Vreem, information merchant and general dogsbody, at your service."

"A pleasure, I'm sure," Doc said, not specifying just whose pleasure it might be. "Let's be off then."

A nearby dropshaft quickly deposited the two at the portal of Madcap, a caf on the ground floor of the building, that catered to plebian tastes, in that its offerings tended towards faux-fatty tasting foods much favored by those with little regard for healthy lifestyles. The pair settled themselves in a rear corner, backs to the wall like a pair of conspirators in an historic spy vid. They both ordered Madmoundburgers, made with beef-flavored soy, along with caffeine-laced cola floats. This was Ujo's normal bill of fare. Doc's preferences tended more towards the epicurean, but this occasion demanded a show of amity and commonality.

"Ah, this is the life, is it not, Citizen?" Doc commented as he reclined in a comfortable lounging chair, munching on his oversized entrée.

"Indeed," Ujo responded. "And a good meal is a welcome respite from the day's toils and troubles."

"I'm sure that your meal is worthy recompense for your toils, but just what troubles might a good citizen such as yourself be suffering?" inquired Doc, probing for information.

"Well, ah, perhaps I overspoke. Maybe not so much troubles as trials, er, quandaries, er, no, better yet, problems."

"And so, problems? Nothing that the Guardians cannot set right, I trust," Doc pressed, cocking his head and smiling encouragingly at Ujo, who was now clearly flustered.

"Ah, well, nowt to make much ado about," Ujo burbled, reverting to the idiom of his upbringing in LiverpoolDome. Well aware of Doc's high standing and considerable influence, he had set out to impress him, not to alienate him. Hastily, he changed his tack. "There's those as might make trouble for honest citizens such as us. Have to keep an eye on 'em, we do." He put a finger aside his nose and winked conspiratorially.

"And I'm sure you do," Doc grinned. "I'm certain that the Sentinels have use for someone such as you, someone who watches out for the best interests of the New Social Order, yes? We'll speak of this again, I'm sure. Perhaps we can be of benefit to each other."

"Without a doubt, sir, I'm sure we can," Ujo replied unctuously, delighted to have a Future as a friend and confidant. "Things are beginning to look rosy for our boy from Blighty, very rosy indeed," he thought.

When Ujo left to avail himself of the caf's 'fresher, Doc took the opportunity to access his records from the Dome's database using his wrist pod and priority access code. As he suspected, Ujo came from a family of n'er-do-wells going back several generations in LiverpoolDome, with a history of behavior bordering on the antisocial. Doc was pondering the many uses he might have for a person of Ujo's character and talents when the man returned from the lavatory.

The rest of the meal was occupied with small talk, and when the two at last went about their own business, it was understood that a loose alliance had been formed whereby each might watch the others' back. This, in spite of obligations and assurances Ujo had made to another player in the drama. Ujo imagined that he was getting the better of the deal, but little could he know how such benefit might go so disastrously awry.

CHAPTER 19

QUINN AND GUS MAKE A DISCOVERY

November 10, 2204

Mid-term break, a whole week for Quinn to devote his full attention to the investigation. Accessing the city's central databank, he determined that F-Kerrick had undergone processing through Usher's Harbour. A convenient opportunity, since his friendship with Gus and Rosie would make it easier for him to go through their files. It would have been much more difficult had Kerrick undergone Awakening in one of the Stildenbachs' establishments.

"Rosie, it's Quinn," Gus shouted as the portal admitted their most welcome visitor. "Have you made any progress with my 'tens' problem? Where do we stand?"

"Sorry, Gus. What with all that's going on, I haven't had time to even look at it. I came to ask a favor. Could you let me look at some of your files? I can't tell you why, but I'm hoping you'll trust my judgment in this matter. It's very urgent and most important."

"Well, you know those files are supposed to be confidential, but since you have high level clearance, and as it could take days or weeks for you to get official authorization, I'll help you any way I can. Does this have to do with your investigation?"

"Sorry, I can't answer that. Just please trust me."

"Quinn. How good to see you," Rosie greeted him as she entered the room. "River's at work, but she'll be home later. Will you stay?"

Quinn laughed. "Of course. Lovely to see you again, Rosie," he said, bending to kiss her on the cheek. "I have work to do here, with Gus' help. In any case, I owe River an apology for neglecting her these past few days, but what with the investigation and my day job and the arrival of C-Sanchez, I've been somewhat busy."

"She'll be delighted to see you. She talks about you .... a lot." She gave Quinn a broad wink. "You and Gus just go and do what you have to do. I have my own work to finish."

She disappeared into the lab, while Gus and Quinn went to the workshop.

"Lo, Professor Braxton," Gabby said as they entered the room.

"Lo, Gabby," Quinn responded. "Hard at it, I see."

"Gus asked me to transfer the old hard copy archives into databases. Then we can recycle them, those documents that we're not required to keep on file by law, and free up some room in the back. Some of the files go back a decade."

"How far did you get?" Quinn asked, fearful that the information he was after might have been destroyed already.

"I'm working backwards. I only have two years of files to go."

Quinn breathed a sigh of relief. The file he was interested in would be among those still on Gabby's worktable.

The folders were scrupulously clean, but nevertheless exuded the mildewed staleness of plastifiber too long in storage.

"What are we looking for?" Gus asked.

"Anomolies," answered Quinn.

"Like?"

"Like I'll know them when I see them."

Gus shrugged and plunged in, handing Quinn one file after another.

"These are neither alphabetical nor chronological," Quinn commented.

"Sorry," Gabby interjected. "I just grabbed armfuls and threw them onto the table. Some of the piles fell over and mixed with others, but they're all there, the last ones I was processing."

"No matter," Quinn said. "There's few enough to go through. Now what's this?"

Quinn had spotted a file with a red tag. No other file had such a tag. "What does the red tag mean?' he asked.

He handed the file to Gus, who took it and looked it over carefully. "Strange," he said. "This file was flagged for an irregularity, but it was filed without action. I wonder why. Wait. Now I remember. The flag is dated early in 2194. We had a rather unreliable intern at that time. Can't quite remember his name, but his work was sloppy. He probably threw this in a filing drawer just before I let him go."

Gus studied the file. It was a history and an approval record for a Future, one who had been Awakened a decade before. It contained all of the relevant papers on the Future, including the application, supporting documents, testimonials, approval stamps, and processing details from storage to Awakening. Something about the paperwork bothered him. The birth certificate was a smeared, crude copy made on a personal copier instead of being a government certified copy. Now he began to examine it in detail.

Quinn looked over his shoulder and read the name on the file; Kerrick, Donald. D.O.B. – 2061-10-12, D. - ?, 2107; A. – 2194-03-04. Birth, death, Awakening. This was it. He could now fill in more pieces of the puzzle, perhaps completing it today.

"This is the one," he said excitedly. "What does the question mark mean?"

"I'm not sure. It appears that the exact date of his death was unknown. Read the file. Note that the birth certificate is not official, it's a crude copy. That's probably why the file was flagged in the first place."

Gus and Quinn hunched over the file eagerly, carefully removing and examining each page. Quinn recorded each significant detail; dates, places, persons, numerical references, for future comparison.

Hours later, Quinn sat with his notebook in front of him, deflated and defeated. He hadn't found the anomalies he had hoped would be there.

"You don't see anything wrong here?" he asked Gus.

"Other than the birth certificate, no, and that might have been just as a result of the turmoil of the times."

"Then I'll just have to start there," Quinn said. He had no solid plan, but he knew one would come to him. "Keep this file aside. I may have to refer to it again," he said, handing the file to Gabby. "And please make a copy of the birth certificate for me before I go. Thanks."

Gus preceded Quinn back to the gathering room where Rosie was already setting out a tray of drinks and wafers. "How about a little snack, boys, while we're waiting for River to get home. It'll be a nice little surprise for her, your being here, Quinn."

"Thanks, Rosie," Quinn said. "I hope River's up for an evening out. I've neglected her terribly of late."

"Yes, you have," Desert confirmed as she paused the tri-vid recording she'd been viewing. River's little sister had been sitting unobtrusively in a corner. Now she crossed the room to help herself to a snack. "Why don't the two of you move in together?"

"Desert," Gus intervened. "Mind you own business. Quinn and River will work out their own relationship, without your help."

Desert humphed and went back to watching her vid. In her first teen year, and having so recently attained puberty, she was, like her older sister, what had once been referred to as a firecracker. She had a strong will and opinions on everything, which she was not unwilling to share with all and sundry.

"How's the investigation going anyway?" Rosie asked. "I heard on the news that the Sentinels are about ready to make an arrest. Was that your doing?"

"I can't claim too much credit yet. We're just wrapping the case, at least I hope so. Gus has been of some help in that, too."

"I have? How? You mean that file we were looking at?"

"Yes, but you can't tell anyone. I have more work to do before we can end this thing."

"But, but …. he's a …." Gus began.

"The less said the better," Quinn interrupted. "Don't jump to any conclusions, Gus. We'll all know soon enough."

He was about to expand on his warning when River walked in. “Hi, lover,” she purred, without a hint of self-consciousness. “Have you come to take me away from all of this?”

“Can I have your sleep shelf when you leave?” Desert asked.

River glared at her. “That wasn’t what I meant, and kindly butt out, little sister.” Desert snorted and turned her back on the group.

“Why don’t we go for a walk,” Quinn offered. “We don’t get to spend enough quality time together.” He guided her by the elbow back towards the portal. “See you later, folks,” he said as they exited Usher’s Harbour.

As soon as they reached the avenue, River put her arm through his and leaned into him. “Mmm, this is nice. We should do this more often.”

“So Desert tells me,” Quinn laughed.

“I’ll have to have a heart to heart with that one when I get back,” said River. “I heard about the latest case. How’re things going? Do you really have a suspect? Did someone turn him in?”

“Not quite yet. I feel we’re getting close, but we need actual evidence to apprehend a suspect.”

“You don’t have enough yet? Couldn’t he be arrested under the Public Safety Act?”

“We’d still need enough for an Arbiter to allow us to do that. Pierre is doubtful about the quality of the information we have now, so I’m gathering more. We should have the results we need before long.”

“I hope this is over soon, not just for the sake of possible future victims, but for the two of us. We need more time together.”

“We will have it, very soon, and then forever,” he said tenderly. River grasped his arm more tightly and pressed her cheek to his shoulder as they strolled down the avenue. Even as their dreams were tempered with reality, they were both nevertheless confident that their future would unfold as it should, no matter what impediments they might face.

November 11, 2204

Quinn pored over the records, document by document, word by word. Nothing jumped out at him. He accessed the Dome's database on the comscreen, but its records provided little elucidation. One more thing to try. Quinn requested access to the database in MontgomeryDome, hoping they had consolidated the records from southern Alabama before the Chaos had destroyed them. What he found gave him hope that a resolution might be possible.

The fragmented information provided by the data files from Enterprise Hospital for October 12, 2061 was revealing. Quinn entered the I.D. code for Donald Kerrick, then scrolled forward and backwards along the list that matched the code with the recipient of each numbered identichip, leaning forward excitedly as the information came up on the screen.

He commed Sera. "Can you come in here? I think I'm onto something."

When she arrived moments later, he pointed to the screen. "These are the I.D. codes for babies born at approximately the same date and time as Donald Kerrick. What do you notice?"

Sera peered at the data, determined to suss out any hidden meaning. After a full minute, she shrugged and turned to Quinn. "What am I supposed to be seeing here?"

"Look at the numbers sequence. Identichips are always coded in consecutive numbers, according to the order of birth in each regional hospital." He scrolled up and down. "In every case here, the numbers are in their proper order, but here, just before Kerrick's number appears, it skips a number. It's one digit off from where it should be. Kerrick's code ends in a 6, and the next one is a 7, as it should be, but the one before Kerrick's is a 4; the 5 is missing. What are we to make of that?"

"Is it significant?"

"On its own, perhaps not, but coupled with all the other anomalies like the unofficial birth certificate, it could be quite important. Chip implant kits are requisitioned from central supply on an as-required basis. If the previous chip kit had been req'd by mistake or had been returned to supply, the number would have still shown up where it should have been. If the chip had been faulty or inadvertently damaged, there would have been a record of its disposition. There's no such record. Where did that chip go?"

"So what do you think happened to it?"

"I'm not sure, but here's a possibility. Suppose that the '5' baby was born and implanted, then suppose somebody replaced that baby with Kerrick, the number 6 baby, most likely because the '5' baby died. The '5' chip would have been cremated with it. The question of why the exchange was made would still remain. And why is there no record of what happened to the child with the '5' chip? All of this must somehow connect to Kerrick and the murders, and I'm going to have to find out the how and why and get to the bottom it all before anyone else gets killed."

"How do you expect to do that?"

"Well, I've reached a dead end here. I'm almost certain that someone tampered with the databank records, to conceal what happened to the child with the missing '5' chip. There's just no more information to be had, no other relevant records, so the only other possibility is to go where those records might still exist."

"You're going afield?" Sera asked.

"I have to," Quinn replied. "Available databank records are incomplete. I have to go through some original archives in the town where this all began."

"Can't you get some local to do that for you?"

"No. I have to do it myself. They won't know precisely what to look for, and I don't want to put out too much information for fear of it getting back to Kerrick."

"Can I go with?" she asked.

"Uh … are you sure you want to do that? It means wearing rad suits and rebreathers and possibly a few days of discomfort, depending on what we find out there."

"Afield! It's an opportunity. How often do we get to leave the protection and comfort of the Dome? Besides, I can help you search. Will it be dangerous?"

"Not particularly, unless there's rogue Outlanders about. I think the area we're going to is safe. Southern Alabama, on the Gulf coast.

Enterprise. Used to be well inland until the ocean levels rose. I can get access to their vaults. Apparently they've preserved fairly complete records from the area in that time period. If there's anything more to be found, that's where it'll be."

Before shutting the databank down, Quinn thought to note the names of the babies born just before and just after Kerrick. The '4' baby was one Jason El-Huseini, the '7' baby an Arthur McCaskill. The names were most probably of no significance in the present investigation, but he thought he had better look into them just in case.

November 11, 2204

F-Kerrick was a creature of habit, if not of epicurean tastes. He could be found most days lunching at Scofield's Deli, an eatery renowned for its fine foods. Belying its name, it featured gourmet cooking. The bill of fare leaning heavily towards dishes developed centuries before in France and Italy.

On this day, F-Kerrick was at his customary table at the back of the caf when Gabby walked in. He'd met Gabby at one of Pierre's soirees and had taken a liking to the young wab. He didn't normally cultivate close relationships with anyone, but Gabby's earnest sincerity in his ambition to one day become a Future had moved him. Consistent with his character, he also viewed Gabby as a potentially useful tool for information gathering or for running errands.

Kerrick waved and motioned Gabby to his table. As the young acolyte seated himself, Kerrick greeted him, "Hello, Gabriel. What brings you to the neighborhood?"

"F-Kerrick. What an unexpected pleasure," Gabby greeted him respectfully. "The Harbour where I work is just around the corner. Usher's. I sometimes pick up soup or a sandwich here."

"Yes. I remember you mentioned that you work in a Harbour. Usher's, you say?" Kerrick said, trying not to show too much obvious interest. "And just what is it you do there?"

"Mostly scut work. Just record keeping and filing and prepping Futures for Awakening and the like."

Kerrick had a substantial bowl of bouillabaisse in front of him and gestured towards it. "Why don't you have a bowl of soup and we can share some pleasant conversation over our lunch? I'm told it aids the digestion."

Gabby was torn between getting back to his duties, and the twin temptations of the fine food that revealed itself in the enticing aromas arising from Kerrick's bowl, and the singular opportunity to converse with a Future one on one. Temptation won out. He ordered faux andouillette sausage avec asperges au beurre, a rather heavy lunch in the French tradition.

"I've always had an abiding interest in the workings of Harbours," Kerrick said. "Even though I've been through the entire process, I don't quite have a grasp on how it all works. I know you have a degree in biogenetics, and that you're working on an advanced degree, so perhaps you could enlighten me."

"I'd be delighted," Gabby replied, and proceeded to explain the procedures between bites of sausage and asparagus. F-Kerrick leaned forward, fascinated. He prompted Gabby in the appropriate direction. "All of this must involve considerable record-keeping," he said.

"Oh, yes, a lot. Most of it's electronic, but we still have to archive hard copies of all of the relevant documentation, with the proper signatures and legal seals. It still amounts to quite a stack of paper and synth. As a matter of fact, just yesterday I was archiving some old documents when Gus and Professor Braxton came in. They looked through some of the files from about ten years back and got quite excited about one of them. I overheard something about a suspicious birth certificate."

"Suspicious in what way?" Kerrick said with furrowed brow. He didn't want to push Gabby too far for fear of alerting him to his interest in the file.

"Don't really know," Gabby replied as he sipped some low-alcohol mock Bordeaux. "They got real quiet after a while, then Professor Braxton took copies of some papers away with him. All very mysterious and hush-hush," he revealed cannily, hoping to impress his eminent lunch companion.

Gabby continued on about obscure technicalities and conservation of resources, but Kerrick had ceased to listen. He was certain that the noteworthy file was his, and now he had to figure out what to do about it. How much did they know? What was in the file that might expose him? Had he become too smug and complacent in underestimating Braxton? Here was something to be very worried about.

"This has all been very interesting," he told Gabby, cutting him off in mid-word as he rose from the table, leaving his soup only half finished. "I have a matter I must attend to, and I regret I must conclude our delightful lunch together. We'll do this again soon." Gabby gaped after Doc as he hastily fled the caf, his mind in turmoil.

There could be no easy answer to this conundrum. It would take bold moves to save the situation, but he had extricated himself from tighter spots than this. His finely tuned instincts for self-preservation had kicked in.

CHAPTER 20

IN THE HEART OF DIXIE

November 13, 2204

Dust devils swept erratically across the bleak and blighted landscape, spawned in the baking, stagnant air of an Alabama autumn. The flyer bucked in the updrafts and settled to the ground in a bone-crunching touchdown. Quinn and Sera, clad in protective gear, hauled their packs out of the craft and made for the terminal building, pausing only to turn and wave at the pilot as he applied power and launched for home. It was only thanks to Pierre that they had been able to arrange this trip on such short notice.

Above the doorway of the dilapidated terminal, paint peeled from a sagging sign that read "Welcome to Enterprise Field in The Heart of Dixie" in faded blue lettering. The expression was ancient, the sentiment sincere and enduring. Good country folk with roots in the soil and arms spread wide in greeting. Even now, more than a few of them were still ready to fight a third civil war for Dixie.

The heat was oppressive, the dust omnipresent. The South, once a rich agricultural economy, was now a dust bowl where the vegetable gardens of the remaining residents were barely sustainable. Regional trade provided for the remainder of their needs.

"Shet that door. You're letting the g.d. dust in," groused a husky voice from behind the aging reception desk. Only the worn soles of a pair of workboots were visible, propped on the counter. A com screen near the ceiling showed a split view of the landing field and an ancient vid that turned out to be "How Green Was My Valley". What bitter irony that title held in this place.

The boots disappeared with a loud thud to be replaced by the craggy, weathered face of a silver haired woman of indeterminate age. She stood and greeted them in a slow drawl, "Welcome t' Enterprise, armpit of creation. Name's Grace. Some folks call me Amazin' Grace, but thet's a whole 'nother story." Her cackling laugh was interrupted by a hacking cough, possibly the result of inhaling too much dust. "Really need all thet gear, do yeh?" She wore baggy, bright yellow coveralls with a rebreather carelessly draped around her neck.

"Thanks," Quinn replied hesitantly, in response to the welcome. He was having some trouble understanding the regional accent. "I figured rebreathers and rad suits were sort of essential here in the Outlands."

"We don't much like thet term Outlands. We much prefer Heartlands or Freedomlands or even boonies, if yeh like. Outlands has an undesirable connotation for us, as if we're lesser folk living in lesser circumstances." She wasn't as hick-country as she pretended, and her accent slipped once in a while, leading Quinn to believe she might be having a little fun at their expense.

"Sorry," Sera said.

"We're new here. We advance booked transport into the town. Is it available?"

"Let me check m' bookin' list," Grace said slowly. She made a show of running through the pages of an old ledger-style volume on the counter. "Nope. Don't see it here. Oh, wait. Yep, here it is, on page one." She chortled deep in her chest. "Just funnin' y'all. Gets kind of borin' out here. Not too much air traffic these days. Y'd be the Braxtons, right? Only bookin' this month. Vee-hikle's out in the lot." She pointed through a grimy window towards a decrepit looking gyrocar perched on its central orb. "It's not much, but it'll get you t' where yer goin'. Only five kay t' town from here anyway. An easy walk, if y'd prefer."

"Thanks, no," said Quinn. "We'll take the car. Do we need a map?"

"Naw. Ain't but one road into town, but look sharp or y'll miss it. Mostly underground now. No more picket fences or quaint front porches," she continued mournfully. "Jest a few trees and dust, dust, and more dust."

"Why do you stay, then?" Sera asked. "You'd be much more comfortable in a Dome, with all you're needs supplied, and you'd be protected in a controlled environment."

"So they keep tellin' us, but it's all 'bout family and tradition and roots and the freedom t' be us. Yeh'd have to have been brought up here t' understand. Look, I've been around. When you get t' town, don't underestimate the folks there just because they talk strange. Y'all probably think we're a bunch o' hicks out here, but most of us have as much education as most of you Domers, and for all of our down t' earth ways, we're just as good as any of you. We're just different is all."

"Don't get us wrong," Sera protested. "We haven't prejudged you, and I believe that we may be more alike than you think. We probably sound strange to you, too."

"Yeh got that right. Don't mind me. I get a little defensive when it comes to m' friends. Just treat 'em right, O.K.? Good luck to yeh."

Quinn grasped Sera's arm and quickly guided her toward the exit, before she was able to get into a wider philosophical discussion of the Domes versus the Outlands. "Thanks, ma'm. We'll have your vehicle back to you in a couple of days."

"Y'all have a good day now," the woman said by way of a send-off, then turned her attention to a short-hopper that was powering up on the runway. Quinn and Sera couldn't imagine what it meant to have a good day out here.

With rebreathers firmly in place, they raised the car's canopy and got in.

"You know how to drive one of these things?" Sera asked.

"Sure," Quinn replied. "I did an hour in a holo race simulator, then one of Pierre's friends gave me a lesson on a real one down in the Dome's parking level. Nothing to it."

He closed the canopy, powered up the vehicle, and moved the steering yoke. The car surged smoothly ahead and promptly ditched itself on the other side of the road. An embarrassed Quinn applied power and managed to regain the blacktop, such as it was, where he followed a wobbly course, veering from side to side until he finally evened out a hundred meters or so further along. He imagined Amazin' Grace's amusement, but didn't look back to see if she was watching. This had probably made her day good.

"Nothing to it?" Sera commented, relaxing her death grip on the passenger seat only long enough to cinch her restraints a little tighter. "Are we having fun yet?"

They sped towards town, raising a plume of red dust behind them. Quinn gripped the yoke with grim concentration. Apparently the smooth and level floor of a parking garage differed somewhat from the fractured, decaying roads in the real world.

The ancient and poorly maintained pavement was cracked and sand-covered, causing the car to bounce and swerve despite the shocks and gimbals supporting the gyroscopic mechanism. What had once been prime agricultural land on either side now lay arid, worn out and useless, a desert, like so many other areas of the continent had become. It could not have fed the teeming millions that had once lived here. The Gulf's rising waters had flooded the lowlands and put Enterprise practically within sight of the new coast. The face of North America had changed markedly in less than 200 years.

It took only minutes to travel the short distance into Enterprise. The place resembled a ghost town of the old west. The buildings that were visible were deserted and tumbledown, drifts of dust piled high against their foundations, weeds and shrubs growing in the streets. Some buildings had collapsed or were tilting precariously leeward of the prevailing winds. The once prosperous town was all but buried in the failures of the industrial age and the Age of Chaos that had followed. It was a sad commentary on the inability of mankind to recognize its own failings and to take corrective action.

A small stone pinged off the car's canopy on Sera's side. She yelped in surprise and outrage. "We're under attack," she shouted. Quinn skidded to a halt.

A radsuit-clad figure approached them, hands upraised in a placating gesture. Quinn popped the canopy as the figure removed his rebreather. “Sorry. Didn’t mean to startle y’all. Just needed to get y’r attention before you passed out of town altogether. Been expecting you. Amazin’ Grace called. I’m Merv Oakes, mayor of our little community. Welcome t’ Enterprise.”

Quinn groaned inwardly. He’d wanted their expedition to remain a low-key affair, out of the public eye. Merv, seeming to sense his discomfiture, tried to reassure him. “Don’t worry. We didn’t call out the brass bands ‘n jumpy girls. Pierre commed me and asked me t’ help. Still, don’t expect to go unnoticed around here. We only get visitors a couple, three times a year. Let’s get y’all inside,” he continued, pointing to a low concrete and steel structure nearby, roofed with a layer of dirt. He replaced his mask and walked towards it. Quinn and Sera observed that the roof was covered with greenery; some shrubs, and orderly rows of what appeared to be vegetables.

Quinn powered up and swung over to the building, slowing the car near the heavy steel entrance doors. Merv met them as they alighted from the vehicle. “Used to be a shoppin’ mall,” he said. “Partly buried by blowing soil. We ‘dozed dirt up the sides and insulated the roof. Plants help to hold the soil in place and provide food for the co-op. Makes a handy refuge from the rays. C’mon in.”

He punched a button at the side of the entranceway, and the doors slid open, revealing a cavernous, dimly lit interior. They descended a double wide staircase which gave on to a mezzanine overlooking what had once been the mall. Most of the shops had been converted to habs, with their fronts closed off for privacy, save for single entrance doors. Some shops remained, carrying crudely lettered signs reading “Enterprise Food Cooperative” and “General Merchandise Supply”. Overhead, light pipes that extended above the soil on the roof brightened the interior and filtered the attenuated but nonetheless deadly rays of the sun.

People lounged on benches or wandered the length and breadth of the edifice, moving in and out of side corridors and up and down staircases to other levels. Their dun colored clothing reflected the gloom of the chamber, all grey floors and wrought iron railings. A few plastic palm trees and shrubs provided the only relief from the drabness of the interior.

"Just over 150 people, 'case you were wonderin'. When we're not workin' t' raise food in the hydroponics plant and the roof gardens, or maintainin' the water purification and sewage reclamation plant, we basically just walk around t' keep in shape. Everyone has a job t' do, so we all contribute one way or another to the common good, just like in the Domes. The glowstrips provide most of the necessities we don't get from the sunlight."

They walked from the balcony down a short non-functioning escalator to the main floor. People looked at them curiously, but otherwise minded their own business. A few of the men cast surreptitious and lascivious glances at Sera, whose clinging radsuit emphasized her voluptuous figure and child-bearing hips. Potential mothers were as much valued as prospective sexual partners in this society.

"Can you direct us to the hospital?" Quinn asked. "We'd like to get to work."

"Hospital doesn't exist any more," Merv replied. "Leastwise not the one y're lookin' fer, the old one."

Quinn's heart sank. Was his quest to end here?

"I 'spect you're really after the records. That's what Pierre said. Y'll find them in the records room in the civic center. Fortunately, that's at t'other end of the mall. Hope y'all find what y're huntin' fer."

The local dialect almost baffled Quinn and Sera, sometimes sending them to their wristpods for clarification.

"If't yeh need overnight accommodations," Merv told them, "Carl Tomkins runs a B&B on the top level near the main entrance. Doesn't git much business, but he's old and enjoys the company when he can git it."

"Thanks, Merv," Quinn said. "I expect we'll be here for a couple of days. We'll look him up."

Merv guided them to the last space at the end of the mall, a converted First National Bank whose cavernous interior now housed the town's offices and records center. He showed them the vault where the historical records were housed. These had been gathered from police stations, hospitals, and administration centers in the area, as it had become apparent that public institutions might not survive the ravages of climate change, air pollution, and the Great Plague riots. They had been boxed up, sealed and sent to the secure vault in the lower level of the Enterprise mall. Here, Quinn hoped to unearth answers to the tragedy that was besetting RichmondDome.

Together, they located the records from the hospital, and Merv left them alone to get down to work.

"What's a B&B?" Sera asked.

"Beats me. Some kind of sleep shelf rental, I expect. Hope he has food. I brought a supply of wafers, just in case."

They dug into the files, which were fortunately in more or less chronological order.

"Exactly what are we looking for?" Sera asked.

"First, locate any documentation related to births on October twelve and thirteen, 2061. Then find files on Kerrick and …." he consulted his wristpod, "El-Huseini and McCaskill. I have a strong feeling our answer lies somewhere there."

It took some hours, but they had finally assembled an impressive stack of musty smelling file folders. They had just paused for a drink and a snack when Merv returned.

He stuck his head in the door. "How're you folks makin' out? Findin' what yeh need?"

"Getting there," Quinn replied.

"Did you know it's gettin' late? It's almost midnight. If yeh want to put y'r head down tonight, y'd best head over t' old Carl's place afore he shuts 'er down fer the night."

Sera glanced at the ancient digital chrono on the back wall. "We kind of lost track of time, we were so busy. I guess we should call it a night and get a fresh start tomorrow, Quinn. It's been a long day."

"C'mon. I'll take yeh over there and introduce yeh. Y'll like old Carl. He's good folk."

The lights were dim along the mall's vast hallways, and few people were about. It was dead quiet, save for the gentle whoosh of the air circulators. Their footfalls seemed to ring loudly on the composite granite floors, echoing in the vast galleries.

Merv rapped authoritatively on the wooden door of what had once been a bookstore. A hand carved sign read 'Carl's Bed and Breakfast'. Muffled shuffling from within, then a voice, "Awright. Awright. I'm comin'. Don't get y'r umbilicus in a knot." The door swung inward and an ancient face peered out at them. "Ah, Merv. These'd be the folk yeh told me about. C'mon in and welcome to yeh." Merv made the introductions, then excused himself as he made for his own hab. Carl was small, well under two meters, his face leathery and wizened, no doubt a result of many hard years in this harsh climate.

In contrast to the dullness of the mall, Carl's hab was warm and cheerful. His furniture and wall hangings featured a Navajo motif, all primary colors and mosaic designs. Antelope antlers and the bleached skull of a steer at first repelled Quinn and Sera, then fascinated them once they realized that they had been recovered, not killed.

"Thanks for taking us in," Quinn said. Sera echoed the sentiment.

"Not 't all. Don't often get a chance t' talk with Domers. Always somethin' t' be learned. Here, have a seat. Make yeselves comf'tble."

Quinn smiled. He'd never before looked on himself as a 'Domer'. "Guess it's all in your point of view," he thought.

"How 'bout a drink," Carl offered, as he pulled out a clear glass bottle half-filled with an amber liquid. "I hear yeh don't have anything like this in the Domes. Try some."

He put tumblers in front of each of them and poured two fingers, actually measuring with middle and index finger. "Just two fingers fer beginners. Thet's all yeh git. Thet's all yeh need. Help yeh sleep better." He grinned and chuckled deep in his throat.

He poured half a glass for himself, and sat back to watch as Quinn and Sera sniffed at the drink and wrinkled their noses. "Just what is this?" Sera asked.

"Oh, don't yeh worry. Nothin' bad ever came of a little fermented mash and a nice hot fire."

They summoned up their courage and sipped the unfamiliar offering, not wanting to offend their host. It didn't go down well, much to Carl's amusement. When the sputtering and gasping had at last subsided, he said, "Now don't yeh fret. Second sip goes down much easier, now thet y'r throat is used to it."

"I think my nerve endings are dead," Sera commented huskily. She bravely assayed another sample with somewhat more success. It wasn't long before both she and Quinn began to feel the effects of the exotic brew.

"This may seem like a rude question, but just how old are you, if you don't mind my asking?" said Quinn as he attempted to control the slight slur that had crept into his speech.

"Not 't all. I'm a hun'ert fifteen. Don't feel a day over a hun'ert."

"Then you were born in ….." began Sera.

"Yep, in the year of the Great Plague," Carl completed her words. "Grew up in these here parts, and never even considered leavin'. Folks 'round here seem to live to a ripe old age. Could be somethin' in the soil. Sure ain't anythin' in the air." He shook his head and chuckled dryly at the irony.

"Then you might remember a local boy makes good story. Do you recall …?" she said.

"Donny Kerrick?" said Carl, jumping in again. "Sure I 'member Doc Kerrick. Who doesn't? Legend 'round here. I was ….. hmmm … let me see …. 'bout seventeen, eighteen when he disappeared. Doc did a lot for us, even though he was a rep fer Virginia."

"Doc?" asked Sera.

"Doc, as in doctor, a fixer, a guy who gits things done. I recall they had a p'rade for him onc't, here in Enterprise. Honourin' a native son. I was 'round fourteen at the time. Whole town turned out. Quite a show. Brass bands and buntin', school choir, t' works. Lots of pressin' the flesh an' the like. Key t' the city. Endless speeches. Bar-b-q. Yeh git t' idea."

Quinn and Sera both felt a thrill of excitement at finding this witness to history. There might be information to be gleaned here, possibly revelations that weren't available in the paper and electronic records.

"Do you remember much about the man himself, about Doc?" Quinn asked.

"Not a whole lot, just an impression of charisma an' a strong 'n forceful personality. I was kinda young then, an' it was a day to have fun, a day off school. If yeh want t' know more, you might try askin' Amazin' Grace, out t' airfield. She's a hun'ert twenty-three, so she might 'member more than me. Sorry to be mentionin' a lady's age."

"You said he disappeared," said Sera.

"Yep. On one of his junkets t' Europe. Went 'n never came back. Never heerd from again. Nobody knew where he'd gone. Probably murdered in a refugee camp or a derelict city. Had a big memorial ceremony fer him in Washington, they did. Had a smaller 'membrance here. Sad loss."

This was the information missing from Gus's file, the meaning of the question mark on the date of Kerrick's death. Was there more to be garnered here?

"Did you ever hear any talk of young girls being murdered or disappearing around here at one time?"

"Naw. Never heard anything like that. Talk t' Grace. She'll set yeh right. 'Bout time I turned in. Need m' beauty sleep, else I'll begin t' look m' age. You can stay up if you like, but breakfast's at 7. Don't be late. T'morrow you can tell me all 'bout the Domes."

"Thanks for your help. I think I'll turn in, too. I'm feeling very relaxed. We must discuss these matters again," Sera said.

"Yes," said Quinn. "We'll chat at breakfast. I'm going to bed, too."

The two followed on rubbery legs as Carl showed them their rooms. To their surprise and delight, they featured real beds, with thick mattresses and luxurious duvets, in contrast to the shelf pads and thinsulate blankets that passed for comfort in the Dome.

"Bathroom's at the end of the hall. Y'r allowed 2 liters of water each for washing up. It's metered so there's no mistakes. Sorry 'bout the restriction, but that's the way we live 'round here. See yeh at breakfast. Night."

Quinn had anticipated the likelihood for the need of an exchange medium, barter being the predominant economic system in the Outlands, so he'd prepared by stuffing his rucksack with trade goods. He wanted to be sure to pay his way and give fair swap for goods received and services rendered.

As he drifted off to sleep, a thought intruded, and he woke up long enough to put a memo on his 'pod to check the old files from the surrounding police services. He had little doubt that there was more information to be mined here.

November 14, 2204

Quinn and Sera awoke just before 0700 to the mouth-watering smell of something delicious frying, overlaid with the heavenly aroma of fresh-perked coffee. There was a brief skirmish for the 'fresher as the pair rushed to find out what was on the menu. Sera won.

"It soy-bacon. Almost as good as the real thing. Can't raise pigs 'round here no more," Carl explained. "Eggs from free range chickens, when and as we can find them. Coffee's shipped in from across the Gulf, from Guatemala. They can still grow it high in the mountains. We trade for local pottery. At least dirt's still good fer somethin' 'round here."

Quinn arrived as Sera was enthusiastically tucking into her meal, and Carl scooped him a generous portion. "Sleep well?" he asked.

"Not as well as I'd've liked," Quinn answered. "Strange bed perhaps or maybe I'm just not used to being that comfortable. I'll probably adapt by tonight."

They sat down together at Carl's solid oak kitchen table to enjoy the bounty of the wilds, available only rarely in the Dome in spite of its plethora of dining options. A citizen would have to be in the right place at the right time in order to take advantage of such uncommon good fortune. There was, it seemed, something to be said for country living.

Quinn and Sera told Carl all about life under the Domes, and answered his probing questions. Several times, Sera had to be restrained from going off on a tangent when the question of the Compilers and the administration of law and order in the New Society came up. Quinn reminded her that politics and religion were not suitable subjects for mealtime discussion, to which Sera responded with a glare and a rude gesture out of Carl's sightline.

Finally, Sera and Quinn were able to push themselves away from the table. "We have to get to work," Sera said. "There're a lot of files to go through and we'd better get started. Thanks for everything, Carl. We'll see you later on."

"Y'll come back here f' lunch, if yeh don't fancy dinin' on those wafers of yers. Just com me and let me know."

"Thanks, Carl. We might just do that," Quinn said, as the two headed for the door.

When they arrived at the civic center a few minutes later, Merv was there to greet them. "Just op'nin' up," he said. "How was yer night at Carl's?"

"Well, it beats anywhere I've slept in the Dome, and the food's great," Quinn replied. "I'll recommend it to all of my friends," he added with a laugh.

"I have civic business t' take care of, so I'll let y'all get to work. See yeh later."

The file folders were just as they had been the night before, and Sera and Quinn dug into them enthusiastically, sorting and taking notes and copies with their wristcomp data collectors. The backstory was beginning to come together, the past revealed.

Although the paper records for the precise allocation of the identichips were missing, the billing records were still intact, and they revealed some anomalous facts.

"Sera, look at this. The Kerricks were invoiced for two babies, but the McCaskills were billed for a D&C and a birthing kit. The supply room records show that three birthing kits and three identichip kits were sent to the birthing rooms in that time period, the numbers ending in 5, 6, and 7, the last two requisitioned together about the time that Donny was born. The chip number ending in 5 seems to have just vanished. There's no record of it being returned or destroyed. Wait, here it is. Just as I thought. That chip was assigned to a baby that died the day before Mary Kerrick gave birth, the day that Mrs. McCaskill entered the hospital, yet the death was registered as the Kerrick child."

"Meaning?"

"Either sloppy record keeping or deliberate tampering with the data. I'd bet on the latter. The discharge dates on the two bills are the same, even though Mrs. McCaskill's procedure was done a day earlier than Mrs. Kerrick's. According to the records, the McCaskill baby's chip ended in

7, but the records indicate that baby was born before the Kerrick child. It doesn't make sense. I'm sure there's been a substitution."

"Well, the El-Huseini baby was born three days earlier, so the logical conclusion is that the McCaskill baby is the one we should be looking at. We have to presume that Mary Kerrick gave birth to twins, then gave one up to the McCaskills, voluntarily or involuntarily, after theirs died. The numbers on the identichips confirm that. Let's check school and police records," Sera suggested.

The information they sought was in the state's central databanks, so the search was quick and easy. Quinn brought up the school records of the two children and put them side by side. He added a scroll of relevant law enforcement records at the bottom of the screen.

Donald Kerrick had been a model student who garnered nothing but praise from his teachers, and was consistently on the honour roll. He had never come to the attention of the police, except for the single occasion when he had rolled a car in a field and was seriously injured.

Apparently, Arthur McCaskill had been highly intelligent but a difficult and withdrawn child who gave his teachers a great deal of trouble. He didn't show up in the police records, but his father had been in more than one dustup with the law.

"Like father like son," Sera commented.

"Not necessarily. McCaskill Senior's crimes were of a non-violent nature. We have to dig deeper."

"I wonder if this is relevant," Sera observed. "Arthur was active in the drama club in high school, but Donald never seemed to show any interest in that area."

"So?"

"In university, suddenly Donald is interested in drama? It shows here that he participated in their drama club."

"Good. We're beginning to see more pieces of the puzzle. Now if we can just fit it all together."

A few keyword searches revealed the pattern of assaults in the area, followed later by several murders, just like the ones in the Dome. These were cross-referenced to several similar crimes that occurred in Mississippi around the same time.

"Now we're getting somewhere," Quinn said. "Except that Donald Kerrick's profile doesn't fit our killer's. He was a model student from a loving family. The records from the school's guidance councilor show that. Arthur, on the other hand, was just the kind of kid we might expect would turn out to be a sociopath. He had a turbulent home life and was a social misfit. Only one problem. It says here that Arthur died in a fire on September 24, 2078. Arthur's parents died in the same fire, along with his older sister. End of story."

"So what now?" Sera asked.

"I don't know. I'm stuck. Any suggestions?"

"We know that Donald Kerrick and Arthur McCaskill are somehow linked. We just have to figure out how. What did Donald Kerrick do after 2078? His profile from our databanks shows a life of significant accomplishment and public service. Even so, you think that Donald and Arthur are most likely the same person, don't you?"

"Not when they were kids, but later on. Donald's sudden interest in drama points in that direction. It's the only possible answer. We just have to find the evidence to prove it, then we have to prove that F-Kerrick is the one committing the murders in the Dome. When was Donny's car accident?"

"Wow! It was on the same night that Arthur died. That can't be a coincidence," Sara said.

"Wait a minute. Let's go back to the hospital records. I think we're on to something. Yes, here it is. I should have seen this in the first place. The blood types of Donald and Arthur are the same, and identical to Mary Kerrick's, all O positive, but Alma McCaskill's is different; AB negative. Whoever altered the records wouldn't have dared to change something so vital to their future health treatment. The same blood type, O positive, is recorded when Donald was transfused after his car accident. That's it. I think I've got it. Just a few more pieces to put in place, and I can turn this whole mess over to Benwright and have done with it."

Quinn and Sera copied all of the relevant records and downloaded what they needed from the databanks, then put everything back where they'd found it. A few last minute details to check on the next morning, then they could be on their way. Now all they needed to do was call for their ride home and spend another pleasant night at Carl's before departing Enterprise. All in all, a very productive and edifying trip.

CHAPTER 21

THE MAKING OF A SOCIOPATH

October 12, 2061

"Push! Push now. Harder! Harder! O.K. Relax. Breathe. Easy now…… Push!" Mary's OBGYN coached her each step of the way, even though she was more than familiar with the routine. The drugs helped some, but it was still a painful experience, just as her previous three birthings had been. She was soaked in sweat, drained of energy, and labour had barely begun.

Her husband Lou squeezed himself into a corner of the delivery room, trying to stay out of everyone's way and, more to the point, attempting to be as much of a non-participant as possible in the ongoing process. He'd been through this before, three times before, each time at her insistence. "You were there for the conception; you'd damn well better be there to help out with the birth. They don't call it labour for nothin'!"

Twins, damn it. That was all they needed. Two more mouths to feed. They loved all of their children, they truly did, but things were getting way out of control. The babies were two weeks early and, as with most twins, the doctor had warned of possible complications during childbirth.

"Brad. It's not working. We're going to have to do a section. Doctor Cross. Anesthetic please, quickly." He turned to the nurse, "Chris, hand me a C-tray. Mr. Kerrick, please wait outside."

"Is she going to be all right, Doctor?" Lou asked.

"Fine, just fine. Don't you worry about a thing. This is routine. She's just having a little trouble this time out. The birth canal isn't as elastic as it used to be. She'll do O.K. I'll let you know as soon as it's over."

Lou made a hurried and grateful exit as his wife went under the laser scalpel. He sweated out the next hour in the fathers-to-be waiting room. He had never been one for the affectations that had overtaken parenthood in years gone by; the 'we're pregnant' era, the 'Baby on Board' placards (even when it wasn't), the 'shared experience' births, the fake pregnancy bellies that some men wore in sympathy, the 'stay-at-home dad' phase. Birthing babies was women's work, raising kids was shared work, providing for the family was a man's job. O.K., so he was male chauvinist, a throwback to the 20th century. He didn't care, as long as his family thrived and prospered. The former was his responsibility, and the latter was made all the more problematic by harsh circumstances. Farming was a precarious business at the best of times, which these were not. The bank was breathing down Lou's neck, and he was teetering on the edge of a financial abyss. The hospital bill would tip him over it.

America had been a failing world power early in the 21st century. Foreign interventions had sapped its strength and cost it valuable political capital and credibility, even among its supporters. Constant battering by natural disasters had drained its treasury and devastated its industrial and public infrastructures. The legacy of the Second Civil War between the red and the blue states, late in the third decade of the 21st century, virtually ended its hegemony in world affairs, as millions died, refugees swept back and forth across state borders, and the land was laid waste. It had never quite recovered from that internecine conflict, as China and India claimed their predestined places as global powers.

The Water Wars of the 2040s, local conflicts, climate change, ozone layer depletion, and self-inflicted pollution of water, land, and air all combined to undermine the foundations of human civilization throughout the world. In many areas, society imploded and otherwise decent people turned on one another in an effort to survive.

In the Americas, by the 2050s, unusually hot summers had taken their toll, once again reducing the heartland to a dustbowl. The aftermath of the Civil War's lingering chemical soil contamination combined with mineral depletion and a continuing drought made for meager crops. Farming was, at best, a marginal way to make a living.

The next few decades were hard living, especially for country folk like the Kerricks. Lou grew up on the family farm, just south of Enterprise, Alabama, his parents barely scratching a living from the blighted soil. This had once been cotton country until the boll weevil infestation early in the 20th century, but cotton had been replaced by peanuts and soybeans which thrived in the sandy soil. Now, even those crops were threatened

When he met Mary on a shopping trip to the big city of Dothan, sixty kilometers away, he was immediately taken with the shy clothing store clerk. Making the trek to Dothan every weekend, he wooed her in the traditional way and had won her heart with his romantic attentions. They were wed in March of 2053, and he brought her back to the farm and into the hearts of his family. Mary was soon heavy with child, and presented Lou with a son, Lou Junior, before the end of the year. Within two years, Mary gave Lou another child; a daughter, Mary, then one more son, Walter.

Lou's mother died in 2060, and his father followed soon after, still pining for the love of his life. Lou and Mary had inherited the farm, such as it was, and stayed on, barely eking out a living as they raised their offspring. At least it was good to have the kids to help around the farm, and each other to rely on. So it was, in 2061, that Mary was once again expecting. Due to her age, 35, and the fact that her last delivery had been difficult, her doctor warned her that the birth might be problematic. Complicating the situation was the fact that Mary was carrying twins. When Lou and Mary arrived at the Enterprise Civic Hospital on the morning of October 12, 2061, they were prepared to endure whatever the fates had in store for them. The twins were premature, but were expected to have a higher than normal birth weight for a multiple birth.

"Mary's fine, the twins are fine," Doctor Bradley announced as he entered the waiting room. "You can go and see your wife as soon as the meds wear off. She's had a rough time and needs some sleep. How are you making out, Mr. Kerrick?"

"Oh, I guess I'll be O.K., Doc," Lou replied. "I'm just a little worried about how we can feed two more kids."

"As to that, I may be able to help you out," the doctor said, taking a seat beside him and leaning in conspiratorially. "It's rather unconventional, and you may have some moral misgivings, but I've got a proposition for you."

"I'm listening," Lou responded.

"We had another expectant mother in here last night. She's the wife of one of this hospital's principal patrons, and, as you might understand, we rely heavily on private donations to keep our benevolent programs going. They already have a daughter, but they badly want a son. Her child died within hours of birth due to an undetected heart complication. She's indicated that she would be willing to pay a substantial sum for a son."

"Can't they just adopt?" Lou asked, wondering why the doctor was bothering him with somebody else's problem. Didn't he have enough of his own?

"That's rather time consuming, and since her husband has made some powerful enemies in the system, he might not be looked upon favorably during the application process."

"And she's willing to pay a substantial amount?" Lou replied, the implications just beginning to penetrate his weary mind.

"Substantial," the doctor confirmed. "I know that you're in dire financial circumstances, Lou, and this is your chance to get out from under, and to give at least one of your children a singular opportunity for a better life. They'll cover your hospital bill and pay off your bank loans, not to mention leaving you with cash in hand."

"I don't know if I could sell it to Mary. You know how it is with her and babies."

"You have to be practical, Lou," the doctor pointed out. "It's a matter of survival, now. Times are tough. I'm sure we can work something out." Not to mention the boost this might be to his personal career, doing a major favor for one of the hospital's important patrons. Such service did not go unrecognized in his business.

A couple of hours later, Lou stood at Mary's bedside, twisting his cap in his hands and looking miserable. The twins were nestled in the crooks of her arms, and she looked contented, if a little the worse for wear after the surgery. This was not going to be easy.

"What's the matter, dear," Mary asked. "The twins are fine, so what's wrong?"

Lou's inner turmoil showed in his face, so he was unable to fool Mary. Soon, the whole story poured out of him. Naturally, Mary was horrified at the proposition. First she cursed Lou, then she cried, then she cursed him some more. He attempted to mollify her, telling her that everything would be all right and that they'd make out somehow.

Mary was exhausted. After a nurse came in and removed the twins, Mary slept at last as Lou dozed in a chair in her room. When he awoke, Mary was looking at him. The twins were once again cradled against her.

"Could you really give your own child away?" she asked.

"Not give away, sell." he said, before realizing that only made it worse. He attempted to justify his position, "Honestly, he'd have a better life than we could ever give him. These people are pillars of their community, and they have lots of money. What can we give our children but misery?"

"And lots of love. We can at least give them that."

"The McCaskills are desperate for a boy. They'll love him too, and give him every advantage in life that we can't. Really, we don't have to do it. I'm just presenting another option, a God given opportunity that could benefit all of us."

"I know. In my mind I know you're right, but I can't ever square it in my heart. I'm a mother. What else could I be?" The tears came again, and she hugged the twins to her. Lou approached her, trying to put his arms around her to comfort her, but she shook him off.

"Hold them," she said. "See how you feel after that." Lou took the twins and sat in the chair, clutching them to him. He knew what she meant, but the wretchedness of their situation drowned his emotions in a sea of despair.

They talked for hours, and Mary remained adamant that the children were theirs and would always remain so. It took time, but Lou, much to his surprise, finally wore her down. She ranted and she railed, but once she calmed down, her pragmatic nature took over. Lou was not normally very persuasive, but the logic of his argument combined with Mary's inherent practicality won the day. Desperate times, desperate measures.

They left the hospital the following day with their one child, Donald. Mary shed a few tears of regret, and Lou couldn't look her in the eye. The other twin was spirited away by his adoptive family, his true identity eradicated and replaced with that of the dead baby. The doctor covertly altered the appropriate records, and just as the dead child had been consigned to the hospital's incinerator, so any trace his very existence evaporated. This was not the kind of covenant that, if revealed, would reflect favorably on the hospital or on any of the participants.

Mary took time to mourn the loss of a child. She knew that he was better off, but she couldn't escape the feeling that she had betrayed her baby and that Lou had betrayed both of them. Time and life's exigencies made it easier for her to forgive herself and to forget the duplicity that had led her to this low point in her life. Raising four kids and trying to cultivate the marginal land kept her mind focused on survival. Now that they were out of debt and had some money in the bank, at least the interminable struggle to keep their head above water had eased.

* * *

The other twin began his new life in an upscale neighborhood in Enterprise, with his adoptive parents, Perry and Alma McCaskill and stepsister Lurene. There was no record of the adoption. As far as anyone was concerned, Alma had given birth to a normal son, without any complications. The truth was hidden in the details of the paperwork. Mary's other twin became Alma's son. The earlobe identichip implant numbers were altered on the birth records. A life removed; a life restored, at least on paper.

Perry McCaskill's life left a lot to be desired. As a youth, he was a bully and a petty thief. His accomplishments in school were unremarkable, as much of his time there was spent in the principal's office and in the detention room, when he wasn't skipping classes altogether. He quit university in his first year, having barely qualified for a position there in the first place, and after finding out that he couldn't quite manage to con the professors as he had his high school teachers. After his parents threw him out, he took on a series of low-skilled, low-paying jobs, and stole from every one of his early employers, losing many a job as a result. Drifting aimlessly, always at odds with society, always arrogant and rebellious, he took to petty theft and con jobs to support himself. Then he met Alma.

Alma was the daughter of a wealthy businessman, and as such, lived a life of comfort and privilege, always expecting from society more than she gave back. When she met Perry, something within her snapped, as she saw in him a part of her life that had been missing.

Pampered from birth, cosseted in the bosom of her family, educated in private schools, and brought up to be a lady, she had been shielded from the seamier side of life. Now, Perry eagerly showed her that aspect, at the same time managing to live comfortably off her family's wealth. Alma's parents looked on her new boyfriend with disapproval and did all that they could to separate them. This just made Alma all the more determined to be with him.

They eloped, and were married on Alma's twenty-first birthday, the day her trust fund kicked in, just the way Perry had planned it. He actually loved Alma, and she him, but there was a disparity in their ambitions. She had a lot, he had none. She wanted to be as rich as her daddy but, now that her parents had cut her off, she came to the realization that the trust money wouldn't last forever. Perry, on the other hand, was content to live the high life until the money ran out, then swindle people for more, or send Alma to beg additional largesse from her folks.

Ultimately, Alma would have no more of it. Realizing that her husband was pretty much useless in the money-making department, at least by honest means, she managed to use what influence she had to get him a job in the state's public service. She craftily maneuvered him into a position where he had access to a good deal of the finances for his department and, with sly suggestions here and there, unleashed his criminal propensities on the unsuspecting taxpayers of Alabama. Perry misappropriated over a half million dollars before they caught up with him. He was appropriately penitent at his trial, pleading guilty and offering to pay back the remaining half of what he had stolen. The judge, taking into account the not inconsiderable bribe he had received, accepted the plea and sentenced him to sixty days house arrest and 200 hours of community service. Perry and Alma came out of it with over two hundred thousand dollars that they had managed to conceal from the justice system.

"All in all," thought Perry, "A reasonably profitable deal. I can live with that."

Fortunately for Perry, his arrest and the subsequent trial received little publicity. Also fortunate was the fact that the state's Progressive Republican Party was not sufficiently diligent with their criminal background checks, and he managed to get a position on their fundraising committee. Now here was a turkey just ripe for the plucking. This time he managed to divert over a million dollars, and the party was loath to prosecute, as it would have materially affected their ability to attract donors. Chalk up another one for the bad guys. Alma was delighted. A night of wild debauchery in celebration of their burgeoning fortune and Perry's narrow escape resulted in the conception of their first child, Lurene. She was born in the spring of 2057.

Their next venture would not have such a salubrious outcome. Perry was caught with his hand in a corporate cookie jar, and those folks were not quite so forgiving. After much bluster about cheating shareholders out of their due, the corporate execs turned him over to the law, meanwhile pocketing for themselves most of what Perry had squirreled away, while claiming that he had hidden it so cleverly that it was unlikely ever to be found. A convenient tax write-off was the result. Perry wound up being sentenced to a two year prison term.

This was where things started to go wrong. Perry whined and pleaded to be kept out of jail. He begged the judge, he begged the prosecutor, he begged Alma to use her influence. He cashed in a few favors by ratting out some of his former criminal acquaintances, and wound up with his sentence reduced to one year. Alma was not amused, since one of Perry's old buddies was her cousin.

"How was I to know?" Perry complained. "You never mentioned him."

"Spineless, that's what you are," Alma retorted contemptuously. "Next time, take your punishment like a man."

Of course, there would be a next time, and a time after that. Over the years, their fortunes waxed and waned, but by the time their second child had been conceived, they were not only reasonably well off, but were viewed by some as pillars of the community. This was mainly due to their generous donations to local causes and to the high regard in which Alma's parents were held. Her parents remained unamused.

Such was the environment into which the young adoptee was brought. They named him Arthur, after Alma's father, and in the hope that the honour of the name might be translated into hard currency at some future time. In the matter of 'nature versus nurture', the issue was decided by the unwholesome influence of the stepparents. While they loved little Arthur, his upbringing took place in an atmosphere of tumult and turmoil. When Dad wasn't off to some country club prison, he was often banned from the house for transgressions real or imagined. Alma's contempt for this ineffectual man only increased over the years, as Perry continued to fail to provide her with the degree of wealth that she coveted. At least Arthur had his doting stepsister Lurene, four years his senior, to provide love and guidance.

Arthur followed in the footsteps of his stepfather when at last he passed through the doors of academia. Many teachers remembered Perry, and were not surprised at the way in which Arthur comported himself in school. He was disruptive and indifferent, preferring to use school supplies as toys and missiles rather than for their intended purpose. The main difference between Arthur and Perry, his teachers found, was that Arthur was highly intelligent, easily grasping concepts and turning in quality work, when he actually chose to do any work at all.

By the time he reached high school, he had begun to bully other students, especially girls. It was abundantly clear that he had a cruel streak, and was often referred to the guidance office for assessment and rectification. Had they been able to examine his home life more closely, a rational explanation for his behavior would have become apparent. Parent interviews cast little light on Arthur's deteriorating behavior, and Arthur wasn't telling.

Although Arthur had never been physically abused by his parents, the psychological damage of a house divided had its cumulative effects. Alma's growing contempt for Perry now extended to all males of the species, and she was becoming bitter and uncivil, even towards Arthur, the male nearest and dearest to her. She would often deride his lack of achievement in school, belittle his intelligence and abilities, and scorn his apparent lack of ambition.

"You're just like your father," she would tell him. "You'll never amount to anything."

Added to that was the unwanted attentions of his sister Lurene. She had entered puberty early, at age eleven, and had begun to fulfill her sexual curiosity by age twelve, Arthur being the object of her research. At first it was just looking and touching, which led to fondling, and ultimately to demands that Arthur perform acts that, at age 8, he was just barely capable of understanding and ill equipped to accomplish. Lurene's sexual curiosity extended to the exotic, and when Arthur was unwilling or unable to perform, she abused him, both verbally and physically.

The physical abuse began with punches and kicks, whenever he expressed reluctance to satisfy her needs. She found an extra thrill in the violence. Finally, it progressed to face-slapping as she straddled his naked body, rubbing herself against his barely erect penis. She climaxed explosively, digging her nails into his sides and drawing blood, then collapsed on top of him, alternately sobbing in ecstasy and laughing hysterically. She begged him to forgive her, licked the blood from his skin and, for the first time, gave him the gift of her mouth on his now limp organ. He recovered and exploded in her mouth, the pain of his swollen face and torn skin forgotten. Arthur was now twelve years old, Lurene 16. They both understood perfectly what they were doing. When, at last, Arthur took her virginity, their bond was cemented forever.

Soon after, Arthur began to dominate their sexual encounters, holding Lurene down and slapping her repeatedly as he entered her. Her body expressed the satisfaction she felt in this new aspect of their relationship.

He found it doubly satisfying when he climaxed, thus what had begun as sexual curiosity, had morphed into a sado-masochistic conspiracy. They were very careful and discrete, avoiding overt signs of the type of bond they had developed, and Perry and Alma remained blissfully unaware.

It wasn't long after Arthur's dominance manifested itself that the assaults began. Young girls, around twelve or thirteen, walking alone near dusk, were accosted from behind. At first, the perpetrator was satisfied with holding them face down with the weight of his body, rubbing himself against their buttocks until his gasps became groans of gratification, then vanishing into the evening. The police, entirely baffled by the lack of clues, settled for issuing a warning to the general populace. The assaults became more violent, as the criminal progressed to slapping and punching his victims after putting a hood over their heads. Sometimes he stripped them and fondled them, but he was too clever to penetrate them. School had taught him all about DNA trace. He would often force them to masturbate him, ejaculating into a tissue then making sure he washed their hands before he released them. Though the victims' descriptions of the attacker were somewhat lacking in detail, even so the police were able to conclude that the assailant was young, clever, strong, and well developed.

By the time he entered high school at age 14, young Arthur had become angry and surly. The pressures of his life were having a cumulative effect. He had few friends, none close, and girls instinctively feared and avoided him. In any case, he had no need of romantic entanglements. He had all he needed at home, and his nocturnal excursions satisfied his darker yearnings. He had briefly contemplated involving Lurene in his nighttime adventures, but decided that his enjoyment of those encounters would be attenuated by concerns over how she might view them, and the attendant risks her participation might pose.

The turning point came when Alma returned unexpectedly early from a shopping trip to Dothan. Passing Lurene's bedroom door, she heard angry sounding male grunts from inside, accompanied by feminine shrieks. Her brain briefly refused to apprehend the sight that greeted her when she opened the door. There was Arthur, naked, thrusting himself deeply inside the equally naked Lurene, his hands around her throat. His frantic groans were all but drowned out by Lurene's cries of ecstasy as she climaxed.

"What? ..... What?" Alma croaked, unable to believe what she was seeing.

The young lovers hurled themselves apart, Arthur onto the floor on the other side of the bed, and Lurene curled up under the covers.

"Just what the hell do you think you're doing to my daughter?" Alma demanded, assuming that Arthur was raping Lurene. "What kind of a beast have I brought into my home?"

Arthur's protestations of innocence had no effect. Alma was livid, Lurene subdued and silent, except for soft whimpers.

Alma took off on Arthur. "I should have known it was a mistake to adopt a whelp from ... from ... those kinds of people." She crossed the room and began to slap Arthur about the head as she continued to berate him. He dove across the bed and fled naked to his room, where he locked the door and curled up on his bed, sobbing. His head was awhirl with pain, the humiliation of detection, and with the new found knowledge that he had been adopted.

There was little discussion between Alma and Perry concerning the incident. Lurene's input was minimal, and she had few qualms about selling Arthur out in order to conceal her own culpability in the matter. Criminal charges were out of the question due to the public disgrace it would have brought on the family. So it was that at age 15, Arthur was packed off to a private school in Mobile. Before he left, he had attempted to inquire of Perry, then Alma, as to his status as an adoptee. More particularly, he was interested in who his biological parents were. His stepparents were hostile and uncommunicative, so he learned nothing.

It was no coincidence that assaults on young girls in Mobile began shortly after Arthur arrived there. By now, he was angrier than ever, in part due to the unjust circumstances of his banishment, not the least of which was Lurene's betrayal, but also due to the loss of ready access to the type of sexual release to which he had become accustomed. The severity of the beatings that he inflicted on his victims increased, as did the cruelty of the sexual humiliations he visited upon them. Even so, he was extremely careful to leave no evidence, especially that of the biological variety. Local authorities were baffled. They had nothing to go on, except for the vague descriptions given by the victims, and the occasional scuffed footprint of a common variety of sports shoe.

Apart from the growing brutality of his assaults, Arthur endured his ostracism stoically and finally buckled down to work in school, at last viewing the benefits of an education as his only realistic chance to succeed in life. His academic accomplishments were outstanding. He acquired two passions in high school; politics and drama. He was fascinated by the process of gaining control over large numbers of people with their acquiescence, and was even moved to join the Young New Republicans. His drama avocation took an interesting turn when, after playing several roles on stage, he found that his forte was actually backstage, in the makeup department. Having made himself up for such diverse roles as Othello and Mark Twain, he realized he had a genuine facility for the art of makeup, a talent he began to use while stalking young girls.

All the while, he was using every resource available to track down his birth family. He displayed a significant aptitude for electronic information retrieval, and was able to tap into the computers of the hospital in Enterprise where he was born. What he found astounded him. It didn't take him long to deduce the course of events that had led him to being given up by the Kerricks and placed in the care of the McCaskills. It was a simple matter of checking area directories in order to find out where the Kerricks lived.

* * *

In the sixteen years since Arthur had been adopted out, the Kerrick family had prospered. The payout of their debts and the infusion of cash had given them a new lease on life. Coupled with that, the drought had ended and the farm had begun to thrive. The blighted soil, with a considerable dispensation of government largesse, had been rehabilitated, and new methods were found to shield the crops from airborne pollutants and the increasingly intense u.v. rays. Peanuts thrived in the sandy soil, and soybeans were grown under protective sheets of biodegradable thermoplas. They even kept a few hogs that grew fat on the forage provided by the remains of the plants left over after the harvest.

The farmhouse now had a new coat of paint, as did the rail fences leading up the paved driveway to the carefully tended flowerbeds fronting the open porch. A new equipment storage building and workshop had been erected in place of the tumbledown barn. All in all, life had become quite comfortable for the Kerricks.

Mary was the second child born into the Kerrick family. Now, at age 22, she pretty much ran the farm. Mary and Lou had passed middle age, and were slowing down. Lou Jr. had moved on, forsaking farm life for a more stable and lucrative career in commerce. The third child, Walter, still helped out by maintaining and running the robot cultivators, planters, and harvesters, and seeing to it that the crops got to market.

The youngest boy, Donny, at age 16, was only a year from finishing his high school diploma in the nearby town of Samson. Like Lou Jr., his ambitions were not agriculturally related. He had hopes of a career in government, and had made an early application for a political science course at the University of Alabama. His academic credentials were outstanding, and his acceptance was all but assured. Donny could not anticipate the upheaval that was about to disrupt his life.

* * *

By age 16, Arthur had managed to assault more than a dozen girls, ages eleven to thirteen; these being his preferred victims. Police in both Enterprise and Mobile were on the alert, but their investigations were at a standstill. It was inevitable that things would take a nasty turn.

Pamela Miller, twelve years old, was Arthur's unlucky thirteenth target. Following his usual modus operandi, Arthur tackled her from behind and pinned her to the ground in a flowerbed beside a secluded suburban walkway connecting housing developments. He then began to rub himself against her while holding her hair so that her face was pressed into the soft soil. How was he to know that Pamela was asthmatic? He took her laboured inhalations and frantic efforts to raise herself up as indications merely of extreme distress, which would have been accurate, had her medical circumstances not been so dire. She was fighting for her life. Her struggles served only to inflame his desire.

When he was finished, he whispered into the ear of the now limp child, "Don't you dare move for at least a full minute. If I see you move I'll come back and finish you off." Then he made his hurried departure, totally unaware that Pamela had aspirated a significant amount of dirt and lay dead where he had left her.

The word spread quickly throughout Mobile. The authorities redoubled their efforts to find the perpetrator, interviewing citizens near the scene of the crime and gathering what little forensic evidence that there was to be found. They were in contact with the police in Enterprise, where a similar rash of assaults had occurred, and followed up on the obvious lead that the person behind the crimes had moved to Mobile. Due to the apparent shrewdness of the crimes, it didn't occur to them to look for a high school student, so they came up empty.

If he'd had any sense, Arthur would have been alarmed by the outcome of the incident. Instead, he was intrigued by his lack of remorse. He had never regretted any of his previous assaults; rather enjoying the afterglow and the memory of them. In this case, the death of his prey invigorated him and increased his sexual gratification when he revisited the assault in his mind, masturbating in his small room back at the private school. He vowed that, with his next victim, he would try out some creative techniques in order to explore this new level of sensation.

* * *

Sarah Lou Gallagher was tall for her eleven years, and somewhat better developed than her contemporaries. Arthur spotted her riding her bike along a walking trail that followed a meandering stream in a nature park some forty kilometers from Mobile. The city was getting to be a hot zone of vigilance and law enforcement, and prudence dictated that a temporary change of venue might be in order. Arthur was able to afford a used gyro wheeler from his meager earnings as a clerk at the local health food store, so transportation was no longer a problem. The wheeler came with a removable sidecar, ideal for transporting goods or whatever else he might need to move quickly.

The unsuspecting folks in Lucedale, Mississippi were not nearly as vigilant as those back in Mobile, so they were not unwilling to let their children roam free. Sarah Lou and two of her little friends had ridden twenty minutes to get to the park and were taking a leisurely jaunt along the creek, looking for a place to picnic. When they found it, they spread their towels on the bank and pulled their lunches from their backpacks. It was an ideal day and life was good. They exchanged stories and gossip, splashed barefoot in the stream, and talked and laughed and giggled throughout the warm spring afternoon.

They were blissfully unaware of Arthur lurking in the woods, watching and waiting for an opening. His chance came when Sarah Lou, announcing that she had to pee before they made the trip home, skipped happily off into the bushes. When she failed to return in a reasonable time, her friends went looking for her. Of course, she was nowhere to be found. Later, they were able to report that they had heard the ascending whine of a gyro wheeler as it powered up and moved away from them on a nearby road. By the time the authorities issued an alert, Arthur had crossed the Alabama state line and was wending his way along an overgrown trail leading to a secluded lakeside cabin.

Arthur had selected his hideaway from a satellite view of the area, noting that it was tucked well back from the nearest road and did not appear to be in use. On his way to Lucedale, he had broken in and cleaned the place up, preparing it for its imminent purpose with a stash of food and water, and a variety of ties and shackles on the bed.

The girl's remains were found ten days later, due to an anonymous tip. Apart from stalking and capturing his prey, and the stimulation of the assault, taunting the authorities was an extra kick. He had tormented the girl physically and sexually for two days before finally killing her, then had allowed sufficient time for the deterioration of forensic evidence before he made the call. Not that there was much in the way of forensics to be found, given the heat of the season and the abundance of insects and rodents in the woods. As a precaution, he had used a condom and, re-enacting that day Alma had caught him on top of Lurene, he had strangled the girl as he was climaxed inside her. This time there was no Alma to interrupt, and he stared into the girl's eyes as her life slipped away.

The killing itself, surprisingly, left him unfulfilled. Anger had followed disappointment, and he had hammered the lifeless girl with gloved fists until the adrenaline surge passed.

"Damn you, Lurene! Just damn you!" he had screamed as he struck the limp body repeatedly, startling himself with the revelation that his outburst might have been about more than just sexual gratification. On the trip back to Mobile, he embarked on a voyage of introspection and self-discovery.

Not that he was about to give up his wicked ways. Three more young girls would meet an untimely end at the hands of the phantom killer. He struck near Alabama-Mississippi border towns, always managing a clean getaway without anyone spotting him. He was growing more cunning by the day. Now was the time to take the next step.

CHAPTER 22

RAGE AND RETRIBUTION

Summer, 2078

Seamus O'Toole opened the front door of his farmhouse to find a polite young man standing there. He told the farmer that he was seeking short-term employment, just for the summer. The fact that Seamus' property adjoined the Kerricks' figured large in Arthur's choice of location. The youth's bearded face and long hair, coupled with an ever-present floppy sunhat and sunglasses, concealed his startling resemblance to the youngest occupant of the adjacent farm. Seamus was glad for the extra help and, as the youngster had requested only minimum wage and room and board, he was hired on the spot. Arthur's new employer was both astonished and gratified to have found a youth who was actually willing to do an honest day's work.

Arthur spent that entire summer and the one after observing the Kerricks, noting their comings and goings and their domestic routines and customs. He kept an eye on Donny in particular, and on more than one occasion managed to get close enough to the family to study them at first hand, sometimes at community picnics or sporting events or at their worship (even though interest in religion had waned markedly in the last half of the twenty-first century). He used at least two of these gatherings to infiltrate the Kerricks' home, knowing that they would be away for some hours, in order to go through Donny's papers and possessions, and to familiarize himself with the layout of the house.

He learned enough to recognize that, for whatever reason, he had been denied a life style that would have been the envy of most of his contemporaries. Familial love emanated from every corner as he prowled the home, opening cupboards and drawers and poking through old photo albums. He even appropriated, for his own pleasure and edification, a couple of data cubes depicting family get-togethers and daily routines.

Autumn, 2079

By the end of the second summer, he felt he knew the Kerricks, and Donny in particular, well enough to make his move. It was time for him to take his revenge on Perry and Alma for the shabby way they had treated him during his time with them, and the cold and callous way they had dismissed him from their lives. He had some ideas about Lurene's fate, too, for the way she had betrayed him. It had come as a shock, during the murder of the little girl from Lucedale, to find out how much he really abhorred his adoptive sister's complicity in his exile.

It would take some careful planning and timing and no small amount of courage to carry out his scheme. His first step was to go to Enterprise and kill Perry and Alma. That was the easy part. He still had a key to the house, and simply let himself in during the day, when nobody was at home. Alma arrived first, and Arthur greeted her with a baseball bat to the head from behind the kitchen door. She slumped unconscious to the floor, and he bound her to a kitchen chair then taped her mouth shut. When Perry entered through the same door not long after, his initial dismay at seeing his wife in such a shocking state caused him to freeze in his tracks, until he was dropped by a single blow from the bat. He, too, was tied to a chair.

Arthur moved the chairs to opposite sides of the table so that the two would see each other when they regained consciousness, then put full place settings in front of them, creating a macabre tableau. "The Last Supper," he chuckled to himself. "The very last." He was truly warming to his mission.

Lurene arrived from work just before suppertime, but this time Arthur confronted her directly. He had dreamed of this face to face encounter for years.

"Hi, sis. I'm home," he said cheerily as she came in by the front door. "How've you been?"

Lurene was temporarily dumbstruck. When she regained her composure, she demanded, "What the hell are you doing here. You shouldn't be here. Dad will kill you if he finds you in the house." Now she was playing for time. She feared what her little brother might be up to, and she used false bravado to mask her terror.

Arthur laughed. "More like the other way round," he said, nodding towards the kitchen. Lurene took two steps down the hall and peered into the room. "What the …" she managed to get out before she, too, was clubbed unconscious. When she awoke, she found herself tied naked and spread-eagled on her bed. Arthur was sitting tilted back on a chair, watching her with amusement. "Oh, God," she thought. "He's going to rape me." That should have been the least of her worries.

"Payback's a bitch, isn't it, sis?" He was enjoying this. His betrayer was actually trembling with fear.

"Now just wait a minute, Arty. You know how much I love you, how much we meant to each other. Didn't I show you how to live? Didn't I open up new worlds to you? You probably think that I sold you out. I never said a word against you, honest. You have to believe me. "

"Nor a word for me, either, bitch. You could've come to my defense somehow, but you chose to say nothing."

"And what the hell do you think I could possibly have said? That we were in love and wanted to spend the rest of our lives together? That would've gone over real big."

"You could have at least told Alma that I wasn't raping you." He had had enough of the whore's lies. He knew her for what she really was. "Shall we have a little re-enactment? Let's see how things might have turned out."

Lurene opened her mouth to scream, but Arthur shoved her panties into it. Without hesitation or ceremony, he mounted her and thrust himself deeply within her. She tried to cry out in protest, but managed only strangled groans. Arthur had not planned to spend a long time on claiming his retribution against Lurene. He put his hands around her throat, almost gently and lovingly at first, and increased the pressure slowly. It was then that she realized that rape was not his sole purpose here, and she began to struggle, pulling on the ties that bound her to the bed, thrusting upwards against Arthur as he thrust downwards. Her resistance only served only to increase his excitement. Now the pressure on her throat was crushing, and consciousness faded quickly. As her life ebbed away, Arthur released his hold on her throat and began to hit her, first with open hands, back and forth on the face, then with closed fists, on her upper body and head. As she passed her last breath, he allowed himself a powerful, screaming climax, still swinging his fists back and forth as he battered his betrayer's face and torso.

That he had no regrets was not surprising to him. After the adrenaline rush and the afterglow of a climax well-earned had abated, he dressed himself and went downstairs. Alma and Perry were still where he had left them. Their deaths would not be so easy. He began with Alma, using a length of baling wire from the farm where he worked. In preparation for this moment, he had fashioned two garrotes with wooden handles. Slowly, almost lovingly, he came up on her from behind and, as Perry watched in wide eyed horror, he encircled her neck and pulled the wire tight, causing it to bite into her flesh, tying it off even as she fought for breath. Then he moved behind the terrified Perry, repeating the procedure with another length of wire, so that each was able to observe the death throes of the other. In their last moments, they strained against their bonds, their faces exuding agony, and, watching them, Arthur felt a swelling of sexual excitement in his groin. He extracted his penis and relieved himself manually, undergoing his petit mort even as they suffered the real thing.

The sun had set when Arthur locked the house up after making sure that no lights were burning. He mounted his gyro wheeler and made the return journey to the vicinity of the Kerrick farm. In the execution of this final phase of his plan, timing was everything. He had noted that it was Donny's habit to go to the local high school dance on Friday nights, and to return home near midnight, driving his parents' car. There was only one route connecting the main highway to the farm, and Arthur waited for Donny to show up near a wooded area along that road.

Just after midnight, the distinctive shape of the headlights of an Arcturus III sedan appeared, moving carefully along the dark and winding side road, the muted whine of its cyclonic engine barely audible above the chirping of crickets and the croaking of frogs. Arthur waited calmly as Donny approached. He'd dumped his gyrowheeler in a flooded gravel pit nearby. If all went well, he would not need it again. Donny glided to a stop when he saw a form illuminated in his headlights.

"Hi," he said. "Aren't you the kid that worked for the Sam O'Toole next door for the last two summers? Need some help?"

"Yes to both," Arthur replied, making his way closer to the driver's door. "I ditched my gyrowheeler. Can you help me haul it up the embankment?"

"Sure. Where is it?" Donny asked, getting out of the car.

"Just over there on the curve," Arthur said, pointing vaguely ahead.

Donny walked ahead of him, into the glow of the headlights, and turned around to face Arthur. "Over there," he asked, pointing. Arthur nodded, and Donny moved off in the direction of the ditch. Arthur moved into the darkness beside the road, and lifted the baseball bat concealed in the tall grass. Moments later, Donny lay unconscious on the pavement. Arthur studied his face briefly under the illumination of the headlights, then carried him back to the car. He bound his hands in front of him and deposited him in the back seat.

Donny was still unconscious when they arrived back at Arthur's boyhood home. It was after 2 a.m., and the neighborhood streets were quiet and deserted. Arthur drove straight into the attached two-car garage, having moved Alma's car to the edge of the driveway earlier. He dragged Donny inside the house and deposited him in the kitchen, near the bodies of Alma and Perry. Their heads were stretched backwards, faces frozen in a rictus of agony, bloated tongues lolling from gaping mouths. Blood had pooled on the floor beneath their chairs, where they had strained at their bonds in their death throes to the point where their wrists were cut through by the thin nylon ropes. They had died neither quickly nor quietly.

Arthur's next act was to go to the bathroom, shave off his beard and cut his hair. He returned to the kitchen twice to make sure that he resembled Donny as closely as possible. He had spent the summer getting a farm boy tan within the limits of avoiding skin cancer, as most sensible people tended to do these days, what with the depletion of the ozone layer and the hazards that presented. He naturally had the same body type as Donny, and took care to adjust his weight over time so that it appeared to be as close to Donny's as possible. He stripped Donny and examined his body minutely for scars and blemishes, fortunately finding none. The only problem he observed was that Donny was circumcised where he was not. "Not really a major obstacle, unless somebody Donny knows intimately sees me naked," he mused.

After he was satisfied that no casual examination could distinguish him from his twin brother, he poured a pitcher of water on him to awaken him. Donny started back into consciousness. He took in his new surroundings, gaping in horror at the contorted bodies of Alma and Perry slumped in the kitchen chairs, looking like they had just finished the meal from Hell.

"What the hell….!" he gasped. The irony of that exclamation did not escape Arthur's notice.

"Relax, brother," he said, moving into Donny's field of vision. Donny gasped.

"Why, you're …"

"Me? Is that what you were going to say? You would have been almost right. I'm your long lost twin brother. We were separated at birth, and now I'm back. Sounds like a plot from a bad soap, doesn't it?"

"Twin brother? But I have no twin brother," Donny protested.

"Long story. Tell you later."

"But why am I tied up, and what's going on here? What do you want from me?" He felt himself losing control of his bladder, the fluid warm on his legs. Arthur looked down in disgust.

"Well, in a nutshell, you got the life I wanted and I got shit, and now I'm going to reclaim what should rightfully have been mine, and you're going to hell. Nothing personal. So just how are things going at the old homestead?" Arthur was drawing Donny out, trying to glean useful information and to familiarize himself with his speech patterns and idiosyncrasies. Eventually, Arthur related what he'd learned of the saga of their birth and separation, and the life that he'd been thrust into. They talked back and forth for the better part of an hour, Donny alternately begging to be released, then attempting to get Arthur to forsake his plan and be welcomed back into the family like the prodigal son. In view of the grisly scene in the kitchen, he knew that there was little chance of that.

Eventually, Arthur tired of the game. "Time to say goodbye, bro. I have a schedule to keep. I don't hate you, so I'll make this quick and easy."

He retrieved a pistol from the kitchen drawer where Perry normally kept it, turned, and fired, all in one fluid motion. The bullet hit Donny between the eyes. "Quick and easy, as promised," Arthur murmured as Donny slumped forward.

It wasn't easy setting fire to a fireproof house, but Arthur had that covered. Using a combination of a timed igniter, accelerants and an artfully arranged natural gas leak, his familial home would self destruct within an hour after he left it, along with the mortal remains of Alma, Perry, Lurene, and, ostensibly, himself. If forensics experts managed to determine the cause of death of any of the decedents therein, it didn't matter. He had thoroughly ransacked the house, and had hidden the plunder in a secure place along his route back to the farm. He wanted it to look like a home invasion and murder. There could be no link to him.

The last part of his master plan would be the most difficult. His greatest fear was that, having inserted himself into the Kerrick family masquerading as Donny, he would somehow give himself away. To forestall this possibility, he was about to arrange to injure himself in a traffic accident; not badly, but enough so that changes in his way of walking, his mannerisms, his speech patterns, or even his memory could be blamed on the accident.

As difficult as it might be to crash a practically crash-proof car, Arthur was confident that he could manage it. To facilitate this, he had disabled the gyros and the instafoam cushioning system, a skill acquired in autoshop. The turnoff from the highway to the farm road where he had waylaid poor Donny was a rather sharp turn, and Arthur, at high speed, aimed the car across a shallow ditch and into the adjacent field, where he cranked the steering wheel sharply to the left. The right front wheel dug into the soft soil, causing the car to swerve right and to roll over several times. Arthur was more or less safe, strapped in and within the confines of a steel and carbon fiber cage. After freeing himself from the seatbelt, he crawled from the overturned vehicle and arranged himself artfully on the ground. He used the tire iron to break his left leg and left wrist, painful as that was, and whacked himself on the head a couple of times for good measure, then hurled the iron bar into the darkness. Mentally reliving his revenge on the McCaskills gave him an adrenalin surge that helped to manage the pain. The rewards would be well worth the effort.

The accident scene was spotted quickly by a motorist on his way to work just before dawn, the still-glowing headlights providing a beacon to guide rescuers to the site. Arthur was stabilized and taken to the hospital in Samson, where his new/former family rapidly gathered to comfort him. They crowded into the emerg cubicle, appalled by his cuts and contusions and the sight of his swollen face and bandage-swathed head. Nobody took particular notice of the small cut on his left earlobe, where he had taken time before torching the house to exchange Donny's identichip for his own. He imagined that he had thought of everything.

"How could this have happened, Donny?" Lou asked, after Arthur/Donny had been patched up and it had become apparent that he had suffered no serious or permanent injuries. "That car was state of the art. It shouldn't have gone off the road or turned over."

"Sorry, dad," the false Donny answered. "I thought I felt the gyros give out on the highway. I stopped the car and got out to look for a problem, and I forgot to refasten my restraints when I got back in. I have no idea why the instafoam failed. I was so close to home, I thought I could make it safely." He lisped and gurgled through swollen lips, a bit of bloody drool escaping his mouth. The image was picture perfect for what he was attempting to convey.

"Never mind," Mary said. "We're just glad you're all right. The doctor said you'll have to stay here for a couple of days, then we can take you home." It was painful for her to see her precious boy so badly injured, but she took comfort in the doctor's reassurance that his injuries were neither serious nor permanent.

And so it was, that on October 4, 2079, Arthur took his rightful place in the Kerrick household as Donny, a member of the family, in good standing. His siblings helped him up the steps and over the threshold of the farmhouse where Donny had spent his first sixteen years, and had now been supplanted by his long lost identical twin.

Arthur/Donny thought, "I'm home. I'll be happy here." He had set himself on a path that would end more than a century later, in a very different place.

* * *

As planned, the McCaskill home had gone up like an aerosol bomb, almost taking the houses on either side with it. An investigation by the police and the fire marshal's office determined the cause of the blast to be arson. Autopsies of the charred remains of four people in the home established that all of them had been murdered by various means. The police did their best, but with so little evidence, remaining, they could not even decide how many culprits there had been, never mind who had done the deed. The most puzzling aspect was the fact that Arthur's charred body appeared to be missing its left earlobe, the one that normally contained the identichip that had been implanted just after birth. No trace of it was found in the debris. Not that it would have mattered. The identichips on all of the others were fused beyond usefulness.

* * *

Donny, having graduated high school the previous spring, had been accepted by the University of Alabama and was due to show up for classes the very day that Arthur was released from the hospital and was welcomed back into the bosom of his family. Arthur called the faculty of poly-sci and asked if he might be allowed to report a couple of weeks late. When he explained his circumstances, they readily agreed. He intended to take the time to bond with his new family and to gauge the success of his deception.

He pretended to be more seriously injured than he actually was, and somewhat addled from the blows to the head. He was slow in responding to conversation, leading the listeners to conclude that he had some kind of temporary mental impairment. This perception on their part had the added benefit of making them more reluctant to initiate a dialogue with him for fear of causing him, and them, embarrassment.

By the time he was well on his way to recovery, he was able to pronounce his masquerade a success. He felt a bit uneasy when he conversed with Mary; there was a feeling, a tension that he didn't quite understand. Had her relationship with Donny been contentious? For all of his self-styled cunning, Arthur felt he was at a disadvantage when Mary was around. He was thankful when the time arrived for him to depart for university.

* * *

"Tuscaloosa. Now here's a new and untapped hunting ground," thought Donny/Arthur, appraising the university campus and its environs as he sought out the registrar's office. Having pre-registered electronically, it took only a matter of minutes for him to introduce himself and get his class and housing assignments. The off-campus billet he had requested, so that he wouldn't have to share with a roommate or be surrounded by other students night and day, was conveniently located within walking distance of the campus, and just down the street from a middle school.

Donny buckled down to his studies in earnest, and for several months had time for little else. He was in regular contact with the Kerricks, and began to feel that he had become one of them. At Christmas break he was able to return to the family farm, where he was welcomed warmly, and even began to feel right at home there. He was still uneasy around Mary, who gave off an ominous vibe in his presence. He hoped that it would not eventually lead to a confrontation. His hopes would soon be dashed.

CHAPTER 23

DEMISE AND RESURRECTION

Autumn, 2080

After his return to Tuscaloosa, Donny worked hard and maintained a high grade point average. He was determined to do well in his deceased twin's chosen field, as politics had been one of his early passions, and success in that area might ultimately offer great rewards. Here, too, he joined the drama club, and distinguished himself in the role of FDR in Sunrise at Campobello. This also gave him access to makeup and wigs, some of which he secreted away for his own future use.

Spring approached and with it final exams. Arthur was too busy to think of anything else but studying, and even when he returned home for reading week, he closeted himself in his room and spent little time with the family. Soon enough, exams were over and Arthur took some time for himself, to just kick back and relax and think about his future. Long suppressed desires intruded upon his musings, and his resolve to remain circumspect in his illicit ventures began to evaporate.

He allowed himself a single, well-planned excursion to Birmingham, the largest city in Alabama, where his movements would be cloaked by the masses of humanity swirling about him. The city, once a bustling industrial metropolis, had been all but destroyed in the Second Civil War almost five decades before, but had rebounded strongly under the coalition government's policy of Recovery and Reconciliation. Barely noticed in his theatrical makeup, he lurked in one of the city's larger parks at dusk, and inevitably a young victim came his way. When he had done with her, she lay in the woods, bloody and mortally wounded. By the time she was discovered, she had succumbed to her injuries and Arthur/Donny was long gone.

Reluctantly, he returned to the farm just in time for spring planting. Even though his place in the family was what he had longed for, Mary's disquieting attitude towards him, a bad vibe that he sensed when she was near, caused him a great deal of apprehension. He had been at home for barely two weeks when Mary cornered him when the two of them were alone in the house.

"You're not him," she declared. "You're not Donny. A mother knows these things."

"How could you possibly deny your own son?" Arthur replied indignantly. "Look at me. Am I not the flesh of your loins, the blood of your blood? Who else could I be?"

"I've been watching you. You're the other one," Mary answered angrily. The rage that had simmered within her now erupted. "I suspected something right after the accident. A person doesn't change that much, even with the injuries. I know who you are and what you are. What did you do with Donny? You killed him, didn't you?"

Arthur was forced to make an instant choice; to attempt to respond with a convincing lie, or to take the problem in hand right now and finish it once and for all.

"Does anyone else suspect that I might not be Donny?" he asked deviously, partially forsaking his pretense. Her response would make his choice for him.

"No. Until this moment, I only suspected. You've confirmed my worst fears. I'm going to have to tell the family, and together we'll decide what's to be done with you." She spat out the words in fury, heedless of the possible consequences.

"I'd hold off on that if I were you. I'm still your son, even though you might look on me as a bad seed. If I'm as ruthless as you suspect, how far do you imagine I'd go to protect myself? Don't you think it likely that I'd be capable of anything? If you want your loved ones to remain safe, it might be a good idea for you to go along with me. After all, we wouldn't want anything to happen to them, now would we?"

Mary turned ashen. "You wouldn't dare. You can't go after all of us," she said defiantly, regaining her composure.

"It only takes one. Which one should it be? Lou? Lou Junior? Walt? Mary? I could take any one of them at any time. You can't possibly protect them all."

"You're a monster. What did I give birth to?" she said, her confidence waning.

"Don't beat yourself up over it. Donny turned out all right, didn't he? I'd probably have been the same, given half a chance ….. but you and Lou didn't give me that chance, did you? You're the ones who sent me to live with those lowlifes. They're the ones who messed me up. Is it any wonder I turned out as I did? That was your mistake, and I paid for it, and now it's coming back to haunt you. You're just going to have to live with it, literally, Mom!" He spat out the last word contemptuously, an exclamation of his contempt for her and what she and Lou had done to him. "So make up your mind. What's it to be? Are you going to risk trying to turn me in, or can we live together long enough for me to do what I have to do and get out of your life forever?"

"Just what is it you have to do?" Mary asked.

"That, for now, is my business, but I promise that none of you will be harmed if you leave me alone long enough to accomplish it. Do we understand each other?"

"Tell me what you did with Donny. I'm assuming he's not exactly safe somewhere."

"Regretfully, you're right. I found it necessary to dispose of him so that I could rejoin this family. It wouldn't do to have two Donnys running around. If it's any comfort to you, he didn't suffer."

"No, it's no comfort at all, and you leave me little choice." Her eyes welled up and her voice cracked. "It goes against everything I believe in to let you get away with this."

"Understood. You're a strong and determined woman. I get that, but it's not all about you. There are four other people involved, and you have to keep in mind what's best for them. So here's the deal. When I go back to university at the end of the summer, that's the last you'll have to see of me. Don't give me a reason to come back. Remember, I'm always watching, or I wouldn't have survived this long."

Of course, Mary had no choice. In order to protect her family, she would have to acquiesce to Arthur's demands. Still, she would bide her time and await her opportunity.

Arthur spent a tense summer on the farm. He kept a close eye on his mother, with his antennae tuned for any changes in the aether. He detected no difference in the family's attitude towards him, so he worked hard alongside them, assuring the viability and prosperity of the farm.

Working from dusk till dawn kept him occupied, and kept his thoughts away from areas to which they might otherwise have strayed. By day's end he was too exhausted to pursue his base desires, even had he the inclination. It was best that he keep his more perverse activities well away from home. His plans for the future demanded it.

* * *

In late September, Arthur returned to the university to complete his degree. Before he left the farm, he had yet another intense heart-to-heart with Mary, assuring her that any attempt to contact the authorities would have unfortunate consequences. He reminded her that he was a survivor, and that he could and would evade any attempt to apprehend him, at least until he was able to pay a visit to at least one member of the family. Mary reaffirmed her promise to keep silent about his true identity, and he departed, much to her relief.

Arthur's graduation year passed uneventfully, apart from several more unsolved assaults on young girls in Tuscaloosa and surrounding communities. In May of 2081, the family dutifully attended his graduation ceremony, blissfully unaware of the threat they were under, and witnessed the awarding of a political science degree, magnum cum laude, to Donald Kerrick. They went out to dinner to celebrate, and Arthur chose the occasion to announce his future plans.

"I've been offered an opportunity to intern with the Liberal Democratic Party's committee to re-elect the President. I'll be working in Washington, at party headquarters and in the West Wing. Even so, I promise not to lose touch with my family, and I plan to keep close tabs on those I love." He turned to Mary and grinned broadly as he said this. She returned his look with a hesitant and insincere smile, and quickly excused herself to go to the restroom to regain her composure. When she finally stopped trembling, she squared her shoulders and put on a brave face before she returned to the table, where the others were showering praise on young 'Donny'. She caught a look from him that conveyed the message, "We understand each other, don't we?" to which she returned an inconspicuous nod. Now, added to her earlier fears was the concern that this vile creature might actually gain power over more than just her family.

A month after his graduation and the joyful family reunion, Donny was to make one final visit to the family farm. Thunder grumbled throatily in the distance as frequent flashes of lightning illuminated the distant clouds from within. The storm threatened, but never came near enough to do more than stir the air sufficient to bend and swirl the tops of the trees far above his head as he lay in wait. His homicidal intent was not out of malice but merely for self-preservation. Of the many deaths for which he was responsible, he had regretted only one. This would be the second.

It would not be long, he knew. Mary attended book club at the library every Wednesday and would be home soon. He waited, his patience rewarded when a car's headlights came up the road and turned into the narrow laneway. The car squealed rapidly to a halt when he stepped into its path.

Mary leapt from the car and rounded on him, her voice quivering with rage. "What are you doing here? You promised to leave us alone. Have you come back to torment us some more?"

He didn't answer. It would have served no purpose. Instead, he raised the pistol he had kept for so long, the very one he had used to kill his own brother. Her eyes widened in fear and belated comprehension, just a moment before the bullet struck her between the eyes. She fell dead beside the car.

"Sorry I had to do that," he whispered as he examined the body for signs of life. "I just couldn't trust you to keep quiet forever."

He lifted her into the back seat and cleared away any signs of the incident left on the ground, just as the rain began to pound down. The car sank quickly in the flooded gravel pit, coming to rest near his abandoned gyrocycle. The flooded pit was too deep to ever give up its secrets. He returned to the place where his own car was concealed and drove home, confident that his secret would be safe now that the last perilous link to his past had been erased.

The next day, a shocked Donny promised the family that he would use his influence, bend every resource to find her, but instead he was able to guide the hunt in the wrong direction. Eventually, even the Kerricks gave up the search for Mary, but never the hope that someday she might return to them.

* * *

Within two years, Donny had managed to ingratiate himself with the upper echelons of the Party and had moved rapidly up the organizational ladder. His drive and ability were recognized and rewarded, and he was soon in charge of recruiting youths to the cause. He had exceptional access to the White House and to senators and congressmen. It would not be long before the name Donald Kerrick was one to be reckoned with both inside the Beltway and in other areas in which the exercise of power was a preeminent occupation.

Now, at the tender age of 22, his bid for recognition and power was bearing fruit. His ambitions were about to be fulfilled. The next stage in his plan would take determination and courage. He could not know that, within a very few years, the rise of the Compilers would give him the singular opportunity he would need to accomplish his purpose more than a century later.

Autumn, 2086

Newly-minted Congressman Donald Kerrick was attempting to look dignified as the media pressed around him the day after the mid-term elections, taking photographs and vids and clamoring for a statement. He'd paid his dues to the Party, worked his way up the ladder, granted favors and collected chits to be cashed in later on. It had all rightly culminated in his narrow victory over the incumbent in his new home state of Virginia, and he was barely able to quell the sense of elation that swelled within him. It was difficult to maintain a stately image when he wanted so badly to gloat. His public campaign had been conducted with integrity and honour. What had happened behind the scenes was not nearly so honourable, but the voters didn't have to know about that.

"Congressman," a reporter shouted. "Now that you're in the House, will you press for the reforms that you promised in your campaign?"

Congressman Kerrick grinned broadly. The answer to the question could have been a simple 'of course', but politicians are not constructed that way. "Damn the torpedoes and full steam ahead," he intoned gravely. Not very original, but the media didn't particularly care. All they were after was a sound bite that would play well as a headline or on the evening news.

After the press had finished tormenting him with more of their sophomoric inanities, he was finally able to repair to the sanctuary of the back seat of the limousine that the Party had kindly provided. This was his world, this was his new life, this was his due. Now would come the important work, just how to exploit the advantages he'd earned. He'd be sure to think of something.

Winter, 2087

"Mr. Speaker, please come in. Have a seat," said Donald Kerrick, graciously welcoming Howard Grantham, Speaker of the House, into his office. "How may I serve the American people today? What can I do for you?"

"Congressman Kerrick, we have a crisis on our hands" the Speaker replied without preamble. "You are in a unique position to serve your party. You're familiar with the proposals made by the Compilers, and you know that many of them have been adopted and are now the law of the land. The Compilers have gained status well beyond our imagining, and even now act as a third party in the minds of the people."

"And the crisis?"

"Well, that's just it. The more public support the Compilers gain, the less for the rest of us. Their very existence threatens our preeminent position in this country, and it seems that funding that we might otherwise have received is being siphoned off by them. The Party is getting quite concerned about their growing influence on the people. We'd like you to sponsor a bill that would limit …."

The import of the request was not lost on him. A visit by the Speaker himself instead of the party whip drove that point home. Donny was well aware that the party would be only too willing to take advantage of the naiveté of the freshman congressman from Virginia. If the initiative went well, the senior party members would take the credit, and if not, the bill's sponsor would take the fall. "Before you go any further, Mr. Speaker, I should warn you that I have a personal interest in the aims and policies of the Compilers, and our party opposes them at its peril. Implementation of the Compilers' manifesto is the will of the people. If we resist the people, then we're in danger of becoming the third party in governments to come."

"Nevertheless," the Speaker insisted, "a decision has been taken to fight back against what we regard as intrusions on the rights and freedoms guaranteed in the Constitution."

"You mean the rights and freedoms of our members to pork barrel and to go on junkets at taxpayers' expense and to gerrymander and generally to loot the treasury and behave like royalty. You're all afraid of losing what you regard as your entitlements." Donny was quite worked up by now. "If you think I'm going to go along with this nonsense, you and the party brass are sadly mistaken. I was elected to safeguard the interests of the people, and that's just what I intend to do."

The Speaker had grown red in the face during the tirade, and responded with equal passion. "If you think you can buck the establishment and keep your seat, you're the one who's sadly mistaken. Measures will be taken to strip you of any rank and privilege you may imagine you possess. Pressures will be brought to bear that you can't begin to envision. You'll toe the party line or you'll resign your seat."

With that he huffed out of the office so rapidly that he failed to see the smile on Donny's face. Donny accessed the small vidcorder concealed behind the flag above his desk, and a satisfied grin played about his lips as he watched the Speaker's entreaties, then threats, issuing from the tiny machine. Now he had them by the balls; he knew it and they would soon know it. Most of the people, those with more than a vague comprehension of political maneuverings, would take a dim view of a political party attempting to use its power to undermine the popular reforms proposed by the Compilers. It only remained for him to select the particular media outlet that he could count on to disseminate the story widely and to whip the prols into a suitable degree of outrage.

When Donny broke the scandal, he had already resigned from the L.D.P. and was sitting as an independent. The wave of popular support he received, the accolades heaped upon him by the general public and by the Compilers in particular, would have overinflated his ego had he not already arrived at that condition. He was lauded as a hero. Much benefit may accrue to champions of the people, and Donny had every intention of taking full advantage.

In the aftermath of the near collapse of the Liberal Democratic Party, the Compilers were certified to run political candidates in every constituency in the upcoming federal election. Their problem was not that they had too few applicants, but too many. It was, for them, a difficult task to select the best of the best, and among those young Donald Kerrick stood out. For him, ultimate power might be just an election or two away. He was already toying with the title 'President Donald Kerrick'.

Autumn, 2088

The contenders had done battle, the survivors hewing and thrashing at each other until only three were left standing, then two, and at last one. When it was all over, it was Edith Eldrich of the Progressive Republican Party who was entitled to don the vestments of office, the purple robes of the President of the United States. The government remained strong, but its control over the people was shaky, its very competence in doubt, as it struggled to deal with the blighted lands, the tainted air, and the scarcity of potable water, as well as a declining economy. With the L.D.P. discredited and the people badly in need of a savior, the Compilers racked up huge gains in this, their first election. The P.R.P. remained in control of both houses of Congress, but the Compilers took their hard-earned place as a formidable opposition, with Donald Kerrick re-elected, and appointed by the grateful Compilers as minority house leader. His meteoric rise continued, propelling him towards the lofty goals he envisioned for himself. Time would tell.

* * *

Emile was holding forth in front of a select group of surviving Compilers a short time after the election. "We owe a great deal to Doc Kerrick for advancing our cause beyond our wildest expectations." Donald's reputation as a fixer both before and after his first foray into politics had earned him the nickname 'Doc', a label of which he was most proud. "In view of the continuing crises gripping the United States, and indeed most of the world, he's agreed to place the advancement of our major agenda points at the top of his priority list. Most especially, he'll push for the establishment of the Domes and all of their attendant social and political restructuring."

"Yes. I concur," Brad said. "Our organization, our philosophy have progressed and matured. Now is the time for the final push. We stand or fall on what happens next, as do the hopes of mankind. Doc Kerrick holds the future in his hands. We can count on him."

The loss of Maria Sanchez and Ranjit Singh and so many of the others earlier that year, both Originals and fellow travelers, had been a serious blow to the cause. Yet most of them, those who had been quick to visit a Harbour, would soon be reawakened to help fulfill the destiny of the Compilers' vision. In the meantime, others took their places and moved the dream forward to its ultimate fruition. Their faith in Doc Kerrick was to prove to be both well-founded and sadly misplaced. The question would only be resolved more than a century later.

* * *

True to his word, Donald 'Doc' Kerrick championed the Compilers' cause in the House. It would take several years, but piece by piece, bill by bill, they achieved their goals. In 2096, at age 35, Donny ran for the Senate and won his seat. Now he would press his advantage and begin to position himself for a run at the presidency, most likely in the election of 2100. Over the intervening years, Doc had distinguished himself with his forceful and able leadership, helping to restore order to the country and in the process saving many lives. He served on committees and boards of inquiry, and became the public face of the Compilers' political wing.

He knew that he was a force to be reckoned with, but as with most great men, a re-examination of his goals and his prospects gave him pause. Was this what he really wanted? Was it achievable? What new opportunities, what alternative futures might present themselves if he changed course? He had the acuity to realize that a candidate for president would come under extraordinary scrutiny. The dark secrets in his past, if uncovered, would ruin him and threaten his liberty and the freedom to realize the ends to which his compulsions propelled him.

He allowed his baser instincts to guide him and decided that his best course lay not in the now but in the then, in the far future. With remarkable self-control, he had suppressed his more ignoble tendencies for all of those years since he had left the farm for good, and had denied himself relief in the greater interest of fulfilling his future plans. Having insulated himself as best he could from his former alter ego, he embarked on a daring plan to assure the fulfillment of all of his ambitions and desires, but in a time and place perhaps far removed from where he was now.

Accordingly, he made his application and confidently awaited the outcome. His public record and the accolades heaped upon him by his contemporaries virtually assured his acceptance as a Future. Yet another sort of candidacy would ultimately end in success.

Spring, 2099

Planning and approval for the Domes project was at last completed, ratified by national governments and finalized by the World Council of Compilers, the new organization that had supplanted the United Nations and had now begun to act a de facto world government. Before long, it issued a call for volunteers with expertise in all areas of planning and construction. They framed it as a patriotic duty; patriotic in the sense of serving the interests of the planet, not those of the few nation states that had managed to survive the ravages of the 21st century.

With his expertise in management and organization, Donald Kerrick saw an opportunity, and volunteered to oversee a segment of the construction of the first Dome, putting his career on hold for the greater good. Ever more tributes followed his selfless gesture. His motives were not entirely altruistic, as he had fully expected his display of patriotism to boost his career. He also had something else in mind.

He was assigned to the project he had requested; supervising the laying of the foundations of one of the first great Domes, near to the plague-ravaged and riot-torn ruins of Richmond, Virginia, in his very own constituency, and close enough to Washington to enable him to remind colleagues and opponents alike that he was still around, still a force to be reckoned with. His part of the project would take over a year, and at the end of it Donny/Arthur had added considerably to his prestige and to his credentials as a candidate for Futures status.

His public service ended in 2101, and he returned to the Senate, a hero several times over. He was proud of what he had accomplished, and followed up periodically, accessing the Dome as construction progressed over the next three years.

"Do all of these tunnels still conform to the original specs?" he asked the site foreman on a follow up visit, a year after his tenure there had ended.

"Sure," came the reply. "We've adhered strictly to the plans. Changed nothing. You should know, Senator. You're the one who supervised the foundation construction."

"I just wanted to make sure nobody's been messing around with modifications that might impair the integrity of the Dome. It's important that everything remain in place."

Doc continued to inspect the foundations and its substructures for several hours after the foreman had gone back to his office. Satisfied, he returned to Washington, only to revisit the site of the Dome several times over the construction period.

The Dome was finally completed in 2104, the same year in which Donald Kerrick's application for status as a Future was approved.

Summer, 2104

"Hello. Anyone home?" Doc's voice echoed in the vast, empty space beyond the dark oak door.

Moments later, Ethan Usher rushed into the room from the back hall, wiping his hands on a rag. "Sorry," he said. "We're just in the process of packing up for the move to RichmondDome. We'd normally have a receptionist there to greet you, but things are in flux right now. What can we do for you? Aren't you Senator Kerrick? I recognize you from the news vids."

"Yes," Doc replied. "I just received approval for Futures' status, and I was hoping to expedite the storage process here. You come highly recommended."

"Well, thanks. Glad to hear that. If you like, we can get the paperwork started right now, and we'll process you as soon as we're moved. Should only take a few days. Everything here's been disconnected and the memory crystals are already in the Dome. Won't take us long to be up and running again."

A week later Doc found himself once more visiting the newly-completed RichmondDome. Usher's Harbour had been granted space in the third ring, fitting for the level of importance accorded its vital function by the Council of Guardians. Doc was the first client in the new location, and he lay on a comfortable lounge waiting to be processed. The office smelled of fresh cut laminate and newly extruded plastic, overlaid with antiseptic spray and a simulated floral fragrance.

"Now this won't hurt a bit," Ethan assured him as he affixed the electrodes to Doc's temples.

"Wish I had a work-time credit for every time I've heard that one," Doc responded.

Ethan chuckled. "No, really. Just relax now and I'll run the preliminary diagnostic. Only takes a few minutes. Then we'll place the crystal and do the download. While that's going on, I'll cull some DNA for storage. You should be out of here in no time."

And so it was done. The endgame was in sight, and Doc could go to his just rewards at any time, confident in the assurance of his resurrection.

* * *

WashingtonDome was completed less than a year later, some 20 km inland from the historic site, and the government was moved under its protection, safe from the ever-worsening conditions outside. Monuments to the presidencies of Lincoln, Grant, Jefferson, Obama, and Falstaff, as well as other luminaries, were moved to mini-domes outside the main Dome, the better to honour their contributions in perpetuity.

Doc worked hard over the following two years, making frequent journeys far afield to offer succor to those who still lived in open cities and refugee camps as they awaited the shelter and security of a Dome. His junkets extended as far as Europe, fact-finding missions in support of the Compilers' ever expanding influence. His expeditions were not entirely altruistic, for in the relative anonymity of foreign lands he found opportunities to slip away and to revert to old, bad habits. Once more, he felt no qualms about satisfying his long-suppressed needs. More than a few young girls found themselves in dire circumstances, but none would live to tell of it.

Doc's final journey was to the fertile plains of southern Ukraine, east of Odessa, where the decaying cities and refugee camps had a degree of self-sufficiency due to their ability to raise their own food and scavenge the land for essential resources. He always anticipated the possibility of an unfortunate end to his risky sojourns, so he put his affairs in order before every departure, concealing any possible evidence of his culpability in former crimes and planting misdirection for potential investigators. His final task before each departure was to visit Usher's Harbour to update his memory crystal.

He even had the audacity to prepare a sort of tribute to himself. "My friends," he wrote, "Do not grieve for me. I have led my life and conducted myself with love and respect for my fellow man. My time on earth was dedicated to serving humanity, my leaving of it a result of that devotion. Having the surety that I will one day be resurrected to continue my service to mankind, I go in peace, with the serenity of mind that attends the certitude of a life well-lived. Lament not. I rest." He had wanted to add the quote, "Nothing in his life became him like the leaving of it; he died as one that had been studied in his death to throw away the dearest thing he owned, as 't were a careless trifle", though he couldn't quite recall the source, but he decided it was a bit over the top, somewhat obscure, and an ultimate distraction from his own brilliant words.

Doc reread the document with some satisfaction. Duplicity had always worked well for him. In the event that he might suffer an early demise, his final words would only serve to enhance his reputation and assure his status on the day of Awakening. After all, who on this earth admired Doc more than Doc himself? He was truly at peace.

"Fools," he thought to himself. "You are so easily deluded. That's the true foundation of my success, in every way. Mourn me, my obtuse friends, for I have further use for you." He chuckled aloud as he sealed the letter in an envelope and placed it where it was sure to be found should he not return from his latest mission. He prepared in the realization that he might one day fail to elude the authorities, that his luck might run out, and that such failure would not be any of his doing, but pure mischance. He knew that, for this last part of his scheme to be effective, he must not be taken alive or identified in death.

The Ukraine was not his final destination, but it was important that others believed it to be so. He intended to travel 1000 km overland to Volvograd, near Russia's border with Kazakhstan, there to pursue his unnatural appetites in that ravaged city where poverty and despair and lawlessness offered unending opportunities. Even had he anticipated the outcome of this unfortunate venture, it would have been unlikely to have deterred him from seeking the release for which he so fervently yearned. He set forth with the supreme confidence of one whose future is secure.

* * *

There were intermittent reports of young girls vanishing from refugee camps and remote settlements, but these were often dismissed as products of the chaotic conditions existing in the world, such anomalies being attributed to the lack of order and control. Some began to turn up dead; brutally assaulted and strangled, and the authorities could ignore the problem no longer.

The Compilers were still attempting to establish some degree of influence over the majority of the displaced populations around the planet. It was taking longer than they had anticipated. By 2106, the new force for law and order, the Legion of Sentinels, had been established, and had begun to investigate the growing list of missing children. With persistence and diligence and the aid of electronic surveillance and data analysis, they began to discern a pattern. Time and place and opportunity, a confluence that began to point in one direction. No one suspect was yet apparent, but the pattern thus revealed provided them with places and dates where increased vigilance might end the reign of terror.

Spring, 2106

The squad moved forward in response to hand signals from their leader, Captain Vladislaw Barinkov. Black uniforms absorbed the faint glow of security lights affixed to the corners of the factory building. A dozen shadows flowed around the structure, enveloping it in an ever tightening ring. Four gathered near a side door, stunners at the ready. The leader raised a hand and counted down, one finger at a time.

They burst through the door, spreading outward in a semi-circle, night vision goggles revealing …. nothing. The empty concrete floor stretched into the distance, populated only by support pillars. They halted in place, listening. A sound, faint, anguished. A soul in peril. Barinkov tapped his com three times, signaling the rest of the squad to reposition.

Upwards they moved, composite soles whispering over metal stairs, ramps, catwalks. Whimpers, quiet sobs echoed in the stillness of the darkened galleries. The muted cries were closer now, only a few strides away, but growing fainter. Barinkov poked his head around a pillar and saw a shape moving in the far corner, crouched beside a small figure, hands on its throat. He switched off his night vision, signaling the three men behind him to do the same, then turned on a floodlight built into his helmet. The larger form moved away from the smaller one moments before the lights came on.

The child lay on a mattress, supine, head bent back over the edge, dead eyes reflecting the bright light. A figure down on one knee beside her, knuckles momentarily pressed against its temples, weeping. It sprang up, a man-shape, naked white body gleaming in the lights from the helmets of the startled Russian Sentinels. In spite of their professionalism, they momentarily froze in place, bewildered by the scene before them, barely able to comprehend the evidence of their eyes. The man reacted more quickly than his stunned pursuers, hurling himself through a nearby door and slamming it shut after him. The Sentinels sprinted in pursuit, only to find the door immovably locked.

"Another route," Barinkov snapped at his second. He commed the rest of his squad to hold the perimeter and watch for the fugitive.

His lieutenant consulted a handheld screen and motioned far to the left. They rushed to the next door and into a side corridor. A phantom darted out of sight around a distant corner. They arrived there just in time to see him crossing a catwalk leading out over the abandoned tank farm.

Storage tanks once filled with the solvents the factory had formerly produced stretched row on row into the darkness. Most of their contents had long since evaporated, vented into the air through safety relief valves as the pressure of the expanding vapors built up within. Nonetheless, many of the tanks held small amounts of the solvents, and large volumes of highly flammable vapors. Even now, their blended odors fouled the still night air.

The fugitive ran, leaping from platform to platform, easily outpacing the heavily burdened Sentinels. Barinkov called up his sniper. It was their only chance to stop their quarry before he vanished into the darkness. A rifle cracked, once, twice. The first shot fractured a rusting relief valve, the second hit the iron tank just below it, sparking the escaping vapor into yellow incandescence. Too late Barinkov realized his error. The tank exploded with a roar, setting off a chain reaction in the heavy fumes clinging near to the ground, denting nearby tanks, and in turn releasing their volatile burdens.

In mere moments the entire tank farm ignited in a series of detonations, as pent up gases heated and burst forth from rents in weakened tanks and from overburdened relief valves. Of the pursuers, nothing remained. Likewise, the pursued was consumed, not a trace to be found. Even his clothing was turned to ash in the resulting conflagration, as the factory building was laid waste.

The ensuing investigation laid the blame for the disaster on Captain Barinkov. Com records supported the finding. As for the perpetrator, no forensic traces were found to help identify him, no witnesses, no evidence of any kind. Even his transport, concealed among the storage tanks, had been reduced to unrecognizable scrap.

The charred remains of the girl were buried and with her the last vestiges of a reign of terror that had gone on for a quarter of a century and had ranged over a large portion of the planet. Of course, the authorities could not know that, for they lacked the information necessary to connect the dots.

Doc vanished, his mortal remains no more than ashes scattered over the ruins of a tank farm in far off Russia. This was not quite the way he had planned his demise, but close enough. Doc's peculiar mindset did not allow him to care much one way or another about the specific circumstances of his passing, though he would have preferred it be more spectacular, more public, more heroic, as befitted his self-image. His Futures' status assured, he knew he would one day rise again, to fulfill his self-appointed destiny.

His friends and colleagues came to believe that he had somehow gone missing in the Ukraine, in pursuit of the furthering of the greater good, in the service of his fellow man. An investigation did nothing to change that perception, as the evidence Doc had left behind prior to his departure bolstered that conclusion. At his memorial, he was lionized, due homage being paid by those who thought they knew him best. His letter was read aloud, and they wept. His reputation grew. Ironically, his eulogy included the quote, "Nothing in his life became him like the leaving of it."

Almost a century would pass before the evil resurfaced.

Spring, 2190

"Joyful Awakening to you," the tech said, welcoming him to the future, in the last decade of the 22nd century.

"Joyful indeed," thought Doc, grinning up at her. "I'm back."

CHAPTER 24

A REVERSAL OF FORTUNES

November 15, 2204

Quinn and Sera were able to wrap up their work in Enterprise by the following day. They called for a flyer to pick them up, then said their goodbyes to Carl and Merv, expressing gratitude for their help, then made their way back to the airfield. Amazin' Grace, still at her post, greeted them like long lost friends.

"Have a good time in Enterprise, did yeh? Looks like y're takin' back a bagful of souvenirs," she chuckled, referring to the case full of files they'd gathered.

"Without a doubt the entertainment capital of Alabama," Quinn declared, playing along. "Carl said that you might be able to fill us in on some happenings around here about a century or so ago, around the time Doc Kerrick paid a return visit. Carl apologizes for telling us how old you are, by the way."

"No problem. Proud of it. So, what d' yeh need t' know?"

"Do you remember anything about Doc Kerrick?"

"Ha! Now there was a case and a half. He was here round 'bout '03, I think. Big t' do. I was on the welcomin' committee, helping t' get things set up and show him a good time when he wasn't busy with official functions. He was cute, I mean real cute. Brought him food 'n treats 'n things in his motel room. Tried to give him more, if yeh know what I mean, 'n here's me a hot little number at 22 years old 'n he never gave me a tumble. Queer, if yeh ask me."

"So you …."

"Tried t' tickle his fancy, yeah, but he was no Bill Clinton."

"Who?"

"Never mind. It was way before even my time. Doc was sociable 'n outgoing, but you never heerd of him attached to any woman. An odd duck."

"Do you recall anything about young girls disappearing or being murdered a couple of decades before that?"

"No. Sorry. Nothin' like thet. Life was kinda peaceable in these here parts, far as I know."

"Well, thanks for your help, Grace. Looks like our ride's here. Maybe we'll see you the next time we decide to vacation in the sun and sand. Drop in if you're ever up RichmondDome way."

Grace cackled with laughter. "I'll do thet, 'n y'll always be welcome t' come see us again. I'll still be around. Count on it. Good luck t' the two of yeh. Y'all come back now, y'heah."

" 'Bye, Grace," Sera said, waving, as she and Quinn donned their rebreathers and walked back out to the tarmac. "I must have been here too long. I'm beginning to understand what she's saying."

They threw their packs and the file case into the flyer as they greeted the pilot, then strapped in and gave Grace a final wave before the craft ascended rapidly into the pollution hazed blue sky. From a great height, there was a rough beauty to the land. It was easy to forget that, on the ground, it was a symbol of mankind's foolishness and failures.

* * *

Quinn commed Pierre the moment he passed through their habs portal. “We’re back,” he said. “What news?”

“We’ve got the Shadows watching your friend 24/7,” he informed Quinn. “They have the building under surveillance, and we’ve arranged for some spy cams to be concealed in the corridor outside Kerrick’s hab. That might take a few days. It took some doing, but I’ve set it up so that the Shadows report directly to me. Nothing so far. What about you?”

“The trip was very worthwhile. We uncovered considerable information from the archived files, and from interviewing some people who were actually there a century ago.” Quinn continued, excitedly outlining what they had found out about the babies being switched at birth, with the apparent replacement of one child with another, the attacks on young girls when Doc was in his teenage years, and Doc’s seeming lack of interest in women.

At the end of it, Pierre deflated Quinn by commenting, “It’s still pretty thin. You don’t actually have anything directly connecting Kerrick to the present crimes, or even to the crimes that took place over a hundred years ago. It’s all pretty circumstantial. As an Arbiter, it’s unlikely I’d even let this case get beyond the hearing stage with the evidence you’ve presented so far. Kerrick has always portrayed himself as a pillar of the community, and nothing you’ve found so far contradicts that.”

“What about when he apparently replaced his brother?” Quinn protested.

“Circumstantial,” Pierre interrupted. “Still no more than conjecture. That he might have been given away at birth wasn’t his fault, and you don’t have any corroboration that Donny Kerrick was actually Arthur McCaskill. You need proof before we can act. Can you present facts rather than inferences and suppositions?”

Quinn was getting frustrated. “So the whole trip was a waste of time?” he asked.

“No, not at all” Pierre replied. “You’ve often said it yourself; good old fashioned detective work. You have to build a case before you bring it before the Council of Arbiters. You need solid evidence, both circumstantial and physical. If you can find witnesses, so much the better, then we can put all of the puzzle pieces together. We still have much work to do, my friend.

I'll keep you posted on the Shadows. Let me know if you find anything more." With that he rang off.

Quinn sat with his head in his hands. Sera, who had been hovering in the background, listening in, attempted to comfort him. "Don't take it so hard. We've made a lot of progress since this thing began, and as Pierre said, what we found in Enterprise fills in many pieces of the puzzle that we can use as evidence against him later on."

"In my mind I know you and Pierre are right, but we have to nail this bastard, and we can't wait until he strikes again. I'm going to have to go back into his hab. When I was there the last time, there was something about it that just didn't look right. He's reconfigured it in a way that puts the dimensions off, but not by much. I'm sure there's evidence there somewhere."

"Why don't you give that job to the Shadows?"

"Because they won't know what to look for, or if they find anything, they might not recognize it as evidence. They're trained in law enforcement, not in investigative techniques. They're likely to be somewhat ham-handed. I've been in there before, and I know what to do."

He commed Pierre again. "Can you get the Shadows to let you know if Kerrick goes out someplace where he'll be away from his hab long enough for me to go in again and look around? I need to have another look. If you need physical evidence, that's where it's likely to be."

"I can do that," Pierre replied. "Aren't you taking a risk that you might get caught, or tip him off, so that he might destroy the evidence or go to ground?"

"Let me worry about that. The risk is worth it if we can get him now."

"Right, then. It might not be for a few more days, but I'll let you know when and if."

Quinn sat back, somewhat placated by the prospect of action in advancing his case against Doc Kerrick. He would have preferred to have been on the move immediately, and the possibility of having to wait an indeterminate length of time was maddening. In the meantime, he and Sera unpacked the case of files they had retrieved and began to re-examine them piece by piece.

November 19, 2204

Vale Chang sat in front of a com screen in the psych ward of Seabrook Hospital. She'd been in there for almost two weeks, undergoing physical and mental rehabilitation. She was still fretful and withdrawn, as the after effects of her ordeal lingered. Now that her strength was returning, she was going through a battery tests to determine if her ability to smell colors was real. She welcomed the diversion and was eager to prove her abilities.

"This test is to determine your ability to recognize colors visually," Doctor Gold informed her. "The screen will flash a series of colors, and all you have to do is to name them."

Vale nodded. "That's easy," she said. "I could do that with my eyes closed."

"We'll get to that later," Dr. Gold said.

When the colors came up on the screen one by one, she correctly identified each of them, as the doctor stood by and recorded the session. "That was too easy. Give me something difficult to do."

"O.K. The reason we're using a screen instead of swatches or tiles is to make sure that paints and dyes don't influence your sense of smell. Now I'm going to put a blindfold on you, and I want you to try again, O.K.?"

Once again Vale nodded. "This is fun," she said.

When the blindfold was in place, the colors were flashed on the screen once more, in random order. Again Vale was able to correctly identify each one.

"Astonishing," the doctor remarked. "I wouldn't have believed it if I hadn't seen it for myself. Next, we're going to put this mask over your nose and mouth. It will feed you purified air, so that no outside odors influence you."

With the mask in place and the blindfold on, Vale was unable to identify a single color.

"Just as we expected," the doctor said. "You do appear to have the ability to smell colors. We'll repeat the tests tomorrow, in a different way, but I'm convinced now. Can you tell me how you do it? What does it feel like to you?"

"Mmmm. It's no different than if I can see a flower and smell it at the same time. Its color is just another type of smell that comes from it."

"What does a color smell like?"

"Something like taste, but in my nose. Blue is sweet and flowery. Red is bitter and spicy."

The following day, the doctor continued the testing.

"In this test, you'll be blindfolded again, and I'm going to bring several people into the room, one at a time. Tell me what you can sense about them."

"O.K. Do I know any of them?"

"You tell me," Dr. Gold replied.

The first person was a nurse, wearing the light pink coveralls of her profession.

"Pink," Vale said immediately. "And pale green."

"Nurse. Are you wearing anything green?" Dr. Gold asked her.

"No, doctor. Nothing."

"Vale, what do you mean by pale green?"

"Nice, warm, loving."

"You can smell what people are like?"

"Yes. Everyone has a color."

"This is an interesting development," the doctor murmured to himself.

The next person to enter the room was Max Ford, the tech who had rescued Vale. She shrieked in delight.

"It's you," she said, tearing off the blindfold. "You're the one who found me. You're green, I mean you're dressed in green, and you're pale green, too. Thank you for saving me."

Max laughed with pleasure. "You're quite welcome, little miss. I'm glad I could be of help."

Doctor Gold recorded all of this with growing astonishment. He amended his test schedule to include a different kind of test specimen. He arranged to bring in an elderly woman who was afflicted with a physical disability beyond the scope of modern medicine to cure. She had spent several years in the hospital, and was deformed, and distressed by her ailment.

"Orange," said Vale.

"Orange?" the doctor asked.

"Yes. She's very unhappy, and very annoyed about something."

"Vale, what kind of person would smell red?"

"Mean, nasty, cruel," she answered.

Several more tests on a similar note proved Vale's ability not only to smell colors, but also mood and personality. But what might that have to do with the suspect in her abduction and assault? He hadn't appeared to be wearing red on the secvid, so could she have been smelling his mood, his persona? What kind of person, in the New Society, would be so mentally warped as to smell red? There couldn't be that many, so would it be possible to use Vale's unusual ability to track him down? These were questions for other experts to examine, and accordingly, Dr. Gold filed his report to those authorities.

The little girl was recovering well from her ordeal, and with a maturity that belied her physical age, showed an unexpected degree of understanding of her unusual abilities and the theories behind them. There would be a few more weeks of treatment and more tests, but she would recuperate with time and loving care.

November 20, 2204

Doc was in a hurry. It was uncharacteristic of him to sleep late. He had an appointment to keep, and he took pride in being punctual. As he stepped into the hall, Ujo Vreem's portal opposite also slid aside.

"Good morning to you, citizen," Doc greeted him.

"And a very good morn to you, sir," Ujo returned, in his usual sycophantic manner. Ujo's eyes widened slightly as he studied Doc's face, and the latter, alerted that something was amiss, began to retreat into his hab.

"Excuse me, I've forgotten something," he said, as his portal slid shut. Rushing to the nearest mirror, he saw what had caught Ujo's attention. In his haste to get ready, he had not properly secured his left sideburn. The bottom half of it was swinging loose, thus revealing its spurious nature. Doc fastened it properly and once again went back into the corridor. Ujo's portal was closed, but Doc was able to hear an excited murmuring directly behind it. He put his ear against the panel and heard Ujo in animated conversation with somebody.

"Yes, I saw him just now," Ujo was saying, apparently into his com, for the exchange was decidedly one sided. "It's urgent that I speak with you. I've something very unusual to report.... This afternoon?...1300 hours?..... All right. I'll see you there." Silence.

Doc slipped back into his hab. "This could be serious," he reflected. "I may have to do something quickly. Vreem is obviously an informer. His recent and sudden arrival here could be a danger signal. I should have picked up on that." With characteristic intellect and cunning, he examined the problem from every angle and arrived at a drastic yet practical solution.

Once more he entered the hallway. He could not know that his luck was still holding, since the Shadows had not yet had an opportunity to install the spy cams. He rapped on Ujo's portal, which slid aside after an eyeball appeared briefly in the spy hole.

"F-Kerrick. What might I do for y'r Honour this day?" Ujo welcomed him as the portal slid aside. He appeared nervous, and Doc recognized that his reversion to the idiom of his birthplace indicated that he was flustered.

"An urgent and personal matter I'd like to discuss with you," Doc replied.

"Well, then, do come in. It's a privilege to have such as y'rself gracing my humble digs."

Doc entered, and was appalled at the lack of taste displayed by his neighbor. It appeared as if he'd appropriated used furniture from the local Relaxation Centers. The place was in a state of disarray such as might have been left by undisciplined children.

"Pardon the mess, y'r honour. I haven't had a chance to clean up today, and the cleaning 'bots are not fully charged," he lied.

"Looks like the place hasn't been cleaned in days," Doc observed.

"Well, there's no need to be rude," Ujo replied, offended.

Doc stepped forward and grasped the smaller man by the throat. "Who are you and what are you doing here? Why are you spying on me and who sent you? You'd better answer me, and tell the truth!"

Ujo croaked and gasped. When Doc slackened his grip on Ujo's windpipe, he was able to wheeze, "No sir. You've got me all wrong. I'm nowt but an ordinary citizen trying to make an honest day's wage. I earn my time credits like anyone else, by serving the interests of our Dome."

"And just whose interests are you serving today?" Doc demanded, tightening his grip slightly.

"No … nobody's. I've done nowt to cause offense to y'r worship. Why're you doing this to me?" It began to dawn on Ujo that he was in serious trouble, and that he'd better be careful of what he said to this obviously deranged Future. "It was just … that is, I was only trying to …"

"To inform on me to the person at the other end of that call you just made on your com," Doc shouted. He hurled Ujo onto the grimy, junk covered couch then tore the com from Ujo's wrist and dialed up the call history. There it was; Quinn Braxton. "So, the game's afoot," Doc murmured, quoting his favorite fictional detective.

Ujo was rubbing his throat as he attempted to rise. Doc swung on him, smashing him in the face with a roundhouse right. Ujo collapsed to the floor, his broken nose bleeding profusely. He groaned and tried to get up, but Doc clocked him once more for good measure, then bent down and administered a tranq with his microjet. Ujo lay pale and deathly still as Doc grabbed a towel to staunch the flow of blood. When it had subsided, he cleaned up the blood on the floor and the nearby wall, then let the 'bots loose to do their usual efficient job of removing any remaining traces. The towels he threw into the dispose-all, where they would be reduced to ashes and flushed away. He dragged Ujo to the portal and peered along the hall in both directions. Satisfied that nobody was about, he slung the unconscious informer over his broad shoulders and carried him across to his own hab. Ujo's day was about to get considerably worse.

* * *

Quinn was at the appointed meeting place minutes before 1300 hours. Ujo was nowhere to be seen. He waited until 1315, then attempted to com his informant. No response. Now he was worried. For all of his many faults, Ujo was reliably punctual. The fact that he failed to answer his com was a major concern. At 1330, after a second unsuccessful attempt to contact Ujo, he left a message for his C.I. to contact him and went home.

When he hadn't heard from Ujo by late evening, he alerted Benwright and requested a trace. The mystery of Ujo's disappearance would remain a minor annoyance for the Sentinels for some time to come. They would not waste too much time and resources on somebody whose lifestyle sometimes involved the necessity to lay low until some or other offence given to his associates might blow over or be forgotten or forgiven.

November 21, 2204

Quinn was certain that F-Kerrick had something to do with Ujo's disappearance, the urgent call he had received being ample evidence of that. The Sentinels searched Ujo's hab, but found nothing untoward in the chaotic mess. As expected, his friends and acquaintances professed to know nothing of his whereabouts.

Quinn was now extremely perturbed, having been stymied at every turn. He knew without a shadow of a doubt that Doc Kerrick was responsible for the five assaults that had taken place in as many months, and felt that he had sufficient evidence to hang a charge on him. Apparently, he was just about the only one. Even Sera still had reservations.

Ultimately, this exasperation exploded in an unfortunate encounter that took place later that day on the patio of the Central Plaza. Quinn was on his way to a meeting with Benwright and spotted Doc enjoying a break from the workaday world, sitting at a table, sipping a synth-latte and soaking in the few pale rays that managed to filter through the grey air and into the Dome. Provoked by the outrage he still felt following the first and each of the subsequent murders, he decided on the spur of the moment to take this unexpected opportunity to confront him.

"Pardon, F-Kerrick. Might I have a word?" Quinn said as he approached. He was barely able to keep his temper in check, and the false civility he displayed was taxing his self-control.

"Ah, Professor Braxton. Have a seat. What may I do for you today?" Doc was fully aware that Quinn was on to him, but remained determined to tough it out with false bravado and persistent denials.

"It's about certain criminal activities that have disrupted the tranquility of the Dome lately. I'd like to know what your involvement might be."

"My goodness. You don't waste time with small talk, do you? But why me? What makes you think I might be involved with such depraved crimes?" Doc was grinning at Quinn, his face a mask of arrogant superiority.

"You left a trail," Quinn answered. "Some of it was intentional, most not. You can't deny your past, no matter your efforts to cover it up. I know who you were and where you've been." He moved closer and loomed over Doc menacingly.

"What do you imagine you know?" Doc said, looking up at Quinn, apparently unperturbed.

"I know you're not who you pretend to be. I've been to Enterprise and I've examined the records. Your past is clouded, and I'm going to continue to dig until I'm able to expose you and prove that you killed those kids. I'm going to …"

The information chilled Doc, but he was determined to brazen it through. "Save your breath and your time," Doc interrupted. "There's nothing to find. There's nothing to prove. Direct your efforts elsewhere. I don't know why you're persecuting me, but let me tell you that going after a Future is a bad idea. Unless you want to wind up on a construction crew mixing perbond, you might want to rethink this course of action."

Doc stood up and stalked off towards the main administration building. Quinn stared after him, realizing he'd made a mistake in letting primitive emotion overrule good sense in confronting him. What had he gained? Had he expected Doc to confess? He recognized that Doc probably suspected him of concealing a recording device, and so had suppressed any hint of a declaration of guilt. Quinn feared the consequences of his rash action and, as it turned out, with good cause.

* * *

Quinn arrived for his meeting with Benwright a short while after his confrontation with Kerrick, only to be informed by the roboreceptionist that the Director was in conference and would be with him soon. After cooling his heels for half an hour, he was finally admitted to Benwright's office.

"Well, you've been busy," Benwright greeted him.

"Oh?"

"A certain Future has informed my superiors that you've been to the Outlands, looking into his past, and he's not happy about it."

"Oh." He had expected consequences, but not this quickly.

"He feels your attentions are unwarranted, and demands that we rein you in. Is your interest in him unwarranted?"

"I apologize for not keeping you informed as to what I was doing, but it was only my personal suspicion, and I didn't have enough solid evidence to bring to you until now."

"You realize you've stirred up a storm of outrage by accusing a Future of wrongdoing. The Council is getting involved, and even C-Sanchez is being informed. You'd better have some pretty good evidence to back up your allegations."

"I think I do, but Pierre Adler disagrees," Quinn said. He ran through the progress of his investigation, outlining every piece of relevant evidence.

At the end of it, Benwright, who had been leaning forward, eagerly listening to Quinn's exposition of the facts, sat back and clasped his hands in front of him. He mused for some moments, then said, "I can see where it might appear that F-Kerrick could be involved in these crimes, but the limited amount of physical evidence we've gathered so far, coupled with the secvids, would seem to contradict your conclusions. The process citizens go through to become Futures would seem to be impenetrable by someone with evil intent or a less than perfect past. Given the indignation you've aroused, my boss, Commissioner Earl has ordered me to suspend you from the case and turn your part in it over to C-Sanchez's independent experts in other Domes."

Quinn was stunned. He opened his mouth to say something, but Benwright held up a restraining hand. "Now you and I have developed a relationship over the years, and I've come to trust and respect your judgment. Turn over your files on F-Kerrick immediately, and to be fair, I'll look them over. In the meantime, if you wish, I'll allow you to carry on a separate and unofficial investigation. I can't promise you any resources, but I have to satisfy the demands that you no longer be allowed to look at F-Kerrick as a suspect."

"Is there nothing else we can do to go after Kerrick?"

"Only one thing I can think of, but it's a stretch. Since Futures are assumed to be citizens above reproach or suspicion, one could perhaps petition C-Sanchez and the Council of Compilers to carry out an in-depth assessment of F-Kerrick's past. The drawback there is that the request would also have to be presented to the Dome's Council of Guardians, and it's almost certain that's where the petition would be rejected. You'd be better off leaving it to me. If there's any substance to your hypothesis, we'll find it eventually."

Of course, Quinn had no choice but to agree reluctantly to Benwright's terms. At least he could still maintain an informal link with the case, and with Pierre's support, he could continue his own investigation. The Shadows might be his last tenuous link to Kerrick.

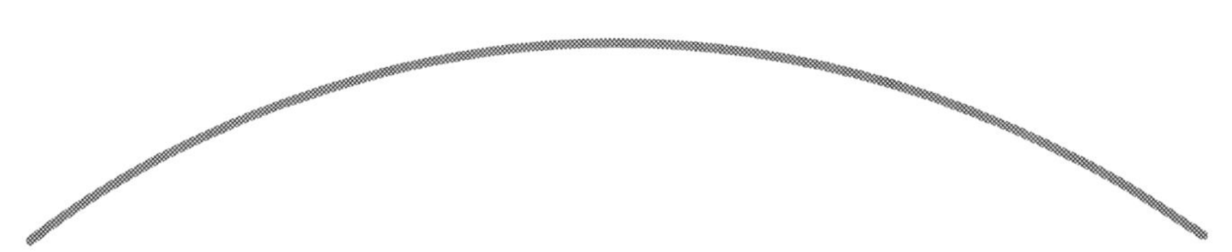

CHAPTER 25

UJO'S BAD DAY

November 22, 2204

Ujo awoke to a world of pain. He found himself shackled to a metal chair, the manacles tight and biting into his flesh. His face was inflamed and sore, his eyes puffy and swollen almost shut. There were bruises over much of his body, and what felt like a couple of broken ribs, as corroborated by the pain he experienced with every breath. He attempted to keep his breathing slow and shallow. His entire body felt cold, the metal of the chair draining heat through his bare skin. He'd been stripped of his clothing.

"You're awake," said a familiar voice off to his left. He forced his head to turn, shards of pain shooting through him at every movement. Through bloated lids he was barely able to see a form sitting there watching him. "You've been gone from us for the better part of two days," Doc informed him. "Drugs will do that to you."

Ujo attempted to force words through swollen, dry and cracked lips. He could manage little more than a croak.

"Come, come now. Surely you can do better than that. You had plenty to say when you were talking to Professor Braxton about me. What, exactly, were you going to tell him at your rendezvous, and what have you reported so far? You can tell me. We're friends, are we not?"

Of this Ujo had his doubts, as he sat bound under the Future's fixed stare. He tried once more to speak, with scant success.

Doc rose impatiently from his chair. He grasped a handful of Ujo's hair and pulled his head back, squirting water into his mouth from a squeeze bulb. Ujo choked and gasped, but swallowed the water gratefully as it ran down his throat and spilled across his bare chest and between his legs, adding to his discomfort. Doc resumed his seat and sat glaring at his unfortunate prisoner.

"Now, Vreem, you have the floor, so to speak. Talk to me."

"Please, sir, I … I'll do anything you want. Just don't hurt me. I told Braxton nowt about you. I didn't get a chance. He arranged for me to be there, across from your hab. I'll inform on him for you if you want. Let me go. I won't tell anyone." He babbled on, terrified at the probable outcome of his confinement.

"Ach," Doc spat. "Just the kind of whimpering and whining I'd expect from the likes of you. Ready to sell anybody out to save your own skin. But I tend to believe you. Perhaps you didn't have time to pass on anything significant. I'm going to leave you for a while. I'll miss your company, as I have no doubt you'll miss mine. When I return, we'll resume our chat. Yes?"

Doc moved out of Ujo's sight line and Ujo heard a door behind him groan on rusty hinges. Through swollen lids, he was able to get a quick glimpse of his surroundings, a carbocrete room about 5 meters square lit by glowstrips on walls and ceiling. Then the door clicked shut and the lights went out. It was the darkest dark he had ever experienced and he quivered in pain and terror. Straining against his bonds produced only agony, but no hint of the possibility of escape. He could do no more than wait for Doc's return and whatever horrors might accompany that.

It seemed many hours later that the door creaked open and the lights came on, though Ujo had no way of tracking time. It could have been a day or more for all he knew.

"I've brought food and drink for us. You might want to enjoy it while you can, my friend," Doc said, setting down a satchel of tools. "Now, where were we?" He smiled, and Ujo trembled, but not from the chill in the air.

Ujo's protestations of innocence and friendship had no effect on Doc, and in due course, his screams, echoing in the chamber deep beneath the Dome, gave testimony to the depravity of man and the futility of attempting to evade karma.

November 24, 2204

It wasn't until Doc pondered the sight of Ujo's mutilated body that he was able to come up with another plan, an alternative to leaving the Dome as a means of evading justice, should Quinn's efforts bear fruit. He didn't relish the prospect of spending the rest of his life in the Outlands, deprived of the creature comforts he had enjoyed for most of his life.

Every newborn for more than a century and a half had been implanted with an identichip in their left earlobe. The chip's circuits eventually merged with the nervous system of the individual, giving a readout not only of their identity and related personal information, but of their general state of health, and the details of their brain activity. Doc conjectured that, if he switched Ujo's identichip for his own, the informer having no further use for his, then he might assume Ujo's identity. It wouldn't be the first time he had accomplished such a feat. After the chip completed its neural connections, for all intents and purposes he would be Ujo.

Doc's actual physical appearance was similar enough to Ujo's that he might pass for the deceased petty criminal by using only a small amount of makeup and prosthetics. He could compensate for the minor difference in height by wearing unfashionably flat shoes and adopting the stooped and furtive posture of one who wishes to attract little attention. If any of Ujo's former acquaintances should spot a discrepancy in appearance ... well... people such as Ujo, he reasoned, had few real friends, and even fewer who would be likely to go to the authorities on any matter short of their own survival.

It would mean, for him, a change of lifestyle, and not for the better. "But not to worry," he thought. "I've been down before and recovered. It's just a matter of time. If things should take a turn for the worse, I'll be ready."

November 25, 2204

Quinn repeatedly paced the length of his office cubicle. He was unable to settle down and work efficiently, so engrossed was he in the challenge of bringing Doc to justice. His suspension from the case and the consequent loss of a large portion of the resources necessary to end Doc's reign of terror weighed heavily on his mind. He would sit at his desk for a few minutes, preparing lessons and marking assignments, vainly trying to concentrate on the job at hand, but his mind would inevitably drift to the murders, and he would soon find himself walking back and forth, searching for solutions.

At the sound of a throat being cleared and he looked over to see Sera leaning on the doorframe. "Agonizing over it won't help," she said. "You've done everything you could. Kerrick has influence and resources and the protection of the status of a Future. We have to look for his weak points. Now that we know who he is, we should be able to penetrate his defenses. Cheer up. At least he won't be able to go after any more children."

"I know, sis, but the waiting is killing me. I haven't heard from Benwright and we're not always sure where Kerrick is. Pierre's Shadows are supposed to have him under surveillance, but he's a slippery character, and I suspect he has resources we haven't even imagined yet."

"You're probably right, but fretting about it won't solve anything. Why don't you take the rest of the day off and we can work on the case together. I have some ideas, and I'm sure you have, too. The solution might be right in front of us. Come on. Let's grab some lunch and get to work."

Some hours later, still reluctant to admit defeat, the pair regarded Quinn's correlation chart, diagramming the relationships among the victims and the times and locations of the crimes.

"It's all there. If Doc is ever brought before the Arbiters, they'll be able to see the whole story right there in front of them. All I need now is to get back into his hab and find out what he's hiding there, then we'll be able to fill in the rest of the gaps in the mystery."

"The biggest one being the discrepancy between the physical appearance of the person on the secvids and Kerrick himself. That's a huge obstacle to overcome," Sera pointed out.

"The explanation for that will no doubt be very interesting. We can speculate about it all day, but I'll bet the answer will turn out to be something simple." In spite of their lack of progress, he felt optimistic and reinvigorated and prepared to face whatever might come. His sanguinity would soon be challenged in a critical and most unexpected way.

CHAPTER 26

THE SHADOWS KNOW

November 27, 2204

"It's on," Pierre informed Quinn the moment he opened his com link. "Kerrick's gone to a community meeting to defend the measures the Council's taking. He's likely to be gone for some time. Take care. If you're right, he's a dangerous man. Keep me posted."

"Thanks," Quinn answered. "I'm on my way."

As the floater glided across the city towards the inner ring, Quinn activated his com helmet and reviewed the tri-d blueprints of a standard bachelor hab's design, once more overlaying it with the measurements he'd taken the last time he'd been in Kerrick's hab. The discrepancies were obvious. Walls and cubbies had been subtly altered so as to conceal hidden spaces. Those spaces were where he would begin his search.

On debarking at the floater station, he looked around and saw Shadows at every juncture. It was undoubtedly a product of his overactive imagination, but here in Lowertown, sinister figures abounded, and he wasn't proficient at telling the good from the bad. When he arrived at Kerrick's level, he moved quickly along the hall and stopped in front of Ujo's hab just long enough to speculate on what dismal fate the unfortunate C.I. might have suffered. Moments later, he found himself inside Kerrick's hab, which appeared just as it had before; tidy and spotless. There were two areas that Quinn had marked for examination, and he quickly set to work.

The first was near the entry, behind the robocleaners' recharging station. A painstaking search revealed hidden catches which gave way when the panel was pressed at two precise spots. Behind was a narrow storage closet, the contents of which were astonishing. There Quinn found two full body expansion suits, just about Kerrick's size which, when worn under his clothing, would make Kerrick appear portly. The space also contained two pairs of gelshoes, neither of them the recalled model, complete with lifts to enhance height. At last, a clear explanation of the discrepancy between the secvid images of the perpetrator, and the more familiar outward aspect of the suspect Future. There were several sets of casual clothing, including hoodies, sized for someone with a morphology somewhat smaller than Kerrick's altered self. In addition the cubbyhole contained lifts, wigs, facial prosthetics and makeup, as well as a spraybulb of synthskin and a loaded tranqspray injector. Finally, tucked behind a wig, Quinn found a roll of red ribbon, as if more proof were needed. He used his 'corder to document what he was seeing.

The second suspicious area was below the window along the outer wall. It appeared that the space, a half meter from floor to sill, had been expanded inwards by some forty centimeters or so, for the full length of the window wall. It looked like a window seat, but was closed and immovable. Quinn spent some time fiddling with it, looking for hidden panels and catches, but was ultimately obliged to give up. He couldn't force any joints or remove fastenings for fear of giving away his intrusion. Being unauthorized, his invasion of F-Kerrick's privacy would be looked upon as criminal activity, no matter the reason. The best he could do was to use a sensor in his com helmet to ascertain that the space was hollow and empty. All of his activities were picked up by his holocorder for later revue.

After once again doing a close inspection of the rest of the hab, Quinn erased the portal record of his intrusion and walked out into the corridor. Looking left and right, he had the eerie feeling that he was being watched. Just before he entered the dropshaft, he spotted a tiny spycam hole in the middle of the blank end wall. A clumsy effort by an inexperienced group, but something Kerrick would be unlikely to notice.

* * *

"Well, isn't he just too clever," Sera said as the two of them watched the holovid playing back on the comcenter. "Who would have thought of a thing like that?"

"He planned this for a very long time. He's reversed what most criminals do. Instead of disguising himself to commit crimes, he's disguising his everyday life, and becomes his true self when he's at his worst. This is why he didn't have to concern himself with being recorded by the sec-cams. He was once in the drama club. He learned to do makeup in university. That's how he does it. He's been playing a part all these years, the role of a decent and responsible citizen."

"So the physical description we've been going on is totally wrong."

"Yes. His mass at Awakening was around 80 kilos. His apparent mass now is over 100 kilos. He must have, over the last decade, gradually bulked up his disguise so as to appear to have gained mass slowly. His plan was very long range. He also uses lifts in his shoes and facial prosthetics to alter his height and normal appearance."

"Couldn't he have done it the other way around, the way normal criminals might do?"

"Yes, but that would have impaired his mobility and his agility. A disguise of that nature would have slowed him down and made his movements less flexible. Any lesser costume wouldn't have had the effect of throwing us so far off the track."

"If he's really so evil, if his rage is so uncontrolled, how could he have restrained himself long enough to carry out such a plan?"

"I don't think he did for the whole time. His first step would have been to curb his base desires when he was in the public eye, during the time leading up to his election to Congress, then onward to his being approved as a Future. From his history in the public service, it appears that he made a lot of trips to refugee camps and ruined cities. Historical records show that many people vanished in those areas during the time of chaos, including a lot of young girls. How easy it would have been for him to go far from civilization to fulfill his perverted desires. He would have had to have denied himself any relief after he was Awakened, at least until he could familiarize himself with his new environment and gradually adapt and change his outward appearance."

"Why the synthskin?"

"I can make an educated guess, but you're not going to like it. I think the reason we found no semen or epithelial cells on the victims was that he sprays his body from the neck down with the synthspray before he goes out to commit his crimes, and removes all of his clothing before he rapes the girls. Notice on the holovid of his secret cache that there's a flexible head covering that exposed only his mouth and his nostrils. He'd have worn it during the actual commission of each crime. It's all very extreme, but it enabled him to leave no significant clues that might have led to his identity."

"How dreadful. What gave him away?"

"If it hadn't been for that one small fragment of a gelshoe, he might have escaped scrutiny. That was the only solid connection we had to him. ACS Travio unearthed the fact that the only two pairs of gelshoes we couldn't account for belonged to Futures, and brought the information directly to me. From there, it was only a matter of putting the pieces together. Now, if that were the only major piece of physical evidence we had to go on, it might not prove anything, what with some 10 000 pairs of those gelshoes in circulation, but coupled with everything else we've got ....."

"So, do we finally have him?"

"I'm certain of it. I'm going to put this all together on a memory crystal and take it to Pierre tomorrow. It's almost two weeks 'til he's due to strike again. With the Shadows keeping him under observation, the Sentinels will have plenty of time to apprehend him. He's not going anywhere. At least I'll sleep well tonight."

November 28, 2204

The urgent call came in the wee hours of the morning, but it wasn't from Benwright. As soon as Quinn answered, he recognized Rosie's panicked voice.

"She's gone. We can't find her anywhere. You've got to help us."

"Rosie, calm down. Who's gone? When?"

"It's Desert. She was in her sleep shelf when we retired for the night. I kissed her on the way by. I got up early, and saw she wasn't there. We checked everywhere. She's not here. Oh, Quinn, what should we do? Help us," she sobbed.

"I'll be right there. Have you called the Sentinels yet?"

"No. Should I?"

"A moment please, Rosie. There's an urgent call on another line. It might be her."

"Professor," the voice boomed from his com. "I'm guessing by now you know what has occurred." The speaker was disguising his voice, just as he habitually cloaked his appearance, but his identity was not in doubt for a moment.

"Kerrick, if you've done anything to …."

"Don't say anything, just let me talk. I have the child. She's in a safe place. She'll be all right, just as long as you agree to my demands. I know you were in my hab and uncovered my secret. I have no choice but to leave the Dome, so you're going to help me. You can have her back once I'm gone. Agreed?"

"How do I know you have her and that she's safe? How do I know you'll let her go if I help you?"

"I'll send you a vid of her later, and you'll just have to trust me on the second question. You don't have any choice in the matter. You will not tell anyone of this. If you do, then Desert's fate will be on your head. I'll get back to you soon. Out."

Quinn sat stunned for a few moments, then recalled that Rosie was still waiting.

"Sorry, Rosie. It wasn't what I'd hoped for. I'll be right over. Don't call the Sentinels. I'll explain when I get there."

"Please hurry, Quinn."

Quickly, he woke Sera up and outlined the situation for her. She was horrified.

"What can I do to help?" she asked. "Do you want me to go with you to the Ushers?"

"No. Stay put for now. I may need you here or elsewhere. I'll com you with further developments and perhaps we can put our heads together and come up with something."

Before the floater dropped him near Usher's Harbour, Quinn had made the decision to defy Kerrick, at least in part. He wouldn't call in the Sentinels just yet, but he had to tell Gus and Rosie. It would go a long way towards lessening their anxiety. Although the information that she was in the hands of a serial killer would be distressing, at least they would know she was safe for the moment. He had to buy some time to consider the situation and try to reach a satisfactory resolution. Desert's safety was paramount, he decided, but if he could somehow entrap Kerrick without risking that, it would be of maximum benefit to everyone. At worst, if he did help Kerrick escape, there would at least be a chance of catching him later on. He was mindful of the possibility that Kerrick might try to revert to his wicked ways in the Outlands, but with a planet wide alert out for him, even the Outlanders would be increasingly wary of a stranger in their midst.

He arrived at Usher's Harbour and the portal slid aside in response to his identichip. Gus and Rosie immediately rushed to him, overwhelming him with a barrage of questions. Quinn did his best to calm them, and when they had become less agitated, he took them to the gathering room and sat them down.

"Where're the kids?" he asked.

"They're still out looking. What news?" Rosie asked.

"I know where she is. You have to stay calm 'til I explain. I found out who's been killing those poor girls, and the killer found out that I know. There's no easy way to tell you this. He's taken Desert to ensure my silence."

Rosie shrieked and burst into tears and Gus gasped, wringing his hands. He put his arms around Rosie as she sobbed in grief and despair, and the two tried to comfort one another. "What … what's to be done?" Gus was able to ask at last.

"Don't panic. He's promised not to harm her, in return for my helping him escape the Dome, or at least to refrain from interfering with his escape. He'll arrange for her release once he's safely away. If we keep our heads and do what he demands, we might all get through this unscathed. Our first priority must be Desert's safety."

"How can we have any confidence that he'll keep his word?" Gus asked.

"We have no alternative. He's keeping her at some secret place, and we have no way to find her or to rescue her. Even if we were to involve the Sentinels, they'd have no better chance of locating her, and she'd be in even greater danger."

"Who is this creature?" Rosie asked. Quinn was mildly surprised that neither of them had broached the question of the kidnapper's identity until now.

"He's a Future, one Donald F-Kerrick, also known as Doc Kerrick in his former life," Quinn answered. There was no point in concealing his identity from Gus and Rosie.

The two just sat there thunderstruck. Gus opened his mouth to say something, but appeared unable to frame a question. "Oh my lord! Those files. I was the one who Awakened him. He came from this very Harbour. I'm responsible for this tragedy."

Quinn placed a hand on his old friend's shoulder. "No, you're not. You couldn't possibly have known what evil you were setting loose. Don't blame yourself."

"I know you're right. Even so, I can't help but feel that I played a key role in all of this," Gus said, hanging his head. After some moments, he activated the com and called the children home. "We can share this with the kids, can't we?" he said.

"Of course. It would be cruel not to tell them. They might have some input into how we should proceed."

Quinn's com chimed. When he accepted the call, he was confronted with an appalling sight. He quickly routed the vid to Gus' comcentre so that they could all share it. There was Desert, bound to a chair, a blindfold covering her eyes. Mercifully, it wasn't a red ribbon, and she was still fully clothed. Gus and Rosie sat gaping in open-mouthed horror at what they were seeing.

"What do you want?" Quinn asked the unseen caller.

"Desert is alive and well, as you can see," the disguised voice replied. "Don't attempt to find her. You won't be able to. And don't try to take me, even if I appear in public. Desert will die of thirst in a matter of days if I'm not available to take care of her. Any foolish or impulsive action on your part will cost her her life. Have patience, and all will end well." The connection was abruptly terminated. Quinn immediately attempted a trace, knowing that the effort would be futile. Doc was too smart to ever allow such an obvious thing.

"We'll get him," Quinn said. "We'll get him soon. This I promise, for everyone's sake. I love that child like a sister. She will be returned safely to you."

"How was it possible that such a creature was approved to become a Future?" Gus asked angrily. He was barely able to control himself, and was trembling with anxiety and rage. Rosie was unable to raise her head from his shoulder, and clasped him to herself as if she could never let go.

"I don't know, but we're going to have to find out, in order to prevent it from ever happening again."

River, Jonathan, and Daniel tumbled into the room within moments of each other, all talking at once, urgently questioning what was happening. Rosie tried to settle them down, but they were persistent.

"Quinn has it under control. If you'll be quiet for a moment, I'll tell you what's going on," Rosie told them sternly, quickly regaining some measure of composure for the sake of her family.

They sat together, looking fearful, while Rosie outline the progression of events. When she revealed the identity of the kidnapper and Desert's immediate situation, River gasped and began to sob, and the two brothers pounded their fists on the furniture and cursed. This time it took Rosie longer to calm them down.

"Quinn is handling this for us. He's assured me that Desert will be all right as long as we do as this monster says."

The siblings expressed the same fears that Rosie and Gus had put forth and Quinn attempted to reassure them. Gus put his arm around River, comforting her as best he could. All five of the Ushers huddled as close to each other as they could get, seeking communal solace in their fear and misery.

"I understand your grief, and I can't alleviate your fears, but we have to face reality," Quinn told them. "We're just going to have to wait until he contacts us, then do what he says. We have to hope that it will go quickly and easily. In the meantime, I'm going to get together with Sera and we're going to look for clues as to where he might be holding Desert. If we can locate her, we may be able to come up with a plan for rescuing her without putting her in any danger."

"Can I come with you?" River asked plaintively. "I might be able to help."

"It might be better if I took one of the boys," Quinn answered.

"Please," she begged. "I need you."

Quinn's heart broke for her. Even if he hadn't had strong feelings for her, he could have refused her nothing in her misery.

"All right. Come along," he said gently. "The rest of you should stay here in case circumstances change. You boys take care of your parents. I might need your help later on."

He commed Sera and filled her in, then told her that he and River were on their way back. "I have some ideas. I want you to pull out the copies of the Enterprise files. We're going to have to get creative here."

CHAPTER 27

BENEATH THE DOME

November 28, 2204

"What are you looking for?" Sera asked Quinn as River handed her a share of the file folders now spread out on the work table.

"Some hint, anything that we might have missed about Doc's past. Something we might have overlooked or not recognized as significant the first time through."

The three of them had spent hours sorting through the files. "Did you know that his mother vanished around the time he graduated from university? Do you think that's important?" Sera said.

"I doubt it'll have any relevance to our hunt for Desert, but it probably has something to do with his attempts to conceal his true identity after he disposed of his brother. I'd bet on it."

More searching, but with scant results, until Quinn pulled up Doc's work record. "Damn. I just remembered something Doc said to me when I confronted him on the plaza. Now it makes sense. He threatened to get me assigned to laying perbond. According to the databanks, perbond was a particularly nasty powder once used as a bonding agent in carbocrete. Mixing it in was one of the dirtiest jobs you could do in construction in the early days of the Domes. Doc was chief construction supervisor when they were laying the foundations for this very Dome. I'd forgotten about that. Its importance didn't register with me until now."

"So?" Sera asked.

"So he'd have known the substructures of the Dome intimately. He'd have had ample opportunity to redesign passageways and hideyholes for his own use. Remember, he's a long range planner. Look at the vids of Desert he sent to prove she's still alive. Notice the background? She's in a carbocrete room. The only place there are rooms like that is beneath the Dome. They've been there for a hundred years."

"Can we use that information to find her?"

"Perhaps. Thulia Traynor was found in a stockhouse with a carbocrete floor, but there was no hint of how he was able to get in or out. I'll bet there's a slab or panel that moves aside to give access. It must have been cleverly concealed, like the ones in his hab. We have to go back there and look for any traces. We might just be able to track him from there."

"Is that a good idea? I mean, to confront him in his home territory. Shouldn't we call in the Sentinels?" River asked.

"I'm not exactly in their good graces right now. Besides, we don't want a troop of Sentinels tramping around down there and alerting him, and he might get wind of it if he has any covert connections in the security forces. No, we have to do this on our own. I'm hoping we can find out where he's hiding Desert without actually running into him."

Quinn suggested that River call Gus and Rosie and let them know what was happening. River's parents were elated to hear the news, and expressed cautious optimism along with an admonition to be careful. The three of them changed into unisuits, River donning a set borrowed from Sera. They loaded gloworbs, a medkit, food and water into backpacks, along with some rope and tools borrowed from the maintenance closet down the hall. Now they were prepared to face whatever dangers the Dome's unfamiliar subterranean world might have in store.

* * *

They arrived at the stockhouse early that afternoon. Quinn managed to persuade the onsite supervisor to admit them so that they could continue the investigation. The supervisor left on a floater van to make a furniture delivery, requesting that they lock up when they left. The Sentinels had long since released the scene of the Traynor killing, having been unable to find any further evidence there. The space was very much the same as it was when Quinn had last seen it. They set down their packs and proceeded to examine the floors and walls.

Since they knew what they were looking for, it wasn't long before River discovered rectangular lines barely visible in the dust near the rear of the building, behind a pile of furniture. During the Dome's construction, Doc had had full access to the original blueprints, showing the Dome as it would be once it was completed, so he had been able to anticipate where walls would be placed and locate the hatch accordingly. It was almost certain that he knew of many such hatches throughout the city.

Poking and prying had no effect, so they began to search along the nearby walls, without result. Quinn had an inspiration.

"There were no walls here when he arranged for the hatch to be installed. It probably opens from below."

"Then how could he access it from above if he needed to, and how can we get through it?" Sera asked.

Quinn had had the foresight to bring his com helmet, anticipating that he might have need of some of its advanced tools. He squatted above the hatch and ran a scan.

"As I expected. The latch is electronic. If I transmit a range of probable wavelengths and codes, something should connect. Make yourselves comfortable. This might take a while." He programmed the com helmet for a series of codes, then set it by the hatch and activated its electronic transmission.

They sat on the chairs and pads that were stored for distribution and waited, while discussing the situation and attempting to anticipate what might be in store. Just over an hour later, they heard the sound of bolts withdrawing, then the hatch moved downwards and slid aside. They all rushed over to look down into the widening gap. Below was a rectangular corridor dimly illuminated by a few glowstrips on the walls, with rungs set into the wall to allow for easy access from above.

"Let's get packed up. We have to go now," Quinn said. He donned his pack and, making sure the other two were prepared, descended into the hole. Once he reached the floor, he turned on a portable gloworb and motioned the others to follow. When they had joined him, he pointed out faint tracks in the dust. "Notice how the footprints come from that direction, where Thulia Traynor was abducted, then continue in the opposite direction. The first set will be when he brought her here, and the others when he left. If we follow the second set, we may find something."

He took the lead, all three of them carrying gloworbs to dispel the shadows. They were able to check their position relative to the surface with geolocators in their coms, so they knew that they were nearing the main avenue that separated Kula and Hanover districts. Here the corridor widened to allow small vehicle access, and bright glowstrips lighted their way. Intermittent traffic in the passage had partially obliterated the footprints. A slight breeze, freshening the air in the caverns, stirred the dust, but traces were still visible.

"What now?" River asked.

"He turned right here, towards the perimeter. If we keep close to the walls, we should be able to see where he turns off into another side corridor, if he does." Having no better option, they moved slowly outwards, following the track away from the center of the Dome. At some point, they passed under the Dome's outer edge and into an area near the outer limits of the foundations. They arrived at the outer wall, where low and narrow tunnels extended left and right. Here, the footprints went off in both directions, and it wasn't clear if either or both were Doc's.

"Shouldn't we split up?" Sera suggested.

"No. Too dangerous," said Quinn. "We have no idea what Doc may have in store for us if we run into him down here. We'll try first one direction, and then the other if need be."

They bore left, moving in a counterclockwise direction around the perimeter, carefully observing walls, floors, and ceilings in the light of their gloworbs. A walk of a kilometer or so brought them to a blank wall, a dead end.

"Guess we'll have to go back," Quinn said, moving his lamp from side to side, examining the barrier.

"I don't think so," River replied, bending over. "Look. The footprints don't reverse. They end at the wall." Sure enough, the tracks went right up to the wall. They surveyed every nearby surface.

Quinn checked the original drawings on his com. "The blueprints show a continuous passage. No barrier. He must have had considerable influence to have had this put in."

"Here it is," Sera said at last, pointing to a black box in a small niche at the junction of the two walls. She inserted her finger, pressed a button, and the end wall vanished.

"Amazing," Quinn said. "It wasn't a wall. It was a modified privacy barrier. We could have just walked through it if we'd known. He must have installed this relatively recently."

River peered beyond the barrier and saw the corridor stretching off into the distant shadows. "Look," she said. "There's another set of footprints going in the opposite direction. The two sets converge just ahead."

They moved forward and had gone only a few meters, following the footprints, when something caught Sera's eye. "Well, would you look at that," she said in wonder.

* * *

Pierre was furious. His normal unruffled manner had been displaced by outrage.

"How could this have happened? How could he have managed to get by you?" He was berating the leader of the Shadows assigned to track Kerrick's movements. "You had coverage of the entrance into his hab and the exits from the building. You had a spycam in the hall. How was this possible?"

Gil Fineman, the target of Pierre's tirade, was attempting to interject a few words of explanation, but was having difficulty making himself heard above the strident salvo being discharged in his direction.

"If you'll just look at the surveillance vids, Honour, you'll see that there's no sign of him leaving his hab at any time. We even had a surveillance cam watching the roof, and he didn't get out that way. Short of invading his hab, we have no way of knowing ..."

"Find him, and do it quickly," Pierre shouted. "He has the girl, and we have to stop him. But be discreet. We can't tip him that we're after him, or the consequences could be grave."

In spite of Quinn's admonition for them to keep Desert's kidnapping to themselves, Gus and Rosie had decided that Pierre should be brought into the picture. They knew that Quinn was working closely with Pierre, and felt that the Arbiter might be able to help. When they had informed him of what had occurred, he had in turn summoned Gil Finemann for a complete accounting.

After Finemann left, he commed Gus. "O.K. We're on it. I've got the Shadows trying to track him. There're only a handful of them and it's a big city, and we have to do this very covertly, so it's not going to be easy. We're hoping that he uses a public portal so his identichip will reveal where he is. Have you heard from Quinn?"

"No. He's doing some tracking of his own. He seems to think he has a solid lead. We don't know exactly where he is, but River and Sera are with him."

"All right. Keep me in the loop and I'll com you if I hear anything."

The Arbiter severed the link then began to wonder if there were anything else he might be able to do to resolve the situation. As a last resort, he could call Benwright, but that would have to wait for the outcome of the dual efforts of Quinn and the Shadows. He didn't want to upset any ongoing rescue attempt by involving too many people. Now came the waiting game.

* * *

"Alert, alert," Gil Finemann shouted into his com. "We've got him. Avalon Mall, rear entrance. His identichip just triggered the portal alarm. All teams converge on the area immediately."

A dozen Shadows rushed through the mall entrances, confounding shoppers and passers-by. Finemann monitored the portals, waiting for another alarm to be triggered. He ordered his men to spread out through the mall, searching for anyone answering F-Kerrick's description. For a long time, nothing occurred. No sightings, no alerts.

At last, an alarm was triggered at a main exit portal. "All teams to the transit exit," Finemann ordered. "He appears to be attempting to board the maglev to WashingtonDome." The major domes on the east coast were linked by underground vacuum tunnels enclosing high-speed magnetic levitation trains.

It took some minutes for them to arrive at the station, but by that time the train was many kilometers along the vac-tube. Finemann made an instant decision to alert his Washington counterparts and ask for their assistance. He gave no details, but transmitted Kerrick's identicode to them so that they could apprehend him when the train arrived. Ten minutes later, when the maglev pulled into the WashingtonDome station, it was swarmed by security forces, but they were unable to find any trace of the elusive Future among the debarking passengers. They thought they'd detected a weak signal from Kerrick's chip, but ultimately, they lost track of it. A fruitless search of WashingtonDome yielded no useful results.

* * *

His escape plan involved switching identities with Ujo. He'd removed Ujo's identichip and replaced his own with it, and now he had yet another use for his original chip. Before placing it into Ujo's lobe, he'd cloned it onto a respondent crystal lattice with an integrated short-life battery. Doc then covered the tiny incision in his own earlobe with flesh-colored healing gel and took the copy of his old chip with him, wrapped in foil, as he made his way to the surface dressed in nondescript civilian clothing. Nobody would be looking for someone in Ujo's persona, so he felt confident that he could move unnoticed through public spaces.

He'd entered the Alban Mall with the cloned in his pocket, and as he did so he unwrapped it and allowed it to trigger the portal sensors, knowing that they would identify him to the authorities, then he seated himself in a caf overlooking several mall levels. He was not surprised when a number of furtive figures quickly appeared and began to search the area. As he had anticipated, Quinn had broken their verbal agreement. Now everyone was involved and all hell would soon break loose. In spite of that, he was enjoying the battle of wits with the professor, a battle he fully expected to win.

Now that he had confirmed that his chip was being singled out for special attention, he walked through the underground tunnel connecting the mall to the mag-lev station at the Dome's periphery. Having triggered the station's portal sensor, he covertly dropped the cloned chip into the open bag of a woman passing near, then left by another exit. Kerrick's chip would continue on its journey to WashingtonDome, where its battery would quickly die. If everyone believed that F-Kerrick had left the Dome, he'd be free to continue his life in the role of Ujo Vreem, or perhaps as someone else whose identity he might conveniently steal. As to his abnormal predilections, he would deal with that matter in due course.

But first, he had one more task to accomplish. He had promised Quinn severe consequences if his directives were not followed, and he was not accustomed to being defied. An object lesson was in order, and he was now on his way to take care of that detail. He smiled in anticipation.

CHAPTER 28

TO THE RESCUE

November 28, 2204

Quinn turned to follow Sera's gaze. A tiny, unobtrusive red light was flashing within a narrow crevasse in the wall. He would have missed it entirely had Sera not chanced to spot it. They moved closer to examine the light. Quinn scanned it with his comhelmet and was able to determine that the light and the box it was attached to were harmless.

"What's that?" River asked, bending to examine it.

"Best guess, it's either some kind of monitor, or a means to access a portal. If it's the former, then we've already triggered it and Doc knows we're here. I'm hoping it's the latter. Either way, we have to check it out."

He set his comhelmet to the task of running a full diagnostic and a wideband wavelength scan, just as it had in the stockhouse. After a few minutes, they were rewarded with the sound of an ancient panel squeaking and groaning in the opposite wall. A portal opened and glowstrips came on, illuminating the stark room beyond. There, tied to a metal chair, was Desert, eyes wide with terror. Her eyes widened even further when she saw the three who entered the room, and tears began to flow down her cheeks as she sobbed in relief.

Astonished at their good fortunate in locating Desert so quickly, they rushed to her, all talking at once. River wept in relief as she fumbled to release her sister from her bonds.

"Are you all right?" she asked.

Desert was now sobbing so hard that she was barely able to speak. "O.K. … yes … O.K."

"Did he hurt you?" Sera asked.

"No … treated me well." The young girl was beginning to regain a measure of composure. "He gave me water … nutriwafers. Promised I'd go home if I cooperated … if all of you cooperated. It was horrible. I was so scared. I didn't … believe him. I thought he might do to me what he'd done ……." She broke down and began to weep once again.

River embraced the trembling child and attempted to comfort and calm her. Sera pulled a thinsulate blanket from her pack and wrapped it around Desert.

Quinn was gritting his teeth in fury. As Desert recounted her story, his outrage increased. He was angry, and more determined than ever to track down the depraved Future and bring him to justice. "Let's get her out of here and to a med facility to make sure she's unharmed."

They moved into the corridor and, using the geolocator and Quinn's comhelmet, pinpointed the nearest surface access.

Sera called ahead for a paramed unit to meet them, and River commed her family to share the good news with them. "Yes, she seems to be just fine. The medtechs will have a look at her anyway once we get outside. She appears to have suffered some emotional trauma, and it might be a good idea to put her under professional observation for a few days, until we're sure she's O.K. I'll com you as soon as we know where they're taking her."

"Here," Quinn said at last. "We can go up here." He climbed the rings set in the wall and triggered the portal. It opened to reveal foliage above, and the concerned faces of two medtechs peering down at them. Sera and River passed Desert up to Quinn, who in turn passed her on to the waiting techs.

When all of them had regained the surface, they saw that they were in greenspace passing through Kula district. The paramed floater was tethered nearby. The medtechs placed Desert gently onto a floater stretcher, and proceeded to examine her and wire her to a monitor. They quickly moved her into the ambulance and lifted off, making for the nearest hospital. River insisted on going with them.

"They're taking her to Kula district hospital," Sera informed Gus and Rosie as the floater vanished into the distance. "Yes, the techs think she'll be fine. Yes? What did he say? No! I'll see you at the hospital." She severed the connection.

"Well, what did they say?" Quinn asked.

"They panicked and contacted Pierre. Told him everything. He's furious. He turned his Shadows loose to pursue Kerrick. They thought they had him but they lost him. He must know by now that they're after him. They thought he took the maglev to WashingtonDome, but they're not so sure now. He might still be here in RichmondDome."

"Thank goodness we got Desert out of there. He has no power over us now. With all of the activity that's been going on up here, with the Shadows running all over the place, I expect you're right. He almost certainly knows that he's been compromised. He probably doesn't know that Desert's been rescued, so he'll be on his way back there to exact some kind of retribution. I have to go back down."

"No, you can't. Don't try to be a hero. He's too dangerous. There's no point in concealing what we know any more. Com Benwright and have him send the Sentinels in there to deal with him."

"I want you to do that. Tell him where we are and wait here until they arrive, then you can direct them to Kerrick's hideaway. I'm going in to try to find him. He can't be allowed to get away again. I'll try to wait for the Sentinels before I act against him, but I'll do whatever needs to be done to put an end to this."

* * *

Despite Sera's entreaties, Quinn was determined that Doc not escape the justice he so richly deserved. Once more, he descended into the tunnels beneath the Dome. It wasn't far to the side corridor where they'd found

Doc's redoubt. He was sure to be headed that way as soon as he realized that his scheme had failed.

Quinn moved along the passage until he reached the modified privacy barrier. Once again, it had been turned on. It must have been on automatic reset; he was certain that they hadn't reactivated it when they left. He proceeded cautiously through it, his glolamp held high. A sharp report from the darkness beyond shattered the silence, and the lamp exploded in his hand. Instantly the blackness enveloped him, and he pressed himself against the nearest wall.

"Projectile weapon," he thought. "He got here ahead of me." Several more bullets buzzed past him and pinged off the carbocrete walls.

The hiss of a portal opening and closing nearby, then silence filled the Stygian void surrounding him. The night vision in his comhelmet would have helped in this situation, but he'd taken it off at the hatch and unthinkingly left it on the surface with Sera. He slid along the wall, his arm outstretched, feeling his way. A few meters along, he felt a smooth edge, a break in the carbocrete wall. Following its contours, he determined that it was a low portal, not far along from the entry to the room where Desert had been held. His fingers traced the outlines of the opening and its surface, searching for some kind of keyed entry or trigger to gain access. At last, he located a simple slide that allowed him to move the panel aside manually, and opening it cautiously, centimeter by centimeter, edged his head around the expanding opening.

Beyond the portal another corridor, low and narrow, cloaked in darkness broken only by a faint light in the distance. The light vanished and reappeared, as if momentarily blocked. Quinn needed no added reminder to exercise extreme caution with the deranged killer lurking nearby. He slipped into the passage and stayed close to the wall, proceeding warily towards the light. Almost immediately he stumbled over something in the darkness, something large and yielding. He fell hard, rolling away from the obstacle underfoot, but picked himself up quickly, fearful that it was Doc himself who had tripped him up. Nothing moved near him, so he proceeded guardedly. He'd gone no more than 30 meters when a nearby movement caused him to advance more slowly and guardedly, back to the wall.

A voice broke the shadowy silence. "Stay right where you are, professor. We wouldn't want anything unfortunate to happen to either of us, now would we?"

Quinn froze, mindful of the projectile weapon Doc had fired minutes before. He could only hope that the Sentinels would arrive soon.

Doc continued, "I had all of you running in circles, didn't I? I hope that you've enjoyed the game as much as I have. Granted, I underestimated you, professor, but now we carry on, yes?"

"No. I don't think so," Quinn stated. "It's over for you. Help is on the way. So now you can tell me, why did you do it?"

"You just have to know, don't you? Is it really important?"

"Everyone will want to know. It might even play a part in the Arbiters' decision as to what to do with you."

"I don't think that's going to be a consideration. I'm not going to let it go that far. I expect you know all about my stepsister."

"The one you murdered, along with your adoptive parents."

"You have done your research well. Yes, her. She introduced me to the wonderful world of deviate sex at a very early age. I seem unable to give that up. She also betrayed me when it became more important for her to save her own skin than to stand by me. Now I get to exact my revenge on her over and over again."

Doc briefly recounted the details of his childhood, some of which Quinn had discovered, and others that he couldn't even have imagined. Quinn considered what the killer from the past had told him. Of course it made perfect sense. It all fit. Those childhood experiences that had warped him forever, starting with his early adoption by the McCaskills, his subsequent abuse and neglect at their hands, and his eventual exile, those events that had turned him into a sociopath. At last Quinn was able to understand the genesis of some of Doc's delusional behavior; the belief that he had been let down in his youth by his loved ones. He would have had to have possessed a certain propensity to fall into that sort of psychopathy in any case, but it explained a lot.

"Civilized people manage to control their behavior. You had that option."

"Don't presume to lecture me on man's nobility or perversity, Professor Braxton. Perhaps I chose not to amend my conduct. Have you considered that I might enjoy what I do? I do it so well, don't you think?"

"I find that somewhat implausible. Nobody could take pleasure in living your kind of life. The sadistic acts that you commit might give you some fleeting gratification, but how could you possibly choose to live a charade of a life, a life of pretense and duplicity, a life without friends or loved ones?"

"Don't assume that you know me just because you know my history. My life is much more complex than you can imagine. I do have my moments, and I do revisit my loved ones, in my own inimitable way." He chuckled at his witticism, the significance of which was mostly lost on Quinn.

"So tell me, why the sixth of every month, and what's the significance of the red ribbon?" Quinn was now stalling for time in the hope that the Sentinels would arrive to put an end to the affair. It was fortunate that Doc liked to talk about himself.

"My stepsister was quite inventive as regarded our sexual activities," Doc said. "She liked to tie me to the bed blindfolded while she did interesting things to me. I often returned the favor. The blindfold happened to be red. As for the sixth of every month, it was more or less an arbitrary date I chose for misdirection. I wanted you running around pursuing useless clues instead of concentrating on areas that might have yielded useful results. Had you going, didn't I?"

Quinn ignored the taunt. "You could always surrender. We don't execute people or incarcerate them for life any more. You can be treated, you know. We deal with criminals and deviates compassionately in the New Society." Silence answered his offer.

The faraway light was once again briefly occluded. Quinn moved carefully toward it, but hadn't gone more than a few steps when a bright flash lit up the tunnel behind him, followed shortly thereafter by a concussive wave that knocked him off his feet. Debris assailed him as he tumbled forward, his head forcefully impacting the floor. His last thought as he blacked out was one of regret that he'd never had a chance to say goodbye to River and to tell her how much he really loved her.

* * *

The entire Usher clan arrived at Kula hospital only minutes after Desert had been taken to emerg for treatment. They crowded against the observation window to watch her as she rested in a lifepod, closely attended by med-staff, with River hovering anxiously nearby.

"She's been tranqued for her own good," River informed them as she exited the room to update them. "The doctor says she'll probably sleep for about a day. Physically, she's in good shape. They're worried about her mental state, so they'll keep her relaxed and monitor her brainwaves for a while, then she'll undergo a course of therapy until they're sure she'll recover fully."

The family peppered her with questions until she threw up her hands and asked an attending to take over.

He confirmed what she'd told them, and promised that Desert would get the best of care.

"Was she assaulted?" Gus asked reluctantly, fearful of the answer.

"No," the doc answered. "She has a few scrapes and bruises, probably sustained during her abduction, and a few abrasions on her wrists and ankles from her escape attempts, but otherwise she's in good shape, physically.'

"And mentally?"

"She may have to spend a few days here while we do a full psych evaluation, just to make sure. I have no doubt she'll recover completely. Don't worry about her. She's a tough little lady. When we brought her in, she tried to get us to take her home."

The family breathed a collective sigh of relief and settled in to await developments.

"Where're Quinn and Sera?" Gus asked.

"I'm not sure," River replied. "When I left they were still outside the exit hatch in the Kulu greenspace."

"Yes. Sera commed us from there. She said they'd meet us here. They should have been here long ago." He activated his com and awaited Sera's response, keeping the connection private so as not to disrupt the serenity of the hospital. As he talked low to Sera, the Ushers saw him go pale. He severed the connection.

"What is it?" Rosie asked.

"Quinn has gone back in after Kerrick. He's determined to catch him. Sera stayed outside to wait for the Sentinels. They've just gone in after Quinn and Kerrick. I hope they're in time."

River went ashen at the news. "I shouldn't have left him. I could have stopped him," she lamented.

"No, you couldn't have," Gus said. "Sera tried, but he was determined. We'll just have to wait it out. Quinn's tough and resilient. Have faith that he'll be all right."

That was easier said than done. With both Quinn and Desert to worry about, it was going to be a long night for the Ushers.

* * *

Sera stood indecisively beside the hatch. Having directed the Sentinels as best she could, she was wavering between going to the hospital to see about Desert or following her brother in his pursuit of Doc. Finally, reasoning that Desert was being well cared for, she once again descended beneath the Dome. The Sentinels and medtechs remaining near the entrance had attempted to dissuade her from following Quinn, but with characteristic Braxton stubbornness she shook them off and followed after him.

She could hear the Sentinels well ahead of her, making their way towards Doc's hideaway. The glolamps they carried illuminated their path and guided Sera in their direction. She had almost caught up with them, nearing the room where they had rescued Desert, when they were all brought up short by a massive explosion. Most of the Sentinels were knocked off their feet as a gout of flame and smoke erupted from a portal only meters ahead of them. Sera was pushed back by the blast, barely able to keep her feet. Her ears rang from the detonation, and it took her some moments to recover.

The Sentinels began to pick themselves up even as the smoke cleared, but two of their number remained on the floor, one of them unmoving. The others rushed to lend assistance and to secure the area. It quickly became apparent that the blast had caused debris to block the entrance to the side corridor, but that there was no further threat to their safety. The two immobilized troopers were carried out of harms way and first aid administered.

"What happened?" Sera asked as she joined the group.

"Don't know yet," replied Captain Medra Powell, leader of the party. "Looks like Kerrick is making sure we can't follow him, wherever he's going."

"My brother's in there following him. You've got to help him."

"We'll do what we can. We're going to need some equipment to clear this mess. It could take a while." She called for backup, med-techs, and a work crew to clear the tunnel.

Sera was frantic, but the rubble was too heavy to clear by hand. Like the Ushers at the hospital, all she could do was wait, helpless to influence events as they unfolded. It seemed that the tragedy was to continue endlessly, with no clear resolution in sight.

CHAPTER 29

THE NIGHTMARE ENDS

November 28, 2204

The service tech carefully backed a rubble-laden floater-excavator out of the tunnel and dumped it well away from the scene of the destruction. He was removing the debris a few centimeters at a time, moving forward cautiously so as to avoid the risk of any further ceiling collapse. Two other techs flanked his efforts, spraying a plastisteel coating on the damaged ceiling to stabilize it until permanent repairs could be made. At last, having cleared the tunnel mouth, he shut the machine down and summoned Captain Powell. Sera lingered close by, far enough away so as not to interfere with the ongoing operation, yet near enough to see what was going on.

The critically injured Sentinel had been removed to the surface, and the other one was being treated on site. He had adamantly refused to leave the scene and insisted on continuing his duties even as the med-techs placed a quickheal synthskin patch over his head wound and cleaned up his cuts and abrasions.

The service tech was whispering to the Captain and both were casting anxious glances into the tunnel mouth, then in Sera's direction. Already frantic with worry, their actions only added to her fears. The

Sentinel nodded several times and motioned two members of her team to join her. The three proceeded a few meters into the tunnel and bent to examine something.

After a few minutes, Medra Powell straightened and moved towards Sera. Sera attempted to shift her position so she could see down the tunnel, but the Sentinel moved to block her.

"Please don't go over there," Medra said. "We've found a body. You don't want to see it."

Sera gasped and took a step backwards, leaning against the corridor wall, her ashen face in her hands. She began to weep, her shoulders shaking. "Are you sure it's my brother?" she managed to ask between sobs.

"I didn't say that," Medra answered. "Because he went into the tunnel just ahead of us, we can only assume it is, until the forensics techs have had a chance to make a positive identification."

"Could it be F-Kerrick?" Sera asked hopefully.

"The body was too badly burned and mangled by the explosion to attempt an I.D. without the proper equipment. The identichip appears to have been badly damaged and the lab boys will have to examine it to see if they can recover the information on it. Don't make any assumptions. Your brother may yet be safe and well somewhere." Her assurances were hardly comforting.

Tears streaked Sera's face as she tried bravely to stifle her sobs. Medra reassured her as best she could, motioning one of the med-techs over to minister to her. Another Sentinel relayed the news to the surface and summoned the forensic techs.

"If it's any comfort to you," Medra said to Sera as the med-tech administered a mild tranq, "The body appears at first glance to be smaller than your brother. Take heart. We'll know soon."

Even so, Sera was not reassured. She wouldn't be able to put aside her fears until the body was positively identified.

An hour later, a startled exclamation came from deeper in the tunnel, as the Sentinels clambered over rubble and explored deeper, towards the distant entrance. "There's another body in here, Captain. I think you'll want to see this."

* * *

Doc was congratulating himself on the apparent success of his scheme. For the second time, he'd used an explosion to mask a change of identity. He'd left the long-suffering C.I. bound and gagged at the tunnel's mouth, plastique strategically attached to the ceiling just above him. Ujo had been kept alive, though just barely, in anticipation of just this eventuality. Reasoning that the explosion would mangle the body sufficiently, Doc had triggered the detonation remotely. An added bonus was the probability that Braxton might have died in the blast, thus erasing the most dangerous impediment to his change of identity and the possibility of a new life.

Once he re-established his identity as Ujo Vreem, he intended to apply for permanent transfer to another Dome, far enough away that it would be unlikely that he'd run into anyone who might recognize him as an imposter, perhaps in Africa or Australia. He might then be able to resume what he regarded as a normal life. Until then, he intended to lay low in Ujo's hab.

"Ah, yes, life is good indeed," Doc considered. "I've done well for myself." He hadn't expected to keep up his original masquerade forever, and had made allowances and preparations to survive any unexpected setbacks.

It had been far-sighted of him in his former life to conceal a gun and explosives in the subterranean labyrinth, along with other supplies that might aid him in the future, after he would be Awakened as a respectable citizen. His position as construction supervisor for the Dome's foundation had afforded him the unique opportunity to make certain adjustments for his own future benefit. He'd been able to have his own 'improvements' added to the blueprints, and once the construction was completed, he'd eradicated any trace of his modifications in the records. Now he was reaping the benefits of his irrefutable genius. He felt somewhat cheated that he couldn't boast about it to the public at large.

He made his way towards the light at the end of the tunnel, an exit well concealed in the woods beyond the limits of the Dome. He'd opened it up the day before, to ensure that it wasn't blocked and to facilitate his rapid escape should it become necessary. That eventuality now seemed to be the case as the Sentinels would soon be hard on his heels if he didn't move quickly.

His plan was to leave the Dome, then return to it through a little used and relatively unknown maintenance portal in one of the light manufacturing facilities surrounding the main Dome, then through a connecting tunnel into the Dome itself. He was tempted to go back down the tunnel to check on Braxton's fate, but restrained himself, reasoning that if the professor were alive and conscious, he might thus imperil his own escape.

He donned a rebreather and walked the remaining distance along the tunnel's gentle slope to the upper end. Reassuring himself that nobody was near his escape hatch, he emerged into the woods in the dusk of a late November afternoon. He closed the hatch and locked it from the outside, then covered it with earth and brush. He knew that the Sentinels would eventually find it and break through, from top or bottom, but at least it would buy him extra time to vanish into the city's populace. He moved towards the Dome's entrance and the start of his new life.

November 29, 2204

The next morning the news swept through the Dome like the first fresh breezes of spring, wafting away the fear and horror of the past few months. The monster was dead and tranquility had returned. The citizens could resume their normal lives and those who had fled in fear could return.

The techs had been able to positively identify the mangled body. The tattered remains of bright red clothing and a body expansion suit on the corpse, coupled with partial information recovered from the damaged identichip confirmed its identity in the minds of the Sentinels.

"He's waking up," River said brightly, bending over Quinn's pale and battered form. Hearing the words, Quinn's eyes popped open to find River and Sera flanking his recovery pod. He couldn't have been more delighted at this turn of events. Not only had he survived, but his two favorite ladies were with him. It took him some moments to recall the events of the previous day, the full implications of his present situation only just beginning to sink in.

"Are you two all right?" he asked, divulging his primary concern.

"Of course we are," Sera answered. "We were never in any real danger, but you …. How are you feeling?"

"Everything appears to be intact," he answered. "I think I'm O.K. Aches and pains and bruises, but nothing appears to be broken."

"There you'd be wrong. The robodoc says that you have a broken arm, along with assorted scrapes, cuts, and contusions. The med-techs said you'll be just fine in a day or two," River affirmed. She leaned over and kissed him on the lips, adding a little extra zest in celebration of the joy of their reunion.

When River had finished, Sera leaned over and kissed him on the forehead. "Welcome back to the world, brother. The med-techs want to keep you here for a day or so, just to make sure the impact of the blast hasn't addled your brain. I could speak to that without the benefit of sophisticated diagnostics."

"Hah," Quinn snorted. "I remember pursuing Doc into the tunnel, but not much after that. I think I tried to talk him into surrendering then everything went black. I thought he had me for sure."

"He blew up the tunnel and himself with it. You're lucky you survived. If you'd been closer to him, you'd be dead, too."

"He's dead? It's all over?" A surge of relief swept over him.

"Yes," Sera said, laughing. "We're all safe again. They positively identified him from his chip and his clothing. He won't be bothering anyone else. Get well soon and we'll all go out and celebrate."

"How's Desert doing?"

"She's coming along well," River answered. "She's up and around, and they've put her in with that Vale Chang girl, the one who smells colors. They're getting along just fine, supporting each other. The med-techs tell me that she's suffered no physical injuries and a period of psych therapy should clear up most of the lingering effects of her captivity."

"So, good news all around. This does call for a celebration, and as for you, my lovely lady ..." He reached for River with his good arm and encircled her waist, pulling her closer and moving his hand downward, stroking her derriere appreciatively. River demurely and gently removed his hand, but once again leaned in to kiss him.

"O.K., you two. Get a room."

"I have one, in case you hadn't noticed, and you're in it."

"I get the message," Sera said, rolling her eyes in mock-distaste. "I'll leave you alone for a few minutes. The rest of the Ushers are with Desert. They'll be in to see you soon. By the way, Benwright wanted to be alerted as soon as you woke up. I'll give you to a few minutes then I'll com him. The Sentinels want to interview you, too. Take warning. It's going to be a busy day."

* * *

"I've convened this final meeting of the investigative task force to thank you all for your efforts during the crisis," Benwright said. "I'll ask all of you to finalize your reports and submit them to me, especially you forensics techs. There'll no doubt be endless inquiries on how this disaster was allowed to occur, so we'll need very complete records to present when they're required. We owe a special vote of thanks to Quinn Braxton, who's still recovering in hospital and couldn't be with us in person today. He's present through a com link, and I'd like to express our special thanks to him for tracking down and exposing the evil that was the late F-Kerrick. Get well soon, Quinn."

A holo-projection of the hospitalized professor hovered near the dais. The entire group rose to their feet and applauded their injured colleague as he watched from his recovery pod. He acknowledged the ovation, inclining his head slightly in their direction and giving a modest royal wave, then faded out his image so that he could deal with the nuisance that had just entered his room.

A media-orb now hovered near him and asked the inevitable 'how do you feel?' questions. Had he been slightly stronger, he might have been able to seize it and hurl it against the wall. He decided to take the high road.

"Well, thank you for asking. Cuts, bumps bruises, and a fractured radius, nothing really. I'll be up and about in a matter of days." His head was swathed in quickheal and his right arm in an electrosonic healing cast. He was scheduled to be discharged from the hospital the next day, but he didn't want the media to know that.

"You're the man of the hour," the media-orb informed him. "How do you like being a hero?"

"I got lucky," Quinn responded. "I was in the right place at the right time, and thanks to my training and special investigative skills, I was able to notice things that others might have overlooked. I don't regard myself as a hero, just a citizen doing his duty."

"And what of F-Kerrick. Do you regret his death? He was a human being, after all."

"Not a human being by any definition that civilized people might recognize. He was the author of his own misfortune, a deeply disturbed soul whose cruelty and cowardice have been unmatched in living memory. He was arrogant and egomaniacal. Ultimately, ineptitude and foolhardiness brought him down. Nobody should mourn him."

The media-orb persisted in its questioning, with Quinn patiently attempting to satisfy the media's curiosity. Finally, the interviewer ran out of questions and left, having probed Quinn's personal life, including his family history and trivid-viewing interests. The citizenry at home and in the parks and plazas tuned into every 'breaking news' bulletin, hung on every word, every pronouncement and speculation as the reports continued hour after hour, endlessly repeated.

Quinn, who by now had turned up his pain meds and drowsed blissfully, was unaware of the adoration and praise being heaped upon him by the populace, notwithstanding the medi-orb's characterization of him as a hero. Just before he drifted off to sleep, he had a thought. Something was nagging at the back of his mind; a question that he should have asked Benwright. He felt that it was something quite important, but he was sure it could wait. Peace had returned and all was right with the world.

* * *

Doc slept. He'd returned to Ujo's hab the previous day, easily passing through the cordon of Sentinels at the building's main portal. The Sentinel who scanned his identichip gave him a strange look, but passed him through nonetheless. Doc figured that there might still be an alert out for the missing C.I., but that he was a relatively low priority. The Sentinel would probably report that Ujo had returned, but it was unlikely that anyone would take notice.

He'd entered the hab, skulking by the Sentinels in the corridor. Some gave him hard looks, as they were in the habit of doing with shady-looking characters, but were too engaged in their own tasks to pay him much heed. They were moving efficiently in and out of his former hab, carrying away evidence. Doc had left behind little that he valued, so he had few regrets concerning his former belongings. By this time they'd probably managed to open up the construct beneath the window and had discovered how it connected to the building's service ducts. It had been a useful way in and out of his hab on some of those occasions when he feared he might be observed in his true aspect, without his Futures' garb. He'd only recently been able to use the newly-completed exit, evading the prying eyes of anyone who might report the comings and goings of a stranger.

The physical and emotional strain of the last couple of days had drained him completely. Even as exhausted as he was, he felt compelled to tidy up Ujo's sleep shelf and the area surrounding it before he deemed it habitable.

He slept the clock around before arising and searching the hab's refreshment nook for nutri-wafers and water. Those would have to sustain him for a few days, until the Sentinels had cleared the corridor and he felt confident enough to venture forth.

The comcenter came to life at Doc's command and searched for his stated preference of news of the recent developments in the case of the child killer. He was gratified to see the reports of his own death, which markedly increased the chances that he would not be exposed in his new persona.

"…. just a citizen doing his duty," Quinn was telling the media-orb. The professor looked little the worse for his near-fatal experience. Battered and bruised, but alive nevertheless. Doc was disappointed. So much for the hope that the blast had removed that particular annoyance from his life.

The image of a smarmy, elegantly coiffed 'caster floated in one corner of the tri-d, as Quinn's figure froze momentarily in place. "The hero of the hour modestly disclaimed credit for ridding the Dome of this vile threat, then condemned the former Future with the following words."

Quinn continued, "He was the author of his own misfortune, a deeply disturbed soul whose cruelty and cowardice have been unmatched in living memory. He was arrogant and egomaniacal. Ultimately, ineptitude and foolhardiness brought him down. Nobody should mourn him."

Doc nearly choked on his nutri-wafer. This was too much. " …. disturbed! … cowardice! ….. arrogant! … ineptitude! … foolhardiness!" He was outraged. How dare a mere professor of biology presume to challenge his brilliance, to insult his superior intellect! No, this must not stand. If Quinn Braxton had failed to understand what had taken place over the past few months, he would soon be made to recognize what should be obvious to all. Donald F-Kerrick was not a person to be trifled with, nor would he suffer fools gladly.

When Doc finally calmed down, some measure of rationality tempered his rage. "What now?" he thought. "A challenge has been issued, though unintentionally. Even so, the gauntlet has been thrown down. What can I do without revealing myself and jeopardizing my safety?"

Having just had a narrow escape, he was unwilling to jump back into the fire. Yet, he could not rest until the affront had been set right. What to do? He'd have to take some time in his new guise as Ujo in order to decide how to address the issue.

* * *

The Ushers fairly tumbled into Quinn's room, all talking at once. They'd just finished their visit with Desert, who was undergoing physical and mental rehabilitation, and they were anxious to see how Quinn was doing and to express their appreciation for his rescuing the youngster. Quinn awoke abruptly from his nap.

"How are you doing, my friend?" Gus asked. "You look well."

"As well as can be expected when you've been shot at and blown up," Quinn replied, laughing.

"River told us about your adventure," Rosie put in. "And it's all over the media. There are even posters and T-shirts and holo-statues out already."

"No!" said Quinn, reddening. "There's no need for such a fuss."

"There is! You're the most famous person in the Ten Domes," Dan said, referring to the group of Domes strung up and down the Atlantic coast, "and maybe in the whole world," he continued proudly, "and you're our uncle and you saved my sister and killed the monster that kidnapped her and those others."

Quinn's blush deepened. He'd never sought the spotlight, was in no way the type who wanted to be centered out. He could only hope that the interest in him would quickly wane and that he could return to a quiet and untroubled life.

Rosie leaned over and gave him a cautious hug, in consideration of his injuries, and a big kiss on the cheek. Each of the men in the family shook his hand and gave him a gentle pat on his good shoulder.

Gus had a tear in his eye, betraying his heightened emotions. His love and pride were showing, not to mention his gratitude for Desert's rescue. "Is there anything we can do for you?" he asked, "I mean anything at all, to show how grateful we are for all you've done for us."

"No, that's not necessary, and I don't need anything," Quinn replied, "but you can tell me all about how Desert's doing."

"We just came from there. She'll be all right. As soon as the investigators finish interviewing her, we're going to have her memory selectively wiped. She'll recall nothing of the incident, and her recovery will be much more rapid. They did the same thing with Vale Chang, and she's returned to being the happy and well-balanced individual she was before she was assaulted."

"Thank goodness for that. I'm glad for both of them. Before I forget, you might want to gather all of the files you have relating to Donald Kerrick and turn them over to the Sentinels. I'm sure they'll want to add them to the archive of this sorry chapter in our Dome's history. It's certain that they'll be needed in the inquiry into what went wrong and how it can be prevented from ever happening again. "

"I'll begin as soon as we get back to the Harbour. I'm ashamed of the role my Harbour played in this wretched affair."

"It wasn't you fault," Quinn reassured him. "No one could have known what the imposter was capable of. The failure wasn't yours. There was nothing you could have done to prevent the tragedy. Kerrick was somehow able to circumvent the best laid plans and safeguards of the Compilers. We'll soon find out what went wrong. Don't blame yourself."

The arrival of Pierre Adler interrupted Quinn's commiseration with his long time friend. "Quinn, my boy," Pierre boomed, "I can't begin to tell you of the firestorm you've stirred up among the Guardians and the Compilers, and even the Sentinels and the Arbiters for that matter. Congratulations, by the way. You made us all proud. Anyway, as I was saying, panic among the administration. Finger pointing back and forth, et cetera. This whole thing's become political very quickly. Apparently, you're the only one likely to come out of the affair unscathed." He paused to take a breath. "Sorry. I do go on. Forgive me. I'm excited. They tell me you're going to be fine. Hello Gus, Rosie, boys. What do you think of our friend here?"

"Couldn't be prouder," Gus said.

Rosie nodded in agreement. "Strong and handsome and a Futures candidate as well, at least that's the rumor," she added with a wry grin. Quinn knew she was putting him on. She mirrored Gus' sense of humor.

"O.K. O.K." Quinn broke in. "Now you're starting to make me self-conscious. I appreciate the adoration, but could you tone it down a bit. If you want to do something for me, fend off the media-orb and make sure they spell my name right. As much as I enjoy your company, I need to get some rest."

"I think he's hinting at something," Pierre said archly. "We'll let you have some alone time for now. I ran into River on my way in. She said she'd be here shortly, after she visits with Desert for a while. Have a nap. You may need your strength soon."

The group eased their way out of the room after many more hugs and handshakes and pats on the shoulder. In truth, as much as he loved each and every one of them, the patient was relieved to see the visitors go. He lay back to await River's visit, fantasizing about future encounters with her in more private surroundings.

* * *

He awoke to a pair of lips pressed to his own. He truly hoped that it wasn't the male nurse who'd been attending him during the day and pressing him to accept a sponge bath.

"Hi, handsome," River said. "Want some more of that?"

Instead of answering, he pulled her to him and drank deeply of her essence as he once more pressed his lips to hers. It was several minutes before they emerged gasping from the deep and passionate kiss. By then, it was evident that his ardor wasn't the only thing that had been raised during the encounter.

"Oh!" said River, noticing the verification of his passion. "Is that for me?"

"Anytime you want it, after I get out of here," Quinn replied with a chuckle. River moved to claim her prize, and would have had not a media-orb appeared in the doorway, venturing uninvited into the room. She quickly withdrew her hand.

"Go away!" Quinn said testily. "I'm not available for interviews now."

"But the public wants to know," the orb protested. "We have a right …"

"You have the right to get bounced off the wall," River growled protectively as she advanced on the orb, which rapidly withdrew into the corridor. She returned to Quinn's side as the medi-orb beat a hasty retreat towards the exit doors.

"Well," Quinn said, "This is a side of you I didn't know about. What a tiger you are."

"When it comes to protecting my loved ones, you'd better believe it." She observed that the moment had passed, spoiled by the intrusion of the media, and that Quinn was once again quiescent. "Never mind," she said. "We'll be alone soon enough, then you'll see what other tricks a tiger can do."

She smiled hungrily, and Quinn returned her smile, hoping he wasn't, in fact, leering. He was anxious to see what tricks she had referred to, and looked forward to being released from care so that he could further explore this aspect of her nature.

November 30, 2204

Quinn sat up in bed, poring over the final reports on the closing stages of the terror on his wristcomp. He felt fortunate that the upper end of the tunnel had been open else the confined pressure wave from the explosion would surely have crushed him. He spotted something in the reports that bothered him and immediately commed Benwright.

"Congratulations, Quinn. Looks like you're the man of the hour," Benwright said when he answered the com. "How are you feeling? What can I do for you today?"

"I was feeling just great until I read the final reports. The Sentinels' report says that the upper end of the tunnel was closed and blocked from the outside. Can you confirm that for me?"

"Probably. What's the significance of it?"

"When I entered the tunnel and confronted Kerrick, the end of the tunnel was open. I could see the light coming in from outside. How did it get closed? We have to know. And how would Kerrick have got past me? Just before the explosion, he was closer to the outer end of the tunnel. The passage was narrow, yet his body was found closer to the explosion than I was. That's just not possible."

"Could you have blacked out temporarily? There must be an explanation."

"Not a chance. And one more thing. I looked over the section of the report that deals with the identification of the body. You used his identichip and his clothing." That portion of the report had finally triggered in Quinn's mind the question he'd been meaning to ask Benwright. "Did your people bother to compare his DNA profile with the records at Usher's Harbour? There's nothing in the report about it."

"Well, no. Given the positive chip I.D. and the clothing, we assumed …"

"He's still alive!" Quinn almost shouted. "Do a DNA match on the body and you'll confirm it."

Benwright was taken aback, but he'd learned not to argue with Quinn's exceptionally logical insights. "One slight problem with that," he said hesitantly, not quite believing the conclusion Quinn had drawn, "The body was flashed this morning. Only ashes remain. There's nothing left to match."

Quinn had been leaning forward in rapt attention. Now he collapsed back into the care pod, defeated. He was certain that Doc was still alive. He had to find some way to prove it before the nightmare once again resurfaced. He had no idea of Doc's future intentions, but whatever he might have in mind, he had to be stopped, swiftly, decisively, and finally.

CHAPTER 30

DNA EVIDENCE

November 30, 2204

Quinn's reverie was interrupted by a flicker of blue at the periphery of his vision. With an imperious sweep of her robes, Compiler Sanchez passed through the portal, leaving her entourage in the hallway, and made for his care pod. There was a broad smile on her wizened face.

"Professor Braxton. I see that you're awake and apparently thriving. Well done! I bring you greetings from the Council of Compilers, best wishes for a full recovery, and the gratitude of the jubilant citizens of RichmondDome for your valiant efforts. Your service will not be forgotten."

Quinn was at a loss as to how to respond. Obviously the Compiler did not know of the turn of events that might plunge their little world back into the gloom of panic and despair. He made an immediate decision not to mention anything until his worst fears might be confirmed or laid to rest.

"Thank you, C-Sanchez," Quinn responded politely. "I'm just glad I was able be of service."

"Yes, yes," she countered. "I watched your interviews. Don't be so modest. You went above and beyond mere civic duty. You risked your life and the safety of your loved ones. Few in our safe and protected world get the opportunity to become a true hero. We're all thankful that you were in the right place at the right time, and had the courage to confront real danger. Once more, our thanks for your service. Is there anything I might do to make you more comfortable or to speed your recovery?"

"No, thank you. They take very good care of me here. I'm on the mend and I'll be able to return to my normal life very soon."

"I've been in contact with the Council of Compilers and you should know that, should you choose to apply for Futures' status, your acceptance would be all but assured, pending your DNA profile results. Given your parentage, I'm certain that would not be a problem. It's the least we could do to thank you for your service."

Quinn was at a loss for words. It was the greatest honour his fellow citizens could bestow.

"You don't have to respond. I know it's all a bit overwhelming. I regret that I must now take my leave and return to GenevaDome to resume my duties there. We will be in touch with you regarding further honours. Farewell until then."

Her eyes were filled with joy as she squeezed Quinn's good hand between her own, then left the room. A medi-orb hovered in wait and pursued her down the hall, peppering her with questions. To her credit, she and her entourage managed to ignore the nuisance until they were safely out of the building and on their way to the airfield. The media-orb finally gave up and floated away, seeking more compliant prey.

"Have I done the right thing?" Quinn was asking himself. "What more could I have done? I've alerted Benwright to the probability that Doc is still alive. Now we just have to figure out if I'm right. No point in stirring up the Compilers until then." He lay back on his pillow and continued to examine the conundrum from every angle. There had to be a solution.

* * *

Doc was still in a state of high dudgeon. He was unable to let it go. Fury unabated, he paced Ujo's bachelor hab, impatiently thumping each wall as he reached it. It was uncharacteristic of him to allow his emotions to get the best of him, but his anger and frustration were unconfined. He felt trapped in the hab, unable to exercise his former freedom or to bring to bear what might be left of his hidden resources. The Sentinels would by now have discovered most of his secreted caches. Few reserves remained to him.

His work was not yet done, yet he was constrained from completing it by his unfortunate circumstances. Yes, errors had been made, but he didn't feel that the fault lay with him. That posturing meddler Braxton, his sister, and the Ushers had conspired to derail his carefully laid schemes.

Perhaps a parting gift for the whole bunch of them, something for them to remember him by. He'd have to arrange things so that they might appear to have been pre-planned. If everyone believed that he'd somehow reached out from the grave to exact vengeance on those who'd brought him low, then the risk to his wellbeing would be minimized. Now, how to accomplish that without stirring up the hornets' nest once more. Patience. It would come to him.

December 1, 2204

The lights in the hospital were dimmed at this early morning hour. Quinn had awakened and sat bolt upright, shaken from an apparently sound slumber by a random thought. Too many good ideas are so frequently lost to the allure of sleep, as they go unspoken and unrecorded. Quinn was determined that it would not happen in this instance. He commed Benwright.

"Lo?" the director answered drowsily. "What's so important at ….. 0300 hours, Quinn?"

"The clothes. What did you do with the clothes and the expansion suit?"

"I suppose they're still in the evidence box," Benwright answered. "Why ……? Aaah. You're after the DNA, right?"

"Right. Can you check, and get the lab to look for trace DNA and compare it with the files at Usher's Harbour? We need to know, and quickly, before something else happens."

"I have to tell you, Quinn, I'm skeptical, but I'll do what you ask, just in case you're right. I'll wake some people up. They'll be irritated to say the least, but I'll make sure they know how important this is. If it were anyone else ....," he trailed off.

"Thanks. Get back to me as soon as you find anything out." He reclined once more, satisfied that he had done all that he could for now. He soon drifted off into a contented sleep, secure in the knowledge that he'd moved yet another step towards a resolution of the crisis.

* * *

By coincidence, another sleeper awoke at about the same hour, also in response to a vagrant thought. An idea that had been percolating at the back of Doc's malicious mind came to the fore. It would take time to refine the scheme and to put it into action. He'd have to move quickly if he expected to press the advantage of his new identity. He lay back, smiling. A victory was a victory, and at this stage he'd take any triumph he could get. He had no qualms regarding what he was about to do. Soon, he slept the sleep of the righteous.

* * *

Elsewhere in the Dome, Quinn slept. The Ushers slept. The unsuspecting populace of the Dome slept too, confident that peace and order had been restored, and that all was right with the world.

December 2, 2204

A much reduced delegation was on hand at the aerodrome to see the Compiler off early on that December morning. Only President F-Benito and Commissioner Chaz Earl attended C-Sanchez as she entered the hangar dome. A small honour guard of Sentinels stood by.

"The circumstances of my departure are much more providential than those at my arrival," the Original said. "It's unfortunate that so much tragedy resulted from the actions of one man. My fellow Compilers and I will scrutinize all of the reports and attempt to ascertain what errors in procedure might have allowed that monster into your Dome. I can assure you that this will not happen again."

F-Benito responded, "We have the utmost confidence that the Compilers will get to the bottom of it and take corrective action. Thank you for your support and advice in this matter. I hope you'll visit us again and take advantage of the hospitality of RichmondDome without the pressures of official business."

"I'm sure I can arrange a vacation here at some time in the future. I'd appreciate the opportunity to explore the ruins of some of the great cities of the east coast, especially Washington and New York. We will meet again, President F-Benito. Farewell."

The formalities completed, C-Sanchez boarded her flier. The delegation remained by the hangar doors as the aircraft was taxied onto the tarmac and took to the sky, its graceful wings unfurling to take advantage of the air currents that swept upwards from the Dome. It rose effortlessly, circling to gain altitude before it set out eastward, and was soon lost from sight in the grey and misty air of the autumn morning.

* * *

The ping of his com on the side table jarred Quinn awake, at about the same time the Compiler's flyer took off. He accepted the call and was not surprised to hear Benwright's excited voice.

"Do I need to tell you that you were right? There were traces of Kerrick's DNA on the body suit, and a lot of one other. We're comparing it to the Dome's database to find out exactly who it was, if indeed it was one of our citizens. It's evident that somebody other than Kerrick was wearing the suit when the explosion took place. We should have the answer within the hour."

"Thanks, Benwright. Being right about this brings me no great joy. I'd rather have been wrong. So it begins again, perhaps. We need the identity of that body quickly if we're to catch Kerrick before he slips our net again."

"I'll com you the minute we have anything. Out."

Quinn disconnected the monitors and got out of the care pod. His personal intern rushed in, concerned that all life signs had suddenly disappeared from the monitor on his desk, setting off alarms.

"You shouldn't be out of bed," he admonished.

"I have important business to take care of. I can't be lying around. In any case, I'm due to be released today and I want to be out of here before the media get wind of it. A few hours early won't matter."

The intern commed the doctor and informed him of Quinn's decision as his patient quickly dressed himself. The doctor hurried to the V.I.P.'s room, but after conducting a rapid scan of his injuries and consulting the robodoc, decided against trying to dissuade him from leaving.

"You can take the cast off by tomorrow. The arm will be healed by then. Don't exert yourself too much for the next couple of days and you'll be fine. Take care of yourself and come to see me before the end of the week. Good luck."

Quinn thanked him and left the facility. He'd not gone far when Benwright contacted him. He was stunned by what the Director told him.

"The body was identified using the DNA records as that of Ujo Vreem. I believe you were acquainted with him."

Quinn gasped. "He was my C.I. I can't believe it. You'd better …."

"Already done," Benwright said, anticipating Quinn's request. "Sentinels are even now converging on Vreem's hab. The building's portal records show that he entered four days ago, after Kerrick was already supposedly dead.

No movement since. Kerrick must have assumed his identity. If we're lucky, we'll have him within minutes. I'll let you know. Out."

Rather than doing nothing, Quinn opted to head for Lowertown to witness Kerrick's capture. He boarded a floater and directed it to the station nearest Ujo Vreem's former hab. He was only minutes from his destination when Benwright commed him once again. The news was not what he wanted to hear.

CHAPTER 31

DOC ESCAPES ONCE MORE

December 2, 2204

Blissfully unaware of the firestorm about to burst around him, Doc had completed his morning ablutions and sat down to have a couple of nutriwafers and a synthcaf from the dispenser when he chanced to activate the comcenter.

" … that something is about to take place in Lowertown," the voiceover reported. "This building seems to be the focus of a Sentinels' cordon. They appear to have the front and back entrances blocked and nobody is being allowed in or out. When we attempted to get a comment from the squad's leader, we were told to desist from reporting anything until the operation was completed. Being a responsible news organization, and in accordance with the Sentinels' wishes, we now return you to the studio until we have received authorization to report more."

At the mention of 'this building', the media orb had transmitted an image of the very building where Doc now resided. Indeed, there was the

Madcap Caf on the first floor, a blue-clad Sentinel turning hungry citizens away from the entrance. He had no doubt that he was the subject of the operation, and he knew he had to move fast.

He'd barely begun to put his latest plans into operation, but self-preservation was the first order of business. Grabbing a few bare necessities, he rushed to the portal and peered into the corridor. The Sentinels had completed their business in his former hab across the hall the day before and had left the place unguarded. Doc took two steps from Ujo's hab and quickly entered his code. As he had suspected, the Dome's administration had failed to change the access codes, there being no reason to do so given the ostensible demise of the former occupant. Unknown to him, his luck continued, since the spycam had been removed from the corridor after the investigation of his hab had been completed.

He entered, allowing the portal to close behind him, and moved towards the box beneath the window. It had been broken open, revealing the hollow space beneath. Quickly, he squeezed into the space and wriggled down the concealed passage. It was a tight squeeze, but he'd passed this way several times before and he was confident that it would once again serve him well.

At last, having changed levels and directions several times, he slid through an opening and once more found himself in a familiar service corridor on the first level beneath the Dome. He was wary, given the commotion above, and his vigilance was about to be rewarded.

"Stand where you are," a Sentinel commanded, moving towards him with his right arm extended, hand upraised in an authoritative 'stop' posture. On full alert, Doc had anticipated that the Sentinels might station men in the lower levels. Without hesitation, he stepped past the outstretched arm and plunged a knife, taken at the last moment from Ujo's hidden cache, into the unarmed Sentinel's neck. A spray of arterial blood immediately soaked Doc's arm and spattered his shoulder and face. The unfortunate man died quickly, a warning scream becoming no more than a gurgle in his throat.

Doc looked up and down the corridor, suspecting that others might be nearby as backup for the raid on the surface. He guessed that the operation had been put together quickly and that its elements were unlikely be well coordinated. That knowledge might allow him to escape the net, though his prospects did not look very good at the moment. He had no idea in which direction safety might lie.

The Sentinels wristcomp pinged, and a message on the screen requested confirmation of his position and status. Doc lifted the device from the limp arm, placing it on his own, then punched a button marked 'Confirm'. The screen showed a flashing spot on a schematic of Sublevel 1 and a line reading 'Status: Operational'. The response seemed to satisfy the caller. Obviously, the Sentinels had never anticipated that one of their devices might be compromised by a lawbreaker, so they had simplified it to the point where anyone could use it.

Doc was gratified to see that the screen also showed the positions of other Sentinels in the sublevels. Now he would be able to map a safe exit route. All he had to do was to decide where he wanted to go. That should be easy. His plan for those who had foiled his otherwise perfect schemes was in its infancy, but being the master of improvisation that he was, he had confidence that it would be fully formed before he arrived at his destination.

First, he had to descend several sublevels, as there were things he needed from one of his subterranean caches, one that he was certain the Sentinels could not possibly have discovered. With the wristcomp guiding his way, he moved forward, eager to press the small advantage he still held.

* * *

"Bad news," Benwright informed Quinn. "He's gone. Looks like he moved out fast. The comcenter was on. He probably saw an early media report of our raid. Any idea where he might be headed?"

"Not a clue. Best guess, he's likely to try for a way out of the Dome. I'm sure you've got all of the transport hubs covered by now, and Ujo's indent code programmed into all of the exit portals. It's a big Dome. All we can do now is remain alert and search for him as best we can."

"Agreed. You know that the media will somehow get wind of this. I'm calling an emergency meeting of the task force. If we thought we had a mess on our hands before, it just got a lot worse. Out!"

* * *

The din of agitated conversation almost drowned out the sound of the Director's gavel as he repeatedly tapped for attention. At last, the excited conversations died down and Benwright was able to address the assembly.

"I guess I don't have to tell you the nature of the current crisis. Not only is F-Kerrick still alive, but he managed to get away once more and we have no idea where he is right now. No excuses. We made mistakes. Due to inexperience and unjustified optimism we failed to follow up on what should have been obvious to us. Now we'll all pay the price. We can only hope that Kerrick has fled into the Outlands, but given his past record, I don't think we can count on that. If he has fled the Dome, we'll pursue him out there in any case.

"It's been three hours since the raid was conducted and here's what we know. Kerrick faked his own death and appropriated the identity of one Ujo Vreem, a confidential informant. He was able to move about the Dome in his new guise, as we had only a low level alert out for Vreem, who went missing over a week ago. He apparently took over Vreem's hab, across the hall from his former hab, and lived there under the very noses of the Sentinels who were investigating his crimes.

"This morning's operation was to have been conducted in utmost secrecy, but nobody thought to tell the media to stay away. Consequently, Kerrick was alerted and made good his escape. He evidently gained access to his former hab and, using the concealed exit we discovered there, managed to reach Sublevel 1. A heroic Sentinel attempted to stop him but was stabbed to death. That's where the trail ends. He could be anywhere by now."

Quinn rose. "I concur with Director Benwright's analysis. Given Kerrick's history and his particular psychopathy, I'd guess that he's still in the city. We have to attempt to get into his head and anticipate his next move. We must put past mistakes behind us and move on, being careful not to repeat those past errors. It's likely that he's in full survival mode right now, just trying to keep out of sight and evade capture. He won't have time to get up to his usual nonsense. The Sentinels are conducting a full sweep of the sublevels, but have maintained a low profile above ground so as not to alarm the populace. The sec-cams are fully manned and Shadows are covertly sweeping the public areas. He can't possibly evade us for long."

A tri-d schematic of the Dome and its sublevels floated in front of the participants, summoned up by a command from Benwright. Superimposed on the image was the position of every Sentinel and Shadowman in the city. "As you can see, all areas are well covered," he said. "We're concentrating our search here, here, and here," he continued, illuminating areas in Lowertown, inter-Dome transport stations, several sublevels, and lesser-used external exits. "I'd like to say that his capture is imminent but, given his past performance, that would be unduly optimistic. What I feel comfortable in saying is that he cannot evade us for long. We know who he is and approximately what he looks like. We know the identity that he has assumed, and we've set portal sensors to search for that individual and issue an alarm. Unless he's gone to ground, we will find him sooner rather than later. Carry out your assigned duties. Keep in touch. Be vigilant. Thank you for coming."

With that, the meeting broke up. Small knots of individuals conferred in hushed tones, examining the tri-d of the Dome and the reports on Kerrick and his recent activities.

Quinn moved to Benwright's side. "You've activated the long range sensors, haven't you?" he whispered. "You can track any citizen within the Dome now."

"What makes you so sure?"

"The fact that you didn't deny it just now when I gave you an opportunity to."

"The security branch said it was a necessary measure. The populace is not to be notified yet, at least until the current emergency is over. I know I can count on your discretion in this matter."

Quinn nodded. "Of course. You have my word." Still, his state of unease was now about much more than the missing Future. "Suppose an individual had no identichip. What then?"

"But everyone has a chip implant," Benwright protested.

"We've already determined that Kerrick was able to remove his and substitute Ujo Vreem's. That's how he was able to elude us. He's probably discarded Vreem's chip by now. What would happen if he removed his chip completely? How could you track him then?"

"We have the ability to count individuals in any given area. If the count doesn't match the number identified by their chip readouts, then we know that an unauthorized person is in that area. That's how we've detected intrusions by some Outlanders in the past at the external portals, since few of them have implants."

"Could you pinpoint such an individual?"

"Only to an area say, about 50 meters across. If there were a lot of people in that area, we couldn't easily pick out the one without the chip."

"That won't help us unless we can lure him out into the open, and I fear that he's too clever for that. Unless he's hiding, he won't be staying in one place for too long. He's proved to be unpredictable in the past, but he's also single-mindedly consistent in the pursuit of his goals. We can use that. I have an idea. Work with me on this. If I'm right, we might have him in custody very soon." Quinn explained his reasoning and his plan to Benwright, who pledged to use his influence and his resources to support him.

The task force's working session supplanted the mid-day meal and would last well past sunset, many of the troubled participants forgetting to take their evening meal so great was the concern for their idyllic world that had been so cruelly turned upside down. Even so, most had little appetite for food. They would have been outraged and appalled had they known that the subject of their deliberations was lurking directly beneath their feet.

* * *

The long range sensors could not penetrate the layers of earth and carbocrete that sheltered Doc. His last safe redoubt was beneath the Dome's central tower, the seat of the city's administrative offices where, even now, the task force was working. Doc knew from the captured wristcomp that the Sentinels sublevel patrols were concentrated at the peripheries of the Dome, since all of his secret caches uncovered thus far had been in those areas. There were few patrols in the central area, as the Sentinels were spread thin, patrolling the vastnesses of the undercity and the Dome's streets and buildings.

After stripping off his clothes, Doc used several water bulbs from his precious cache to wash off the Sentinel's blood. Next, he used Ujo's knife to carefully excise the identichip from his earlobe. That would confer on him a modicum of anonymity, since it would never have occurred to a citizen to be without one, nor to the authorities that a citizen would be abroad in such a circumstance. He knew that public portal sensors could be set to monitor individual identichip transponder signals, and that they also counted individuals passing by them for the purpose of optimizing traffic flow. Again, luck was with him. Had he known about the activation of the long range identichip sensors, he would have smiled at his foresight in removing the chip.

Once more, he patched up his earlobe and used his makeup skills to alter his appearance, then dressed himself in the slightly padded green unisuit of a service tech. He might pass casual visual inspection, but if a Sentinel approached him with a portable chip reader, he'd be in trouble. Still, he had his knife and the will to use it.

Finally, he attached a mini-battery to Ujo's original identichip, and placed it into a tiny capsule. He had one last use for it. His proximity to the central tower afforded him a singular opportunity, one based on his knowledge of the tower's construction and purpose. Outside air, drawn in at the tower's apex, was humidified by water jets as it entered through the louvers and baffles and filters and purifiers near the top. He attached a hollow tube to a port in one of the uptake water tubes at the tower's base and inserted the capsule containing his identichip. A timer would open the valve at the appropriate moment and allow the chip to rise in the water pipe. It would be propelled to the top of the tower, where it would lodge in one of the spray jets, close to the Skylounge's floater station. That was all the advantage he required.

Now he turned his thoughts to the problem of Quinn Braxton and the Ushers. Quick, efficient, complete, then disappear. That must be his credo, else all could be lost. He would allow himself a single day in which to complete his task, then he must absent himself from the Dome, successful or not. "Thus it is ordained," he thought as he moved to the endgame. He was nothing if not melodramatic, seeing himself as somewhat of a latter-day Moriarty.

With the dead Sentinel's wrist comp as a guide he set out on his mission. It took some tinkering to ensure that the device's transmission capabilities had been disabled, so as not to give away his position. A query immediately popped up on his screen, requesting his position and status, but he ignored it. As he moved along the corridors beneath the Dome, he was easily able to avoid patrols, Sentinels in twos and threes that showed up on his display. Several patrols moved towards his last known position, but he was already well away from there, and they would find nothing.

He ascended level by level towards the surface, accessing a service portal into the same mall from which he had abducted young Viola Secouri, openly using his identity as a service tech to blend into the unsuspecting masses that flowed to and fro. He briefly considered the possibility of taking a floater to his destination, then discarded the idea as unworkable, since floaters used identichip information to deduct the cost of the journey from the individual's time credit account in the central data banks. No chip, no trip.

Doc moved cautiously along surface streets, confident that his latest disguise would conceal him as just another anonymous leaf in a forest made up of the teeming thousands of citizens eddying around him. He strode from street to street, maintaining an unhurried pace so as not to attract undue attention. When he spotted a Sentinel along his route, he casually moved to the opposite side of the thoroughfare, away from any potential short-range electronic snooping. His fear wasn't that he would show up on a scanner, but that he would not.

It was late afternoon as he neared his destination, the light of the autumn day beginning to wane. Glolamps throughout the Dome brightened to compensate. Having skirted the patrols below, he must now return to the gloom of the caverns in order to reach his goal. The nearby park afforded access through a hatch concealed in a copse well off the pathway. He wasn't unduly concerned about being noticed, as his service tech's guise conferred on him the authority to be there. Once more in the undercity, he was in his element, a covert world of solitude and shadows. He moved along familiar corridors, dodging patrols as he stalked his prey.

* * *

Desert was happily playing with Vale Chang in a corner of the Ushers' gathering room. Quinn had asked for and received permission for them to be allowed out of the hospital on temporary leave. Both children had undergone a directed memory wipe, erasing the horror of the abductions and abuse from their young minds. Now they were once again able to experience the innocent joys of childhood.

Apart from the occasional giggles and shrieks from the tweenies, there was an eerie silence in the household. Quinn had chosen to share the secure information concerning Doc's escape with the Ushers. In view of their suffering at his hands, he felt that they deserved to know that he was still on the loose, still dangerous. They maintained a grim vigil, waiting for something to happen, taking comfort in their familial proximity.

"Don't worry," he had assured them. "I've arranged for protection on all sides. He won't be able to get at you here."

As dusk blanketed the Dome, Quinn's com pinged. Benwright's voice shouted excitedly as he answered it. "We've got him. Ujo's identichip just triggered an alarm near the Skylounge. If Kerrick's in the tower, there's no way he can get out now." Quinn had put the com on speaker, so all in the room were able to hear.

"On my way," Quinn responded. "Have to go, folks. We've got Kerrick trapped in the tower. This will all be over very soon." He paused only long enough to give Sera a hug and a peck on the cheek, and for River, a long and passionate kiss.

Cries of "Be careful" and "Good luck" from the Ushers sped him on his way as he rushed through the portal. The Ushers exchanged significant glances as Quinn made his hasty exit.

"Well, all we can do now is to wait," Gus said.

"Yes," Rosie affirmed. "Quinn knows what he's doing."

Time stretched on endlessly, as it tends to do when the future is uncertain. At last Rosie said, "I hope Quinn knows what he's doing. At least he'll keep us ….." She broke off abruptly, staring.

Vale had raised her head as if paying close attention to what Rosie was saying, but she was not. Slowly, she rose to her feet, moving her head from side to side, appearing to test the air. Desert was looking at her in astonishment, trying to figure out why she'd suddenly left the game they'd been playing. Vale walked towards the back wall of the room in a half crouch, as if stalking prey. The expression on her face was one of single-minded concentration, her movements and demeanor positively feral. She stopped at the wall and pressed herself against it, hands splayed beside her head, as if listening to something beyond.

She uttered a single word that chilled Rosie to the bone as she comprehended its significance. "Red," she whispered.

* * *

Doc had finally managed to reach the tunnel beneath Usher's Harbour, having negotiated the labyrinthine passages of the undercity, and the many detours necessary to avoid Sentinels' patrols. He was now in the service corridor, beside the wall of the sublevel workshop where the departed were prepared for flashing.

He'd used a little-known backdoor into the central computer to tap into the Usher's private com system and had then configured it to capture pictures and sound from the rooms where the built-in cameras of each comcenter were located. As he watched the family in the gathering room on his wristcomp, he was gratified to hear that his diversion at the central tower had worked as planned, and that even now the Sentinels were actively pursuing him elsewhere. He would have preferred that Quinn remain where he was, to share in the just retribution that was about to be visited upon the clan. Perhaps Braxton could be dealt with at a later time. At least his sister would be present for the denouement. Now all that remained was for him to gain access to the Harbour, complete his mission, then follow his escape plan. He removed a package of stabilized construction explosives from his pack and set about his work.

On the upper level, the family heard a muffled 'crump' from below. They withdrew to the corner of the gathering room farthest from the corridor leading to the basement door, huddled together in expectation of what was to come. What followed a short time later was not a complete surprise.

* * *

"Welcome. We've been expecting you," Quinn said. He was standing next to the stairs leading up to the main floor, Benwright at his side.

Doc had just stepped through the hole he'd blasted in the wall even as the carbocrete dust settled. "What? ..... But how did you? ..... I just saw you ......!" he stammered, consternation written on his face. He attempted to back out into the corridor, but a scuffle of feet and the sound of stun weapons powering up persuaded him that that particular avenue of escape was now denied him.

"What you saw was a vid, prepared in anticipation of your actions. Your diversion activated prematurely. It gave us plenty of time to figure out what you were up to and to prepare," Quinn said, grinning coldly. "In any case, we had anticipated that you might come here to exact your particular brand of warped vengeance, so your scheme would not have succeeded no matter what you did. Vale Chang alerted us to your arrival."

Doc stood frozen to the spot, looking left and right in the vain hope that an alternative plan would come to him, a way to flee the trap that had closed about him. "How could you have known? I could have been hundreds of kilometers away by now. It's impossible that you could have anticipated my plans."

"Yet we have," Quinn said as Benwright moved towards their immobile quarry, restraints at the ready. The close proximity of Sentinels to his rear persuaded Doc that his journey had come to an end and that resistance was futile. He had foreseen everything but this.

"Your particular sociopathy was a predictor of your actions," Quinn continued. "I guessed that you'd be unable to leave it alone, the fact that we foiled your plans and defeated you, forcing you to run. You just had to avenge yourself on those you blame for your downfall, one last blow to salve your massive ego. As clever as you imagine yourself to be, you're driven by compulsion, not logic. Your history validates that thesis."

"My history?" Doc said, as Benwright fastened the restraints in place behind his back. Doc had briefly considered using the knife still in his possession to take Benwright hostage, but was too numbed by the turn of events to act.

"Oh, yes. We know all about you, Donald-Arthur Kerrick-McCaskill. What you revealed to me in the tunnel, combined with what we were able to reconstruct of your past from old records, gave us an exceptionally detailed account of your unique psychopathy. You're not the most prolific serial killer in history, but you've definitely had the longest run. That's over now."

Doc felt let down, disappointed that it should all end like this. No epic confrontation with his implacable foe, no struggle on a high precipice, no last minute reprieve for the hero of his own life story, himself. Instead, abject defeat and subjugation at the hands of those he considered to be his inferiors. His shoulders slumped in disgrace then, silent and subdued, he allowed himself to be led up the stairs.

* * *

After a seeming eternity of waiting, the Ushers were not surprised to see several Sentinels emerge from the rear corridor into the gathering room, weapons upraised. Behind them, Doc, his hands bound behind him, closely escorted by Quinn, Benwright and another group of Sentinels. The adults gawked; the children looked on in baffled silence.

Vale recoiled in nameless fear. "Red," she stated once more. Though she had no recollection of the events that had almost cost her her life, she still retained the ability to 'see' people's auras.

"It's over," Quinn informed them. "This one won't be causing anyone grief ever again. He'll be held under tight security. It's up to the Arbiters to deal with him now."

As the killer from the past was led away, escorted by Benwright and the troop of Sentinels, River rushed to Quinn and embraced him, holding him tight. "Don't you ever leave my side again. I can't bear the thought of what might be happening to you when I can't see you and feel you near me."

"That won't be happening anytime soon, darling. I suspect we're all going to be taking a much-needed break to get over this. As for the two of us, I know of a holo-pod with our name on it. What would you say to a virtual world tour, with lots of rest stops? Say, about ten or fifteen days, or so?"

The passionate kiss River bestowed on him necessitated no further answer. Gus and Rosie hugged each other and their children, including Vale Chang. Quinn and River turned to Sera and included her in their embrace. Relief had morphed into the joy of living and deep affection that bound this particular group of people together. The future was beginning to look a lot brighter.

CHAPTER 32

THE TRIAL

December 3, 2204

"What now?" Arbiter Coleman asked. "What can we possibly do with him?"

"Perhaps a formal trial?" suggested Arbiter F-Karl.

"I fear not," Pierre Adler replied. "We still have twenty-first century case law on record, but not the means to implement it. The kind of justice we require here, for an offence of this nature, was once dealt with by jury trial. We can't possibly subject our citizens to the psychological trauma that they would suffer by being confronted with the evidence that must be presented during such a trial."

"We could wipe their memories afterwards," Arbiter Leung proposed.

"I think not," Pierre continued. "The trauma during the trial itself would probably send some of them mad. In addition, Kerrick would require an advocate, somebody familiar with case law of this type. There are precious few of those on the entire planet and, I'd wager, none who would be willing to take on the defense of such a monster."

A conclave of Arbiters had been convened shortly after Doc had been apprehended at Usher's Harbour. Their task was to decide on the disposition of a criminal the like of which had not been seen in living memory. There were four Arbiters present in RichmondDome and another dozen sitting in by remote transmission. Their tri-d images crowded one end of the meeting room of the Department of Justice in the central tower. The combined age of those present easily topped a millennium, their collective experience only slightly less. These were the finest legal minds on Earth.

Arbiter Boseman from MadridDome spoke up. "Might I suggest a Supreme Court-type hearing, that is, trial by Arbiter? I see no viable alternative."

"Yes," agreed Pierre. "At the very least, justice will be seen to be done. We could appoint teams of Arbiters to ensure that all of the legalities are observed and that the rights of the accused are upheld. One team would present the evidence for the prosecution, and the other, any defense that they might be able to mount."

"Defense? Are you serious?" Arbiter Rafstanifari inquired.

"Very much so. I believe that the only possible mitigation of Kerrick's offences might be in his background, in his childhood. Insanity was often used as a defense in the past. Professor Braxton has gathered a considerable body of facts relating to the offender's early years which might serve as a defense. All else would involve protecting his right to a fair trial. Naturally, a neuroscan would be in place when he testifies."

"He'd be allowed to testify?"

"It's his right."

"And the scan would show if he's lying?"

"Yes, a neurobiological brain scan would do that. However, if he really believed that his testimony was the truth, then the scan would indicate that he was telling the truth. That much we'd have no control over. If his testimony contradicts the witness and physical evidence, then we'll know for a certainty."

"And as to the final disposition of the accused once convicted?" Arbiter Karl asked.

"Assuming that Kerrick is convicted, which is a more than reasonable supposition, then we might have a problem," Pierre answered. "We don't have the twenty-first century options available to us. Obviously, the death penalty is out. Exile is no alternative. It would be inappropriate, given the nature of the crime. We don't dare foist this monster off on the Outlanders. We have no prison facilities, and such an option has often in the past been condemned as cruel and unusual punishment, at least where a life-term would be concerned. We do, however, have a solution that's been offered by some of our best and brightest. Sera Braxton and River Usher are waiting outside this chamber to present to us a most unusual proposal for the disposition of a criminal of Kerrick's nature. Let's call them in."

They listened in spellbound silence as the two women made their proposal, complete with holo-charts, diagrams and animations. When the presentation was complete, a collective sigh of relief swept through the room. Here was the answer to their dilemma. Here was justice with compassion, the very embodiment of the New Society.

December 10, 2204

"You asked to see me?" Quinn said as the Sentinel admitted him to the sterile white detention room, then left, closing the door behind him.

"I did," Doc answered, from his supine position strapped to the bed. "I wanted to explain ...."

"No," Quinn said angrily. "There's no explanation possible or necessary. We know everything about you that we need or want to know. If you feel some compulsion to unburden yourself, there're plenty of psych personnel willing to listen. I've wasted more than enough time on you."

"It's not like that. You don't understand. Just five minutes, that's all I ask."

"What? You think I owe you something? You think I owe you as much as the time of day?" Quinn asked fiercely. "I expect that you want to attempt to justify all that you've done, to beg forgiveness for the lives you've destroyed. Or is it that you merely want to sing your own praises about how clever you've been, how successful at your macabre craft. You already did that in the tunnel."

"Me? Beg forgiveness? I thought you knew me, Professor. It's not in my character. As for bragging, my deeds speak for themselves, for good or ill. I thought you might appreciate some insight into how it's possible to circumvent the safeguards built into the acceptance process for Futures.

Even though it's unlikely someone like me might ever again exist, you should know how to prevent it, just in case."

"Is this your idea of community service?" Quinn asked sarcastically. "Perhaps some way to moderate any sentence that the Arbiters might impose?"

"Not at all. I know what I am and what I've done. There is no way I can make amends, even if I were so inclined. If I had it to do all over again, I doubt I'd be capable of doing things any differently. I can only surmise there was just enough iniquity within me such that it was there to be nurtured by my stepparents and my stepsister. But for them, I might have turned out to be a decent and productive citizen. Who knows?"

"I doubt that the label decent would ever have been applied to you," Quinn sneered.

"Even so, the Compilers should tighten their procedures for qualifying Futures and for testing them after Awakening. You've traced my career path in my former life, and you know that in spite of my, shall we say … uh … cravings, I did dedicate myself to serving the people. If I'm allowed a restricted wrist comp, I'll record my suggestions for them. I neither want nor expect any favors for this, nor is it to be taken as an indication of remorse. Nobody would believe it, anyhow. And then there's the matter of the Compilers themselves.

"What's that supposed to mean?"

"Ah. Of course you don't know. Being a Future and a Guardian, and having virtually unfettered access to databanks confers on one a range of knowledge not available to ordinary citizens such as you. Perhaps you might be interested in what else I know?"

Quinn was indeed interested, though he attempted to conceal his degree of curiosity from the disgraced Future. Mindful of what Sera had been telling him and Benwright's unwitting revelations, he realized that he had little choice but to accede to Kerrick's request in order to find out what vital information he might possess.

"Well? What's it to be? Can I count on your help?"

Through gritted teeth, Quinn was able to promise Kerrick his support, but only for the good of the New Society. After that, after the trial, all he desired was to get on with his own life and never again to see or hear of Kerrick. And so it was that Quinn found himself in the curious position of advocating for the former Future before the Council of Guardians and requesting favors on his behalf. In the interests of the common good, Kerrick was granted that which he required to fulfill his promise to Quinn.

December 25, 2204

The trial began without fanfare. It was held in closed chambers, the only observers permitted being the media, without recording devices. There was to be no reporting until after the trial was over. The proceedings were officially recorded and the vids sealed and archived in the Dome's vaults. Citizens and scholars would be granted access to them upon application, but only after they had read a précis of the trial to ensure that they were up to the disagreeable task ahead. All of the legalities would thus be observed and justice would be served.

When the trial ended, when all possible evidence for and against had been presented, the Arbiters came to a unanimous guilty verdict, then handed down the penalty that Doc deserved, though there were those would dispute that characterization. Even in such a nonviolent and tolerant society, many citizens felt that his offences warranted a much harsher punishment, yet everyone agreed that, short of reverting to the barbarism of the time from which Doc had come, there was little else that could be done to redress the crimes that he had committed.

As the Sentinels escorted him from the courtroom, his face a passionless mask, he was at last mute. He had nothing left to say that had not already been said, nothing left to do but to face his destiny.

EPILOGUE

Summer, 2076

"Wake up, sleepyhead. Vacation or no, there's chores to be done," Mary admonished.

"What time is it?" Arthur groaned.

"Just after six. If you want breakfast before you head out, you'd better be at the table in ten minutes."

As she left the room, Arthur rolled over. Donny's bed had already been vacated and tidied up. Within the allotted time, he dressed, made his bed, and splashed some water on his face. He arrived at the breakfast table just as Mary was dishing it up and Donny and the rest of the family were digging in.

"What's on today?" he asked.

"The usual," Lou replied. "You and Donny recall the roboharvesters for servicing, after you slop the hogs and feed the chickens."

No use grousing. Every member of the family was expected to do his or her share, and that was just the way it had always been.

The warm summer sun and clear blue skies stood in stark contrast to the storms of the previous day, and the crops were responding gratefully to the bounty from above by returning bounty in kind. Donny and Arthur set out shoulder to shoulder to complete their assigned tasks. They shared a home, a family, and everything that went with it, just as they had once shared a womb. Their common interests and avocation cemented their bond of brotherly devotion.

Arthur's little world was as ideal as it could be. All of his needs were provided for and he was enfolded in a cocoon of warmth and love. What more could one ask? And yet, he felt a certain disquietude, a sense that his life was not being fully realized. He wanted more, outside of the boundaries of his small and restricted existence. There was an unfathomable itch, a feeling that gnawed at his very being, something begging to be released. It came to him in the night, haunting his dreams and sometimes unsettling him by day. Bizarre images of anger and violence. Perhaps someday he'd learn what it was that bothered him so and act to satisfy those strange, unrecognized yearnings. Until then, he'd just have to make do.

January 29, 2205

"Do you think it's working?" River asked.

"Can't be sure," Sera responded. "Brain activity seems to indicate that he's on the go, doing something in his virtual world. Wish we could access exactly what he's up to."

"As long as he's behaving himself. We wouldn't want him reverting to any bad habits. We can't punish him as he deserves, but we won't reward him, either."

"No. The program will see to that. He'll stay bound up in his own mind where he can't harm a living soul, until the day he dies. He'll remain in the sensory-dep tank, all tubed and wired up, till it's time to dispose of his mortal remains. With the nanobiobots regulating his every system, he'll stay fit and healthy for many years to come."

"So the Arbiters have pronounced, and accordingly the program will provide for all of his psychological needs," River said. "The 'bots will provide the rest."

"Yes. I can't thank you enough for supplying the history and e-artifacts that allowed us to make his world real for him. I couldn't have done it alone."

They continued to observe the monitors for some time, assuring themselves that all was well and that they had come up with the most humane, the best possible solution for the problem at hand.

* * *

When Sera arrived home, Quinn was sitting at his desk, documents and tri-d's covering its entire surface. His brow was furrowed with worry. As Sera approached him, he handed her a small green volume, its title standing out in gold leaf; 'The World According to the Compilers'.

"We have to talk," he said.

* * *

In a sterile room under constant guard and monitored by sec-cams inside and out, the program continued its work, ticking on day after day, season after season, year after year in the virtual world where Arthur 'Doc' Kerrick now resided. It modified itself as circumstances required in order to provide the reality necessitated by the mind of its prisoner.

The program laboured on through the day when River and Quinn were wed in the real world, through the day when they had their first, then a second child, and on after they were both granted Futures status, along with Sera, for their service to their Dome. Sera ceded the family hab to Quinn and River, and moved in with her aceball player, along with her current ladylove, and soon enough both women were carrying potential Futures. All of this happened against a background of political and social turmoil in which Quinn and River and Sera would play no small part, and which would have an outcome that nobody could have anticipated.

It toiled on through the years when Arthur Kerrick's virtual self experienced an awakening and he embarked on yet another voyage of self-discovery, this time with the girl next door, and even on past the day when their families gathered around them to celebrate his realization of marital bliss with her which, as far as he was concerned, would last for all eternity.

THE END

About the Authors

Barry Epstein is a retired high school teacher with a lifelong love of literature. Born in England in 1941, he moved to Canada in 1947 with his parents, and now lives on the shores of Manitoulin Island in Georgian Bay with his wife Darls and their cockapoo Marlee. He occupies his time with writing and gardening. This is his first novel.

Darls Epstein shares with her husband a love for the English language and for wordplay, a passion she acquired at an early age. Born in 1941 in southern Ontario, she met her husband in Sarnia in 1965. The concept of the Domes was hers, and she and Barry worked together to flesh out the story.

Glossary

Compiler – a member of the worldwide governing body that has administered the affairs of planet Earth since the advent of the 22nd century.

Fitman – a person exceptionally dedicated to fitness and health.

Future – one who has earned the singular honour of being allowed a second life as a reward for his service to his fellow man.

Guardian – a member of a local governing council

Hab – home, dwelling

Harbour – a Safe Harbour where memories are stored and DNA gathered so that Futures might be resurrected at a later time.

Ordinary – a person with an unproven, imperfect, or defective genome.

Original – a member of the original group of Compilers who, in the mid to late 21st century, created the elements of the New Society.

Sentinel – a policeman

Shadowman, Shadow – a detective, a covert operative

Wab – wannabee, acolyte, aspirant